*This Must Be
the Place*

This Must Be
the Place

Kate Racculia

St. Martin's Griffin
New York

THIS MUST BE THE PLACE. Copyright © 2010 by Kate Racculia. All rights reserved. Printed in the United States of America. For information, address St. Martin's Press, 175 Fifth Avenue, New York, N.Y. 10010.

www.stmartins.com

Designed by Meryl Sussman Levavi

The Library of Congress has cataloged the Henry Holt edition as follows:

Racculia, Kate.
     This must be the place : a novel/Kate Racculia.—1st ed.
        p. cm.
     ISBN 978-0-8050-9230-1
     1. Boardinghouses—Fiction. 2. New York (State)—Fiction. I. Title.
     PS3618.A328T48 2010
     813'.6—dc22

                                                              2010001434

ISBN 978-0-312-57166-5 (trade paperback)

First published in hardcover format by Henry Holt and Company

First St. Martin's Griffin Edition: July 2011

10 9 8 7 6 5 4 3 2 1

For Mom and Dad

Contents

Part III

This Must Be
the Place

Sixteen Years Before

Amy considered the postcard: a boardwalk scene. Throngs of people wandering in the sun. Sparkling blue ocean to the right, cheery awnings on the shops. She sniffed. The man beside her on the bus stank of tuna fish and cigarette smoke.

This must be what it feels like to die, she thought.

She was sore all over, sore and too tired to be scared. She suspected this *was* what it would feel like to die: to give up everything that came before, to just—cut it off. Tear it out. She wasn't religious. Her parents died before they had a chance to impart much wisdom on the nature of immortal souls, and her grandfather, when she first went to live with him, told her he was allergic to church. But she suspected there was something beyond what she knew. Beyond what she could touch and smell. She suspected there was a sort of transition period, where you had a chance to say good-bye to your old self and your old life, and this was hers, on this Greyhound, her sandaled feet propped on her back-pack, with nothing but a postcard on which to mark her passing.

Not that she ever intended to mail it.

She'd never intended to, not even when she bought it. She'd been waiting for Mona to finish her shift at the pizza place—and by *finish her shift* Amy meant *break the suction with her boyfriend's face*—and was killing time in one of those boardwalk junk shops. The boardwalk was full of junk; there was shit *everywhere*. Key chains and T-shirts and snow globes (how lame was that, snow globes at the beach?), and stupid little sculptures built out of shells; Amy, of all people, could appreciate tiny objects, but there was just so *much*. It made her think of how many people there really are in the world, and whenever she thought about that, she felt suffocated and insanely lonely, which was classic irony when you thought about it: that realizing she was one of a million billion or whatever made Amy Henderson feel like she would never be anything but alone.

She bought the postcard because the guy behind the counter was giving her weird looks and she wanted to prove to him that she wasn't loitering, even though she was: she was a fucking grown-up. She had money.

She smoothed the card over the top of her leg: OCEAN CITY MISSES YOU! said bright red letters across the sky. Hardly. She chewed her pen and turned the card over to the blank side and wrote, *Mona, I'm sorry.*

She didn't know what else to say, so she filled out the address. She still wasn't going to send it, but it felt good to state the facts: *Desdemona Jones, Darby-Jones House, Ruby Falls, New York.*

Maybe she should apologize a little more. *I should have told you*, she wrote.

What was the one thing she wanted to tell Mona? What could you put on a postcard—knowing that some nosy postal worker would probably read it, and you barely had enough room to say anything important anyway?

You knew me better than anyone—I think you knew me better than me.

That would make Mona happy. Mona wanted to be someone's best friend more than anything in the world. It was a little pathetic; but then sometimes it made Amy a lot happier than she wanted to admit.

Mona would worry, so next she wrote: *Don't worry. I swear I'm happier dead,* which was a little mean, because it would make Mona wonder whether Amy had flung herself off a cliff or across some train tracks or taken a whole bunch of pills and gone to sleep. But Mona should know better. If Amy hadn't done any of those things while they were still stuck in Ruby Falls, she sure as *hell* wasn't going to do it once she finally escaped.

It was getting late, and Amy wasn't so tired that she didn't know how hungry she was. She'd bought a few bags of pretzels at the last bus station, and now she crunched into them happily, her lips shriveling from the salt. She started to remember where she was going, and that of course made her remember where she'd just come from, and she thought of Mona, who would have been so scared when she found her just—*gone*.

She didn't know why she'd done it. She woke up early and knew today was the day (or rather, yesterday was the day; she'd been on this bus for something like twenty hours now), and when you knew something, there was no point in not-knowing it, just like there was no point in waiting. What day was it, the eighteenth? She uncapped her pen and wrote *August 18, 1993* on the top edge of the postcard, where the stamp would go. Her stomach and her knees and her butt hurt, and she was grateful to be in the window seat, even though it was dark and there wasn't much to see. She pressed her forehead against the cool glass.

She thought she was in Indiana, or Kansas maybe, by now. Hollywood was closer than ever. Her future was closer. The world flickered by, unspooling like a reel of undeveloped film.

The darkness of the bus, close and warm, reminded her of sitting in the dark of a movie theater on the boardwalk with her father, a million years ago, it seemed: the summer before he died, when she was four and he took her to see *The Clash of the Titans* on a rainy day when it was too cold to go to the beach. "This is Ray Harryhausen's masterpiece," he whispered to her. "You think those skeletons in *Jason and the Argonauts* are cool, wait till you see Pegasus. Wait till you see Medusa. Wait till you see the Kraken." She remembered sucking the chocolate coating off each Junior Mint and thinking it was funny that there was sand on the floor, like the beach just couldn't stay away, and then the lights came down and she forgot about the mints and the sand. She left the earth completely. She traveled to Olympus. She rode the back of a white winged horse. She shrank from the red death rattle of Medusa and goggled at the great titan of the sea, the Kraken, as it rose screaming from the depths to claim the sacrificial Andromeda.

And he—Ray Harryhausen—had created them! Had *built* them, improbably, from wire and clay and plastic and feathers; built them and given them movement, and desire, and souls. Harryhausen, come to think of it, was the only god she had ever learned to worship; he created a world in his movies that captured her, that thrilled her, that felt like home. It was a world she'd spent her entire life trying to find.

And now she could see the doorway, just a little down the road, waiting for her to walk through.

She sat up and grabbed her pen.

Anyway, I left you the best parts of myself, she wrote. *You know where to look.*

There was nothing more to say.

Part I

1 ❧ The Runaway

Arthur Rook didn't know.

He woke up on Friday morning when Amy rolled out of bed, but the running of the shower sang him back to sleep. When his alarm buzzed at seven he woke again, shaved and dressed and fed himself and Ray Harryhausen, the cat, and stood on the curb in front of his apartment complex in Toluca Lake, just north of Hollywood, waiting for a ride to work. Like every morning in Los Angeles, it was colder than Arthur, who grew up in Boston, thought LA was supposed to be. He squinted at the sun, hugging himself. He saw his breath on the air. He wished Max Morris would show up already, hopefully with coffee, or maybe those little homemade donuts Max's boyfriend Manny made, that Max didn't like and didn't have the heart to admit. Manny put little notes in with the donuts—always a pun (*You're my favorite in the hole world!* or *Donut what I'd do without you!*)—and Arthur felt a little guilty devouring sweets specially packed for another person. When Arthur asked Max why he let Manny go on thinking he liked the donuts—wasn't he worried some day Manny would discover the truth and be hurt?—Max shrugged and said sometimes you let the people you love believe what they want to believe.

Why? Arthur had asked.

Because you love 'em, Max had said.

There. Right then.

That was the moment it happened, they would tell him: at 7:48, while Arthur was waiting for Max to show up in his stuttering silver Geo, thinking about Manny's donuts.

Arthur got into the car when Max arrived—late, sans both coffee and donuts—and the two of them headed down Cahuenga into Hollywood, creeping in a sludge of traffic. Max apologized for not bringing any breakfast, and Arthur lied and said he'd eaten at home, and when Max called him on it, they pulled into a gas station and Arthur ran inside for two cups of coffee and a box of Ho-Hos.

"You eat like a freaking teenager, Rook," Max said. "One of these days your metabolism is going to implode, creating a black hole that sucks this entire universe into it."

"I am the destroyer of worlds," Arthur said. He was tall and thin and had a recurring nightmare in which he grew thinner and thinner until he was a skeleton holding a sword and shield, like the vengeful dead in Harryhausen's *Jason and the Argonauts*. When he told Amy, she smiled and said she'd still love him if he were a special effect. She laughed—*I might even love you more*—and Arthur thought, *Of course you would.*

Max parked in the faculty lot of Hollywood High and they hauled their equipment into the front hall, just like they had last year on school picture day and the year before that. Then Max disappeared to speak with their office contact, and Arthur, chewing a Ho-Ho, unpacked the lights and the backdrops and the cables and cords. It was 8:45—8:43 was the time of the first missed call on his cell phone.

From 9:15 to 10:30, Arthur stood behind the tripod and told one hundred and fifty freshmen to smile like they meant it. This was his favorite part of the job. It was the reason he became a photographer: for love of the moment when his subjects showed themselves to the camera and to him. Arthur loved people. He didn't really understand them or feel like he belonged among them, even, but he adored being a witness to their existence. He loved how various they were, how fragile and tough and strange and each his own universe: self-contained and whole. He was a Watcher. Amy told him, one afternoon six months after they met, that he would be unbelievably creepy if he weren't so damned good.

"You think I'm good?" Arthur had asked. He didn't care if Amy thought he was creepy—he *was* a little creepy, he knew that; anyone who goes through life preferring to watch than participate will trend that way—but he had been enchanted that she thought he was good. "You mean pure of heart?" he asked. "Valiant?"

"Not quite," Amy said. They were in bed. "The truly pure don't know how to do *that*."

"Sometimes they do," he said. "When they've been driven to it."

Amy grinned at him. "What I mean," she said, "is that you believe other people are basically worth living for, and it shows."

"You mean I'm an optimist."

"I mean you *see* people, you see people all the time, and you don't get bored or tired of them. You don't start to hate them. How do you manage?"

He remembered the weight of her hand on his face, the pressure of her thumb against his cheek.

"How do you do it?" she said.

"You give me too much credit," he said. "I hate them plenty."

"You are such a liar. Name one person you hate, one person."

"Adolf Hitler. Douchebag."

Amy laughed.

"Cigarette-Smoking Man." Arthur counted on his fingers. "Iago."

"I mean one *real* person—"

"Short people who recline their seats all the way back on airplanes."

"—I mean who you *know*, personally, that you hate."

Arthur kissed her to buy himself time to think. "That guy," he said. "That guy at the restaurant the other day."

"Which guy?"

"With the bad suit and the tacky tie."

"Who yelled at the waitress and made her cry?"

"Yeah, him," he said. "I *hate* that guy."

Arthur couldn't hate people, any more than he could hate water or grass or stone. Ordinary people, like the chubby freshman girl slumping on the padded stool in front of default Backdrop A (Mottled Blue Slate), were too magnificent and too oblivious to *hate*. He asked for her name and homeroom.

"Jennifer Graves. I'm in Mr. Woodbridge's." She was pale and had flat brown hair, pulled back in an unforgiving ponytail. There was an angry red spot on her chin.

"Jennifer, hi," Arthur said. "I'm Arthur."

"Hi," she said.

"You don't look like you want to get your picture taken."

She crossed her arms and scowled. "What gave you that idea—oh, do you have eyes?"

Arthur smiled at her. "You know what they say about high school?" He ducked to look through the viewfinder.

"That they're the best years of my life?" She had a truly scorching glare. He framed her in the camera sight. "These are my glory days?"

"Only the strong survive," he said.

She twitched a smile. He saw it through the lens and captured it, plucked it out of time and space and made a digital copy in ones and zeroes. And in two months when Jennifer Graves's parents opened the folio of their daughter's freshman-year portraits, Arthur thought they'd see someone familiar in her eyes, her lips, the lift of her cheeks. Not the sullen unhappy girl who slammed her door and said mean things just to say them. They'd see the little girl who'd known the joy of running naked through a sprinkler. Who'd spent the better part of 1994 lumbering around the house after her delighted little brother, pretending to be a Tyrannosaurus Rex. They'd see a hint of the person Jennifer would grow up to be, after she'd bested this phase of her life simply by outliving it.

They'd see what Arthur Rook had seen.

Max took over for the sophomores. Arthur stepped outside with what was left of his cold coffee and watched the traffic roll by. It had never felt right to him to have a high school this close to so many cars, so much exhaust. There was a gas station down on the corner, and the Walk of Fame was only one street up. He could see the top of the theater where they held the Oscars. Growing up in Los Angeles was unfathomable to Arthur—Los Angeles period, as a place where people lived normal lives, was unfathomable. When he first arrived, it had felt like the city was teasing him, rubbing up against him in a way that felt embarrassing and unreal, like a stranger crowding him on an otherwise empty bus. Alien vegetation, spiny and thick-leaved, sprouted beside walkways and highway medians or waved their triffid fronds high above his head. The world smelled of fresh-turned earth, of wet dirt. The murals that lined Hollywood Boulevard—Bette Davis, Bob Hope, Marilyn Monroe—rippled like mirages on storefront security gates, disavowing anything so pedestrian as death. There were a million pictures of corpses in Hollywood: eyes smoldering, cowboy hats tipped forward, skirts blowing up around their thighs forever. The city romanticized eternity by reminding you how many people were already dead, and in the presence of so many beautiful zombies, Arthur felt doomed.

Then he met Amy. He'd been in town for a month—a long dreadful month, with no job secured, no apartment rented, no friends met. No validation that his decision to come to LA—once so appealing for its diametrical opposition to Boston—had been anything other than a poor decision. He'd driven around the boulevards of North Hollywood aimlessly, refusing to get on the freeways (he had never owned a car, had never had to develop any quick instincts behind the wheel). When he accidentally turned onto Mulholland Drive, he was so frightened by the hairpin curves that he drove straight back to his motel and didn't go out for three days. He didn't speak to anyone in that time without the assistance of a telephone, and when his mother told him that no decision is absolutely permanent and he could come back to his old room any time, he didn't say no. He said, *I'll think about it.*

Fantasizing about flight yet refusing to leave Los Angeles before he'd properly seen it, Arthur mustered his courage and drove down to Hollywood. He passed the Chinese Theater and a man dressed as Dr. Frank-n-Furter stuck out a beautiful fishnetted leg and tried to wave him down. Arthur waved in return but didn't stop. He passed the Roosevelt Hotel and the Chateau Marmont and the Viper Room, knew he would never be cool enough to step inside them, and was grateful for it.

In-n-Out Burger—now, that was more his speed. He pulled into the In-n-Out on Sunset and parked. In the lot there was a boy in a white paper cap holding a board in front of him like a cigarette girl, taking orders from the cars in the drive-thru line. It was a long line—it was lunchtime, he realized. He also realized he was hungry. He didn't remember when he ate last, though he did know it had been something from the vending machine at the motel.

But his appetite, and his fledgling good mood, evaporated the moment Arthur Rook stepped inside the Xanadu of Southern California fast food. White-capped workers buzzed with efficiency, their red aprons held together with large wicked safety pins; customers casually ordered items that weren't even on the menu (a double-double? a Flying Dutchman?). The restaurant was tiled like a bathroom or a hospital, bright red and clean white, and rows of red palm trees marched across the walls, the rims of the drink cups, the paper place mats lining the trays. Everyone else knew what to do but him; everyone had a place here but Arthur, the out-of-joint socket, the improper cog in this beautifully humming machine. And now he was at the counter and the girl behind it was smiling broadly, and behind her another happy worker was murdering potatoes with a diabolical contraption that was half guillotine, half garlic press. The giant silver handle came down on a naked potato, and it splintered into pale fingers.

"What can I get for you, sir?"

I do not belong in this place.

His eyes flew to the hand-painted menu above her head. Hamburger, cheeseburger. No other options. No one else had ordered just a hamburger or a cheeseburger. Would they know, could they tell, if he tried to fake it?

"Sir?" The girl at the register was stunning. Everyone in LA was beautiful, even the girls at the In-n-Out. It made him sad, and he didn't know why.

Arthur opened his mouth but nothing came out.

"Sorry, I didn't catch that."

The machine was slowing. He, Arthur the interloper, was screwing it up. He had a sudden violent premonition that it was too late for him to escape. He would be crushed by this city, eaten, and then forced to wander it forever: nameless and alone in an undead town.

"He'll have a double-double and an order of animal fries."

It was a girl's voice, behind him: strong and bright and sure. It continued. "And I'll have a two-by-three and a Neapolitan shake."

The voice stepped beside him and smiled, and the lonely Watcher, invisible for so long, was seen at last.

Seen by a beautiful girl—a woman. Maybe twenty-five. Tall, like him, with straight dirty-blond hair and wide open eyes and broad shoulders. She had a geometric body, all angles and planes and edges except for her breasts—large breasts that Arthur, at the same time as appreciating the hell out of them, imagined she might have hidden under sweatshirts and oversize flannel shirts for years. The way she held herself now felt new and unpracticed, as if she had only recently learned how to be at ease but had learned it and learned it well. Arthur smiled at her like a man granted his dying wish. The machine around them began to purr again, and he opened his mouth but still nothing came out.

"Don't mention it," she whispered.

That was how Arthur Rook met Amy Henderson. Amy, who would sit down with him at a table in the sun, who would explain the difference between a double-double and a Flying Dutchman and then wipe a dot of ketchup from the corner of his mouth with her left fingertip. Who would teach him how to navigate, how to survive, how to fall in love with LA's charmingly daft will—finding its resolve to exist for its own superficial sake perfectly romantic and not a terminal fool's dying delusion. Who would teach him to fall in love with her. Who would be his friend and his lover and then his wife, who would be his home, who could create life from metal and rubber and wires for the sake of a few frames of film, and who would, at 7:48 on a Friday morning in early October, send ten thousand volts from the tip of the same finger that had wiped the ketchup from his lips through all the chambers of her heart.

Amy, who would be killed instantly.

Amy, who would make Arthur Rook a widower at thirty-two.

"Hey, Arthur, your phone." Between students, Max jerked his head at Arthur's coat, draped over an open equipment trunk. "Been ringing like crazy."

Arthur set down his empty coffee cup and flipped his cell phone open. He had ten missed calls.

☙

Of the ten calls missed, there was only one message, left by Amy's boss, Stantz. His real name was Bill Bittleman, but he loved *Ghostbusters* and wanted everyone to call him Stantz—everyone Amy worked with loved at least one movie like a religion; they loved movies, period, but there was always one movie above the rest. Bill Bittleman's was *Ghostbusters*.

"Arthur, I'm so sorry—oh, Christ, Arthur, I'm so sorry," said Stantz's message. "Call me. Call me on . . . this phone, this number, I couldn't find your number so I looked it up on Amy's . . . phone. Call me *immediately*. Where *are* you?"

Arthur was cold. Freezing.

His fingertips were numb when he redialed Amy's number. Her picture appeared on the tiny screen of his phone: Amy with Ray Harryhausen draped across her shoulders like a fur wrap—a very alive, very pissed-off wrap.

Why was Stantz using Amy's phone?

"Arthur!" shouted Stantz. "Arthur, I—I don't know how to tell you this."

Bill's voice cracked. Bill was crying.

"It was an accident," Stantz said. "It was just a stupid accident, a stupid—"

Arthur heard a high whine. The sound of crystal vibrating.

⚶

Arthur was lying in bed in the dark, under the covers, fully clothed. His sneakers were still on and his mouth tasted like tin. He couldn't remember Max dropping him off after work. He didn't remember if he'd fed Harryhausen. He kept more regular hours than Amy, so feeding the cat was his—responsibility—

⚶

Arthur was standing in the shower. A freezing cold shower. He was resting his head against the tile in the corner, and when he stood back, he felt a ridge pressed into the skin of his forehead. His throat was sore. His hand—hurt—Jesus, what did he do to his hand? His knuckles were raw and stung, bloody, under the cold spray from the showerhead. He turned off the water and stepped out of the shower and there were little red polka dots all over the bathroom sink, and Arthur saw that someone had punched the bathroom mirror. It hadn't shattered but it was cracked in one corner and dangling off the cabinet's glide track.

He wrapped a towel around himself and opened the door.

Ray Harryhausen was lying in the middle of the hallway, his furry bulk puddling over his paws so that he looked like a striped brick with a cat's head.

"Are you hungry?" Arthur asked him. "Did I feed you? Huh, Harry?"

Harryhausen, who tended to be either inert or asleep, wasn't exactly behaving oddly by lying in the middle of the hallway, but something was wrong about it. Something was wrong about *him*. Arthur and Harry had never liked one another—Harry was really Amy's cat, had been her roommate for years before Arthur came along—

Amy's cat—

Harryhausen made a horrible, horrible noise and Arthur sank to the carpet on his knees. Everything that had happened that day, everything he lost, flooded back as a nightmare: Max driving him to the hospital, to the morgue. Standing there while Stantz, red-faced, explained that Amy had blown a fuse while working on an armature and went back to the breaker and there was a wire—that was old or stripped—Arthur couldn't understand, didn't want to—wires were crossed. Electrons flew. Into the tip of her finger (her left index, he had kissed it a thousand times) and up her forearm (pale underside, purple veins) and through her bicep, her shoulder. Straight down into her heart. *Fibrillated*, they said.

Fibrillated.

Stantz kept talking—about the sound and the blowback and the smell—and Max told him to shut *the hell* up, and the morgue was cold, and Amy was blue and dull and not-Amy. Her left hand was angry and swollen. Burned.

Did she have a will?

I don't know, Arthur said. She liked grapefruit and coffee together for breakfast.

Did she want to be buried or cremated?

I don't know, he said.

She wore his old concert T-shirts to bed and sang him lullabies as Axl Rose (*Good night to the jungle, baby!*) and Mick Jagger (*Hey! You! Get into my bed!*).

Any family?

All gone, he said. Just me. Just her and me.

What would you like to do with the body?

Max took him home—Max took him home and got him into bed

and Arthur was pretty sure Max held his hand for a while and kissed him on the forehead—and then Max left.

Harryhausen made the horrible noise again. Arthur had never heard him cry before. Complain and hiss, sure, but this was completely different. This was deep and wild; it sounded like he was scraping it from the bottom of his tiny cat lungs. Like it was tearing his throat open.

Arthur sat on the carpet and stretched his legs out in front of him, in the hall, in the dark, and dripped cold water out of his hair and down his bare chest and tried to swallow but he didn't have any spit. He ached.

He lurched forward and his body tried to vomit but there was nothing in his stomach. Harryhausen jumped to his feet, hissing, and padded away, enormous fuzzy gut swaying from side to side.

Arthur didn't know anything. He didn't know if Amy wanted to rest in the ground or flame out into a million tiny particles. He didn't know if she'd made a will, or if there was an object, a memory, she wanted carried on by someone else in her name.

He didn't know and he was never *going* to.

He had to be dreaming. None of this was even remotely possible. He was thirty-two. Amy was thirty-one. They were young and full of blood. Their bodies and their minds were still their own to control. He couldn't imagine Amy—her body, Amy's body—lit with electricity. Had she flown? Had she fallen? Had she looked like she was dancing?

She liked to dance.

Of course Amy hadn't made out a will, it was too soon—but he didn't know that, not for certain. And just because she might not have officially left a will didn't mean Amy didn't want certain things done or said or given after her death. Just because Arthur didn't know what Amy wanted him to do with her body didn't mean *Amy* didn't know.

Why hadn't she told him?

Why hadn't he asked?

What else didn't he know?

What else hadn't he—the Noticer, the Watcher, the Good Seer of so many strangers—not known about his wife? What had he missed? What could he still see, if he looked hard enough?

He pressed his back against the wall for leverage and slowly, gently, pressed himself up from the floor. He blinked back stars. He could do this—if he, Arthur Rook, could see anything, he could see his wife. It didn't matter that she wasn't here. He could see.

He started in the bedroom. He looked through her dresser and saw her yellow-and-black striped socks, her grandfather's enormous green sweater, the blue lace bra she wore on their third anniversary that made her pale skin glow. He smelled Amy all around, but he didn't see anything he didn't know. He looked under the bed and saw her purple bowling shoes, also the white open-toed pumps she named Marilyn (left) and Norma Jean (right). He looked in the bathroom, in the broken medicine cabinet and the hamper. He tossed razor blades she would never use and unopened tubes of toothpaste and dirty clothes on the floor, and still he didn't see anything. Arthur was slowly drying from his shower but he was cold, only wearing a towel, and shaking so viciously his teeth chattered in his skull. He ran to the kitchen and looked in every cabinet and in the refrigerator, and all he saw were the plates they had bought together, the cups and the bowls they'd eaten ice cream and cereal and hot soup from. An unfinished gallon of milk, leftover Thai take-out, half a grapefruit swaddled in plastic wrap that she'd been saving for breakfast tomorrow. Arthur saw all these things but he did not see Amy—only trace evidence of what she'd worn, what she'd eaten, what her body had done.

"Where ARE you?" Arthur shouted, scaring himself. *"I know you're here!"*

He heard Harryhausen crying again, followed the sound to the living room, saw Amy's monster movie posters—*The Clash of the Titans* (her One Movie, her religion), *The Thing, The Beast from 10,000 Fathoms*—and saw his own reflection in the framed glass. He tossed the cushions off the couch and found thirty-six cents and a single blue sock. There was nothing else—nothing that he didn't know—no clues to solve, no hints, no indication.

Nothing to see that hadn't already been seen.

Shuddering now, muscles twitching with cold and fear, Arthur returned to the bedroom. At some point he had begun to cry. He sat on the edge of the mattress and told himself to calm down, that he'd just proved he knew everything there was to know about Amy Henderson. He'd seen her. He'd seen *all* of her. She hadn't told him what he didn't know because there wasn't anything to tell.

She hadn't known either.

Arthur choked on nothing.

Harryhausen hissed at him and Arthur looked up, and there was Harry, in front of the closet—how stupid Arthur was, not to have looked in the closet. He didn't have the strength to stand, so he crawled over to the door and pushed it open, and there were all his pants and shirts and Amy's skirts and dresses, hanging silently, companionably. Suspended. Sleeves waiting for arms that would never fill them. Collars waiting for a throat that had grown cold and still. Shoes entombed and stacked in bright paper boxes. And Arthur, exhausted, fell over on the carpet, hating himself for not being able to see.

He blinked. He breathed. The pile was rough on his cheek. He felt Harryhausen walk by his head and closed his eyes and wished he could just fall away and forget everything, could make it untrue, could make it unhappen. He tried to will himself to sleep for a long time and couldn't. He opened his eyes again.

And Arthur's eyes, which had only needed time to adjust to the dark, saw a shoebox. A huge shoebox on the floor of their closet that he'd seen a million times, that he remembered moving into the apartment, even; but a shoebox that—despite its bright pink cardboard, the word GUMBALLS! like a cattle brand on its side, big enough to hold a pair of black stiletto boots (pictured) that Arthur had never seen his wife wear—had always been effectively invisible, tucked neatly beneath the hems of their everyday lives. He had never opened it. He had never asked Amy what it contained. He had never even been curious until the day his wife disappeared.

It was so very pink, even in the dark.

He lifted the lid.

He saw Amy.

❧

At eleven o'clock the next morning, Arthur Rook's apartment would be broken into by Max Morris, who, after Arthur didn't answer any of his phone calls, would worry the door open with a credit card only to find the tiny one-bedroom he'd never actually stepped inside ransacked. Gutted. The refrigerator door open, motor wheezing. Papers strewn across the hallway and the bedroom floor. A trail of empty duffel bags and packs like shed skins leading from the hall closet to the bedroom, where, on a bed littered with clothes, an empty space the size of a large case told Max that Arthur had packed and fled. Arthur Rook would never know, but Max, who was a little in love with him (he couldn't help it; he'd never met anyone so guileless), would put everything away as best he could. He would fold the clothes and place them in drawers and on hangers. He would find Arthur's cell phone on the living room floor and feel a little less hurt that Arthur hadn't answered any of his calls. He would stack the papers neatly on the kitchen table and close the refrigerator but throw out the milk (probably spoiled). He would leave the blood in the bathroom. He would see the cat food dishes on the counter and guess that Arthur had taken Amy's cat with him. Then Max would steal a lukewarm beer for his efforts, and call the police, and sit in the living room and wait for them to arrive, examining a picture of Arthur and the late Amy Rook: huddled together on a beach somewhere, the wind whipping her hair across both of their faces. And Max would hope that his strange, quiet, runaway friend, wherever he'd gone, would be able to find his way back home.

But Arthur's home had ceased to exist. Its ghost had called to him and told him where to run.

2 ~ Freaks and Worthy Souls

Oneida Jones was a freak. It was nonnegotiable. It was absolute. It was common knowledge among both her fellow classmates and the population of Ruby Falls at large, but it wasn't until after her twelfth birthday that she ever considered the possibility that it was something to be embraced rather than raged against. Her fellow sixth-graders thought she was a freak because she had huge frizzy hair and dark eyebrows that touched in the middle of her forehead, because she demanded that Mr. Buckley teach them about Japanese internment camps, and because she was named after a spoon (not true). Ruby Falls, in the most general sense, considered her the freak reminder of the downfall of her mother, Desdemona Jones—the Fallen Prom Queen, as Mona was fond of calling herself, even though the title was something of a misnomer; Mona technically never made it to the prom.

Mona, the teenage daughter of Gerald and Mary Jones, pillars of the community, their boardinghouse a veritable Ruby Falls institution, ran away in the spring of 1993—and reappeared that August with a baby. Suddenly there was the infant Oneida and Mona, jiggling her on her hip, refusing to be denied or swept away: in her senior year at Ruby Falls High, shopping in the same convenience mart where all of Ruby Falls shopped, acting as though nothing remarkable had happened. Nobody ever said anything to Oneida about her mother, not directly. But she had spent her young life interpreting the awkward pauses and silences in conversations with the old guard of Ruby Falls, her grandparents' friends and colleagues, who thought her mother ought to have accomplished something more respectable with her life than having a kid at sixteen and baking wedding cakes for a living.

Oneida thought it was a perfectly acceptable way to live; Mona never gave her reason to think otherwise. When she was old enough to ask questions about her father, her mother always said the same thing: he wasn't ready to be a dad but I was ready to be a mom, so I brought you home. Her grandparents had always been kind and loving. If they had ever felt awkward around her, it must have been during her infancy, because she didn't remember anything other than juice boxes, endless hands of rummy, and pockets in cable-knit sweaters full of butterscotch candy, sticky in crackly orange wrappers. They were dead now, and her mother ran their boardinghouse, the Darby-Jones, a rambling mansion built in 1899 by her great-great grandfather, William Fitchburg Jones, and his business partner, Daniel Darby, who had sold hardware, farm tools, and milking equipment to the dairy farmers who still made up the entire tax base of Ruby Falls.

Oneida spent her childhood wandering the old creaky hallways of the Darby-Jones, variously hiding from and pestering the tenants over the years: Alice Cooper, an octogenarian who went to church every day to pray for the soul of that "devil rock musician who slanders my good name"; Roger Beers, an old hippie who worked for the post office and taught her the intro chords to "Smoke on the Water"; Kitty Grace, the former home economics teacher at Ruby Falls High who worshipped John F. Kennedy and had a small tattoo of his profile on her shoulder blade. It was a childhood almost completely devoid of other children. It wasn't until she went to kindergarten that Oneida understood not everyone had a working knowledge of mah-jongg, knew what *glasnost* meant, or had played with a stereopticon. Once the other kids figured out Oneida had more in common with their own parents and grandparents than with them, they found her largely uninteresting; once Oneida insisted that they would like learning about canasta and the Andrews Sisters, that the ancient set of encyclopedias in the den was a thousand times more fascinating than the Internet and she wanted to tell them all about it, the brand of *raging weirdo freak named after a spoon (not true!)* became permanent.

But one month to the day after her twelfth birthday, during a science lesson about the properties of light, Oneida Jones woke up. The tiny voice in her head, that had whispered *You're weird, nobody likes you, they all think you're a freak,* from the moment she climbed on the bus in the morning until she opened her front door in the afternoon, stopped speaking. In the silence, Oneida could finally hear what was happening around her. Jessi Krenshaw was asking Mr. Buckley to explain the difference between reflection and reflaction—*again*—and Mr. Buckley replied in his most sanctimonious tone that light reflacted when it bounced off a surface at an angle.

"What does reflacted light do? Like, can we use it for anything?" asked Jessi.

"Reflaction," said Mr. Buckley, "is one of the main principles behind lasers. It's the reflacting power of light that make lasers possible."

Oneida felt like she'd had a bucket of ice water dumped over her head. Exhibit A: Mr. B had never shown signs of a speech impediment, which, to her mind, was the only excuse for thinking *reflact* was a word. Exhibit B: He was wrong. He was *just wrong.* Refraction occurred when light passed through substances and appeared to bend; refraction was what happened in prisms, not lasers. She knew she was right because she'd spent the previous weekend poring through the L volume of the *World Book Encyclopedia* (*legislature, light, lunar eclipse*), not to mention she'd done the homework. She looked around the classroom. No one else was paying attention: they were scribbling in notebooks, winding hair around fingers, staring into space. And Mr. B just kept saying it: "Light hits the pavement and reflacts in all different directions"; "If light hits a mirror, do we think it will reflect or reflact?" Oneida put her hand over her mouth to quell the wild whoop of laughter that was building in her body, because she had just figured it all out: If being a freak meant she was the only one in the room to realize her teacher was a complete dumb-ass, then she'd be a freak and be proud of it. In that moment, she consciously chose the lonely, superior life of freakdom. It was a life she was already living anyway, but she accepted it on the basis that it was better to be lonely and right than stupid with friends.

That was the credo by which her entire existence took shape, the mantra that she'd repeat to herself when she moved up to the combined junior-senior high, through middle school and into her freshman and sophomore years, whenever her mother asked if she was having trouble: she never had friends over, she never asked for a ride to the movies or the mall. Better lonely and right than stupid with friends, she'd think, and tell Mona that the other kids weren't interesting. They didn't understand her and it was pointless to pretend she cared about useless things like who was taking who to homecoming and who said what on Facebook and blah blah boring.

"They can't all be bad," Mona would say. "There were plenty of boring people in my class, too, but there were a few worthy souls. You just have to figure out how to recognize each other." Oneida, aside from finding this almost impossible to believe, chafed at her mother's suggestion that the reason she didn't have any friends was because she wasn't trying hard enough. What the hell did her mother know? Mona didn't have to spend the day bouncing from class to class, struggling to stay awake and interested, when all she really wanted to do was curl up with a book and teach herself what she really wanted to know—which, incidentally, was *everything*, something she was fairly certain was absent from the curriculum at Ruby Falls High.

And then her sophomore year Andrew Lu transferred into the district, and Oneida understood what her mother meant about recognizing worthy souls.

Andrew Lu was beautiful. He was an athlete with skin the color of milky tea and warm dark eyes. He was also the only Asian in the entire school system, and rumor held that he had been born and raised in China until he was eight. He spoke three languages—English, Chinese, and French. He signed up for cross-country, the fall sport for smart jocks, and when he walked through the hall, cool rolled off him in waves. Oneida didn't understand how anyone under the age of eighteen could possibly be as comfortable in his own skin as Andrew Lu was. She envied him. He fascinated her. She wanted to ask him how he did it: how could he be so confident and yet so *different* from everyone else?

They had the same American History class, and Oneida, who sat three rows behind him to the left, would spend the whole period waiting for him to answer one of Mrs. Dreyer's questions. He'd raise his hand, and she'd notice how smooth and muscular his upper arm was, and then he'd answer the teacher's question correctly and confidently, without stuttering or rambling or adding extraneous detail, as Oneida was wont to do whenever she was called upon because Dreyer didn't think she was participating enough. One day, after Oneida had given a miniature treatise on the Whiskey Rebellion under such duress, Andrew Lu had actually turned around, made eye contact, and smiled. Oneida felt she'd been plugged to an electric generator; her entire body was shocked. It made her violently aware of a hunger she didn't even know she had, and she'd spent the rest of the day hiding in the drama club's prop closet, in the loft above the auditorium stage, sulking and crying and generally feeling sorry for her freakish, friendless self.

⌀

The fates aligned: Mrs. Dreyer assigned Andrew Lu and Oneida Jones to the same group history project. The worthy souls were being given a chance to recognize each other at last. That the other members of their group were two of Oneida's least favorite people at Ruby Falls High, not to mention in the world, hardly seemed relevant. That is, until they were sitting in her kitchen and wouldn't shut up.

"I don't know why anybody still cares about the Beatles," Dani Drake said. She jiggled her leg against the kitchen chair and rubbed her temple with her pen. "They're just . . . they're so *done*, you know? Everybody knows they're, like, the gods of pop music, but who cares *now*? You know? God is dead, so if the Beatles are God, wouldn't it follow they're *also* dead?"

"Who would you rather we write our reports on?" Oneida asked. She reshuffled her stack of loose-leaf history notes until all the pages were straight and neat. Oneida was proud of her compulsive tendencies. They made her feel older than fifteen, more in control, able to stop herself from grabbing a hunk of Dani Drake's bangs and bashing her head-first into the kitchen table.

"Oh!" said Dani with mock urgency, gazing heavenward. "Oh, you're right! There's no other band in the history of music that could possibly be more important than the Beatles! How stupid of me!"

Wendy chuckled into his can of soda, which surprised Oneida: she never would have thought Eugene "Wendy" Wendell possessed anything approximating a sense of humor. What he did have was a reputation: he was to be feared and avoided. It was commonly known that he drank grain alcohol with every meal, kept a Bowie knife duct-taped to his thigh, and that the white rope of scar running from his temple through his eyebrow was the result of a broken bottle fight with a hooker from Syracuse. The hooker won, but Wendy was still a badass mother-fucker. It didn't seem right for him to chuckle, even if the joke was mean.

"Guys—I don't think the Beatles are irrelevant, but for the sake of argument who else could we write this report about?" said Andrew. Oneida felt a little hurt. She tried not to hold it against him; being a good leader was mostly a question of diplomacy, after all, and Dani Drake lived off the bones that were thrown to her. Andrew had become the group's de facto leader, a position Oneida would normally have insisted upon holding herself had she not been immobilized by his physical presence in her house. In her kitchen. She wanted to run her hand through his thick black hair, wanted to will Dani and Wendy into nonexistence so she and Andrew Lu could sit and talk, just the two of them, on a Saturday afternoon, talk about anything and everything: *The Scarlet Letter*, which they were reading in English. What was his favorite movie? What had it been like to grow up in China? She wanted it so badly that she felt a little sick.

"I vote for The Clash," Wendy said.

"Uh, 'scuse me—*no*." Dani wrapped her bright blue gum around her finger and pulled a long strand from her teeth. "They're basically the Beatles of punk."

"The Sex Pistols are the Beatles of punk," Wendy said.

"*No*." Dani leaned forward on her elbows, the better to challenge him. "The Sex Pistols are the *Stones* of punk. Want to quit talking out of your ass?"

"Want to kiss it?"

"Ooh!" Dani chirped. "Nice one!"

In what was clearly an attempt to neutralize the situation by ignoring it, Andrew pulled out the assignment sheet their history teacher had passed out three days ago and studied it intently. The project required them to write their own research paper around a single theme and then give a group presentation on four "remarkable lives," as Mrs. Dreyer had put it. Oneida's group had at first been excited to pull musicians out of Dreyer's old ball cap, but whether to write about four separate musicians or four members of a single band was proving difficult to decide.

Oneida was torn between wanting the session to continue indefinitely—no matter how much she wanted it, Andrew Lu would most likely not stick around for cocoa and conversation without the excuse of a school project—and wanting Wendy and Dani out of her face as quickly as possible.

"We have to write about the Beatles," she finally said, adjusting her glasses.

"No shit, Shirley," said Dani.

"Well, they're the only group we've mentioned so far where there's a lot of information about all four members," Oneida said to Andrew. "So unless you want to get stuck writing about, you know, the *other* guys in U2, we have to write about the Beatles." She tapped her pencil on her notebook.

"That's a great point," Andrew said. Oneida felt her stomach tremble. She flushed and grinned. "I'll take George," he said.

"John!" Oneida said, raising her hand.

"Frick, I guess I'll take Paul," said Dani. "I look forward to exploring his pathological desperation to be liked and the ensuing artistic toll on the genius of John Lennon."

Wendy rubbed his scar. "That leaves . . . what's her name? Yoko Bono?"

"You're really witty for a sociopath," Dani said.

"Ringo," Andrew said. "Ringo Starr, Wendy. OK?"

Wendy shrugged.

In a flurry of closing notebooks, the study group disbanded. Dani clomped through the kitchen and onto the side porch, and the relief Oneida felt upon hearing the screen door squawk behind her was palpable. If pressed, she probably wouldn't have been able to quantify exactly what it was about Dani that drove her insane, but the cumulative effect of her gum-snapping, Beatles-trashing, obnoxiously quippier-than-thou ways incited Oneida to imagine acts of great physical violence befalling her. Oneida wouldn't have said that she and Dani were enemies—nothing had ever occurred between them around which to base an epic loathing—but *damn*, they irritated each other.

"You don't like her very much, do you?" asked Andrew Lu. He stood beside her on the porch as they watched Dani Drake weave her bike down the unpaved gravel drive. His sudden proximity made her jumpy and she nodded, not trusting her voice. She needed to be comfortable around him. He wrinkled his nose and leaned into her side—he was only slightly taller, so the effect was of Andrew Lu pinning his hip to hers, like they were contestants in a three-legged race—and mumbled conspiratorially, "That makes two of us." Then he hopped off the side porch and climbed on his own muddy bike. He even waved as he pedaled off.

Oneida wasn't sure it had actually happened. She raised her arm to return the wave a beat late, and ended up waving at Andrew Lu's retreating backside. She thought about how warm he had felt when he leaned into her, how ridiculously aware she had been of his solid mass. Oneida Jones was not the kind of girl who touched other people lightly, and she didn't take it lightly when other people touched her, no matter how fleeting the gesture. It wasn't that she didn't like to be touched; she just didn't trust it, or trust herself to interpret it.

She tucked a curl behind her ear and gnawed first on her right thumbnail, then her left. What she had wanted to happen—had it happened? Had Andrew recognized her worthy soul? Wind rustled through the trees, exposing the pale underside of the leaves. Her mother always said that when the leaves turned over, it meant a storm was coming. It was late September but it still felt like August: humid and gray, the air thick and anxious.

A thump from behind snapped her to attention. Wendy was still in her kitchen, opening and closing the cupboard doors.

"What are you . . . doing?" she asked, her arms popping with gooseflesh. She had volunteered for the first study session because nobody else did, plus the Darby-Jones, by its boardinghouse nature, had a perpetual open-door policy. But she felt defensive about Wendy rifling through her mother's pots and pans—intruded upon—and her body tensed.

He shook his soda can, the few remaining drops swishing quietly. "Just wanted to recycle," he said. He crushed the empty can between his palms and tossed it into the sink. It made a bright metallic *clank* and Oneida frowned, thinking of the vintage porcelain basin her mother adored.

Wendy walked right up to her and examined her face intently. He didn't blink. He was less than a foot away. The only thing she could think to do was stand very, very still.

"So," she said, her voice catching. "Are you looking for something?"

Wendy didn't say anything. He stared. He still hadn't blinked. His scar, up close, was mesmerizing, a twisted vine of white and pink that cut a half-circle down from his temple, so that his eyebrow was like a line of Morse code: a dash and a dot. Oneida focused on the scar for too long—long enough for Wendy to realize she was staring at it.

"I've been thinking," he said.

Wendy thrust a spoon at her. Oneida flinched, badly.

"Hey," she said. Her mouth seemed to have dried up. She coughed. "Hey, what are you doing with—"

"What does the back of this spoon say?" he asked. "Can you read it for me?"

She gritted her teeth. "It says Oneida," she said. "So what?"

"*So you're named after a spoon.*" And he grinned, a huge wolf grin that sent a cold charge up the back of her neck.

"I'm not going to discuss this with you," she said. "But let's just say that both the spoon and I are named after the same geographic location and Native American tribe."

"Oh—oh, I see. What's your Indian name, Chief Red Spoon?"

"*Hey!*" she said, but Wendy just laughed.

"Shouts with a Spoon?"

"Get out," she said. She knew she was blushing horribly and she hated it, hated it, hated it—hated this stupid body of hers and its stupid blood. She shoved Wendy hard. He held up his hands in a *don't shoot!* gesture and backed up until he was on the porch.

"See you around," he said, "Sitting Spoon." Then he cackled and kicked the porch door open. For the first time since making the word her own, since co-opting it out of a sense of personal pride, Oneida spat it out as a gasping curse as she watched Wendy disappear.

"*Freak,*" she said.

❧

Less than thirty minutes later, the thunderstorm hit. Rain poured down the windows of the Darby-Jones in unbroken streams, splashing off the sills, flooding the driveway, dripping into a blue saucepan on the side porch that Oneida had to empty constantly. She tossed another panful out the door and returned to the creaky pink- and orange-striped beach chaise where she did her best thinking, hidden away from the hustle of the rest of the house, nestled among lawn chairs, coolers, and a cracked flowerpot she had painted with misshapen pansies in the first grade. She'd brought the E volume from the old set of *World Books* in the study; E was one of her favorites (*Egypt, Einstein, electricity, elephants*), but today she wasn't interested, not really. Today she was a mess of nerves: because of Andrew Lu, because of Eugene Wendell, and because of the thunderstorm itself, which made the porch shudder and groan.

She hated being teased. She hated that Wendy thought it was funny to upset her, because—why? Was she absolutely *hysterical* when she got upset? But she knew how to cope with being teased. What she couldn't cope with were secrets, and Andrew Lu was a complete mystery, as inscrutable as the Chinese characters she had watched him doodle on the cover of his notebook. An echo of the voice she'd quelled at twelve piped up: *Why would he like you? Why would Andrew Lu, who is beautiful and brilliant and smells like coconut and coffee, whom strangers smile at when he walks through the hall, who has probably eaten sushi with real chopsticks and has traveled farther away than Syracuse—why would he like you?*

It was a question she couldn't answer, so she slapped the encyclopedia shut, rolled on her side, and watched the rain pour down. Wind filled the porch screens like sails, and Oneida shivered in the light mist. It was barely four o'clock but it was dark, and the darkness made her feel tired and worn out. She closed her eyes. She didn't see the yellow taxi rolling up the Darby-Jones driveway until it was close enough for her to hear the tires crackling in the loose gravel, popping like corn beneath the rain. At first she thought she was dreaming. She had never seen a taxi outside of television; there were no taxis in Ruby Falls. You could walk the entire length of downtown, past the convenience mart, post office, dry cleaner, gas station, library, Milky Way Bar and Grill, and town hall, in about fifteen minutes. The car had a checkered stripe running from hood to trunk. Gingerly, she craned her neck, still sore after flinching from Wendy, to watch the car disappear around the front of the house. Barely five minutes later she heard her mother unlatch the main door and welcome the passenger into the hall.

Oh, great, she thought. *Another stupid mystery.*

She sat still on the porch. She heard her mother's scratchy alto welcoming the new tenant, asking for his coat, telling him to leave his bags at the foot of the stairs. Then Mona launched into her standard tour of the Darby-Jones, her voice drifting nearer as she made her way through the main communal rooms—the front hall, the dining room where Eleanor Roosevelt once drank a milk shake, the TV in the den, and the library; past the rear study (off limits to tenants, reserved as her daughter's study space) and the kitchen.

Her mother's bare feet slapped against the original antique tile as she described how the right side of the pantry was divided into equal spaces for each tenant but the left was strictly for Mona's personal use and house dinners. Had she mentioned that, for an extra two hundred a month, he could be included in the meals she cooked six days a week, excluding Fridays, when tenants pooled their money for take-out? The stove was gas; the left rear burner was finicky and needed to be lit frequently. The pots and pans were to be treated as though they were children, and if he was ever discovered using a metal scouring pad on anything Teflon, he would be lashed to a snowblower and dragged through town. Mona had a dry delivery, and when the mysterious new tenant didn't laugh or even chuckle awkwardly, Oneida wondered if he or she thought her mother was actually serious.

"And this," Mona said, stepping onto the porch, "is the side porch. Where we keep the lawn darts, watering cans, and my daughter." She smiled at Oneida and gestured for her to join them, which Oneida did, crossing her bony arms over her chest and leaning in as Mona hugged her shoulders. Her mother always smelled of flour and frosting, the result of years of mixing, baking, stacking, and piping sugar onto wedding cakes, and Oneida inhaled deeply. "Oneida," Mona Jones said, gesturing to the man standing in the kitchen, "this is Arthur Rook. He's taking the rooms over the garage."

Arthur Rook looked lost. He was very tall and thin, not skeletal like the tall boys at school, who had stretched the same amount of skin over bodies that grew half a foot taller in the space of a summer, but she could picture him as one of those stretched-skin boys in the not-too-distant past. He was far younger than any of the other tenants, and she wondered what he was doing in Ruby Falls. He had dark hair and really needed a shave. His eyes were very dark and very bright, and he didn't blink. He was looking at everything—no, he was studying. He traced the outlines of all the vague, inanimate lumps on the porch, as if he were searching for something he'd left there years ago but would only remember once he saw it again. Arthur Rook's gaze finally made its way to Oneida, and when their eyes met she felt a strange tickle in her throat, like she was supposed to say something to this stranger, or he had something to say to her. He acted as though he knew something she didn't, which, as always, annoyed her.

A crack of thunder snapped Arthur from his trance. He shuffled forward and offered Oneida his hand, which she shook.

"Nice to meet you." His voice was uneven, as though he hadn't used it in a while.

"Where did you say you were from, Mr. Rook?" Mona asked.

"Los . . . Angeles." Arthur Rook shrugged, anticipating Oneida's knee-jerk response, she realized, of *So what the hell are you doing here?* "I had to leave," he said. "I was tired of it." He shook his head. "You need a decoder ring to order a hamburger."

"Oh, come on," said Mona. "Everybody knows about the secret menu at In-n-Out."

At that, Arthur Rook's face turned ashen and his eyes lost their intense focus, flicked back and forth, shone. In the awkward silence that followed, Mona offered to show him his room and he agreed—a little too quickly, Oneida thought, for a man who claimed he was just tired. She wasn't sure which mystery bothered her more: what Arthur Rook was doing in Ruby Falls, or what her mother had said to make him look like he wanted to cry.

3 ⁓ *Will and Testament*

Stepping into the Darby-Jones was like walking into a movie. Arthur had occasionally visited Amy on set, and each time he'd been struck by how unconsciously discomfited he became around Hollywood people. Even the crew seemed hyper-real and hyper-constructed: the grips too muscled, the PAs too loud and neurotic, and the effects team—of which Amy was an utterly devoted member—too wild-eyed and berserk. The air would thicken and spark with anticipation as the crew waited for scenes to be set up, for directors to be happy with camera angles, for stand-ins to be lit, and for stars to be made up. Arthur, the observing husband, would hover on the periphery, grateful for the insulation of his camera. The telephoto distance granted him immunity from the shared delusion that keeps a movie set pulsing: the conviction that all involved are creating something that is, in any way, real.

Ruby Falls also felt like a shared delusion and Arthur, again, immune. It was too atmospheric to have occurred naturally: the shadows too deep, the clouds calculated, too puffy and too perfectly slate-gray. The roadside forest was aggressively bucolic out the window of his taxi. The town center, anchored by a single blinking red light at a single intersection, spiraled out into the requisite townie bar and grill, small convenience mart, and post office with photogenically fluttering American flag. It was Mayberry. It was Stars Hollow. There would be irascible widows who solved clever murders. He had traded the alien terrain of Los Angeles for a land that was no less imaginary—absolutely unreal and cute as hell.

The town was nothing compared to the Darby-Jones itself. The house loomed out of the leafy darkness, four stories tall, wide and rambling and tucked into the woods like the haunted Victorian mansion it probably was. Arthur blinked as his taxi driver pulled around to the front. There's nothing inside, he thought: nothing but bare timber and studs holding up magnificently ominous exteriors. All interiors would be shot in a featureless concrete box in Studio City or Burbank. Real people didn't live in places like this, because real places like this didn't exist.

And Amy had grown up here? No wonder she believed in make-believe.

Amy had told him very little about her childhood. He knew she'd watched hundreds of movies. Her father, who died when she was very small, had introduced her to the Saturday afternoon matinee, to Toho International pictures, *The Seven Voyages of Sinbad*—and to the works of her idol, Ray Harryhausen. He knew she spent her earliest years dreaming of making monsters and had started small—with modeling clay and toothpicks—before finding an erector set at a flea market and discovering the beauty of the hinge, the joint, the electricity that would one day kill her. Arthur had met her grandfather, a quiet man who wore green suspenders and sock garters at all times, even with shorts, when he came out to California—only once—to visit. He flew in to San Francisco and they all drove to Monterey for the day, where the old man was overwhelmed by every public place they went. It was the first time in his life he'd ever been in crowds that large, and they flustered him; he spent his last two days in town watching the PGA Open from the safety of his hotel room. He'd raised Amy after her parents were killed in a car accident and died himself shortly after Amy and Arthur were married. Amy didn't fly east for the funeral because, she said, "He doesn't care. He's dead." She had never given any indication that this place—this *Ruby Falls*; even the name sounded made-up—was a storybook of a town or that visiting it would be anything other than boring and unnecessary; that it was anything other than the place where she'd dreamed of so many imaginary creatures, the place she'd had to escape.

Arthur inhaled. The air smelled like home. The trees—their leaves were beginning to turn.

He'd missed these trees.

He handed the cabdriver two hundred of the dollars he'd pumped out of an ATM at LaGuardia (he'd emptied as much of his accounts as the ATM would allow) and felt lucky for remembering, in his haste, to bring the emergency cash Amy kept in the freezer. *Brilliant, right?* she'd said, folding fifties and hundreds into origami stars and wrapping them in tinfoil. *So they look like hamburger patties.*

Last night he'd stuffed them down the side of his backpack, fresh from the freezer, and they'd cooled the space between his shoulder blades as he waited in line at LAX for a ticket on the first flight east, which turned out to be a half-empty red-eye to New York. He hadn't used the backpack—a beast of a bag that Amy, when she was drunk one night, succeeded in climbing all the way inside—since he took it to Europe as a senior in high school, on his Spanish club's trip to Spain. He'd imagined slinging it from breathtaking site to breathtaking site, hostel to hostel, but in reality had only unpacked it once in a Marriott in Madrid, which depressed him. It was built for adventure, for spontaneity, for a night like the night Amy died: a night where Arthur crammed whatever clothes his hands closed upon into it. A pair of sneakers, two cans of cat food. The book on Amy's nightstand, which he'd lent her.

The big pink shoebox that he'd seen in the dark closet.

In the cab in the driveway of the Darby-Jones, Arthur had removed the shoebox and replaced it with a cat. He'd been able to bring Harry-hausen, in the little cat crate that Amy called his hibernation pod, aboard the plane as carry-on luggage, but now he worried that the Darby-Jones would be pet-unfriendly. So Arthur maneuvered Ray Harryhausen out of his pod and into the top of his backpack. Harry was fast asleep, which was the only reason Arthur was not killed instantly.

It had never occurred to him to leave Harry behind in LA or in the care of Max and Manny, even. It had never occurred to him to call Mona Jones. Or to call—anyone. At all.

He thanked the cabbie and opened the door and stepped sideways into the dream Amy told him to run to.

Arthur stood on the porch of the Darby-Jones—an enormous porch, from what he could see—that wrapped around the house on all sides and was full of rocking chairs and had a hammock at one end, swaying in the breeze. He adjusted the pack on his shoulders and heard his furry passenger sigh. The pink box he held under one arm. The strap of his camera case bit into his shoulder.

There was a neat hand-printed sign in the window. ROOMS TO LET, it said. *M. Jones, Prop.*

He pressed the white button beneath the house number and heard a round low chime, muted by the closed door.

Mona Jones opened it.

She was not what Arthur expected. He had assumed she was Amy's age, his age—thirty or thereabouts—but she looked much younger than he felt. Her hair and her eyes were dark and she wore a black T-shirt dusted around the hips with flour in the shape of hands. Her face and arms were similarly dusted with freckles. She was warm and smelled of vanilla, and Arthur couldn't begin to understand why Amy had never sent that postcard. Why she hadn't kept in touch. Mona Jones looked like a best friend.

"Hello," she said. Her voice was deep. "Here about a room?"

Arthur cleared his throat. "Yes," he said.

His backpack grunted.

She held out her hand. As Arthur shook it, studying her face, her brown eyes, he was stupefied by her presence in this strange movie set of a world: she was warm and she was not acting. She was real. She was another person, another person like himself, who had known Amy. Had loved Amy.

If the postcard was to be believed, she was Amy's only heir.

☙

The postcard was dated August 18, 1993. It read:

> *Mona, I'm sorry. I should have told you. You knew me better than anyone—I think you knew me better than me. Don't worry, I swear I'm happier dead. Anyway, I left you the best parts of myself. You know where to look.*

It shocked Arthur silly. He had read it in the dark on the day Amy died, lying half naked on the floor in his closet, hands shaking after he plucked it from the depths of the pink shoebox. In the shoebox was the collected detritus of Amy's life: photographs, picture postcards, and greeting cards, ticket stubs and buttons and trinkets that, for her own reasons, she hadn't been able to part with. It was a museum in miniature, teeming with memories, with the residue of the recently departed. Bursting with Amy, and with him.

The first thing he had pulled from the box was a bumper sticker: MY CAT IS ON THE HONOR ROLL. Beneath that were photos from their last trip to Catalina Island, bright sunny images of catamarans and ocean water blue-green as candy. An old cherry stem, tied in a knot, dried and tough and still smelling of sugar. A tiny clay Kraken—the monstrous sea creature that destroys the city of Argos in *The Clash of the Titans*—molded by Amy's teenage fingers in green polymer clay, that had been her good luck totem. More photographs of Amy and Arthur at Catalina; at Knott's Berry Farm; swaddled in a bright green blanket and illegally sucking down tequila behind the dunes at Point Dume (that day—oh, that day, he remembered *that* day). Amy defying hygiene, lying on her stomach on Hollywood Boulevard, lips pursed in a kiss for Harryhausen's pink granite star. A ticket stub, faded and bent, from the Neil Diamond concert they'd seen at the Hollywood Bowl for their first anniversary.

Amy had warned him, on their first date, that she was the least sentimental person in the universe. *You lied to me*, Arthur whispered, and flattened the In-n-Out napkin from the day they met across his palm, his phone number at the motel written in red pen.

All pictures he remembered taking. All things he remembered happening.

Until Arthur broke through the top strata to the world beneath.

Only Amy could explain the significance of the wrapper peeled from a bottle of Red Stripe with *Don't let the bastards drag you down* scrawled across it. Only Amy knew where she'd picked up the green Lucite-heart key chain, cracked through the middle. Only Amy could explain why she'd wrapped a set of perfectly round, silver-edged cuff links made of ruby-red stone in yellow tissue paper and tucked them safely in a plastic Easter egg. He held them in his hand. They were beautiful and heavy.

And then *the* postcard. To Mona Jones at the Darby-Jones House in

Ruby Falls, New York. The town where Amy grew up. The town Amy never talked about. To Mona Jones, who knew her better than she knew herself. Mona Jones, to whom Amy had willed something—the best parts of herself, of her (happier-that-way) dead self, with five simple words of direction: *You know where to look.*

Arthur had found Amy's last will and testament: a postcard written over a decade and a half ago and never sent.

Run, Amy told him, and pointed. *There.*

He would have to tell Mona Jones everything.

❧

"I'll tell her tomorrow," Arthur said, and Harry half-wailed, half-hissed, which Arthur interpreted as *You lie.* It was true: he *did* lie. He didn't know what to say to her. He didn't know how to start. She couldn't know that Amy was dead, and if Amy had meant something to her—even years ago—he didn't want to be the bearer of that news. He didn't have the stomach to tell anyone that Amy was gone.

He hadn't told his parents. He hadn't told his brother. He hadn't told his landlord. He just—left. When he thought about Max or Manny or the fact that he clearly hadn't shown up for work today, he heard the sound of crystal vibrating. It hurt. But when he stopped thinking about them, he felt fine.

Harry hissed again.

Maybe he wouldn't tell Mona either.

Maybe he could—

But that was selfish. He was doing this for Amy, not for himself. He was honoring her wishes. He was—

He felt sick. He couldn't think. His rooms stank to high hell of cat piss, which didn't help.

Harryhausen had woken up just as Mona was opening the door to Arthur's rooms, and Arthur, spooked, had dumped the cat-filled backpack in the bedroom and hustled Mona out. In the ensuing thirty-second window, Harry doled out vicious retribution for his confinement. Arthur's entire wardrobe was now soaking in the bathtub (thank God his rooms had their own private bath), but the only soap he could find was a pump bottle of Dial on the sink. He'd done his best to work up a lather, but the bathtub was now a rank stew of urine-soaked T-shirts and cheap liquid soap. He would have to venture out tomorrow, no matter how painful the thought, if for no other reason than to buy cat litter.

Amy used to tease him about teaching Harryhausen to use the toilet. *You can train cats to do it—I've seen it on TV!*

"Sure," he'd said. "You can train *cats* to use the toilet, but the problem is, Harry doesn't know he's a cat. He thinks he's your husband. Your husband who chooses not to use the toilet out of spite because of, you know—"

"You."

"*He* never agreed to an open relationship."

Harryhausen was now licking himself indiscreetly on the green love seat in the apartment's main room, which was large and airy, with shining hardwood floors and trim and neat, if slightly shabby, furnishings. There were bright red curtains in the windows (currently all open) and a matching spread on the double bed; the walls were painted various shades of light green and eggshell yellow. The place was loved and a little Christmasy, which made Arthur feel safe and sleepy. He pictured Mona Jones and her daughter Oneida—what the hell kind of name was that?—with the radio on, dancing and singing, rolling paint all over the walls to the beat of an Elton John song: "Saturday Night's All Right for Fighting," maybe. That's the scene this set was built for, an iconic scene. No: a cliché. Mona would sing into a paintbrush and Oneida, shy, would only dance when her mother grabbed her by the hands and spun her.

Arthur's head hurt. This room, this place, made him—he didn't know what it made him.

He was tired in his bones. He hadn't slept on the flight so much as marked time while he breathed. He hadn't slept on the trains from the city upstate to Albany and points west, and he hadn't slept on the long cab ride out to Ruby Falls, two towns beyond East Bumblefuck, just south of the End of the World. And when had he eaten? He sat on the love seat beside Harryhausen and closed his eyes.

When he opened them again, it was late. It was night. Several years at summer camp in New Hampshire had taught him that night in the country feels different: it feels empty. Void. Alarmingly black and solid with silence. He turned to Harry.

"We should go to bed," he said.

Harry licked his paw and brushed one ear flat to his head.

"That's right." Arthur sniffed. "Wash everywhere."

He couldn't smell the cat piss anymore, which was a very bad sign. It probably meant he was brain damaged, which would explain the static when he stood, the weakness in his legs and his arms, and the nagging sensation that there were things he should be doing or seeing or saying, important things, pressing things, that had nothing to do with his being in this—movie. This television show. This world that Amy, Creator of Worlds, Maker of Monsters, manifested just for him: her past still living, still breathing, still knowable. Her self. Her secrets.

You know where to look.

He wanted them all to himself.

"Come on, Harry," he said, because he needed to hear the sound of his voice. His good voice. Sounding like Arthur Rook, even if he wasn't thinking like Arthur Rook. *You'll go to sleep and wake up again and everything will make more sense; you just have to get to bed—just get to bed, Arthur.* Tomorrow it'll make sense. Tomorrow, you'll see.

"I'll tell Mona tomorrow," he told Harry, who scampered ahead of him into the bedroom. "I'll tell everyone."

Harry leaped to the bed and turned back.

"No, you won't," he said, with Arthur's voice.

✦

Arthur opened his eyes. Where was he and how had he gotten here?

He remembered.

Arthur gasped and shoved twenty pounds of feline off his chest and saw a framed poster beyond his feet, opposite the bed: a picture of neat wedges of pie and cake in meticulously ordered rows, the pastry equivalent of a military drill, and he thought, in quick succession:

I am wearing sneakers in bed.

This is the second time in two days I have worn sneakers in bed.

I am—

Amy is—

Amy is hiding. Amy is here.

You know where to look.

He gasped again, for air, for anything. Everything sang out: his head and his arms and his wrists and his ankles and his hips and his back. His chest. His stomach. His throat constricted, and he heard himself give a strangled little howl that terrified him.

It was still dark. The clock on the dresser—an old-fashioned alarm clock, silver bells like double berets—told Arthur it was four-thirty in the morning. Arthur felt he could cut himself on this world; the air itself was sharp and razor-bright, and here he was: breathing needles into his body like a chump. *Well, maybe that wouldn't be so bad,* he thought; *maybe it would feel good to bleed.* He shook his head and didn't care that there were other people sleeping nearby and shouted, full voice, for Harry.

Harry didn't answer.

"Come on, Harry." Arthur swung his feet to the floor and stood up quickly and almost passed out. Running on fumes, he thought. When Amy worked late, she'd call on her way home from the workshop or movie set: *Tank's empty, running on fumes—gonna hit the In-n-Out; you want?*

Arthur stumbled into the living room. Harry was on the coffee table, lying on the pink box, his tail dangling over one side and twitching happily. He was asleep and dreaming, and Arthur was murderously jealous of this cat—this *cat*—who could sleep atop the museum of Amy and have beautiful dreams. Arthur wanted beautiful dreams. Arthur wanted Amy, the best parts of Amy, that were hidden here if only he knew where to look; he wanted them for himself. And Amy *wanted* him to have those parts. Otherwise she wouldn't have shown him the shoebox in the dark, wouldn't have pointed him at Ruby Falls and told him to run. She had had almost *sixteen years* to send that postcard to Mona Jones, and she never did. If she really wanted to name Mona her heir, she would have.

She didn't. It was clear, it was so clear—Amy wanted Arthur to know. Amy wanted Arthur to use the contents of the pink shoebox to give himself beautiful dreams and, in dreaming, to solve the mysteries she'd left behind. *To know where to look.*

No, Arthur thought. No, that's insane. Amy didn't know. Amy couldn't plan—wouldn't want—

Arthur Rook was good. But Arthur Rook was lost and shocked and more alone than he knew how to bear. When Amy, who hadn't even said good-bye, spoke to him in signs and wonders, he grabbed onto them with both hands. He turned them over in his mind and saw that they were real enough, that they were what he wanted. They took away the red drone in his brain, the sound of crystal vibrating. Mona Jones, who had seemed so real for an instant on her front porch, was another clue, another sign, another wonder. He could use her to find what Amy wanted him to find—he could use her like he had used the postcard. Like he would use the photographs and the clippings and the bottle caps and the key chains. He would use them all to see.

Harryhausen yawned in his sleep. Arthur scooped both hands around Harry's giant belly, up and off the box, and dropped him on the love seat. Hugging the shoebox to his chest, he bolted back into the bedroom and shut the door. He knelt and was just about to slide the box beneath the mattress (the better to dream beautiful dreams) when a light caught his eye—a light outside, through his window.

He froze. He heard Harry digging under the edge of the door, growling, trying to get in.

There it was again—a white dot that swung back and forth in the trees outside his window. He crept to the window and cupped his hands around his eyes.

Someone was in the trees outside. Someone—he saw a hand on a branch, a leg through the waving leaves—had climbed the tree outside his window at 4:30 in the morning. He squinted and saw another hand, holding a flashlight. A flap of fabric, light-colored. Maybe the hood of a sweatshirt.

There was a whip crack and then a body appeared in mid-air, a magic trick falling to earth. Arthur watched as a broken branch and a boy hit the ground fifteen feet below. The branch bounced. The boy—a teenager, in a hooded sweatshirt, thin as a rake—landed with a grunt and rolled to his side, moaning and coughing. The moaning told Arthur he was at least alive and, given that confirmation, Arthur felt no particular need to call for help. He was watching a movie: a movie he was part of, but a movie nonetheless. It was too early for secondary characters to die sense-lessly. This little stunt was clearly just this character's introduction.

The boy stood and rolled his head on his neck. He opened his eyes to gaze longingly to the left of Arthur, at the other end of the house. Arthur stared at the boy and felt like he was watching himself, had traveled fifteen years back in time to witness a moment he had never been brave enough, in high school, to attempt: an alternate history playing out before his eyes. The boy blew the house a kiss and staggered away in the dark.

"Did you see that, Amy?" Arthur whispered. "What do you think . . . what do you think it means?" He sat back on his feet and laid his palm flat on the lid of the shoebox. Then he closed his eyes and flipped the box open, stuck his hand inside, and fumbled until his fingers closed around something small, something paper and delicate, that felt right.

Arthur opened his eyes. Between two fingers he held a cookie fortune. *Someone*, it said in tiny red letters, *from the past will return to steal your heart.*

Arthur spoke and knew it to be true. "The boy is in love with Mona's daughter," he said, and slumped forward. He was asleep before he hit the floor.

4 ᥱ *Dinner at the Darby-Jones*

Arthur Rook didn't go to dinner for four days. During that time, Oneida saw him come out of his room only once, to ask for a cup of laundry detergent—which was particularly odd, because he didn't ask to use the washing machine. When she told Mona about his strange request (which she had complied with, because, after all, she was a good landlady's daughter), Mona gasped, pressed her hand to her throat, and said, "Dear God. You know what they say about strange men who drink laundry detergent."

Arthur appeared, like the ghost that supposedly haunted the third-floor broom closet, to all the tenants of the Darby-Jones in turn, in increasingly odd anecdotes they discussed over dinner. Anna DeGroot was the first to see him, on Sunday afternoon. He came up behind her when she was locking the door to her room and, without even introducing himself, asked if she could direct him into town. "Scared the absolute crap out of me," Anna said, jabbing her fork in the air for emphasis. "And I really didn't know what to do with the question. Did he want a ride? Did he want to walk? If that was the case, did he understand that town was about two miles away?"

"So what'd you tell him?" Mona asked.

"I offered him a ride, of course." Anna shrugged. "You know I've got a soft spot for strays."

Anna was the town's veterinarian. She had moved into the Darby-Jones four years ago when she divorced her husband, and Oneida, despite realizing it was strange that Anna continued to rent a single room from her mother long after she could afford to move out on her own, couldn't imagine life without her. She was a short, plain woman with curly brown hair pulled back in a ponytail with the aid of copious bobby pins and clips, as though her hair, should she not take special pains to hold it back, would explode. She spoke to everyone as though they were frightened animals, in soothing, measured tones that cultivated confidence, security, sleepiness. She was gentle but firm; Oneida could imagine her at the clinic—smelling slightly of disinfectant, dander, and the indistinct tang of animal fear—setting cat bones, wrapping cones around the heads of mutts, soothing an anxious German shepherd moments before putting it to sleep. The euthanizist within Anna both unnerved and awed Oneida. She suspected, beneath the curly, fuzzy exterior, that Anna possessed a core of titanium steel, one that allowed her to kill family pets as a matter of everyday business. No doubt it was this same strength of will that allowed her to screw around with Sherman Russell, the high school shop teacher and another resident of the Darby-Jones, without anyone—other than Oneida—knowing about it.

Oneida had discovered their affair the previous spring when she woke up thirsty in the middle of the night, went to get a drink of lemonade from the kitchen, and passed Anna's rooms on her way to the stairs. At first she'd been afraid Anna was having some kind of fit or was being strangled, but then, in a humiliating moment of clarity, she understood. Sex was happening. Behind that door. In her house. *Right now*. She'd run back to her room, not caring who heard her feet pounding along the creaky hallway. Oneida had seen enough movies to know that kids occasionally stumbled on their parents having sex; it was usually played for comedy, but, at the time, Oneida didn't see anything remotely funny about it. She felt dirty, like she'd been spying and had found out something she couldn't forget. It was equally disturbing as an object lesson in the dangers of getting exactly what she wished for: maybe she didn't want to know *everything* after all.

The next morning, Sherman Russell, a short man who wore plaid flannel shirts and motorcycle boots and let kids she wouldn't trust with a pencil operate giant saws, had greeted her over his morning cup of coffee nonchalantly. Were they all pretending it hadn't happened? That Oneida hadn't heard the queen bed with the carved acorn newel posts thumping against the floor and the wall, hadn't heard Anna's voice, sounding alternately alarmed and thrilled, calling Sherman's name?

Anna poured herself a cup of coffee shortly thereafter, offered a cordial good-morning to all, and opened the *Ruby Falls Register* to the sports section. Oneida realized that what was going on between Sherman and Anna was a secret. More than a secret—it was illicit. Maybe they thought her mother would kick them out if they were discovered, which didn't make any sense at all to Oneida; if anything, Mona would just insist that they each continue to pay rent before blessing them to boink with impunity.

More likely, they were keeping their relationship a secret for her sake. *Most of all,* Oneida thought, and giggled into her bowl of cereal, it was so patently ridiculous, *most of all, you've got to hide it from the kids.* Well, the kids find things out, and then she heard another song in her head: *The kids are quite aware of what they're going through.* She felt happily full of knowledge, buzzed on information. It was a complete reversal of the way she'd felt the night before, and she understood it wasn't the knowing of things she craved—but the knowing of things that other people didn't.

Which made gossiping about Arthur Rook over dinner the highlight of Oneida's day. Anna continued by saying that Arthur had accepted her offer of a ride into town, and they had both gone into Avery's, the convenience mart whose limited selection Ruby Falls depended on for its basic necessities. "So we meet up at the checkout in about twenty minutes, right?" Anna said. "I've got the usual: bread, lunch meat, veggies, toothpaste. And I'm trying not to say anything to this poor guy, who's clearly—*clearly*—bonkers, but I'm watching all this random stuff roll by on the conveyor belt—"

"Like what?" Oneida asked.

Anna bugged her eyes.

"Rubber cement. A pad of multicolored construction paper. Scissors." She paused. "Toothpicks, I think. Tape. String. And kitty litter."

"It's a good source of fiber," Mona said.

Sherman grumbled something into his lasagna. Oneida assumed it was a tacit condemnation of arts and crafts; it was common knowledge that Sherman and Mrs. Brodie, the art teacher at Ruby Falls High, despised each other. Rumored reasons spanned from a long-ago love affair that ended badly to a war over parking spaces in the faculty parking lot. Oneida suspected Sherman hated Mrs. Brodie because Mrs. Brodie was a hippie, and Sherman, who kept a sawed-off shotgun under his bed, did not truck with pacifism of any sort.

"Finally, I couldn't help myself." Anna dabbed at her lips with her napkin. "I tried to be kind of jokey about it, but I pretty much asked him what the hell he was doing. I think I said something like, 'Is this some new Hollywood diet?' because he looked a little taken aback, as though never having been formally introduced meant I wouldn't know anything about him.

"Anyway, he shrugs it off but I can tell I've made him think of something, because he runs back into the aisles for a second. And when he comes back, he has a jar of peanut butter and a box of Froot Loops."

"At least he's not starving himself," Mona said. She wound a string of molten mozzarella around her fork and slid it between her lips.

Sherman laughed gruffly and passed his plate to Mona for a second helping. "Joker doesn't know what he's missing. More for us, huh?"

"You saw him too, didn't you, Sherm?" Anna asked. There was something almost professional about their rapport, Oneida thought. Their casual familiarity, covering for a greater intimacy, felt studied and cautious to Oneida, so the end result was that it didn't feel casual at all. She didn't understand how they could ever think they were fooling anyone.

Sherman nodded and swallowed the giant lump of pasta and cheese he'd just shoved into his mouth. He propped his elbows on the table and splayed his hands, setting the scene. It was the same stance he took whenever he explained a new project in shop, meant to convey the responsibility and seriousness required to operate large machines designed to rend and tear. "It's night, late," Sherman began, flexing his fingers. "I forget which night: Monday; let's say Monday. I go down to the kitchen for a snack and this joker is sitting at the table with a glass of something red in front of him."

"Like blood?" Mona took a sip of water. "So he's a vampire?"

"But here's the thing—all the lights were off. So I don't see the kid until I flick on the switch and suddenly he's just there, with this glass of red junk, and he doesn't flinch or jump or say anything. Kid just looks up at me and sort of blinks, and he looks—kid looks drunk, frankly, and

I've seen enough drunk kids in my life to know what they look like. Glassy eyes. Kind of hollow and dead."

"Rude," said a quiet voice, crackly as paper, that belonged to Bert Draper, the oldest resident of the Darby-Jones, and also the quietest and most likely to fade into the background. "Inexcusable," she clarified, with a sharpness that signified the conclusive judgment on Arthur Rook.

Roberta Draper had lived at the Darby-Jones all Oneida's life and all of Mona's as well. She was eighty-seven years old and the very last of the Drapers, who had once owned the largest dairy farm in Ruby Falls. She was so pious Oneida wondered why she never became a nun. She had lived the life of a nun, with or without the habit—she had never married, kept herself cloistered in her rooms, and made no secret of her disapproval of everything: chiefly, Mona's decision to raise a child without a husband and civilization at large's decision to become a cesspool of sin, flesh, and tabloid magazines, to which, despite reviling them, Bert was utterly addicted. Mona would pick up a copy of the *National Enquirer* or *Us Weekly* whenever she went to the grocery store and leave it in a highly visible location for Bert to pick up, condemn, and eventually take back to her room to peruse. Maybe that's why she never became a nun, Oneida thought. Bert was excellent at recognizing sin but terrible at resisting it.

Bert was mobile for a crone pushing ninety; she walked with a cane but she didn't really need it. She liked having something to announce her presence, and the cane's sharp clomping could be heard throughout the house whenever Bert was on the move. There were five separate rooming quarters in the Darby-Jones, two with their own baths. Bert had one of these, and it comprised the majority of the top floor. Mona had offered to move her into the second-floor rooms-plus-bath—the space Arthur Rook now rented—but Bert had insisted: all she needed was her cane, and she could manage all four flights of stairs quite well, thank you very much. The end result was that Oneida, Mona, Anna, and Sherman would be sitting at a dinner table full of cooling food as they listened to Bert's cane clomping closer and closer, a blip of archaic sonar, until finally—finally—Bert Draper would shuffle into view, gush that they needn't have waited for such an old bag of bones, but radiate pleasure that she had, in fact, managed to teach the younger generations the importance of manners, of propriety, and, most of all, of self-restraint.

General conversation moved from Arthur Rook to other topics too mundane for Oneida to bother paying attention to. She watched as Bert chewed her lasagna and stared into space. There was something about the methodical working of her jaw that made Oneida think the lasagna was incidental, that Bert was really chewing on the puzzle that was Arthur Rook; from the look on her face, it tasted vile.

⚜

By Thursday, Arthur Rook was presumed dead. In a running gag instigated by Mona, mother and daughter were going to have to kick down his door, haul out his corpse, and drag it down the driveway for the trash guys to pick up. Oneida didn't know why this was the funniest thing she'd heard in forever, but it was—she lost it every time Mona described how the two of them would have to heave his lifeless body down both flights of stairs, arms and limbs flopping like carp, and how, by the time they got to the first landing, they'd be so fed up they'd just fold him into a ball and roll him the rest of the way down.

Oneida was always the first to crack; she couldn't help it. She'd tuck her chin down, squeeze her eyes shut, and press her lips close together, but a laugh would always burst through the dam, strangled and sharp: a goose honking into a trombone, as Mona had once described it. And Mona would be smiling at her, beaming even, but otherwise a paragon of control in the face of abject hilarity. She didn't know how Mona did it—how she could be so ridiculously hilarious and never laugh at her own jokes. All she knew was that Mona was the only person who ever made her laugh, really laugh, and she remembered how much she loved her mother—really loved her—every time it happened.

"So what do we think his problem is?" Oneida asked. "Other than being dead."

Mona shrugged. "Being dead strikes me as enough of a problem, don't you think?"

Oneida had already peeled more than a dozen carrots and was slicing apples for cobbler. She stared down at the creamy white flesh falling away under every stroke of the knife. "He's just so different from the other tenants. Seems kind of weird, is all."

Mona tapped her spoon on the edge of the pot, loosening blobs of squash. "Don't worry, Jones. I can smell bullshit a mile away, and Arthur Rook was standing next to me." Oneida looked up, stricken, and Mona smiled. "I know he's hiding from something," she continued. "Maybe his wife kicked him out. Maybe he lost everything in a bad stock trade. Maybe he's having a psychotic break. A good landlord doesn't care. He paid cash up front, he was polite, and, in case you didn't notice, he's cute as hell. Maybe he'll liven things up around here."

Oneida's cheeks and forehead burned. She hated it when her mother talked about men. It mortified her to think that her mother could be physically attracted to someone, would want to date him, kiss him, have sex with him. Sex as a general topic was embarrassing enough, but as it related to her mother? Insufferable. She tried not to think that she'd been infected with the Ruby Falls groupthink—this was the attitude that got her mother into trouble in the first place—but she couldn't help it. Even worse was realizing she accepted herself as the Trouble Her Mother Got Into, that her existence had kept Desdemona Jones from going out into the world and having a bigger life. These spasms of baseless guilt overtook her more often as she grew older, as she understood her own mad desire to leave Ruby Falls far behind. She pushed it down into her stomach and swallowed.

She tossed a hunk of apple into her mouth and watched her mother waltz around the kitchen. Mona Jones, cooking, reminded Oneida of a ballroom dancer: she made it look effortless and elegant, something she'd been born to do. Her piecrusts were flaky, buttery clouds of pastry; her homemade pastas were rich but magically weightless; her wedding cakes were elaborate pieces of sugar architecture built on carrot, cheese, lemon, and chocolate—delicate islands of edible ingenuity that had informed Oneida's first daydreams of fairy-tale castles, imaginary lands, enchanted woods.

Oneida knew her mother could have opened her own restaurant in New York City; she could have built an empire of books and cooking products, her signature on a line of stainless cookware, aprons, and high-heat spatulas. But Mona was living in obscurity in Ruby Falls, unappreciated, her marvels of gastronomy wasting away in the bellies of ex-hippies and lonely old ladies on Social Security who wanted nothing more exciting to eat than pot roast on Monday, chicken on Tuesday, spaghetti pie on Wednesday, meat loaf on Thursday. Wasting away in her own belly, Oneida thought, and touched her rumbling stomach.

Mona spun between the table and the stove, checking the meat loaf, stirring the sautéing carrots, layering the cobbler in a single fluid motion, a few curls falling out of her ponytail and drifting through the air as she twirled. Mona had had her thirty-first birthday last spring, and she seemed young even to her daughter: she still wore ponytails, brightly colored T-shirts, jeans, flip-flops. Oneida could picture her walking through Ruby Falls High—which Mona said hadn't changed a bit since she went there—holding a science textbook and humming some old grunge classic. She was pretty, fair and dark-haired, so she'd run with the popular kids—but she'd be nice to Oneida: smile at her in the hall, pass her the basketball in gym, commiserate about the cafeteria food as they stood in line together. All the normal teenage things that Oneida didn't think she had the capacity to even understand, her mother would teach her to like. Mona would have been her friend, she knew—and she found herself wishing, absurdly, that she could go back in time and be a friend to her mother as well. The kind of friend who would've told Mona over and over again, You owe it to yourself to get out of this stupid town; you're a genius; get out, get out! The kind of friend her mother would call When She Got in Trouble. The kind of friend who would say—what?

Give it up?

Get rid of it?

She shuddered involuntarily, a spasm of the stomach and the spine that had nothing to do with the cool breeze ruffling the white kitchen curtains. Maybe that was the core of her true freakishness, what the world at large recognized in her: she wasn't even supposed to be here. It didn't matter how much Mona loved her. Her mother had made the wrong choice.

She set the table and made herself forget that particular truth about herself.

By the time Anna and Sherman were sitting down, Oneida was calmer. She was a little worried she might remember and put herself off dinner entirely, but the arrival of Arthur Rook, looking slightly rumpled and as though he hadn't actually meant to stumble into the room at that precise moment, was more than a distraction. It had only been a few days since he'd asked her for detergent, and she was surprised how different he looked from the Arthur Rook she'd built in her mind, the Arthur Rook who had taken on comically mythic proportions: who sat in his room and made cat litter and string art on construction paper, who got drunk in the kitchen in the dark; the corpse she and her mother would have to kick to the curb. Arthur Rook, to Oneida's surprised eyes, looked tired and distant but overwhelmingly a real person.

"Hello," he said. "Is it OK if I, uh, join—"

Mona pointed to the seat on her left. "Of course," she said. "Please, Mr. Rook, sit down. We're having meat loaf. And let me be the first to say that I'm glad you're not dead."

Arthur Rook hesitated slightly, looking from Mona to the chair to the other people at the table, and Oneida thought for a second he might bolt. Mona must have sensed it too, because she said, "Welcome back to the world. Small as it may be."

"Arthur." He took the seat. "Please call me Arthur."

"Anna DeGroot," Anna said, turning to shake Arthur's hand.

"Right," Arthur said. "Thanks again for taking me to the store."

"I'm Sherman Russell." Sherman waved from the other side of the table and Arthur, still looking slightly dazed, returned the gesture.

"Nice to meet you all." Arthur unfolded the paper napkin Oneida had placed beside his plate.

Thursday was always meat loaf night, but Mona had decided to switch the usual mashed potato complement for fresh snap peas and carrots and the first acorn squash of the season. Oneida, as usual, had been in charge of the biscuits and was proudly relieved that not a single biscuit had been scorched that evening.

It all smelled fantastic, so Oneida wasn't the least surprised when Arthur, barely concealing the note of desperation in his voice, said, "When are we going to eat?"

Mona's face cracked in a wry smile. "We don't eat it, Arthur. We just like to look at it."

Arthur's brow furrowed. "I'm sorry," he said. "I don't—"

Oneida rolled her eyes and blushed when she realized Anna had seen her. She gave Oneida a little disapproving narrow of the eyes and Oneida slumped in her seat.

Sherman, uncharacteristically, threw himself upon the sword of conversation and asked Oneida how school had been that day.

Oneida's ears detected the *clomp* of Bert's cane—she was on the first floor and would be in the dining room in another thirty seconds or so, and yet the idea of making thirty seconds of conversation with Sherman about school still seemed interminable. Sherman acted as though he and Oneida were fighting the same war, he a general and she a soldier in the same trench day after day, and he frequently talked to her about the troublemakers in his classes as though they were Oneida's friends and she could offer them counsel: "Why don't you tell that Hearst kid to knock it off? He's pratting around with the lathe; there's going to be trouble," or "Can you talk some sense into that Baxter moron? Kid's gonna lose a finger if he's not careful."

She took a sip of milk. "OK, I guess. Pretty boring."

"Any big tests coming up?" Anna asked.

"Math quiz on Friday about the quadratic equation. And I have my group history project. That's due in a couple weeks."

"Is that why that punk kid was here last weekend? That Wendy what's his face?" Sherman, anticipating Bert's arrival, pulled her chair out. "That kid's gunning for trouble. I caught him with a tube of fake blood a week ago; you know what he was going to do with it?"

Sherman didn't continue. With a start, Oneida realized it hadn't been a rhetorical question. She shrugged, said that she didn't really know him, he was just in her group. She neglected to mention Wendy's new favorite thing to do was grin madly at her if they passed in the hall, after which she'd hear a mocking falsetto *Spoooooooooon!* as soon as he glided into her blind spot.

"There's only so many things you can do with a tube of fake blood in wood shop, none of them good," Sherman said. Bert accepted Sherman's distracted offer of a hand and allowed him to maneuver her to her seat. She thanked him quietly and immediately bowed her head, assuming, as Oneida saw it, that the rest of the Darby-Jones tenants were too far gone to even bother asking to join her.

"Tragic Jigsaw-related Dismemberment," Arthur muttered. "A hand, a foot, a finger. Kid kind of sounds like fun."

Sherman bristled. Oneida felt a little giddy. She thought Sherman was a windbag—not a bad guy, but a windbag, and ridiculously out of it—and she agreed with Arthur: Wendy was a jerk, but that didn't mean she couldn't see the potential for comedy in the situation. She smiled, and when she looked up she caught Arthur Rook watching her, noticing her smile. He looked desperately happy, relieved, almost, to have discovered the appearance of a tiny alliance, and she looked quickly away.

"And who is this young man who sits before me?" Bert Draper, all prayed out, adjusted her glasses on the tip of her nose and squinted at Arthur. "Is this the boy who's been hiding from us for days? We will overlook your abhorrent rudeness, young man, but only this once."

"I'm . . . thanks," Arthur said, more confused than penitent.

"Now tell us about yourself. Where do you come from. Where is your family from. What do you do, and what are you hoping to do, now you are here." Bert fired statements, not questions.

"Bert," Mona said, reaching for the platter of meat loaf. "Let's eat before it gets cold."

Bert harrumphed and wriggled in her chair. She reminded Oneida of a chicken settling over an egg, fluffing and adjusting herself, anxiously, jerkily. Roberta Draper gave Oneida the creeps. She was practically mummified, her skin wrinkled and parched; the face powder she used flaked off like dust. Her eyes were hard and dark, and that was what bothered Oneida the most: whenever she talked to Bert, she knew—she knew—Bert was withholding information. Bert had seen more people come and go, and more things happen, in their home than Mona and Oneida put together—and for whatever reason, for now, Bert Draper was keeping it all to herself.

It was also terrifying to watch Bert Draper eat. She didn't have false teeth, but she didn't possess a full working set of originals, either. Little flecks of moistened half-masticated food would work their way between her remaining teeth and through her lips, dropping to her plate or dotting the wildly patterned orange and turquoise scarf she wore, not because of drafts but because, Oneida knew, she was sensitive about the folds of skin that hung loosely from her neck. Having to eat Mona's stupendously tasty dinners within ten feet of Bert Draper was a lesson in culinary sadism: it was painful, but the food tasted too good to stop.

"This," Arthur Rook said, and paused between swallows to breathe, "this is the best food I've ever eaten." He took a long swig of water and exhaled. "I want to . . . to *hug* this food." His cheeks were bright pink and he was smiling. He had a huge smile, Oneida realized, one that made him look like a completely different person—like someone who might be fun to have around, and not just because it was always fun to have a weirdo you could gossip about behind his back.

"You haven't answered my questions, young man." A crumble of ground meat trembled on Bert's lips as she addressed Arthur.

"Which question was that?" Arthur asked. His hand wavered; his fork, carrot speared on its tines, seemed to have forgotten the way to his mouth.

"What brings you to Ruby Falls?" Bert asked.

Arthur's eyes flicked up and to the right and then back again, to Bert's face.

"What brings *you* to Ruby Falls?" he said.

Oneida squeaked.

"I was *born* here," Bert said. Her eyes narrowed. "I've lived in this house for twice as long as you've lived on this planet and you will show me some respect—"

"Bert," Mona said quietly.

"I don't mean to be disrespectful," Arthur continued. "I don't have anything to hide. I'm not—"

"So answer the *question*, young man."

Arthur looked at Mona—looked right *at* Mona—for help. He might as well have said the words: *Will you tell this old bat to back off?* Oneida saw it. Anna saw it, Mona saw it, and Bert *certainly* saw it.

Bert glared at Mona and ran her tongue over her front teeth.

Mona inhaled. "Bert, please," she said. "Give him a break." She nodded at Arthur. Oneida noticed the glow of gratitude staining his cheeks again, as though he'd made a friend for the first time in his entire life. Arthur Rook's hunger was as naked as it was unsettling, and Oneida cringed, embarrassed for him. "If he wanted to kill us in our sleep, he'd have done it by now."

Oneida heard the gentle teasing in her mother's voice, but Bert reacted as though she'd been smacked.

"You're despicable, Desdemona. Making excuses—*flirting*, in front of your daughter, with a stranger. A *married* stranger."

Arthur was married? Oneida squinted across the table, but Arthur's left hand was half-obscured by the salt shaker.

Mona balked. "I am not *flirting* with him, Bert." She turned to Arthur. "I'm so sorry for this, Mr. Rook."

"Arthur," Arthur said.

"You—" Bert stuttered. "Desdemona Jones, your parents would be ashamed of you. *Ashamed.* Apologizing to *him* after what he's said to *me*?"

"What did he say to you, Bert, really? What did he say that was so unforgivable?"

"He didn't say *anything*—that's what's so unforgivable. And you—do you have no idea what you have in this house, you silly girl? What you should be protecting? I know more about these rooms and everyone who's ever slept in these beds and eaten at this table than you can suspect—and that includes you, Miss High-and-Mighty—and I know why and how to protect it. I know *everything* that goes on here"—it wasn't Oneida's imagination that she spat those words at Anna and Sherman—"but I can't be held responsible for your secrets when you let the wolves in at the door. Good night to you all."

She pushed herself away from the table and Sherman, belatedly, tried to assist and only succeeded in handing Bert her cane. The assorted weirdos, daughters, mothers, and lovers of the Darby-Jones sat together in silence at the dining room table, the emphatic clomp of Bert's cane the only sound in the entire house. Mona looked over at her daughter, and the faint sheen of fear in Mona's eyes gave Oneida a horrible chill. Whatever Bert meant by her parting remark, Mona not only knew what she was referring to but agreed—*agreed.* Oneida's mother had a secret, and Bert knew what it was, and Oneida, apparently, wasn't to be told. Despite the meat loaf, the carrots, the fluffy lumps of squash, Oneida's stomach suddenly felt vast and empty as the Darby-Jones itself: a cold, hollow space echoing with each strike of Roberta Draper's cane.

⚕

Oneida begged off clean-up duty on account of an upset stomach. Which was the truth: Bert's words had churned her insides something awful. Mona sent her off to finish her homework and go to bed early, and Oneida left without a word. It made her feel sicker to think it, but she didn't want to be around Mona. She didn't want to be alone with her mother and be unable to ask what Bert had meant when she spoke of secrets—or, worse, be able to ask, and find out, and then not be able to un-know.

She and Mona occupied the two bedrooms in the Darby-Jones's rear second-floor wing, their rooms both opening on the main hall and separated from each other by a bathroom, which Mona called the Green Room: a shared walk-in closet and vanity that Mona had to cross to reach the shower and sink. Oneida's was the smaller room but by far the better: it occupied one corner of the house and had three windows, one with a built-in window seat that overlooked the Darby-Jones property. A giant maple tree grew less than six feet from the edge of the foundation, and the branches had to be trimmed every spring to keep them from growing right into Oneida's room. She protested the trimming every year, because she liked the idea of being able to climb out her window and down the maple tree, liked having the option of escape. The tree turned a brilliant orange-red in fall, and the late afternoon sun shining through the leaves plastered against the window filled her room with golden red light. Like stained glass, Oneida thought. Like her room was not only secluded but sacred.

Without taking off her sneakers, Oneida flopped on top of her bed and pulled her blue blanket up to her chin. Homework. She had homework to do; not much but hopefully enough to keep her mind off what had happened at dinner. She stuck her foot out from under the blanket and snagged her school bag, dragged it to the side of her bed, and rooted blindly for the ratty school-owned copy of *The Scarlet Letter* that

Ms. Heffernan had passed out on Monday. It was falling apart, the pages stained with Coke or coffee or worse, corners bent and ripped. It occurred to her that this was the exact opposite of a good distraction, as she couldn't picture Hester and Pearl without seeing Mona's face and her own, an infant in Mona's arms, in the framed picture Mona kept on her dresser: a candid taken by Oneida's grandmother not long after Mona came home from New Jersey. She could have been any baby: big head, big dark eyes, sexless and round. But Mona looked like a statue—a Greek statue, noble beneath the folds of the same blue blanket Oneida lay under—as resolute and unyielding as a piece of marble. With the face of a kid, not much older than Oneida was now, the implications of which Oneida grasped more with every passing birthday.

She hated her brain. It chewed on things—it churned—whether she wanted it to or not.

Mona's secret was the same as Hester's. It had to be. The more Oneida thought about it, the more obvious it became. It was the central secret of her entire existence, after all: a secret that had been addressed and sidestepped for so long she'd forgotten there was a real answer, beyond the vague, conciliatory *he wasn't ready to be a father*—an answer Oneida hadn't known she was dissatisfied with until that moment. Mona had given her the impression that her father was a nonentity, not worth the time and energy it took even to think about him. Oneida tossed the book aside, spinning with the realization that she had been brainwashed so easily by her mother, had so willingly dismissed the person who had provided fifty percent of her DNA. How could she have lived this life for so long without taking the time to look at it, really look at it, critically?

Bert knew. Roberta Draper knew who her father was.

She stood up and paced. The sun had set and Oneida was surprised by how dark her room had become. She flicked on the overhead light, and the sallow, artificial brightness it threw over everything, coupled with her alarm, caused her to see familiar objects and find them strange. Her bookshelf, painted by Mona with tiny pink and red polka dots, looked diseased instead of cheerful. The blue and yellow ribbons, stamped in white ink with images of microscopes and atoms and words like SCIENCE, EXCELLENCE, and MATHEMATICS hung limp from her corkboard, unable to remind her what she'd done to earn them. A jumble of shoes beneath her dresser and a sleeve, red and black striped, dangling from a half-open drawer, held no meaning for her, had been worn by someone else. And her collection of music boxes—Mona gave her a new music box every Christmas—looked grotesque and frightening, the light bending shadows across the shining porcelain faces of rabbits and cartoon characters. She loved her music boxes, adored their precision and mechanical cunning, but in that one moment everything changed. Nothing in the world now seemed sadder to Oneida than to be frozen in wood or china, never playing a new song, twirling in place forever.

She felt she needed to do something, but rushing up to Bert's room and demanding the truth was far too frightening to imagine. And despite this new ardent feeling of unease about her mother, Oneida knew she ought to confront her first, give her the benefit of the doubt, before plying Bert as a last resort. But not tonight, she thought, wringing her hands. Not tonight. Right now, tonight, she would open her window. Her room was too hot, too stuffy.

The old wood of the window frame was stiff, and her leverage—sitting on the window seat—was poor, but she gave it a violent push and it rattled up. Cold air rushed forward, and she eased her knees over the sill, her forehead against the screen, which she decided to raise, too. Soon there was nothing between Oneida and the outside world, and she breathed in the cold air of early fall and felt calmer. The leaves of the maple tree rustled in her face.

The bottle was tied to the nearest branch. Oneida watched it sway in the breeze for a full minute before she understood that, unlike her other possessions, it actually *was* a foreign object. She barely had to lean out her window to grab it, and when she pulled it closer, the piece of twine that bound it to the maple tree snapped, eaten by the elements. She wondered how long it had been there. What would have happened if it had fallen and she had never found it—whatever it was?

Oneida crossed her legs on the window seat and examined the bottle. It was old, stoppered with a cork, greenish with raised letters, like the bottles she'd seen in antiques shops and flea markets. The embossed glass read BAKER'S TONIC, but a more recent hand had printed a message in tight, controlled script on a dingy label, half torn off: IN CASE OF

EMERGENCY, BREAK GLASS. Oneida turned the bottle over in her hand and saw, inside, a tiny scrap of brilliant blue cloth, loosely rolled to resemble a rose—or a cinnamon bun, maybe. It looked soft and downy, velvety, folds undulating from deep midnight blue to a bright azure. Oneida smiled when she realized how much better she'd feel if she could just touch that fabric, rub it against her cheek, feel it warm and rich between her fingers.

She placed the bottle on the windowsill, too worn to wonder, as she would have on any other day, how it had come to hang from the branch outside her window, who had tied it there, when, and why. For now it was reassuring enough to know that, in the course of the coming emergencies, she would have a glass to break.

5 ~ *In Dreams*

Arthur had always been a dreamer. As a kid he'd rush to breakfast, fresh from adventure, eager to learn what his brother David had seen while he slept. Dave, disappointingly, seldom with anything to report, would slowly blink his ten-year-old lids and shrug, but Arthur had ridden through a pink sky on a cloud of blue cotton candy. He'd been kept in a cage beneath a witch's kitchen table, fattened up for Thanksgiving, and then watched while the witch's relatives arrived like actors milling on a stage with tablecloth curtains half-lifted: a parade of stark black high-buttoned boots with vicious heels that had excited him like no dream ever before. He'd even once dreamed himself onto the bridge of the Starship *Enterprise* and had been whipped into a froth of anxiety because he was *supposed* to be on the *Millennium Falcon*; he was in the wrong universe entirely, and Spock had neck-pinched him to shut him up.

In Ruby Falls, Arthur dreamed all the time.

In Ruby Falls, Arthur couldn't tell when he woke up or if he ever woke up at all.

The past week—the week that had been the source of such speculation among the other residents of the Darby-Jones—Arthur had spent dreaming of his Amy. He saw her. Once she was reading a book on the couch and the lower half of her body was a mermaid's tail, a glittering mass of dark gray-green and blue scales that ended in two veined furls, waving slowly in an imaginary current, mesmerizing Ray Harryhausen.

Once he'd seen Amy lying next to him in bed at night, and when he reached for her he'd felt her—she'd been warm and real—and it wasn't until he tried to kiss her that he understood he was making out with a pillow, and Harryhausen was watching him in disgust from the windowsill. But then Amy walked out of the bedroom carrying the pink shoebox under her arm, and Arthur could swear that both Harry and he turned to look: they had both seen her, he wasn't still dreaming, and maybe he never had been.

His eyes ached from trying to see her. His head hurt from *looking* so hard, all the time, at the pieces of Amy in the shoebox. At first he didn't realize the systematic deification of the shoebox's contents had any religious implications at all, but after days of scrutinizing, recombining, and installing them around his temporary home, it was hard to ignore that he had become a zealot. Scraps of magazine articles and photographs were taped to the wall in neat patterns: in steps and pyramids, wheels and sunbursts. A winding line of postcards—for Los Angeles, for New York, for Santa Cruz and the Mystery Spot—swooped above the red-curtained windows like a smoke trail. Fast-food toys and plastic mood rings slid back and forth on a red string clothesline stretched several times from wall to wall. He was an obsessive detective, embedding himself in his biggest case, plastering his periphery with as many obscure objects as possible—waiting, praying for the larger pattern to reveal itself. For the unseeable to be seen.

Amy showed herself in flashes, smelling of oranges and sunblock: turning a corner, walking away, absorbed in a book. Closing a door or pushing a curtain aside. She would move in and out of rooms, heedless of Arthur calling after her, to speak, to say anything, to please talk to him. If only she could tell him about the objects in the shoebox, Arthur knew he would understand.

She never said anything. She wouldn't even look at him or stop whatever she was doing, and Arthur would lose himself for a moment, and when he opened his eyes again she would be gone and he would wonder when he'd woken even though he didn't remember sleeping. He had to try harder; he knew that was the answer: he had to look deeper, he had to look more, he had the power to find what she'd left behind if only he wanted it enough. And he did want it, more than he'd ever wanted anything else. So every day he sat on the green love seat and blindly chose a clue from the shoebox and waited for Amy to speak to him, or through him, and teach him how to see.

In the box, Arthur found a small monkey made of pink plastic, looping tail like a giant question mark, that had been hanging from Amy's margarita glass on their first real date. After lunch at the In-n-Out, Arthur had been the first to cave: he'd phoned that night, not caring how desperate it made him look. He *was* desperate—friendless, confused, and lonely—and Amy was his lighthouse, leading him back to land.

"You must think I've got a pretty free schedule, Rook." Her voice crackled through a bad connection. "Calling for a date less than twenty-four hours in advance."

"Yeah, you're the social pariah here," Arthur said.

Amy laughed. "Come on, who doesn't love a guy with a social disease?"

Arthur, giddy, couldn't stop himself from singing back to her,

"*'Cause no one wants a fella with a social disease!*"

The silence on the other end was sudden and painful, and Arthur panicked. "Sorry, that was . . . stupid, I just . . . I was in *West Side Story* in high school. I was a Jet."

Then he realized she was laughing, a slow-build kind of laugh that was imperceptible over the phone: a full-body laugh that shook her shoulders and tipped her slowly forward at the waist. He would see her laugh like this many times in the coming years, would often be the cause.

She exhaled and laughed more audibly this time. "Oh, Rook," she said, and then: "I just want you to know—it's OK, I understand."

Oh, God. "What?"

"When you're a Jet, you're a Jet all the way. *Hasta mañana.*"

The next night he picked Amy up at the apartment she shared with an actor named Desmond, who was eating Nutella out of the jar when Arthur knocked. Desmond was short and very handsome, and, Amy whispered close in Arthur's ear as they descended the rickety back steps, desperately in love with Keanu Reeves. "All over his walls," she said. "All over the ceiling, completely papered in magazines and pictures. It's like a . . . a receiver, or an amplifier, that room. Like the sheer force of his desire will bounce around the walls, intensify, and emit a Keanu-seeking beacon that will summon him in the flesh." She shrugged. "He's completely insane, but you have to respect that kind of passion."

They went to a dive bar in Burbank because Amy said it had the best thin-crust pizza in town, and it did, something Arthur would only truly appreciate years later, after he had more of a basis for comparison. The pink plastic monkey had been dangling from Amy's margarita glass, swinging from the salted rim by its tail. Over a huge pizza, margaritas, and a pitcher of beer, Amy told Arthur about the joy of bringing inanimate objects to life. Arthur told Amy about his parents worrying that his artistic ambitions meant he'd be living in their basement for the rest of his life; about David breaking his leg on Arthur's thirteenth birthday—which David absolutely did on purpose, he was so jealous Arthur was getting a Nintendo—about his mother's cancer, her chemotherapy.

Then Amy told Arthur about coming to LA with no money and no place to stay; living in a YWCA; temping, waitressing, building creatures late, late into the night, beasts of clay and wire grappling across her lumpy moonlit mattress; the window that barely opened; the cracked mirror.

Arthur told stories from school, about his classmate Roger, who took photographs of photographs and called it photographography; about Eva, his mentor and favorite professor, born in Russia and unapologetically Communist, who took a series of photographs of her students slapping each other with fake fish. He said she would have loved art school, would have loved the absurdity of the pretension, the inventive mire, the melodramatic gossip and politics of creative people. He asked to see her monsters, said he wanted to see them very badly, and realized, with the sudden impact of a meteor striking the earth, that the rest of his life would be completely different if he didn't kiss Amy before the night was over.

"I need to kiss you tonight," he said, drunk enough to think he ought to warn her. "If I don't kiss you, you're going to go away. Change into a pumpkin or a mouse with a little apron or something."

"I think you're the one who needs to get kissed tonight," Amy replied, the slight slur in her voice making Arthur realize, with relief, that she was a little drunk, too. "You've been here *how* long and you haven't been kissed? That's what this town is all about, you know. Getting kissed, getting off, same diff." She belched daintily. "We should go find someplace right for a big Hollywood kiss."

"Where are we, Burbank? Which way's Hollywood?" Arthur slid out of the booth and took Amy's hand to help her. Her fingers were long and cool, and she curled them around his. "This isn't what I thought Hollywood would be like."

Amy held the door for him and they stumbled out of the bar together. "Nobody expects Hollywood," she said, "to be a lot of crummy strip malls and adult video stores and car dealerships and ninety-nine-cent stores and parking lots and . . . and . . . fothermucker, I'm too drive to drunk. So you are. I mean, you, too."

There was a Laundromat next to the bar, and Arthur leaned his forehead against the window. The bank of dryers hummed across from him, concentric circles rolling together, spinning merrily under the fluorescent haze. An overweight woman in a purple T-shirt folded a flat bedsheet.

"We can go down to Sunset or Hollywood, or maybe up to Mulholland. Mulholland is amazing. Totally lives up to the myth." Amy wove her arm through Arthur's, clasped his hand, and rested her forehead on the Laundromat's glass beside him. "It's dark and winding and so high up you can see the whole town at your feet. A million lights. It's a black carpet of stars." He felt her body expand and contract with a sigh. "Or we could watch these dryers all night."

"So beautiful," was all Arthur could add. Whereas before all he'd seen were the circles, now Arthur saw the colors swirling within—a blue smear, a pink comet, a yellow blur, roiling together like Roman candles, damped by heat, trapped behind glass. This was a new Hollywood to Arthur—this wasn't the zombie city that had been slowly feasting on him for a month, up until two days ago. And it wasn't the fairy-tale gloss, scored and production-designed and glowing with impossibility.

It was a Laundromat next to a bar. It was a beer in his blood and a woman, holding his hand, breathing beside him.

It was better than anything he'd ever known.

He pushed himself away from the glass and Amy followed. Arthur certainly hadn't planned it to be so graceful, had never attempted anything of its kind before, but whether it was the fault of the alcohol or some vestigial Hollywood magic didn't really matter. He swung Amy out the length of his arm and reeled her back, dipping her gently over his extended knee, so that the tips of her hair were brushing the cement when he kissed her. Arthur heard violins and brass swell over the thrum of the dryers, and when they pulled apart, upright and breathless and unsteady, as much from the kiss as the beer, Arthur was filled with an overwhelming gratitude for having found Amy at all—and for not dropping her on her head and killing her.

"I can't believe I did that," he said.

"I can't believe you did, either," Amy said. "Let's do it again." And she went limp in his arms, curving her head and her neck away from Arthur with all the grace befitting a drunken mermaid.

Now the pink plastic monkey dangled by its curlicue tail on the red string clothesline.

In the shoebox, Arthur found a small purple pill that turned out to be a tablet of Easter egg dye (as determined during a highly scientific experiment in the kitchen late at night, when Arthur, seeking solitude, had nonetheless underestimated that lumberjack shop teacher's desire for a nightcap). He found an old framed photograph of two teenagers, a boy and a girl, standing on the edge of the ocean, hands clasped, bodies forming an M, the surf running around their ankles in twin parabolas. He found a loop of anonymous ride tickets, old and blue and bent into perforated zigzags. He hung the tickets over the photograph like a piece of bunting and finger-painted the glass around the figures with red-purple dye. The strangers held hands and smiled and refused to tell him their names.

The objects in the pink shoebox—the things Amy left behind—told him to put them together like so many puzzle pieces. He was moved to make things with them, to take them apart and reassemble them in new configurations. He was a trained artist, for God's sake—he could collage the clues. He just couldn't create the solution.

Arthur had his bachelor's degree in fine art, with a concentration in photography. He took all the required fundamental classes—figure drawing, design basics, and some torturous mixed-media classes taught by grad students who gave As to any kid who thought to juxtapose the sacred, the profane, and the commercial by stenciling the word *fuck* over an oil painting of Mickey Mouse—but Arthur had been miserable at creating anything that required the most basic level of hand–eye coordination, had been inept with a brush and beyond awkward with charcoals. He had survived fundamentals by force of will alone, bought a camera and rented lab space, and never looked back.

The barely passing grades in drawing and painting made semester breaks less than pleasant during his freshman and sophomore years. Arthur came from a family of welders, overnight assembly-line foremen, typists, teachers, nurses, office managers, one podiatrist, one mechanic, and one cop. They were blue-collar Bostonians—Somervillians, specifically—and gave Arthur his first object lesson in loving those you didn't really understand: namely, that it went both ways. Neither he nor his parents could pretend they really grasped the other, and Arthur, inspired by a lifetime of pawing through glossy *National Geographics*, shook like a leaf when he announced he wanted to go to school for photography. His parents were mystified but not terribly surprised and eventually agreed, setting one condition: that he go to State. They wouldn't even consider helping pay for a private art education, something Arthur's father referred to as "setting a pile of money on fire and trying to piss it out." And when Arthur's first set of grades rolled in—As and Bs in his required general ed courses, an A in Visual Theory, and two Cs and a D in Figure Drawing, Mixed Media, and Intro to Painting—his father had tugged on his chin, taken his firstborn son aside, and explained that if he wanted to see naked girls, he didn't have to be an art student; he should just go to more parties. It wasn't healthy for a young guy to see naked girls in class twice a week and then *draw* them, for chrissake. But Arthur held on (and kept to himself that he had, in fact, met one of the models from his figure drawing class at a party and had thus seen her naked in a purely social context), and as soon as he left behind the required charcoals, pastels, paints, and pencils, even his father was impressed.

The justification for his decision first revealed itself to Arthur while he was developing a roll toward the end of his first semester in Intro to Photography. The assignment had been to capture an everyday object in such close detail that it was rendered unrecognizable, transformed into its purest lines and shapes. At the time, Arthur had been dating a busty voice major named Beatrice who wore great smears of purple eye shadow and sang Madonna songs in the shower, a different one every day. One morning, the chorus of "Like a Prayer" wafting over the whine of dormitory water pipes, Arthur had crawled out of her single dorm-issue bed, grabbed his camera, and gone on photo safari in her underwear drawer. They had only been together for half a week—the single dorm-issue bed had seen first and second base and was steadily rounding on third—but, in accordance with the whole Beatrice package, Arthur had expected her underwear drawer to be the undergarment equivalent of the Taj Mahal.

The few pieces he'd already seen had suggested as much, but they proved the exception, not the rule. His first thought upon seeing the perfectly folded rows of clean white and cream panties and matching bras—with a few garishly lacy pieces jammed together in the corner like an aberrant splotch of plumage—was that he had opened her roommate's underwear drawer by mistake. But no. Beatrice the busty voice major had a single; she had no roommate. What she did have—a compulsively tidy drawer of cotton underpants and full-coverage beige bras—flustered Arthur but didn't stop him from snapping two dozen hastily composed photos before Beatrice, dripping and humming, returned.

It wasn't until he developed the film that he understood what he'd felt standing over Beatrice's underwear drawer, which, in the fantasies that occupied the majority of his waking life, had once existed as a teeming mass of black and red lace and strings and straps whose purpose and function he had yearned to explore as a conquistador yearns for undiscovered country. It was a more sophisticated and wholly unexpected emotion that took Arthur as he pinned the dripping photographs up to dry. They weren't the most beautifully composed shots he'd ever taken, but he had aced the assignment: none of them looked like underwear.

They looked like snowy fields. Freshly pressed hospital linen. Blank canvas. Scoops of silken ice cream. And the twinge of disappointment Arthur thought he should have felt at discovering the full-coverage cotton girl lurking beneath Beatrice's cabaret exterior vanished. What took its place was a genuine tenderness and another kind of intrigue—for another person, a real person with the capacity to surprise him, not merely live up to his wildest fantasies and expectations. He got an

A-plus on the assignment and maintained his artistic integrity (and girlfriend) by refusing to reveal the original subject of the pictures.

The photos turned out to be stronger than Arthur's relationship with Beatrice, which combusted in less than a month over irreconcilable differences (Arthur thought it was perfectly reasonable to prefer a midnight show of *Monty Python and the Holy Grail* to a kegger at the fraternity that required every pledge class to kill a chicken, and Beatrice disagreed). When he brought his portfolio home over spring break and his father saw the pictures of Beatrice's underpants—and the A-plus they had earned his son—he clapped Arthur on the back. His parents framed two of them and no one ever suspected they were anything more salacious than fitted sheets. If he could trick his parents into decorating their family room with pictures of his girlfriend's panties, then truly he had found his calling.

Which only made the opinion widely held among his art-department friends harder to refute: that he was batshit crazy for wanting to move to Hollywood—which he did, batshit crazy or not, two and a half years after graduation. He knew as well as they did that all the serious photographic art was going on in New York City. Didn't he want to take serious pictures, and make serious art, in a city that was *closer*? And didn't he know that Los Angeles, choking on paparazzi, was where good photography went to die? He had shrugged off their disbelief with the assurance that he knew exactly what he was getting into; of course he didn't want to spend his life hounding celebrities for blurry money shots, but he wanted to be a portrait photographer, like Dorothea Lange, Diane Arbus, Richard Avedon. Of all the things and places he'd observed, faces fascinated Arthur the most, and what better way to worship the subtleties of the human face than by taking pictures of it for a living, in a town where all everybody did was look at one another?

Plus—and Arthur couldn't explain this to his friends and his family without hurting their feelings—he needed to leave. He had grown up in and around Boston, but it had never felt like home to him. He knew there was more—or, at least, there was *other*. As soon as he had enough money to make the trip, rent a place, and live on long enough to find a job, he went. He couldn't grow up to be like his grandfather, who had never left the house in Somerville where he'd been born—who didn't know how the dirt sounds when it crumbles over the edge of the Grand Canyon, had never eaten hummus or seen a camel anyplace but a zoo, had never heard blues played below the Mason-Dixon line, where it just sounds better. Of course, Arthur's grandfather was perfectly content knowing that he didn't know and hadn't seen as much as he possibly could, but Arthur wasn't. He never could have imagined Amy's face—the way the hard lines of her nose and her jaw worked together instead of against each other—if he hadn't seen her for himself, if he had never left the place where he was born. He hadn't even imagined he would ever love anyone enough to marry her before he met Amy.

And now he didn't remember who that person had been. The Arthur Rook who dropped a large cardboard box of pots and pans and sheets and towels and pillows and an iron his mother insisted he would want, just trust her on this, at the FedEx in Harvard Square—the Arthur whose brother threw a going-away party the Saturday before his flight with red Jell-O shots and illegal Cuban cigars and a surprise appearance from some of his college friends, two years gone from his life and already grown far apart—the Arthur whose parents both took the morning off work to drive him to the airport, only to stand beside him while he processed his itinerary and then wave from the other side of the security checkpoint—that Arthur Rook hadn't existed in almost seven years and would never exist again.

And the other Arthur—the Arthur in love with Amy and Los Angeles, who went into elementary schools on picture day and told kids to say *flatulence*, which only worked with the smart third-graders and then grades five and above—who took freelance head shots on the side and was skeptical when his boss told him the entire studio was going digital and then so sad that it meant he'd be getting rid of the darkroom and Arthur would have to find someplace else to process his prints—who ate dinner with Amy, who slept with Amy, who had an occasional fight but nothing big with Amy, who stayed in on Friday nights and got up early Saturday mornings to go for a run with Amy—that Arthur Rook was gone.

In his place was a new Arthur, an Arthur who dreamed and ached and couldn't see.

The morning after his first supper with the other tenants, Arthur woke up muddled with guilt and still full. He had reentered society for two reasons, both self-interested: he had smelled Mona's meat loaf cooking, and he had realized that it was time to take the next logical step in his investigation.

It was time to use Mona.

But he hadn't counted on that strange old woman, had never intended to make a scene, and he certainly hadn't counted on the effect Mona's cooking would have on him. After nothing but sugar cereal, peanut butter, and water for the better part of a week, Mona's meal hit his system with the intensity of a controlled substance, and for one heady moment Arthur could see again: could see Mona, smiling sympathetically from across the table. He was excited to think Mona's taking his side against the other tenant—that wizened old woman whose name he couldn't even remember—meant she liked him. She would talk to him again and she would tell him things about Amy and about the contents of the shoebox. Which stirred his unease, since he had to make sure *he* didn't tell her too much in return. He couldn't let Mona see the postcard that bequeathed the best parts of Amy to the one who would know where to look. It would be difficult, but necessary, to get at the truth that Amy wanted *him*—and only him—to discover, and if that meant keeping a culinary genius in the dark, so be it.

Harry was lying beside Arthur in bed, practically spooning him.

"Morning," Arthur said. Harry sighed.

Arthur smelled sunblock and oranges and sat up, swinging his legs over the side of the bed.

Maybe he was still dreaming.

He stood. He heard a thump as Harry leaped down and Arthur filled his lungs and took a step and then another step. This really did feel like dreaming: his head was light and very far away.

Mona was singing in the kitchen. Arthur heard her as soon as he opened his door, and for a moment it jarred him. But he refused to wake up.

The old hall boards creaked under his bare feet. He wasn't sure where he was going, only trusted that he would know when he arrived. The hall was more like a balcony or a parapet: a landing that wrapped around the hollow core of the house on all four stories, connected from floor to floor by short staircases that curled like fruit peels. Arthur had never been in a house like this; it was an optical illusion or an impossible illustration, and it made him feel unsteady and wary and watched.

He passed a large framed black-and-white photograph at the top of the main stairs, of two young men in old-fashioned suits with tight collars and matching silver watch fobs, facing each other in fanatically straight high-backed chairs. Behind one chair stood a woman with a grim expression and dark curly hair.

He looked at the two men. He looked at their faces. The man on the left had thick black hair, a long nose in a pale young face, and a smile that revealed itself only after Arthur had been staring at him for a long time. The man on the right, with the woman standing behind him, had short light hair and a spectacular brush of mustache, and a small notch, like a bite, out of one ear. A fighter, Arthur thought. But he didn't look unkind; his eyes were tipped at the corners, lifted. The men in the photograph were smiling. The woman looked like someone had just drop-kicked her kitten.

They wore their secrets like their buttons and their chains and their cuff links—too small to see but essential, giving everything its shape and place.

Their cuff links?

Arthur screamed.

The men in the photograph—MR. DANIEL DARBY and MR. AND MRS. WILLIAM FITCHBURG JONES, as the brass plate screwed into the overbearing gilt frame proclaimed—wore matching, perfectly round, silver-edged cuff links that Arthur had seen, that Arthur had held in his hands, that Arthur had unwrapped from a piece of yellow tissue paper inside a plastic egg. He would bet every dollar he had ever owned or would ever make that they were ruby-red and heavy and beautiful, and this—this was more than a clue, this meant—he didn't know what it meant other than that it was something he was meant to see.

"*Mona!*" he shouted. He pulled the picture off its nail and held it at arm's length and laughed.

"Hey!" Mona's shout startled him, and he clutched the frame to his chest.

She was standing in the foyer, wiping her hands on a blue and pink towel. Her dark hair was pulled back in a ponytail, and she was barefoot, and she wasn't smiling her usual smile. She was angry and afraid.

A tiny part of Arthur woke up and was horrified to know none of this was a dream. It never had been. He was freezing cold. He saw what he looked like to Mona: he tried to remember if he had taken a shower that morning (he hadn't), or shaved (he hadn't, in days), or put on a shirt, even (he hadn't—nor had he put on any pants). He stepped away from the wall, still clutching the frame, and Mona, her brow creasing, started up the stairs.

Arthur's throat clogged as he tried to speak.

Mona froze on the third step. The blue and pink towel hung limp from her hands. "What?" she said.

"I saw—" Arthur tried.

Mona resumed climbing, flicking the towel over her shoulder. She propped one hand on her hip and the other on the banister and glared at Arthur: at his dark blue boxers, his matted chest hair, his rooster legs, as Amy called them. Arthur sniffed and drew farther back. He crossed his arms over the frame, pressing cool glass against his sternum.

"Arthur," Mona said. "What in the blue *fuck* do you think you're doing? You steal shit off the wall. You—yesterday, at dinner, whatever *that* was. You're disrupting my other tenants, one of whom keeps a shotgun under his bed. I live in the sticks but I'm not stupid, so tell me why you're here, why you're really here, before I call the state police." She flipped a cell phone out of her pocket with the elegance of a magician revealing a bouquet of flowers beneath a silk handkerchief.

His hands shook. "Oh, God, no—no no no. There's no reason to call the police. I'm not going to hurt you." Everything was shaking now. His teeth began to chatter, and he felt heat rise from his chest to the top of his head. "I'm sorry, I'll go—"

"I'm dialing," Mona said.

"No! No, please, I'll go; I'll leave right now. I just have to get my cat. Oh—" Harryhausen, who never missed an entrance, came padding down the hall out of Arthur's open door.

"You have a cat?" Mona said, her voice rising three octaves on the word *cat*.

"Ray Harryhausen." Arthur pointed dumbly at the ball waddling toward them. Mona stopped dialing at the sight of Harryhausen and stared, thumb frozen over the cell phone's number pad. Her jaw loosened and hung; her mouth opened.

The cat oozed into a sitting position at the top of the stairs and closed his eyes, spent by the journey down the hall.

Mona flipped the phone shut and didn't speak.

Arthur felt Mona looking at him but couldn't look back. He was so ashamed. Of everything he'd done and been planning to do—of everything he would still do, given the chance. He was so close. He could almost see—he could almost see *everything*.

"Give me the picture," Mona said, holding out her hand.

Arthur's arms refused to let go of the frame and brought it back to his chest, pressing cool glass against his warm skin.

"I'm sorry," he said, and fumbled along the railing in the direction of his room. He was still looking back at Mona when his bare foot caught fur and he heard a wild gut-ripping shriek; the noise was horrible, and so close that Arthur wasn't sure if it came from himself or the cat. Then he felt his center of balance shift, felt gravity yank his chest and pull him down. His shoulder hit the first stair. He curled protectively over the frame, rolled forward so that his tailbone connected next, and then: over to his shoulder again. This pattern repeated several times until it stopped with an abrupt collision with something cold and unforgiving. He hit his head. His elbow hurt.

He heard a thudding and then Mona's face was hovering, darting back and forth with unnatural speed. He squinted and closed his eyes, but that prompted Mona's head to shout *No don't do that!* so Arthur didn't. His arms were still hugging the photograph close to his chest, but it no longer felt cool and smooth: it was prickly, sharp, warm, and sticky. Mona's voice faded in and out; he heard a series of electronic beeps like a heart monitor, and as his vision grayed and blurred, he saw—something.

Just to the right, just—there.

What was that? It was—

Arthur Rook, who could see in the dark, closed his eyes. And when someone shouted *Stay awake, Arthur!* he didn't listen.

⚬

He saw Amy, but she was different this time.

She was actually there.

He heard a metallic rattle and tried to move his head, but something stiff was binding his neck like a collar and he couldn't look. He stopped trying. Amy was leaning over him. Her hair and her eyes were darker than the last time he saw her, and the space around her head was smeary and soft. She looked like a senior portrait, or a studio still from the forties, a photograph taken through a lens coated with Vaseline.

"Hi, Amy," he said, or he thought he said. Amy didn't act like she understood him. She looked up, away from him, and asked a person Arthur couldn't see a question he didn't understand.

"I missed you." He tried again. "I missed you so much."

Amy leaned in closer and Arthur, who had never been in love with anyone the way he was with Amy, felt perfect relief flood his veins with warmth. He had found her. He was flying. Oh, thank God. He smiled.

"He's smiling," Amy told the invisible person. "Is that good or really, really bad?" Her eyes were afraid.

"'S good," Arthur said. "You came back."

"Amy never came back," Amy said, strangely. He felt her thumb passing back and forth over his hand as she held it. She spoke again to the invisible person. "Can I have a hit of that?"

There were so many things to tell her. There were so many things to say, so many . . . and he was so tired, suddenly, and so calm. He was going to take a nap, but first—

"Hey, Amy," he said, "I met Mona. She's . . ."

His throat clicked. He was so thirsty.

Amy cocked an eyebrow. "She's what, Art?" she said, and grinned.

"She's beautiful." Arthur sighed and fell under.

6 ↗ *The Relativity of Normal*

"**M**y mom is insane." Oneida couldn't stop once the first words were out. The tremor in her voice was a warning even she couldn't heed. "I mean, totally crazy, gone, taking the red-eye to Nuts Vegas. So this weird new guy falls down the stairs from the second floor, right? His blood's still probably in the front hall. Mom rides in the ambulance with him, waits around till the doctor's all like, *He's going to live but he might have some memory issues*—like it matters, since he's a *complete stranger* and we know *nothing* about him—plus his chest is all torn up and bleeding, because he fell on a picture frame that he tried to steal, like, off our wall. So he's got all these disgusting stitches all over his body, but here's the part where Mom goes completely off the deep end: he's *here*. He's still living *here*! She helped him back up to his room and she's *taking care of him*. She's *insane*!"

Andrew Lu was completely silent. Oneida wondered if she'd called the wrong number.

"Andrew? Are you there?"

"Uh. Yeah. I'm here. That's pretty . . . crazy."

Oneida rolled back on her bed, wedging her head between the pillows. "I know, right? It's like she *wants* us to get hacked to bits in our sleep by this psycho. I mean, *he lives in our house*. And he's . . . all fucked up." It was a kick to say *fuck* on the phone to Andrew Lu. "Do you think I'm safe? God. I braced my desk chair under my door, but if he wanted to get in here—like, really wanted to—that chair would only slow him down."

"I wouldn't worry." Andrew cleared his throat. "Actually . . . it doesn't sound all that crazy to me."

"What?" Oneida was hurt. She finally had an exciting story to tell, to catch his attention, and her worthy soul didn't get it?

"She probably doesn't want to get sued by this guy. If he fell down her stairs, he could go after her with a lawyer or something. Maybe she thinks that if she helps him get better, he won't press charges." There was a clicking sound in the background, like Andrew Lu was typing. Probably talking to his friends on the computer, Oneida thought, flushing; probably telling them that she, Oneida, was bat-fucking insane.

There was a long pause. Robbed of the only interesting thing Oneida could think to talk about, or think about, even, she chewed her lip in silence. There was more clicking from Andrew Lu's side.

"Sorry about that," he said. "I was just finishing up an e-mail to my grandmother in Hong Kong. She expects me to respond to e-mails in, like, less than twenty-four hours. If I don't, the next time I talk to her she'll be all *you have no respect for me* and blah blah blah." Oneida didn't know what to make of that information, so she stayed silent. She felt as though she'd wandered out into the middle of a frozen lake just in time for a thaw.

The clicking had stopped. "So," Andrew said, "what's up?"

"Not much."

"So you . . . called to tell me your mom's insane."

Yes, she thought, *I had to tell somebody, and the somebody I normally tell these things is the one who's lost it.*

"Did you have a question about the history project? Something you wanted to talk about without the other guys around?"

If she had ever loved Andrew Lu before, it was a pale imitation of the tidal wave of affection that washed over her at that moment. She sat up and dangled her legs over the side of the bed.

"Yes," she said. "You're right."

"I'm good like that," Andrew said. "Don't you kind of wish it was just the two of us working on this thing? You know, Lennon and McCartney, together again."

Oneida stood. One hand held the portable phone to her ear while the other flapped and spun wildly at her side, a downed live wire. This was the most astonishing conversation she'd ever had with anyone. She watched herself in the mirror to make sure it was happening, to see her pantomime of jubilation for herself.

"Yes, I do!" she said, pointing up at the ceiling. "This is why I hate group work. Inevitably, someone like you or me has to carry the dead Wendy—oh, did I say that out loud? I meant dead *weight*."

Andrew kind of chuckled on the other end and Oneida dropped to one knee, made a fist, and pumped her free arm triumphantly.

"It felt like you were holding something back in class the other day," Andrew said. He wasn't wrong; when they'd spent class time meeting on Wednesday, Oneida had felt particularly in love with Andrew, particularly aware of the blue-black of his hair, particularly invested in the way his arms and shoulders moved under his red Cornell University hoodie. That she was holding back an intense desire to touch him, and not a piece of group business, hardly seemed relevant.

Oneida hopped in place. "Here's what I was thinking," she said, and hopped again.

"OK, go ahead," said Andrew.

Oneida sprang from leg to leg, willing her spontaneous calisthenics to provide their own divine inspiration. She hopped over to her dresser, scanned the pile of books and the dusty bag of little-kid makeup she hardly used—the ninety-nine-cent lip glosses and nail polish that showed up in her Christmas stocking every year—and saw her music boxes. Her four favorites stood side by side in a row. Mona, tucking her in at night, used to wind all four up simultaneously, filling Oneida's room with a hideous twinkly cacophony. Sometimes they'd sit side by side on Oneida's bed and slingshot underwear at them, which was how Oneida learned of her mother's abiding love for Tom Jones.

"We should form a band," Oneida said, and sucked in a breath.

"Like, a *band* band?" Andrew sounded less than enthused.

"Early Beatles songs are pretty simple, right? How hard can it be to learn to play one? It'll make our presentation absolutely awesome." She wiggled her fingers in the air. "So much extra credit, you won't believe it. It'll be like we're drowning in extra credit. Extra credit from heaven. Think about it."

There was a pause.

"You'd do that? You'd sing in front of the whole class?"

"That's the point: we'd all sing." Oneida was bouncing around her room like a rabbit on speed; the more she bounced, the more genius her idea seemed, the less it even mattered what Andrew thought of it. "We'd have to rehearse ahead of time, of course, but it'll be fun. And Dreyer will think it's amazing. You saw how happy she was when we told her we'd picked the Beatles. She loves them. She probably went to one of their concerts, like, fifty years ago."

"Why couldn't you bring this up in front of Dani and Wendy?"

Oneida stopped bouncing. "Come on, Andrew. You know Dani hates everything I say, no matter how kickass it might be. So if when we get together tomorrow, you and I are a united front—bam! We're a band." Oneida threw herself backward on her bed and curled happily on her side. She could already see the two of them in Andrew Lu's garage, strumming lazily and singing "Love Me Do," which sounded so simple, so easy. Hour after hour, rehearsing with Andrew Lu—after school, on weekends. Taking a break in the Lu kitchen, his mother handing Oneida a fresh-baked chocolate chip cookie and a glass of milk. The promise of standing in another kitchen, with another family, appealed to Oneida with a ferocity that would have been frightening had everything with Mona been normal—rather, had Mona never revealed herself to be a secret-keeper, and an insane one at that. *Get me out of here,* she wanted to say to Andrew Lu.

"OK, then," Andrew said. "Bring it up when we all meet together and I'll totally support it."

"Perfect!" said Oneida.

"So I guess this ends our clandestine group meeting," Andrew said. "I'll see you tomorrow at Wendy's."

"That's so weird," Oneida said, unable to let the conversation end. A long Saturday afternoon stretched out before her, with very little home-work to distract her from the image of her mother sitting on the edge of Arthur Rook's bed, checking the bandages on his chest and spooning chicken soup into his mouth. Saturday afternoon was the time for watch-ing dumb movies on cable with her daughter, not babying a creep.

"Going to Wendy's house? Seriously," Andrew said. "I mean, I'm the new guy and even *I* know that guy's unstable. I bet he volunteered because his parents need fresh meat."

"Last year's stockpile is running low." Oneida twisted her hair around her finger and pulled it taut from her head. "We should show up at the same time and never let each other out of sight."

"I think we'll be fine. We can toss 'em Dani."

"Dani'd make a pretty lame stew. Maybe they could grind her up, make Daniburgers."

"Ha, gross," Andrew said, and then, more firmly, "See you tomorrow."

"'Bye," Oneida said. With a click, the connection to Andrew Lu and the rest of the world died, without her being prepared for the loss of either. She lay still on her bed for a while, listening to herself breathe and trying not to think. Waiting for a reason, she thought, to feel normal again.

The relativity of normal was something Oneida had never truly appreciated until she'd come home from school the day before and almost stepped in the pool of dark congealed blood in the front hall. Her foot froze in midair over the basketball-sized puddle, her brain having issued an immediate moratorium on movement until it had a chance to figure out what the hell was going on. That was blood, wasn't it? Real human blood seeping between the yellow and blue tiles of the foyer. And if there was blood in the foyer, and it was dark and starting to dry, and her mother hadn't cleaned it up yet—

The moratorium repealed, Oneida flew through the house to the kitchen, where her mother's baking equipment lay spread over everything. A lump of fondant had dried to a hard white stone in the big blue mixing bowl. She ran through the dining room, the study, the family room, and back through the foyer again, though it wasn't until she thought to call her mother's cell phone that her energy had any focus or direction. Her hands shook as she held the kitchen phone to her ear and when it went directly to her mother's voice mail—*You've reached Desdemona Jones and the White Wedding Baking Company. Leave a message and I'll return your call as soon as possible. Thanks for calling; it's always a nice day for a white wedding*—Oneida dropped the receiver and slid down against the green cabinets, hugging her knees to her chin and chewing her lip until she pulled a strip of skin free with her teeth. She stared at the fridge opposite her, dotted with magnets and old school papers tattooed with As and 95s and 92s and 100s in red ink, but nothing else. Her mother had left no note. There was blood in the front hall; there was no note; there was no Mona.

She didn't know how long she sat there, but it was long enough for the sun to set, for the chill of night to settle over the house. She was kneeling over the pool of blood with a roll of paper towels and a bottle of Windex when the front door opened and Mona, struggling under the arm of Arthur Rook, came home. Oneida saw them before they saw her. Her mother was concentrating hard on maneuvering the tall man through the door and into the house, and Mr. Rook, wobbly, disheveled, eyes large and glassy, looked like he wouldn't notice his own hand if he held it in front of his face.

"Mom," Oneida said, but her mother didn't notice. She wasn't sure if she'd spoken out loud, so she tried again. "Hey, Mom," she said, and stood up, Windex in hand.

"Oh—oh, honey, I'm sor—" Mona, spent, couldn't finish, and Oneida wasn't sure the state her mother had arrived in was any more comforting than the grim worst-case scenarios she had imagined while waiting. Mr. Rook leaned against Mona heavily, his head bobbing, and Mona staggered across the hall. Her face crumpled and the look she gave her daughter—imploring, remorseful, and, worst of all, pitiable—made Oneida want to run up to her room and never come out. But she did exactly what her mother wanted to ask for but couldn't: Oneida took Arthur Rook's other arm and the two of them carried him upstairs.

As soon as they laid him on his bed, Mona sent Oneida downstairs to reheat a bowl of chicken soup, and Oneida, no longer sure if any of this was real or not, was stunned into complicity. When she returned with the bowl of steaming soup on a tray, her mother was leaning over Mr. Rook, dabbing at his chest with a cotton ball. She tipped a bottle of iodine against the cotton she held in her hand and Oneida, thankful she had already set the tray on the dresser, saw where the pool of blood had come from: a mass of jagged lacerations across Mr. Rook's chest, trailing lumpy stitches and red welts. He had been shaved, and the black bristles against the raw pink of his skin made Oneida's stomach turn and cheeks color. Head tilted back on the pillow, eyes closed, mouth slightly open—he was absolutely pathetic and, worse, Mona was gazing at him with the rapt, tender attention Oneida had never seen directed at anyone but herself, struck low with the chicken pox or the flu. This time she *did* run to her room, without saying a word to her mother, without dinner, and without any intention of ever coming out again.

There was a knock on the door about fifteen minutes later, and Mona entered before waiting for Oneida to respond. Oneida was curled up in her bed, under the sheets, only visible from the eyes up. She watched her mother sit on the edge of the bed beside her and felt Mona's hand run through her unruly hair.

"I am *so* sorry, Oneida," she said. Oneida blinked. "He tripped on the stairs while he was holding a . . . picture frame. You know, that photograph in the main hall. It—it all happened so fast, I got in the ambulance with him and didn't think how long it would take, how long we'd be at the hospital."

Oneida hurt in a way she had neither a name for nor the words to talk about. She let Mona go on.

"They kept him awhile to make sure his brain wasn't—I guess his concussion was minor compared to the cuts, thank God." Mona took her hand out of her daughter's hair and pushed her own back from her forehead. She sniffed loudly and pressed her fingers to her temple. "I feel terrible. Arthur Rook is not a well man."

"So why is he still here?" came out before Oneida could evaluate its impact on the situation.

Mona acted as though she didn't hear Oneida's question. "I should have left you a note, I know . . . or told Anna or Sherman or—where are they? Have you seen them?" No, Oneida thought; nobody was around. She rolled over, away from her mother. Mona didn't seem to notice the intentional diss and kept right on talking, about how sudden it had been, how she had acted without thinking, how it would never happen again, and how his cat was wandering around the house, be careful about leaving the front door open.

A tiny flame of rage sputtered in Oneida's chest. She had never felt anything remotely resembling rage toward her mother, but there it was:

a spark of resentment, pure and sharp, that she knew neither how to control nor if she even wanted to. How dare her mother leave her like that all afternoon? How dare she care more about a strange man than about her daughter? How dare she put her, Oneida, through that hell of uncertainty and barely do anything to atone for it? Oneida learned on Friday evening that true anger is completely cold and completely silent. Her mother, hand wavering, touched Oneida's cheek and kissed her good night, but Oneida remained motionless, empty, mute. She hated her mother. She hated her mother for making her love her like that: blindly, foolishly, without asking questions, assuming an understanding that clearly didn't exist. She'd been abandoned and betrayed by her best friend.

It was only seven o'clock but she forced herself asleep and didn't wake up until just after midnight. Her mouth felt mossy, so she climbed out of bed and padded into the bathroom that connected her room with Mona's. When she spat the last of the toothpaste into the sink and turned off the water, she clearly heard a sob from her mother's room, a short truncated howl that produced no reaction in her own heart, no flare of sympathy or compassion. *Good*, Oneida thought, and flicked off the light. *Cry yourself to sleep. See how it feels.*

⁊

Since Friday night, Oneida had only spoken to her mother three times and looked her in the eye twice. From all appearances, Mona hadn't noticed. She acted like it was perfectly normal for her to spend an hour in the morning and an hour at night changing Mr. Rook's dressings, feeding him, keeping him company. And that horrible cat—Ray something—had free run of the house: Oneida would find it sleeping on her bed, rolling on her dirty clothes, rubbing up against her legs when she thought she was completely alone. Home was not home anymore, and Oneida could hardly wait to get out of the car and away from her mother. Which was saying something, considering Mona's old station wagon was idling in that freak Wendy's driveway.

"So I'll pick you up at five?" Mona said, the chirp in her voice suggesting she was dropping Oneida off at the mall instead of the cave of a raging teenage psychopath. Oneida nodded and opened her door, closing it again on Mona's admonitions to *have a good ti—*

She walked up the cracked flagstone path and didn't turn to see Mona drive away. The Wendell house had been hard to find, the driveway marked by nothing more than a dented gray mailbox one stiff breeze away from toppling off its post. The driveway itself was endless, meandering and rutted. When it finally ended, the only sign of nearby habitation was a bright green door set into the side of a hill, a hill that gradually revealed itself to be the front of a house, so weather-worn and gray it looked like it had always been there. The door was at least freshly painted, but Oneida saw no doorbell or knocker. She pulled her jacket tighter and rapped on the green wood, praying that Andrew Lu was already inside.

The door opened before she had a chance to drop her hand. She jumped and let out a little shriek because there was Wendy: standing in the doorway, silent and still. He was wearing a black T-shirt with an anarchy symbol drawn on it in what looked like red nail polish.

"Hi, Spoony," he said and swung the door wider. "Enter."

Oneida heard rock music playing from somewhere within the house, then a very loud cymbal crash and singing. Wendy rubbed his scar and said, "Seriously, get in here."

Oneida did as she was told. The Wendell house was little more than a dark cramped hallway that stretched in either direction into darkness, the walls coated in synthetic wood paneling. The music came to a jumbled halt and a few voices filled in the silence. The sounds were coming from somewhere beneath them and to the right, and Wendy, noticing the curiosity that Oneida was unable to contain, motioned for her to follow him down the hallway.

"Um, is anyone else here already?" she asked.

"Nope," Wendy replied.

"Oh." Oneida wished she'd worn her watch. A watch would give her that tiny hint of control: over knowing exactly how early she was, how long she'd have to wait until someone else showed up—and, should she become lost in the bowels of the Wendell residence, how long she'd been held captive. "My mother is always early, sorry about—"

"You're late." Wendy didn't turn around when he spoke. He continued to stalk down the dark hallway, so that Oneida couldn't help but notice how skinny he looked from behind. His bony elbows jutted out of his sleeves like twigs, and his jeans hung off his butt like a scarecrow. Oneida heard her mother's voice clear in her head: *This boy has no ass.*

"I'm gonna show you something," Wendy said, spinning to an abrupt halt. "And I'm gonna make you promise never to talk about it with another human being, living or dead." He spat in his hand. "I'm gonna make you shake on it, and if I ever hear you broke this promise, I'll kill you. I know you know I can."

The music started again, much louder, much closer. Oneida's heart was beating so hard and fast she felt light-headed and gross. The impulse to run back down the hall, run outside, run to her mother—Mona couldn't have made it to the end of the driveway yet; it was too long—was checked by a new voice in her head, terrifying and obstinate: *Your mother would say you're being ridiculous, that she had to get back to Mr. Rook. Your mother would drive away without you.*

Wendy's black eyes blinked. "Wow," he said. "You're so easy to mess with, it's not any fun." He kicked his foot into the wall and a door, barely distinguishable in the murk, swung open.

There was no way Oneida could have been prepared for what lay beyond the door from what she knew of Wendy and from what she knew of the realm of possibility in Ruby Falls. A short flight of stairs led down into a cavernous white room, light streaming in from an enormous picture window that looked out over a rolling valley of trees rippling yellow and red against the blue fall sky; the house was built into the side of a hill. The white walls were covered with brightly colored paintings, some of which Oneida recognized with a start: a garish portrait of Marilyn Monroe in robin's egg blue and bubblegum pink; a man in a bowler hat, face obscured by a bright green apple. But in the center of the room, surrounded by overstuffed and mismatched chairs and sofas, was a band. A girl with long blond braids, a few years older than Wendy or herself, was hunched over a green electric guitar, and an older man, chubby and bald, played an acoustic guitar with a plug snaking out of the bottom. Most shocking of all was the drummer: she was also blond, wore a bright blue tank top, and looked at least ten years older than Mona.

Wendy pointed at the drummer and said, with not a small amount of pride, "That's my mom."

Oneida didn't recognize the song or understand any of the lyrics other than the chorus, which repeated *here comes your man* again and again, but she liked it immediately. It had a driving, bouncy beat, and the guitars sounded—to Oneida, who had never played an instrument other than that idiotic recorder she was required to learn for three weeks in the third grade—bright and happy. It made her feel hopeful, like the plodding beat could pick her up and carry her to its destination; it made her think of ticking second hands, dripping faucets, the little red line that traced the path of Indiana Jones's travels across old brown maps. When Wendy's mom brought her sticks down with a finality that made Oneida clap before she could help herself, she felt as though she'd traveled somewhere far away, miles from Ruby Falls.

She caught herself after only two claps when Wendy snickered at her. "Dork," he said, and walked down the stairs.

"Eugenius." The bald guitar player hailed Wendy and reached for a can of beer perched unsteadily on the arm of a nearby chair. He took a swig and noticed Oneida. "With a girlfriend."

Oneida was too far out of her depth to muster the requisite indignation and denial. She floated down the stairs, past the band and after Wendy, as though it were a particularly bizarre play she was watching from behind a curtain.

The blond bass player winked at Wendy as he passed and addressed Oneida directly. "He's going to want to make it to first," she said, "but for God's sake don't let him steal second." Wendy's drummer mother told the blond to quit picking on her baby, and Oneida, who didn't know how much weirder this could all get, decided she was having a hallucination. Her body was probably passed out in the driveway, her face smushed against the gravel, her brain a million miles away.

"Come on," Wendy said, and pushed through a swinging door. Beyond this door was a more quantifiable entity: a kitchen, looking completely normal and therefore twice as odd in comparison with the room they'd just left.

"Beer?" Wendy asked, clinking bottles in the refrigerator. "No, wait. You're not a beer girl. Let me guess." Wendy steered her gently onto a bar stool and observed her, one hand on his chin. "Kahlua and vodka. That's the kind of girl you are."

A bell went off in Oneida's brain. "Stop," she said. It felt right, so she said it again. "*Stop.*"

Wendy pulled two cans of soda out of the refrigerator. "Again," he said. "You're ridiculously gullible. You've really got to work on that."

She jumped off the bar stool, tensed for escape. This was all too strange, too unexpected, and Oneida was tired of trying to live in a world she didn't understand. She had expected a gun rack, a rusty car in the driveway, a mother or a father who didn't say much and didn't stick around, old orange carpeting, and a lingering odor of cigarettes and wet dog.

"This is freaking you out, isn't it?" Wendy snapped open his soda.

"Not at all," Oneida said, her voice squeaking.

He handed her a can of soda and she accepted automatically. After she'd held it for a few seconds without moving, Wendy popped it open for her.

The silence was heavy with the thudding of drums from the next room. Oneida sat back down on the stool and propped her legs on the top rung. She was surprised—though, in retrospect, she knew she shouldn't have been—to feel a surge of insatiable curiosity. Eugene Wendell was a psycho, a genius, or a hybrid of both. For her to shut down and run away would be in direct opposition to her life's pursuit of information. Learning Wendy wasn't who he appeared to be was like tripping head-first into a pot of gold: if she didn't crack her head open, it would be the greatest secret she'd ever have the opportunity to discover.

"So you're, what, the Partridge family?" she said. Shocked at her own daring, she gave Wendy a penetrating stare and took a sip of soda.

Wendy looked relieved. She was glad she'd decided to play along. "Not quite," he said. "That's not my dad, that's Terry. He works for my dad. But that *is* my mom, and that's my sister Gwen."

"Your sister's name is Gwen Wendell?"

Wendy's face split into a wide grin with too many teeth. Oneida, a little faster but still slower than she liked, caught on.

"Her name is Patricia," Wendy said. "And I will personally remove every last drop of gullibility out of your body if you let me."

The coy familiarity of what sounded halfway between a threat and a promise brought Oneida to one shocking conclusion—he was flirting with her. Wendy Wendell was flirting with her, and Oneida wasn't sure she minded all that much. She took another sip to hide the fact that she had no idea how to react to this information, other than with blind terror.

"So where's your dad?" she said, grasping desperately for a way to reroute the conversation.

"Business trip," Wendy said.

"What's he do?"

"Assassin for hire."

Oneida was ready this time. "Whatever," she said, and couldn't help returning Wendy's grin.

"He's a professional art forger."

Oneida set her soda can on the countertop with a sharp aluminum click. "I don't know why I bothered asking."

"Fine, he's a security guard, and he's at a security guard conference in New York City. You want to see his itinerary? Three days of nonstop action and adventure. There's a lot of badge flashing and glowering and monitor-watching." Wendy had a habit of talking out of the side of his mouth and not looking directly at her, especially if he thought he was saying something funny. Oneida wasn't sure if she found it annoying or cute—for the moment, at least, she was fascinated to discover she had any opinion about Wendy Wendell at all beyond fear and/or loathing. This couldn't be the same Wendy who had brought fake blood into Sherman's woodshop, who prowled around the boys' bathroom in the science wing and sold cigarettes to seventh-graders; who told the computer lab monitor to go fuck himself and the horse he rode in on. This Wendy didn't even look like the same person. He looked skinnier and taller, less hunched and hulking. Cleaner, somehow, and brighter: Oneida had never noticed that his hair was brown with a little black mixed in, that his ears were large and kind of funny-looking, and if he stood in front of a bright light—as he did now, crossing in front of the kitchen window—they glowed seashell-pink as the light passed through them.

She slid off her stool and walked around the kitchen, trying to place this new Wendy in his natural habitat: the bright curtains over the sink, lemons and limes dancing across the fabric; the small stack of breakfast dishes on the counter; the wall behind the kitchen table, painted a deep citrus green and lightly scuffed level with the tops of the chairs; and the lingering odor of coffee, a little burned. Discovering Wendy's Technicolor underbelly gave Oneida a feeling of power, the rush of the privilege of information. It was a power she always felt like wielding.

"Why?" she asked him. "Why do you make everyone at school think that you're this crazy badass who picks fights with hookers? Brings a knife to school?"

"I was wondering how long it would take you to ask." Wendy finished his soda and tossed the empty can into the sink. "It's something I learned from my dad: life is art." He tilted his head as though he were searching for the right words, but Oneida was sure he knew exactly what the right words were and was only posturing for her benefit. "It means," he said, "that your whole life is a creation. What you make it, literally. And you can use your life to totally mess with other people's heads."

"And that's art?" Oneida asked.

"Oh, yeah. Art is anything that makes you think differently."

"But," Oneida said. "I don't think differently about you. I mean, *now* I do, but . . . at school, everyone who thinks you're crazy—they just think you're crazy."

"But I'm not, and that's the art part of it. It's subversive, it's surreal. The misconceptions of other people—that's the medium I work in."

Oneida rolled Wendy's words around in her head. She could feel his eyes on her, watching her think.

"I don't—" she said. "I don't get it."

Oneida didn't realize she'd said the one thing guaranteed to hurt Wendy the most until his face drooped and something in his eyes went dim and distant. It was as though this new Wendy, articulate, animated, and—God, it was still too bizarre to believe—flirting with her, disappeared behind a scrim of the old Wendy, and Oneida felt the usual anxieties leach into the pit of her stomach. She already missed the new Wendy. She liked the new Wendy, liked the way she felt when she talked to him.

"I mean, I do get it," Oneida lied diplomatically.

"You do?" Wendy said, furrowing his brow and rubbing his scar. "So you were fucking with me?"

"Your misconceptions . . . are the medium I work in?" Oneida offered. When Wendy laughed she felt a spark of pleasure cut with a thin slice of fear. Something was happening in this kitchen that she wasn't prepared for, not only because it was completely unexpected but because it had never happened to her before, and there was no way to anticipate this strange wrenching sensation in her chest: what it would mean, what it would make her do. Her whole body seemed to be vibrating slightly, humming in anticipation. Was this what it felt like to—and here she was too pragmatic, too cynical, to even think the words *fall in love*, so she thought back to what Mona had said about recognizing worthy souls. Was this, then, what it felt like to recognize yourself in someone you'd seen a thousand times before, that you thought you already knew? She laughed too, a shaky laugh that sounded a little too high and wobbly to be her own. She looked up and Wendy was staring at her, and smiling, and everything was too bizarre, too new, to be true.

"Wow," she said, and bugged her eyes, blinking, trying to wake up.

"I know it's a lot to take in. My alter ego and all." Wendy shrugged and crossed his arms over his chest. Oneida poured the rest of her drink down the sink, her stomach too antsy for her to add any more sugar. "You can still call me Wendy, if you're more used to it," he said, and before Oneida could think to ask what else she might call him, Wendy leaned in and kissed her.

Oh, sweet holy Jesus, telegraphed Oneida's brain in the instant it was still capable of rational thought, before the truth of Wendy's mouth on hers became inescapable; before she stumbled back into the refrigerator and Wendy, attached, stumbled with her; before her back was pressed up against magnets and shopping lists and—she thought she remembered—an orange photocopied flyer for the Ruby Falls Halloween Carnival that Oneida hadn't gone to since she was eight; before she realized her hands were flapping weirdly in the air because they knew they belonged someplace but didn't know quite *where*, and it was weird and wet and warm and she could taste a banana he'd had for breakfast; before the full gravity of that moment stamped itself on the rest of her life, and certainly before she thought about Andrew Lu.

"Oh my God," she garbled, lips still tangled up with Wendy's. "Oh my God, what about Andrew?"

Wendy's face was enormous when it was this close to hers. She felt herself going cross-eyed looking into his pupils. "He's not coming," Wendy said, and leaned in to kiss her again, but she pressed both hands against his chest and asked what did he mean?

Wendy's eyes flicked back and forth cautiously. "I mean," he said, "that he's not coming."

"What about Dani?"

"Uh, not coming either."

Oneida's heart trilled. "Why aren't they coming?"

"Because I called them last night and told them not to?"

Oneida pushed Wendy away and pulled her hair back from her face. "Oh my God," she said, more to herself than Wendy. "This was a setup. You never meant for the group to meet. You just wanted to get me here. What the hell do you want from me? Why did you show me, tell me—what the hell is going on?"

Wendy was upset—really upset, not acting, not posturing. Oneida could tell because his eyes were wide and he was looking at the floor instead of her. He shrugged. "I dunno," he said. "Maybe because you're the only person in our whole retarded school who might be worth getting to know?"

Oneida paused, momentarily won, and if Wendy had been paying any attention he might have been able to stop himself before going on.

"And if I don't have real sex soon, I will *die*."

She didn't know she had the capacity to be so wholly self-conscious, to feel every part of her body explode from pale to scarlet with a single pump of her heart. Somehow she made it out of the kitchen and through the main room, the band thumping away on that same song (*here comes your man here comes your man*), and down the Wendell driveway. Her heart was tight and baffled and her head was no better.

She would walk the two miles home.

No—she would run.

Part II

7 ❧ Mona Should Have Known

Mona should have guessed. She should have known the second he rang her doorbell and stepped into her hall, should have seen it in his dreamy demeanor, the disconnect in his eyes, his apparent lack of interest in both hygiene and social activity. It couldn't have been any plainer if she had turned his hand over and found, scribbled across his palm in blue ballpoint: *Amy was here.*

Amy had always had a way of making men lose their minds. Not their hearts necessarily, though sometimes the hearts came part and parcel—it looked as though Arthur, torn up in all senses of the word, had made the full investment. The boys who fell for Amy in high school were geeks and geniuses, quiet boys with wet eyes and acne and a murderous desire to touch the boobs of a girl who knew William Gibson wasn't Mel's brother. Mona had long ago diagnosed it as a case of like liking like, of dorks recognizing in Amy their own zeal for the arcane, their passion for a single activity that would never matter as much to anyone else as it did to them. For Amy, that single activity had been making monsters; for the boys who went nuts over her, that single activity quickly morphed from playing *Magic: The Gathering* in their wood-paneled basements to obsessing over Amy. The end result was always the same: they would make an overture, Amy would stonewall them with a cold silent stare, and they would slink away like beaten dogs. One of them, Ricky Ettinger, fashioned a homemade mace out of a baseball and thumbtacks, swung it at the family dog, and was sent to the psychiatric hospital in Syracuse for a month. Amy took no responsibility for her role in their madness, and Mona, who silently thought

Amy didn't have to be quite so mean to them, would nonetheless roll her eyes and nod in solidarity.

Mona suspected she must have lost her mind a little over Amy as well—how else to explain a decade of best friendship? Amy Henderson was selfish and self-centered, so self-involved as to be completely inno-cent: she legitimately forgot to call you for an entire weekend when you'd made plans to see a movie together. She was driven and obsessive and exhausting. But she had the ability to convince you that if you had a real dream, no matter how ridiculous or insane—she wanted to make mon-ster movies, for shit's sake—you could will it into reality through noth-ing but frenzy and focus. It was something Mona had only ever thought to believe in when she was around Amy.

Amy came with her own universe, her own reality. If you stood close enough, you were enveloped the way an extra or a piece of set dressing becomes part of a scene: present but invisible. They met when they were both kindergartners at Ruby Falls Elementary, when Amy slipped on a patch of wet October leaves on the playground and Mona helped her back to her feet. Amy had fallen in mud, smearing the seat of her purple Health Tex corduroys with brown, and no sooner had Mona steadied her than the shrieks of laughter began. But even more memorable that day than the taunts of *poopy pants baby* was Amy's response to the situ-ation: she'd squinted at her tormentors, the kids already growing into the bullies they'd spend their entire lives being, shrugged, turned to Mona, and said, "Whatever. Screw 'em."

Mona still remembered how she'd imagined the word *screw* as a cartoon, like the letters and words on *Sesame Street*, squeezing into her delicate five-year-old ears and burning as it went. "Ouch," she'd said, and clapped her hands to either side of her face. Amy had laughed ("Oh, come on, it's hardly a swear") and asked if Mona had ever seen *The Clash of the Titans*.

That was the kernel of their friendship, and in many ways it never altered beyond the basic structure set on that cold afternoon when they were five: Amy would do or say something that would either shock or amuse Mona, Mona's reaction would snap Amy out of her self-absorption long enough for Amy to realize what she'd done, and then they'd go watch a movie. They'd watched many, many movies: monster movies, horror movies, science-fiction movies, movies about hideously mutated lizards and hairy wolf-men from other planets and slimy serpents born of man's meddling with science, come forth from the sea to teach their creators a lesson. If there was a creature waddling or stomping or slithering across the screen, Amy wanted to see it; and Mona was genuinely eager to learn why this beast, this being born from someone's imagination and given three dimensions (or two dimensions, rather, that looked like three) meant so much to her friend.

Mona knew her parents weren't entirely happy that she was joined at the hip with weird Amy Henderson, raised by her shut-in grandfather in that ramshackle trailer house out in the woods, but the more time Amy spent over at the Darby-Jones, the less Mona's parents seemed to worry. Amy charmed. Amy was polite. Amy, when Mona's parents weren't around, was fond of proselytizing to Mona about how very small-minded and claustrophobic the world of Ruby Falls was, how sad and lame were the lives of everyone they knew, but that was why Mona loved her. Amy had passions, and for a girl like Mona—who, most days, felt as formless and doughy as a hunk of clay—Amy was magic. It was a magic inextricably linked with the dreams and promise of her childhood, which, in retrospect, had been the *specific* dreams and *specific* promise of only one of them. When she tried to recall what she had wanted out of life as a child, Mona could only remember wanting to be Amy's best friend—until Amy took herself away and Mona grew up without her.

And now she was back.

Harryhausen. The last time Mona saw Harryhausen, he'd been a kitten. She'd gone to visit Amy in Los Angeles, just once, years after Amy ran away, when Oneida was barely out of toddlerhood and Mona was barely an adult. Harryhausen the kitten had thrown up in her suitcase when she had less than an hour to make it to the Burbank airport. And now, after a span of time nearly as long as her entire friendship with Amy, to see Harryhausen the cat, full-grown, puddle himself into a massive pile of fur and fat on *her* staircase—and then in the ambulance, when Arthur was mainlining morphine and grinning like an idiot, to hear him say, *Hi, Amy. I missed you.*

Mona, her back pressed against a wall of cubbies stocked with needles and tubes and bandages, had squeezed Arthur's hand and he had called her beautiful—*her*, Mona—which was a shock, but then, hey, we've all said crazy things under the influence of hospital-grade opiates. His eyes rolled white and he fell under again, and the EMT, dabbing gauze on the weeping lacerations all over his chest, said quietly, almost to herself, "She's right here. She's here." The EMT had hay-colored hair, and there was a weird smell, a sharp chemical trace that made Mona think of seeing her father for the last time in the ICU, and then Mona realized that the EMT was as confused as Arthur and thought she really *was* Amy, and she laughed, far too loud, because how the fuck had any of this happened?

Mona didn't know how to begin putting the pieces together. She only knew that all evidence pointed to Amy Henderson, the friend she'd had in another life, and the task of reconciling the two Monas— the loyal sidekick and best friend with the landlady baker and single mother—overwhelmed her. Christ, what could she possibly have to say to Amy? What would Amy have to say to her?

All of this crashed into Mona well after midnight, after she brought Arthur home and put him to bed. And then, tucking Oneida in, she'd felt a mixture of terror and dread, overcome with the horror of time (and the loss of it), and it had taken all her strength to walk to her own bedroom, wash her face, brush her teeth, kick off her sneakers, and slip out of her jeans and T-shirt before collapsing to her knees on the floor, pants still around her ankles. A sixteen-year-old weight resettled itself across her shoulders like an elephant shifting its haunches. Mona wound her fingers into the deep green shag carpeting that had been in her room all her life, that Amy had loved because it was the perfect height for tiny monsters to prowl on safari.

What had Amy done?

What did Arthur know?

She crawled into bed and pulled the covers up tight to her chin and thought about the Amy she had known—and how could she be any different? Amy was unchangeable, Amy was still sixteen—and that Amy hardly told anyone anything, so it was a safe bet Arthur Rook had no idea, really, what he'd stumbled into. The silver band Bert had made such a stink about at dinner was, indeed, right there on Arthur's ring finger—so did that mean Arthur and *Amy* were husband and wife? (Had she cheated on him, left him?) Not that she ever expected Amy to send a wedding announcement or, hell, invite Mona to her wedding, but—when had *that* happened? She pictured the sleeping Arthur, flat on his back in what had once been her parents' bed, and tried to imagine Amy sleeping beside him, as she may have. She couldn't. Mona would have chosen a mad genius for *her* Amy to marry, if she ever married at all. Someone with wild intelligence in his face, knobby hands, a fantastic beard. Not a blandly cute, unremarkable space cadet whose overall aesthetic might be best described as High School Biology Teacher.

Did you even want to tell me, Amy? she thought, pulling the covers over her head.

So Amy now, as Amy had been then, was shut tight as an oyster, working her grain of sand without comment. Mona had always been the one with some secret to share or crush to confess. Only twice in the course of their friendship had Amy shared a secret with Mona, and both times under the explicit conditions that Mona promise not to tell anyone, ever.

Both times, Mona had promised. She wondered how many secrets Amy had told Arthur, and if that had anything to do with his broken brain. When Amy made you promise not to tell, you ended up swearing to more than you ever expected.

The first time she promised, they were both thirteen. Mona remembered seventh grade as a perpetual state of frustration with Amy: they were best friends. They each had half of a jagged-edged heart charm necklace, but if Amy wouldn't pay any attention to her or tell Mona any of her secrets, what was the point? They'd been sitting on opposite ends of the blue corduroy couch in the den downstairs, painting their fingernails and half-watching a Godzilla movie. Mona had just confessed to Amy that she wanted Eric Cole to ask her to the middle school spring dance. Amy hadn't said a word in reply.

"God, Amy. You're not even listening to me."

"I am so listening to you."

"No, you're not. I could tell you the most horrifying, the most secret and private thing I've ever told anyone on the planet, and you'd say, like, *George Lucas would sell his soul to be Ray Harryhausen.*"

"Lucas *would* sell his soul to be Harryhausen." Amy flexed her hands and blew on her fingernails, freshly painted a sparkly green.

Mona could still feel it—the anger rising in her spine, making her sit up straighter. She could picture herself on that ratty couch, now almost twenty years older and still darkening the den downstairs, could still feel Amy sitting beside her, eyes glued to the television. As easily as cuing up a song, Mona could recall the indignation of having her supposed best friend not bat an eye at her confession—because Eric Cole was an asshole, the kind of kid who threw rocks at stray cats, and yes: Mona would go to the dance with him if he asked her. Why? Because he was cute. No: he was *hot.* He was *dangerous.* But wasn't Amy supposed to warn her? Tell her Eric Cole was no good? Wasn't her best friend supposed to care?

"Whatever, Eric Cole's just a substitute," Mona said. "Because I'm *really* in love with Ben."

Ben Tennant lived on the third floor of the Darby-Jones, in the same room that would one day be the site of so much veterinarian-on-shop-teacher embarrassment for Oneida. He was one of the youngest renters ever to live under the Darby-Jones roof: in his mid-twenties but hypnotically adult to anyone under the age of eighteen—and beautiful. He had eyes as blue as paint and thick brown hair that curled at the base of his neck in ringlets like glossy chocolate shavings. He smiled easily and often, and he had a real live dimple on his left cheek when he grinned wide enough to laugh. When he first introduced himself to Mona at dinner, she hadn't been able to stop her stupid mouth from asking what grade he was in—and no, he wasn't a student, but he *did* go to high school with her every day. He was the substitute music and drama teacher at Ruby Falls, a position that had only recently been created after the band director wrecked his car (and himself) in late March, creating a temporary position in the music department and, more critically, a directorial hole in the school musical—a yearly event which, aside from the undefeated women's volleyball team, was one of the few sources of extracurricular pride to be found at RFH. Ben rented at the Darby-Jones to avoid having to drive back and forth every day from Syracuse, where he lived with his fiancée, who was getting her master's degree from the university. He would move out of the Darby-Jones in late May when the music program director came back to school on crutches; and though he would return for the next five years to direct the spring musical, he never lived at the Darby-Jones again after that spring.

But that spring, he was a part of Mona's life every single day. Having Ben not only drive her to school but eat dinner with her, watch television with her, and hell, *sleep* (in the same house) with her, allowed Mona a degree of popularity unheard of for a seventh-grader—the very lowest on the junior-senior high pole. It surprised her with its tangibility: you could *feel* it. The air was different when people you didn't know were talking about you moments before you entered a room. Her back would twitch and she'd realize she was being watched, being discussed. As genuine as people's curiosity seemed to be—*Do you see him in his pajamas? What does he like to eat? What does he watch on TV?*—Mona suspected that none of the Ben fan club thought she deserved her good fortune. Their questions were hungry and slightly vicious; her answers were received with greedy smiles and slitted eyes. *Who was that Mona Jones*, she heard them say in her heart, *to have this beautiful man in her life? She wouldn't even know what to do with him.*

Amy never made her feel stupid about Ben. Amy, as usual, barely gave Mona the impression that she knew Ben existed or that Mona was experiencing her fifteen minutes of fame by association. Amy had never asked if Mona and Ben shared a bathroom (Amy *knew* Mona never shared a bathroom with a tenant; it was one of the Darby-Jones rules). Amy never giggled into her hand about how funny Ben was—*did you hear what he said in rehearsal last night?*—or waxed rapturous about how Ben had placed his hand on her shoulder while blocking a scene. So it shocked Mona completely that Amy's reaction when Mona said *I'm in love with Ben*—and who wasn't, just a little?—was to turn white and tell Mona to shut up.

On the television, Godzilla belched a column of fire at Mechagodzilla.

"What?" Mona coughed. "What, Amy?"

"You're not funny." Amy examined her nails. "I know you think you are sometimes, but you're not."

At thirteen, Mona was in the early throes of realizing she might be, with a little practice, a funny girl—she could make her mother laugh so hard she had to put down the newspaper and wipe her eyes with a tissue—but she still felt clumsy with her humor, a little kid wielding a great big rubber bat. The feeling she got when she made people laugh intentionally—and laugh genuinely—convinced Mona her natural sense of humor was worth training, honing, and putting to use, but it was still awkward and unpredictable. Who could you practice on, other than your friends? Weren't they supposed to be your first and most forgiving audiences? It hurt her pride, especially since Mona hadn't even been trying to be particularly funny. She wished she could remember what had made her think to say she was in love with Ben in the first place. It was an impulse, like everything she said or did; the space between Mona thinking and Mona saying was half of a half of a heartbeat.

"Amy, I'm sorry. What did I—"

Amy sighed and laid her palms flat on her legs. Her nails looked like they were covered in sparkly algae.

"You didn't *do* anything." She stared straight ahead at the television. "Don't worry about it."

Mona chewed the inside of her cheek. Amy sighed again. She opened her mouth and shut it and Mona realized what was happening.

Amy had a secret. Amy was going to tell her something—*finally!*—something that they alone could share. Something that would prove they were friends.

"Ben Tennant . . . sucks," Amy said. "And—I can't tell you any more unless you promise not to tell. Anyone. Ever. Do you promise?"

Amy's voice was odd, colorless and small, and Mona felt apprehension tickle her belly. Maybe she didn't want to know Amy's secrets after all. But no—no, right here: this was what best friends were for.

"I promise," Mona said, and held out her little finger for Amy Henderson to wrap her own pinkie around, a cold, bony little digit that Mona would always remember for the way it shook: the only part of Amy that wasn't absolutely sure of itself.

"I *am* in love with him," Amy muttered. She turned away from the television but didn't look at Mona, didn't make eye contact. She talked to the couch cushions. "I—I can't believe I'm such an idiot. I wrote him a—you know he's lived in New York and London and California, and he's done—he's been in shows and—um, a few weeks ago we were just talking . . . here." Her eyes flicked around the den. Mona remembered. She'd gone to the kitchen for snacks and came back and there were Ben and Amy, watching television together. "He wants to make movies, too. To write and direct his own movies. He's the first person I ever talked to about it that didn't think I was completely insane, and, you know, I just—it felt so good to meet someone who's like me. I feel so alone sometimes. You know?"

Mona winced. *I don't think you're insane,* she thought, but didn't say. *I don't think you're alone.*

"So I wrote this . . . letter. A note, really. On a postcard, I thought he'd think that was funny—it said *Wish you were here* and I changed it to say *we* instead of *you.* I didn't want anything from him other than— I just wanted him to *know.*" She shrugged. Her pinkie, still wrapped around Mona's, squeezed harder. "And he stopped me in the hall and said he had a question about some of the sets? For the show? And I'd been helping Chuck Woz with some of the—whatever, you know— anyway. In his office he told me—he just—"

Amy closed her eyes and unhooked her pinkie. She scrunched herself back into the crook of the couch arm and pressed both hands flat against her face.

"He told me I was being *inappropriate.*" Her words were muffled and thick.

She was crying. Amy was crying and Mona was paralyzed. She had never, ever, seen Amy cry before—not when she talked about how her parents died when she was five, the summer before Mona met her. Not when she sprained her ankle in gym so bad she had to use crutches for a week. And certainly not when they watched that video of *Beaches* Mona's mother rented from the drugstore, which had reduced Mona to a gibbering pile of snot. But now Amy was crying over Ben Tennant, and Mona, who had always thought Amy's heart was invulnerable (to boys *or* to best friends) felt time stop and reorder itself. She was aware of the musty smell of the couch. Dust motes hanging in the sunny indoor air. Amy's long-fingered hands covering her face, a halo of messy strands of dirty-blond hair escaping the rubber band that tried to hold them back. Maybe three seconds passed, but it felt like Mona lived a lifetime between realizing that Amy was crying and that she had no idea what to do about it. Should she hug her? Should she re-grab Amy's pinkie, would that be more reassuring? Why didn't she know what to do?

Before Mona could act, Amy took her hands from her face and sat back up on the couch, perfectly straight. Her cheeks were deep pink. "Screw 'im," she said, and snuffled, once. Then she grabbed the remote and turned up the volume. And they sat in silence and watched Godzilla ravage some nameless Japanese province until Mona's mother, carting a basket of clean laundry, stuck her head in the den and asked them to turn it down.

"I'm sorry," Mona said, when her mother was gone, and winced again, because it sounded so weak and pathetic and was representative of only the tiniest bit of what she actually was: sorry for Amy, sad for Amy, and sorry and sad for herself for getting precisely what she wanted: a secret to prove how well they knew each other. That they were best friends, relatively speaking.

"Me, too," said Amy, and then, by way of consolation, "Eric Cole's a dickhead. You can do better."

The other secret was joint, tied up with the summer they ran away, when they ditched Ruby Falls and hid out on the Jersey Shore. That was the Amy that lived in her mind now, a tall girl with splotchy sunburns on her shoulders and legs, always moving, whether she was running down the beach or the boardwalk. Mona, stretching her own legs under the bedclothes, wondered what Amy had become. Who Amy was now. Still moving, Mona suspected, still going forward. Still running.

Amy ran all the way to Hollywood after that summer in New Jersey, and Mona didn't see her again until Oneida was four. Of all things, after years of not speaking, Amy called her on the telephone. Simple as that.

Mona's mother didn't recognize Amy's voice and covered the mouthpiece, grumbling about telemarketers. But Mona's hand went numb within seconds of taking the phone and she had to lean against the kitchen cupboards to stay upright.

"Hi, Mona," was all Amy had to say.

Mona tried to say hello, but all that came out was a series of huffing sounds.

"Look, I know you're probably . . . still . . . pissed." Amy sounded so much like herself, so much like a direct transmission from the past, that Mona's eyes pricked with tears. She barely remembered herself at that age, and here was her best friend, exactly the same, a time traveler. "And I can't tell you how much—I can't thank you."

The line went silent for a second and then Amy choked, whether on a laugh or a sob, Mona never knew.

"So listen," Amy said, her voice stronger but her words hesitant. "I—did some work on this movie, and there's going to be a premiere in a few weeks out here, and I—I have tickets—and it's a real movie, Mona. You might have even heard of it, it's called *The Big Kahuna* and it's got freakin' Keanu Reeves in it, and it's about surfers terrorized by a creature-from-the-black-lagoon-style monster, and I was chief assistant on the underwater creature animatronics and"—Amy gulped in a breath—"I'd really love it if you were here. I—"

Mona didn't think there was a medical term for the way her heart was frozen, stuck between beats. She hadn't said a word yet. It wasn't until her mother touched her cheek, concerned, that she realized how warm she was, how all the blood in her body was rushing to her head. She was going to explode if she didn't speak.

"Amy," she said. Her mother's eyebrows shot into her hairline. "Amy, I would love to come—I wouldn't miss it. When?"

"Next month. April tenth—you can come for the weekend, I don't know what your—you know—schedule—"

"I can make it," she said, because she could; God knows, she didn't work anywhere outside of the Darby-Jones. "One thing—um."

"What?"

"Should I bring Oneida?"

"Oh—who?" Amy asked.

"The baby?" Mona said, and thought, *I will pass out. I will pass out.* "I . . . kept her."

Amy's silence grew between them, long and loud enough for Mona to wonder if she'd gone deaf in one ear.

"Wh—how did—I didn't know you—"

"Yeah."

Amy coughed.

"Well," she said. "Shit, Mona."

"No, never mind. It's OK." Mona's conscience flared. This was Amy's big dream starting to come true, and whatever choices Mona had made with her life had nothing, really, to do with any of it. "I'm sorry, Amy, I won't bring her. She's kind of a pain in the ass, frankly."

"She would have to be," Amy said, and then laughed nervously. Mona could hear Amy's shaky inhalation, three thousand miles and a million years away. "OK," she said. "I mean, if you don't want to—it would be fine with me if you wanted to bring . . . her, I'd—"

"I'll bring pictures," Mona said.

Which she did. And which Harryhausen, the stupid kitten, vomited on as they lay helpless in her open suitcase on the floor of Amy's apartment. That was one of the few clear memories Mona had of the last weekend she spent with Amy; that, and sitting in the dark of the Chinese Theater as Amy's dreams came to life in front of her. Nothing more substantial than light and sound, the Big Kahuna, as Keanu—basically playing Johnny Utah in a monster movie—called it, *was*. It existed as a living, breathing being, a being Amy had helped create out of sheer will with the aid of nuts, bolts, and rubber. Mona thought the Kahuna favored Amy, even: it was long and broad (the easier to slip through narrow crevices to devour its unsuspecting prey), singularly determined, and persistent as hell: it was going to eat Keanu if it was the last thing it ever did. Of course, the Kahuna didn't succeed; he was obliterated with a small portable nuclear device. As the timer on the bomb ticked down to zero, Amy's hand shot across the armrest, grabbed Mona's, and squeezed, and when the beast exploded in a geyser of red pulp, Amy's eyes shone with tears. That was the third—and last—time Mona saw her cry.

The rest of the weekend was a blur. Mona knew they drove around Mulholland and looked over the city, hunted for vintage vinyl, ate falafel (for Mona, for the first time). They went shopping at the drag stores on Hollywood Boulevard and Amy convinced Mona to buy a ridiculous pair of black stiletto knee-high boots she still hadn't worn. They never looked at the pictures. Mona, at the time, had been too tentative and too awed by the unfamiliarity of her surroundings (since that summer in New Jersey, she had not been out of Ruby Falls for longer than a day) to bring them up; and neither did Amy, apparently content to show off her new town and her new life rather than revisit the old one. When they parted at the airport, they promised to keep in touch, though Mona suspected neither of them would or expected the other to. They were living parallel lives and that was fine. That they would always be connected by the past was important, but their futures would be separate. She felt a little sad, even, that Amy had invited her to share this event— that there was no one else, no one new, in her new life to be her premiere plus one. Not that there was anyone new in Mona's life (other than Oneida). But as she settled into her seat on the plane, Mona was more relieved than sad: Amy's story had a happy ending, and Mona felt she could finally start working on her own.

But what had she done with the past decade? What story *had* she written for herself? In the dark, in her bed, Mona struggled to connect the threads that swirled around the rope of her life, a rope that might as well have been braided from Oneida's thick mane of hair. The death of her parents: her mother first, her father fifteen months later, both of heart disease. The men, who, after Oneida, had amounted to a grand total of three, only one of whom she'd been desperate enough to sleep with—and only then until she woke up one morning and realized she was sleeping with Eric Cole, who had been a dickhead in the seventh grade and was an even bigger dickhead now. She had started her own business. That made her very proud and very happy. But nothing brought as much form or joy to her life as her daughter. Her new best friend. And Mona Jones loved her life, when she really thought about it: she loved waking up early every morning to make an enormous pot of coffee (Sherman couldn't teach kids how to hammer a nail until he'd had at least three cups); sharing companionable cereal-eating silence with Oneida, or, if the silence felt like it wanted to be broken, talking about whatever paperback her daughter brought down to read over the morning meal; seeing Oneida off to school; cracking her knuckles and the spine of her sketchbook and spending the afternoon elbow-deep in confectioner's sugar and flour, whipping ingredients into someone else's idea of the perfect cake for a perfect day. And then whipping ingredients into her own idea of a perfect meal at the end of a normal day. Talking with her daughter, tucking her daughter in, and falling asleep with a book of her own, her finger pressed between two pages. It was a good life. It was a comfortable life—beautiful, even. It was *her* life and she lived it in the present tense.

But Mona Jones should have known better. Just as she should have diagnosed Arthur Rook's obsession, she should have known her childhood wasn't through with her. In all those movies she and Amy watched, all those creatures born of horrific science experiments, all those heroes tormented by the loved ones they failed to save, there was one constant: the past was never past. It always came back to kick your ass.

＆

Mona liked Monday mornings. She liked the bustle of Sherman and Anna and her daughter stirring from their weekend routines, blinking back sleep, guzzling coffee and orange juice as they gathered the will to face another weekday cycle. Bert, who ate breakfast in her top-floor belfry, wouldn't come down until lunchtime. The hours between eight and noon on Monday were the first in approximately forty-eight that Mona had to herself—to read the paper, to check her e-mail, to nurse a cup of creamy coffee with her feet propped on the arm of the couch, something low and moody playing on the stereo. Pink Floyd, maybe, or early Garbage. Nine Inch Nails, if she needed energy for a day of hard work.

But this Monday was very different, and Mona, uncharacteristically, didn't mind. She was too curious about what had happened to land Arthur on her doorstep to begrudge him her hours. She did begrudge him Harryhausen, though: she could hear Amy's cat galloping like a tiny fat pony up and down the stairs and then into the kitchen, around the table, and out into the front hall again. Mona didn't know a creature with as high a ratio of fat to muscle as Harryhausen could move that fast. She wondered if Amy and Arthur had a small apartment, if this was the first time in years the cat had this much room to run. Yet another question for her patient when he was aware enough to be asked.

She lifted Arthur's breakfast tray and breezed carefully out of the kitchen. Oneida was standing in the front hall, brushing her hair back into a ponytail before the school bus came. Mona smiled, as she always did when she watched her daughter try to tame the follicular explosion that passed for her hair, and hoped Oneida didn't catch her. Her daughter had been even more awkward and quiet lately, and the last thing she needed was an indication that her mother was laughing at her. Mona wasn't sure what was going on in Oneida's head—she supposed some of the tension came from the Arthur Rook situation, which Oneida thought was bizarre in the extreme and which Mona didn't have the energy, at the moment, to explain to her. In time, she might. Mona didn't feel like sharing Arthur with her daughter—it didn't feel like any of Oneida's business. Which was odd, but true: Arthur was the first thing in a long time she didn't want to share.

Mona was in awe of her daughter. She freely acknowledged it might not be the healthiest way to raise a child; to think your kid was totally the shit surely wasn't the most objective method of child rearing. She couldn't look at Oneida without remembering the very first time she held her and the sensation of absolute terror blooming in her chest that made it difficult to breathe and impossible to think. She remembered an intense urge to throw the baby, to get it away from her body; had gone so far as to imagine herself hurling this squirming lump in her arms like a football, spiraling through the air, and then turning and running before she saw if anyone was around to catch her pass. But her arms were locked, rigid and shaking. Her body refused to give up this baby, no matter what her brain wanted.

She didn't actually fall in love with Oneida until she was five or six—it was definitely after her trip to Los Angeles—when it became clear that Oneida was insanely intelligent and just as bizarre. Finally, Mona had a captive audience: someone who always laughed at her jokes and would make her laugh in return, who wanted to hang out with her, wanted to learn from her. It was a relief: for as insistent as she was that she not give the baby up for adoption, she couldn't ignore her disappointment during the first years of Oneida's life. Those years had been an endless maelstrom of diapers and sticky fingers, sleeplessness, and the endless, maddening frustration of trying to communicate with a tiny creature who didn't even know how to talk. Her own parents took the lead during Oneida's infancy and were unfailingly supportive. She didn't know, in hindsight, what she had done to deserve such grace from the people whose lives she'd altered radically without once considering how it might affect them, but she didn't question it. They were both dead; she missed them. It was enough to go on, to run the house, to be a grown-up, and to raise their grandkid. Their awesome, brilliant grandkid.

"Have a good day, O," she said. Oneida may have mumbled something in return, but it was lost as she closed the door behind her.

Mona balanced Arthur's breakfast tray on her hip as she turned his doorknob—he'd lost the privilege of a locked door the second he stole that photo off her wall—and wasn't surprised to feel Harryhausen hurtle between her legs as she stepped into his room. Mona had left everything the way she'd found it: the postcards on the wall, the clothesline, the little piles of photos and stubs; and the weirdly familiar-looking pink shoebox on the coffee table had struck her as the pieces of a play already in progress, props it would be best not to rearrange. She had no idea what Arthur was thinking when he'd made such a spectacular disaster. It was a mess, yes, but Mona suspected it wasn't senseless—Arthur had been defacing and cluttering her property to a tune only he could hear, but to a tune nonetheless. She found it strangely charming, that this was what happened when he had a mental breakdown. Because that's clearly what was going on here: Amy must have left him or cheated on him or otherwise rejected him. There was no other explanation.

She knocked on the bedroom doorframe.

"Room service, sir," she said, in a clipped British accent. "Are you decent?"

Arthur was awake and sitting upright in bed. He was wearing one of her father's old button-down shirts, the easier to tend to the wounds on his chest, and had the formidable beginnings of a reddish beard. Harryhausen leaped onto the covers with all the grace of a flying pig.

"So what'll it be first?" Mona locked her elbow and held his tray aloft. "Change your dressings or breakfast?"

Arthur didn't respond. He inhaled and blinked and drew his lips back over his teeth.

"Allow me to tempt you." Mona jiggled the tray enticingly. "For your first meal of the day, which is surely the most important, I've put together a delightful combination of juice, toast, and eggs, fresh scrambled with a hint of butter in the pan, slowly and gently coaxed into delightfully fluffy clouds of unborn chicken."

Arthur's brow creased.

"Yeah, I went too far with that." She slid the tray onto the dresser.

"Let's change your bandages. Maybe by the time I'm through ripping off all your chest hair, you'll have forgotten I said it."

Arthur cleared his throat. "You talk like . . . television," he croaked.

Mona squinted. "That a good thing or a bad thing?"

Arthur smiled a tiny smile and cleared his throat again. He shrugged.

Mona sat on the edge of the bed, tucking one leg beneath her. "What do you remember?" Mona asked.

Arthur wiggled his toes under the covers, to the right of Mona's hip. Harryhausen tensed to pounce.

"Your name?" she prompted.

"Arthur Rook." His voice was dry from disuse. "I grew up in Somerville, Massachusetts. Phone number was 617-879-8446. I have a younger brother named David, lives two streets over from where we grew up, my parents are David Senior and Nance, and I—I moved to Los Angeles. Then I came here. On a plane. And a train. And then a cab."

"What's your cat's name?"

"Harry." He swallowed. The grin was gone, which told Mona he remembered plenty that he wasn't telling her. He ran his hand over his cheeks. "*I'm* hairy. What day is it?"

"Monday. Do you remember who I am? What happened on Friday?"

"Yes." He coughed. "Your name is Mona. Jones. This is your boardinghouse. I had dinner with a vet, a shop teacher, an old woman, and your daughter. And then I saw—red. Stones. In a photo . . . frame—oh, did I break it?"

She nodded. The hospital had given her what was left of the photograph after they were sure they had taken all the pieces of glass from Arthur's chest. The picture of William Fitchburg Jones and Daniel Darby that had been at the top of the stairs her entire life was still whole, albeit covered in Arthur's blood. She thought it looked kind of cool, actually—anyone else might have thought it was grossly macabre, but Mona appreciated that Arthur had managed to bleed with an artistic sensibility: Daniel and William, sitting in those tortuous-looking Victorian chairs, were covered by a deep red-brown swath like an ink wash. The reddish stroke brought depth to the photograph, and she saw things she had never seen before: the notch out of William's ear, which fit with the family story about his stint as a boxer that she always thought was apocryphal. Daniel looked so handsome, so young—Daniel in the picture was probably younger than Mona was now. Arthur's blood gave them life. She had already reframed it.

"I'm so sorry," he said. "I—I had no right to destroy . . . photographs. Family."

"I forgive you," she said. Arthur's eyes wiggled back and forth. Mona, desperately curious and heartened by Arthur's relative lucidity, decided that today was the day. There was no point in waiting for him to get healthier, no point in waiting for him to heal, before she brought up the subject of Amy. Too much time had gone by for Mona to pretend she had any more to spare.

"I'm not usually crazy," Arthur said.

"I doubt that," Mona said, and took a shot. "You'd have to be crazy to marry Amy."

Arthur made a noise. It was quiet, and it was awful. It was a noise Mona thought only animals knew how to make, and only when they'd been kicked for the hundredth time by a cruel master: a cry that dies in the crier's throat, a cry that gives up. That realizes there is nothing to be done but be kicked, that there is no reality but this and there is nothing and no one to save.

Oh, no, she thought. *No*. She didn't want to know Amy's secrets, she didn't want to know them, she didn't want to know—

"Arthur, you don't—" Mona held up her hands, bracing for an impact she never dreamed would come.

"Amy died," Arthur whispered. And he closed his eyes and laid his head back on the pillow. The silence in the room wrapped itself tight around Mona's head, muffling the sound of Ray Harryhausen, purring, purring, like the dumb animal he was.

8 ∾ *How Eugene Fell*

Once upon a time, long before he ever tricked Oneida Jones into coming to his house alone, Eugene Wendell could think of things all day long and not once, not *one* fucking time, would sex come into it. And then one day, without warning, the most normal, boring things, like a remote control or a butter dish or a tube of toothpaste, began triggering fantasies so compelling and urgent that he'd have to excuse himself to masturbate in the most private (hell, closest) bathroom possible. When he first discovered his brain and body's new favorite trick, he'd thought it was amazing: twenty-four hours a day, seven days a week, Eugene Wendell would get off at the literal drop of a hat. It was awesome.

But then, just as suddenly—and improbably—it got old. He couldn't concentrate. He was getting bored. Neither hand was coming up with anything particularly interesting on its own (or together), and he realized he'd kill for the ability to finish so much as a homework assignment without thinking about sex. It was a curse. It was his curse, his alone, and one afternoon, cramming for a history test and momentarily distracted by the image of Dolley Madison with her feet in the air, Eugene realized what he needed: a girl. He needed another variable to make things interesting again, a goal toward which he could channel some of this errant sexual energy. It was so simple, so elemental, it hadn't even occurred to him.

Or maybe he hadn't thought of it because finding a girl was going to be impossible. He went to school in the middle of the middle of nowhere, he only had his learner's permit (no license for another six months, or so his parents thought); and Eugene, despite the fury of his uncontrollable desire, did not slum. He had standards. He actually cared who he porked, wanted to respect both the porkee and himself as porker. He considered this yet another sign that he was the undiscovered diamond of Ruby Falls: a quality guy, a brilliant guy, who would be duly appreciated by the rest of the world in time.

Tossing aside his history book—*American Passages*, it was called, though everyone at school referred to it as *American Assages*, which Eugene thought was a stupid joke because it didn't really mean anything, it just sounded like the word *ass*, ha ha ha, that's so freaking clever—he opened last year's yearbook. His entire class, all forty-three souls of varying intelligence and humanity, stared back at him from a single double-page spread, tiny black and white heads that produced an almost universal spasm in his gorge. He really hated them. He barely knew why, or how he had become the kind of person who hates others. It was like the urge for sex: one day it just happened, and he didn't know how to make it stop. He hoped one day it would go away, but from what he had already seen of adult behavior, he wasn't counting on it.

He scanned the pictures, taken almost a year ago. Everyone already looked older than these versions of themselves, leaner, less chubby. Jenny Heckle had shaved her head over the summer (she had potential, he supposed, but she seemed so mad all the time; he didn't think he'd be safe with her), but there she was, crystallized on last October's picture day, long blond hair draped over one shoulder. Next to Jenny was David Katz, one of the few people Eugene didn't want to punch in the face. Annemarie was a huge bitch. Janice was dumb as a dump truck. And just like that, Eugene was at the bottom of the page, staring at Heather Zink (ugh, no) and feeling more frustrated than ever. Usually he didn't tease the urge, didn't get it all worked up for nothing, and this was why. He thought about Dolley Madison again (trying to find her under all those skirts and petticoats, like doing the breaststroke through waves of bedsheets) and went into the bathroom.

When he came back he picked up his yearbook, growled under his breath, and was about to toss it back into the pile of crap on his floor when his brain hiccupped and he thought: *Oneida Jones*. He hadn't seen her picture; where was she? She should have been between Carrie and David, but she wasn't; and then he saw at the bottom of the page *Not pictured: Oneida Jones.* Mysterious. He tried to summon Oneida and came up with a vague outline of big dark hair and dark furry eyebrows over dark-rimmed glasses. He had barely paid attention to her, ever, but more importantly the thought of her didn't make him feel like throwing up. It made him want to remember what she looked like, if they'd ever spoken, and why he didn't hate her in the same lazy way he hated certain other people he barely knew and yet still knew enough to loathe.

She was listed in the index next to a single page number, and it took Eugene a solid minute to locate her in the Key Club group picture. He had it narrowed down between two pale blobs surrounded by dark hair-clouds when she popped out of the lower edge of the picture. The photographer had set them up on the chorus risers, but Oneida was standing on the ground, off to the side a little, arms crossed and not looking at the camera. *I'm not one of these stupid sheep*, she said to Eugene. *I'm in Key Club because I'm smart and I'm here because they made me come, but I see things they don't, or can't, because they're all too busy saying cheese. Also, my tits are a lot bigger than you remembered.*

The next day in school—as though Eugene needed a sign that he was on the right track, which he didn't—Dreyer assigned group projects in American History and called Oneida Jones's name two seconds after she called his own. He had been trying to get a good look at her all day, and when she turned her desk in to form a group circle, a little part of Eugene he didn't even know existed cracked in half and flooded his entire body. He wasn't sure if he was happy, horny, or an unholy combination of both, but it took every bit of his considerable will not to giggle out loud.

Because Oneida Jones was a hot mess. First of all, that hair—holy shit, it was insane; there was so much of it, and it was so curly and thick. It reminded Eugene of the buffalo hide his Uncle Phil had hanging in his dining room, so dense and furry that, when Eugene was little, he could grab two hunks of it in his hands and lift himself up off the floor. Oneida's ponytail ballooned behind her head like a cloud the color of dark chocolate, and if her features hadn't been angular, or her face so pale and grave, she would have disappeared into all that hair completely. But her nose was long and straight, her chin stubborn, and her eyes large and greenish behind her glasses. Eugene, really looking at her for the first time, was reminded of how blind everyone at Ruby Falls High was, for someone like Oneida Jones—basically a hot female Wolverine, minus the adamantium claws—to be essentially invisible.

The idea of a hot female Wolverine, or more specifically, of Oneida in Wolverine's yellow and blue costume, flashed over Eugene like an instant fever. He ducked out for the bathroom when Dreyer's back was turned. When he came back, so relaxed he felt positively noodle-y, Oneida glared at him and slapped a paper on his desk without uttering a sound. It was a description of the assignment, and she'd written on the top in red capital letters FIRST GROUP MEETING @ DARBY-JONES SAT 2 P.M.

Eugene was thus presented with his first deadline in what he had already begun to think of as the Oneida Project. He had three days until that first meeting: three days to figure out the best path to Oneida Jones's brain. Her heart, he figured, would follow: winning her brain seemed a bigger challenge, more befitting his talents. After dinner that night, when Eugene would normally retreat to his bedroom and attempt to do homework, which would normally result in marathon masturbatory sessions involving any number of historical and/or literary females (they were reading *The Scarlet Letter*—what else was he supposed to do?), he sat in the living room with a can of root beer and watched night fall over the hills through the giant picture windows.

By the time he was sitting in total darkness, Eugene was forced to admit that he had no idea how to get in Oneida's brain. He was *shit* at this. He didn't understand women, though he did understand enough about Oneida to know that you could potentially understand women and still not understand her. He had no precedent for any of this, no practice, and no confirmation that his instincts weren't broken. He had last kissed a girl named Lily during the one and only summer he'd spent at camp. She'd tasted like cherry Kool-Aid, and she'd kissed him back at first but then freaked when he licked the sugary red stains from the corners of her mouth. It had been an unsettling situation, to say the least.

Eugene usually prided himself on being the only person with his eyes open, the only person with a clue, and to be this thoroughly stumped before he'd even attempted the Oneida Project? He belched softly and crushed the root beer can between his palms.

From her bedroom in the back of the house he could hear his sister practicing her bass guitar, ripping through a song by the Violent Femmes that their father had sung to them when they were babies (or so he told them; Patricia might have remembered, but Eugene had to take his word for it), to teach them how to count.

She sounded good. Of course she sounded good, he thought; all she did was play that bass, every hour of every day, when she wasn't working at the McDonald's on Route 31. Patricia was four years older than Eugene, and had graduated from Ruby Falls High the previous spring. She had never pretended to want to go to college. She was going to save up some money (her *own* money, she was adamant), move to New York City, and start a band. Help turn some rat hole into another CBGBs. Eugene thought it was pretty embarrassing—and so, so uncool—that Patricia was realizing her counterculture queen dreams by working the drive-thru at McDonald's, but when it came to Patricia, he'd learned long ago to shut up and stay out of her way.

It hadn't always been like that. When Eugene was still a kid, Patricia had treated him like her favorite toy and Eugene had loved every second of it. He was her audience and her roadie, carrying her amp around the house and nodding sagely when she decreed this particular corner of the living room to have the best acoustics. She taught him everything she knew about music, about punk and rock and roll and new wave; she played him *London Calling* and Talking Heads and taught him to thrash around like a lunatic without breaking his neck; she promised to pierce his nose with a safety pin when he was old enough to "really appreciate it." Eugene adored his sister, probably because she was a younger, blonder version of their father, Astor, whom, if it was possible, Eugene adored even more. But that had been years and years ago, before the thought of girls in general and his sister in particular became equal parts troubling and enthralling—and, in Patricia's case, a little terrifying.

Lately, Patricia's status as a post-graduate lame duck had thawed something between them. They had spoken to each other—not merely to convey vital information but conversationally. She had pulled him into her room to play a new album for him, had asked what he thought, and genuinely seemed to care about his opinion. Eugene tried not to think he was acting like a kicked dog, pathetically happy to be shown a little kindness from the master who had done the kicking. Because he *was* happy, desperately so, that Patricia seemed on the verge of rediscovering her favorite toy, even though it was a toy she had already broken once.

Eugene shuffled through the thick carpet in his bare feet and grinned as a blue-white charge leaped from his fingertip to the metal knob of Patricia's door. He pressed his cheek to the cool white paint and heard her growling along with the bass line.

Patricia's playing got louder, and he opened the door. She was wearing the same red sweatpants she always wore and a lumpy gray sweater that might have belonged to their father at some past, even skinnier, place in his life. She sang in her bird-thin little voice, nodding at him to come on in.

She had arms like bendy straws; they both did. Wendells were not exactly hearty. They sang together through four headaches, five for loneliness, six sorrows, seven n-n-no tomorrows. "Eight!" rumbled Eugene, plumbing the gravelly pit of his voice. It still surprised and pleased him, how deep his voice had become. A part of him was irrationally afraid it would go away, that the Gods of Puberty would realize they'd given him the wrong throat and take it back.

Patricia took the second to last line—nine, for a lost God—her reedy little body and voice wavering. They landed feet first together on ten, ten, ten, *ten for everything everything everything everything!*

Patricia let the bass flop listlessly against her side and, by way of a greeting, flipped her little brother off. "What's up?" she asked, unslinging the strap from her neck.

"Not much," Eugene said, fidgeting in her doorway. "You're a girl, right?"

Patricia looped her thumbs in the waistband of her sweatpants. She had terrible posture.

"Last time I checked. You're a boy, right?"

"I didn't mean it like that," Eugene said. He felt awkward, but the only place he could think to sit in her room was on her bed, and *that* wouldn't be weird. Not at all. "I have a question. About girls."

This improved Patricia's posture markedly. She crossed her arms and leaned back appraisingly. "Holy flipping crap," she said. "Little Wendy has a crush. Who is it? You've got to tell me now, you can't just—"

"Oneida Jones," Eugene said. He thought he trusted Patricia.

She froze, and her eyes widened. "Shut up."

"Is that OK? Should I have run it by you first?"

"It's just that . . . God, Wend, do you know anything about her? Like, at all?"

Eugene crossed his own arms and leaned into her doorframe. "Do *you*?" he said.

"I know she's a complete freak."

"Like we're not?" Eugene said. He didn't like the way this conversation was going. His heart started to beat faster.

"Oh, way freakier." Patricia raised her brows at him knowingly. "Like, scary freakier. You know what they say about her?"

Eugene backed up a little bit. Patricia advanced.

"She has a taste for the blood of virgins. Male virgins."

"Oh, shut up!" Eugene said, flushing. "You don't know anything about her, do you?"

"Ha! No clue," Patricia said. "But I'm sure she's a hot piece of snatch."

"Shut up," Eugene said.

"Excuse me: I'm sure she's a lovely young piece of snatch." Patricia grinned at him and threw herself backward on her bed. "So what's your question?"

Eugene noticed for the first time that his sister's room was a total pit. She was lying on the bed but the mattress was barely visible under a giant pile of dirty clothes and blankets and pillows. The posters on the wall, of Kim Deal and Flea, were coming untacked at the corners and rippled with age. Books and guitar tabs littered the floor, and a small pile of rumpled McDonald's uniforms was emitting the unmistakable funk of fast food service, of grease and salt-infused polyester.

"Has Mom seen this mess?" he asked.

"That's not your question. And, like, none of your business." She sat up, crossed her legs, and patted the empty space opposite her. "Oh, come on!" she wheedled. "It's like I finally got that little sister I asked Santa for."

Grimacing, Eugene perched on the edge of her bed and rubbed his nose, wishing she would open a window and let in some fresh air. Patricia twiddled her thumbs and asked if she could paint his nails.

"How do I get to a girl's brain?" he spat out.

"Skull saw." Patricia rolled her eyes up at the ceiling. "I don't know. It depends. I mean—what's this girl like?"

Eugene shrugged.

"I see. You don't know her, but you like her. How very boy of you." She grabbed her feet with her hands and fluttered her fingers and toes. She was built like a pretzel, all skinny, looping limbs. "OK. First thing: you can't get her anything lame like flowers or candy or jewelry or a stuffed animal; Jesus, God forbid. And the fact that you're aiming for her brain tells me—frankly, Wendy, it tells me you don't know what the hell you're doing."

"Well . . . why else would I be asking?" Eugene said, his voice squeaking.

"Obviously, because you know I know." Patricia narrowed her eyes. "What's her name? Ono?"

"Oneida."

"The hell kind of name is *Oneida*? Never mind. What's the first thing you think of when you think of her?"

"Hair," Eugene said. Patricia's unblinking gaze made it hard to think. He looked down and away. "Uh . . . big hair. Dark. Glasses." He rubbed his eyes, trying desperately to come up with associations that didn't have anything to do with sex, the female anatomy, or bodily fluids.

"Big hair. Dark glasses, I can see the attrac—"

"Raw," said Eugene, and Patricia froze. "She's like a raw nerve. She's a mess, and she's probably super smart and messed up, and when you look at her you think she might snap and . . . bite you, or something."

"Kinky," said Patricia, and pointed at the door for Eugene to get out. "Seriously, go steal some shit from Astor's office. Every fucked-up girl likes a piece of work."

⁓

Astor Wendell's office was a museum. It had once been a spacious two-car garage, but since the Wendells only had one car, an all-weather tank of a vehicle it would have been inhumane to contain indoors, it had been reappointed. The walls were painted pristine white and it was brighter than daylight, thanks to the specially filtered overhead fluorescents Astor ordered direct from the wholesaler. There were two easels set up for Astor's business partner Terry, who played rhythm guitar and had a face you both trusted implicitly and forgot twenty seconds after he left the room. The floor was a mess of paint and gesso, of little bits of wood shaving and glops of varnish. Eugene loved the sloppy chaos of the floor and had spent many hours as a kid staring into its patterns the way other kids lie on their backs and stare at clouds. He thought of it as the physical proof of his father's genius, saw, in the colorful lumps and splatters, years of hard, brilliant labor.

Against one wall was a slotted rack that had held, briefly, Warhols and a Basquiat; a Chuck Close; Dalís and a Balthus; a Magritte and a Gauguin, and one time, memorably, a Munch. The only piece that had never left Astor's shop for a private collection on the other side of the world was a small Miró that hung over Astor's desk, which Astor was particularly proud of because the painting hadn't even been in storage when he swapped it for the forgery. Eugene never found out how he'd managed to get the original off the wall and out of the frame, but Eugene suspected it was even more illegal than Astor was usually comfortable with.

Eugene's father was a professional art forger. He used his position as a security guard to scope the art in museum storage, and, depending on what style of painting he felt like mimicking at the time, borrowed a piece for a week or two and replaced it with a copy before anyone knew the difference. Terry, his partner, was the point man, moving the originals through a mysterious organization of contacts Eugene variously imagined as either leggy and brunette or coldly Russian. Astor usually completed two or three forgeries a year and, depending on how quickly Terry could move the originals, they earned enough for both families to live comfortably, though not extravagantly. No need to attract too much attention, Astor said, not when you've already banked enough to send your kids to college three times over.

The fact that his father was a forger did not trouble Eugene. It didn't seem particularly dishonest to replace one painting with an exact copy, especially since it meant he got the Christmas presents he asked for. In fact, when the young Eugene fully understood what his father and Terry were up to, he thought it was hands down the coolest thing ever. The first time he recognized one of his father's forgeries in the real world he was on a school field trip, and he stood and listened to the wandering crowd until his frantic teacher found him and dragged him to the school bus idling outside. Some people had passed by without a word, a few stuck their faces up close to examine the brushstrokes, one little girl said it was the prettiest thing she'd seen all day, but none of them knew it was a fake. And so Astor's philosophy clawed deep into Eugene's brain: as long as you saw what you expected, it was real enough. And you better believe Astor Wendell wasn't going to let that inefficiency in the marketplace, so to speak, go without being exploited.

Eugene, for the bulk of his childhood, was insanely, stupidly happy. The Wendells had plenty of money and plenty of time to spend together; there were no bedtimes, no asparagus and Brussels sprouts, no forbidden movies. Everyone he loved was unbelievably cool, which made him unbelievably cool by association; which in turn made the fact that he had few friends in school their loss, not his. He never doubted his father's livelihood, nor that the Wendell nuclear unit was of a similar mind.

Until Eugene was ten and Patricia fourteen, and the Wendells went on vacation to New York City. For a week over summer break, they stayed in a renovated warehouse studio in Brooklyn that belonged to a friend of Astor's from his aborted stint at art school (where he'd also met Terry, and where, Eugene suspected, the wide web of leggy brunettes and calculating Russians originated). The four of them took the train into the city and ate souvlaki in the Village. They ran giddy laps around the plaza at Rockefeller Center, and a tall man walking a Great Dane through Central Park let them play with his dog for a while.

They went to the Metropolitan Museum of Art, but it wasn't until after dinner—when his parents got into a fight that started, as far as Eugene could tell, when Astor knocked over a carton of fried rice—that Eugene thought of the way they'd been hurried out of the modern art wing and how odd it had been. He and Patricia had been standing in front of a giant painting of three people on a grassy mountain, trying to figure out whether the girl in a red jacket, lying on her side, was dead or just napping, when Astor gently pressed his palms against their backs and steered them toward the exit. "Your mom feels like she's gonna barf," he said, but when they walked down all those steps to the street, their mother didn't look sick at all. She was eating an ice cream cone and handed everyone orange popsicles before they got into the first cab that pulled up.

For people who hardly ever fought, they sure knew how to do it well: the main studio, a huge empty room with high ceilings and exposed brick walls, echoed and rang. Eugene had closed the metal fire door that separated the kids' room from the rest of the loft, which had the unpleasant effect of making the fight muffled and tinny, like it was happening in the soundless black of deep space. Patricia rested her chin on her knees, her thumb in a paperback copy of *Flowers in the Attic*. The windows were open on Brooklyn. Night had fallen and the air was humid and hot, and strangely silent whenever their parents' voices dipped too low to hear. The lingering odors of renovation, of fresh paint and sawdust, made Eugene's nose itch. They both sat in silence on their inflatable mattresses until Patricia said, "You know we're all completely screwed, don't you?"

Eugene, already tensed by the argument, jumped at the sound of her voice. "No, we're not," he said.

"Oh, yes, we are," Patricia said. "What do you think they're arguing about? Mom just said something about looking over her shoulder *waiting for the hammer to fall*—doesn't that sound screwed to you?"

Eugene shrugged. Patricia sat up on her knees, the air mattress bobbing across the concrete floor.

"I bet the cops are tracking him," she said. "I bet Javert's got the scent."

He shrugged again. They had rushed for tickets to *Les Misérables* the day before, but he had fallen asleep shortly after intermission.

"Eugene, think about it. What he does is *illegal*. If he gets caught, what happens? Do they send him to jail? Maybe he runs away, goes on the lam; what happens to Mom? She loves him like crazy. I bet she'd run away with him. What happens to us then?"

Eugene's head felt fuzzy and far away, sour with paint fumes. "We'd go live with Terry," he said.

"Don't you think if they knew about Astor, they'd know about Terry? So now Terry has to run, too. Do we go to a foster home? Do we get split up? Shit, Eugene, our entire family would be *gone*."

"You know, I remember, when I was your age I thought he was a god. Like Robin Hood or Billy the Kid, some kind of superhero." There was a spike in the argument, and they both turned to the door instinctively. "It isn't normal," Patricia said, "what he does and who we are. *We . . . are . . . so . . . fucked*."

And then Patricia was crying—sobbing, really—and Eugene was genuinely afraid. Patricia had been like this for the past six months or so, quick to cry and cry violently, and Eugene had made a conscious effort to keep out of her way whenever she looked volatile. He didn't understand where this well of emotion came from and what triggered it to overflow so furiously. It sounded now like Patricia blamed it all on their father, which—was she crazy? Asking what would happen if he got caught was beside the point, because he *wouldn't* get caught: he was Astor Wendell. He *was* Robin Hood; he *was* Billy the Kid; he *was* a superhero. If anyone was fucked, it was Patricia, and Eugene was just scared and confused enough to tell her so.

Patricia stopped crying instantly. Her face froze mid-wail, her mouth still open, her eyes wide and red, and her cheeks damp with tears. "What did you say, you little asshole?"

"I said *you're* the only one around here who's fucked up, Patricia," Eugene said.

Afterward, Eugene could only partially reconstruct the events of that muggy night in Brooklyn, in the old loft where the Wendells stayed on their last family vacation. He remembered his sister standing up and throwing her copy of *Flowers in the Attic* at his head; he remembered deflecting it and the tiny slap as it hit the floor. He remembered Patricia hauling him up by the collar of his T-shirt, remembered her shouting at him, *Wake up, Wendy, wake up and grow up*, and then he remembered she let him go and he fell. The rest was gone completely, but when he opened his eyes in the hospital, he had ten stitches snaking through his eyebrow. He'd smashed his forehead on a can of paint left over from remodeling, before hitting the concrete floor. He had nothing to worry about; he would recover completely. But Eugene Wendell didn't come home from that vacation whole. The germ of Wendy came with him, and over the next five years Wendy woke and grew up.

He couldn't will himself to forget what Patricia thought of their father, even though he tried to do just that—with a small degree of success—for a full year. It made him feel jumbled and panicky to consider that either his awesome sister or his awesome father was wrong; if it turned out to be the former, he lost a sister. If it turned out to be the latter, not only did he lose a father, his father was a criminal. Astor was no better than a thief in Patricia's eyes, a few lucky breaks away from getting caught and thereby annihilating the only life Eugene had ever known, with the only family worth being a part of.

But was it, anymore? His sister was making it easier to dislike her every day. His mother and his father hadn't fought since Brooklyn, but Eugene could sense a strange static between them. Even Astor was acting differently, had stopped boxing and scuffling with his son and started asking, if Eugene so much as sighed, if he was *all right*. For the first time in his life, Eugene spent hours alone in his room, listening to music and trying to convince himself it wasn't necessary to decide whether his sister or his father was the crazy one.

He was dangerously close to siding with his sister when Astor stepped in and tipped the scales, permanently, in his favor. In the three days that had passed since his eleventh birthday, Eugene had been unable to stop playing Patricia's gift, an album called *Doolittle* that went a long, long way toward convincing him his sister deserved to be first in his heart. He was obsessed with the first song, which he didn't understand at all: it was a lot of shouting and then something about slicing and eyeballs. But its innate awesomeness was impossible to deny, and he cranked his stereo as high as it could go, set the track to repeat, and thrashed around his bedroom like a little lunatic.

He was sweating and gasping for air when Astor opened his door.

"Good song," he said. "Turn it off. I want to show you something."

Astor led Eugene down to his office, where an ancient movie projector was already set up, and asked him if he knew what that song was about. Eugene, still winded, could only shake his head and suck in a shaky, painful breath. "Black Francis is screaming about this movie, son," Astor said, starting the projector and joining Eugene on the ratty couch. He had a funny expression, halfway between pride and anxiety, and Eugene had a sudden, strange intuition: that this moment was going to change his life, to solidify what had started in Brooklyn, and scar more than his eyebrow.

He was right. For a black-and-white movie with no sound that lasted all of fifteen minutes, it was the most astonishing thing he had ever seen. Eyeballs were carved in half with straight razors. There were breasts and butts and dead donkeys on pianos and armpit hair and ants crawling out of holes in people's hands, and he made Astor show it to him three times, but each subsequent viewing failed to make any more sense than the first. In fact, the less he understood it, the more he loved it.

"Who—?" he said, pointing at the projection on the white wall of Astor's studio, and Astor said "A couple of serious surrealist wackos named Luis Buñuel and Salvador Dalí.

"Provocation. Juxtaposition. Dream logic. Following your impulses, no matter how bizarre—that's what the surrealists were about," Astor said.

"They sound awesome," Eugene said.

"I'm sure they were. They were also probably assholes, but hey, sometimes the world needs creative assholes." He reached over and grabbed Eugene's head in his hand and shook it, a kind of full-frontal noogie. "Noble creative assholes."

Eugene laughed. His skin prickled. He hadn't felt this close to Astor in ages. Certainly before Brooklyn.

Astor closed his eyes and leaned his head back against the couch. He still looked young, had all of his dark brown hair, though he wore it short and neat. Both Wendell kids took after their dad, with their long thin frames and beaky features. Eugene, watching his father beam at him, knew he was looking at the one person he loved most in this world and, in that one moment, was so full of awe for his father that Patricia lost the debate forever. Astor Wendell was a superhero doing a stupid thing, but his son Eugene believed in him utterly; believed that what the world needed was this particular noble creative asshole. His forgeries were an amazing, incredible thing—not just a work but an *act* of art— and if Patricia was too concerned about her own comfort and well-being not to appreciate that, Eugene was done with her.

Eugene Wendell wanted to be just like his dad. But with neither the talent nor the resources to forge actual art, he chose to forge the one thing he could create: himself. It would be relatively easy, since he was already something of a blank canvas at school. Eugene did his work, participated when it was required of him, went home. He didn't exist on the fringes so much as the dead middle of the road and was therefore invisible. But all that would change with the Wendy Project, his first great surrealist work.

The Wendy Project didn't go into full production until Eugene was a freshman in high school, though he had been planning it for about a year, teaching himself to walk a certain way, talk a certain way, glare a certain way. Wendy Wendell was a complete screwup, a cartoonishly violent, antisocial motherfucker, who got into scrapes with hookers and drug dealers—a touch Eugene thought struck just the right absurdist note, given their immediate surroundings (unless, unbeknownst to everyone, some sick bastard had taught cows to turn tricks).

Wendy was introduced to Ruby Falls High through a series of carefully orchestrated rumors. Eugene dropped notes on the floor in the auditorium, fake gossipy missives between people "who had been there," people "who had seen him" punching football players in the neck at away games; he scrawled cryptic, menacing graffiti in all the bathrooms. To act the part, he slumped and lurched through the hallways; made a game of seeing how long he could go without blinking. He committed tiny disciplinary infractions. Nothing he did was grave enough to warrant suspension or a black mark on his permanent record, just the occasional detention or stern talking-to. More importantly, he made people wonder what he might be capable of.

And then all Eugene had to do was sit back and watch it happen, as the faithful sheep of RFH played their part in the Wendy Project: made a nonexistent bully out of thin air and words, from their tiny minds, hungry for scandal and violence. Occasionally a rumor would make its way back to him that was so hysterically distorted from anything he had ever started that Eugene allowed himself a moment of grudging respect for some of the darker, more perverse imaginations of his fellow students. He couldn't be entirely contemptuous of them, he supposed; after all, they were a key component of his work. They had placed him at the top of a tower and left him mercifully alone, protected behind a dense bramble of thorns and black eyes and broken bottles—and the greatest work of art ever perpetrated by a surrealist who had barely begun to shave.

The first six months of the Wendy Project had been an amazing time in Eugene's life. He had come home from school every day with a giant grin on his face, elated that he had pulled it off. Eugene Wendell, the quiet skinny kid who hadn't been much of anything for years, was suddenly revered and feared. In the spring of his freshman year, it started to lose some of its appeal, but he was committed. He was bored, he supposed; even the greatest teenage geniuses get anxious to move on to their next work. So he started masturbating to alleviate some of the boredom, and that had turned into a great work of its own. Shortly after his masturbation habits kicked into high gear, he started to feel angry for no reason, to hate things in ways he had never hated things before. Thus Eugene was faced with the unpleasant truth that perhaps his projects would have to wait, at least until he got laid—unless, of course, he made getting laid his next great work of art.

⚘

Eugene flicked on the light beside the door and Astor's office was suddenly so bright his eyes watered. When he could focus again, he saw that his father had been working on a small landscape. The nearly completed forgery sat quietly on its easel, side by side with the original. It looked a little too tame for a girl as messed up as Oneida; besides, he needed to palm something Astor wouldn't notice was missing. He felt a little bad about raiding the office without asking first, but Astor was working late at an opening and wouldn't be home until close to midnight. Oneida—and Eugene's libido—couldn't afford to wait.

There was a small bedraggled suitcase, old and brown, on Astor's desk, and Eugene snapped the latches open. Neatly arranged inside was a random assortment of knickknacks, old yellowy papers and plastic junk, the kind of garbage you saw in flea markets and antiques shops and junk drawers that hadn't been cleaned out since before he was born. He had no idea what his father was doing with it. More importantly, there was so much junk in the case it would be impossible for Astor to miss any of it.

Eugene pulled out a long, thin strip of dark blue velvet that had been rolled tight like a cinnamon bun. It felt nice between his fingers, warm and rich. This had been a good idea, and Eugene felt a little sideways affection for Patricia. She wasn't a bad person, or an uncool person, under it all; she just didn't get their father. Which was her loss, really.

Eugene shuffled through the suitcase. The papers were very old, brittle and crumbling, and comprised an odd assortment of playbills and photographs and pages torn from what might have been science textbooks, full of old-fashioned illustrations of constellations and birds and rickety flying contraptions. He had never seen this suitcase before, but its contents gave him a pleasant sensation of déjà vu, as though they were scraps he himself had saved for some special purpose he couldn't quite recall. A green glass bottle with a fat corked neck, tucked in the bottom of the case, gave him an idea. He rolled up the dark blue velvet, which he had been rubbing absently during his investigation, and jammed it in the neck of the bottle. Perfect: a flower for a freak.

Eugene held the bottle at arm's length and smiled in spite of himself. It felt right, perfectly right, to give this weird flower to Oneida Jones, who was weird herself and weirdly beautiful. It was the first time he had thought of Oneida as beautiful, and it made him smile again. He saw himself holding out the green bottle to her, saw her face redden in his mind, and watched in dismay as his mental version of her knit her brows together and glared as though he were dangerously deranged.

"Shit," he said. "I can't give this to her."

Wendy would never give anything like this to Oneida, nor would Oneida ever accept anything from Wendy. He would do better to stuff it anonymously in her mailbox or hang it outside her window than walk up and say, "Here. This is for you." She'd run away or smash it at his feet, and he wouldn't blame her; in fact, he'd be a little disappointed in her if she didn't. Eugene had delivered a sucker punch to his own gut: he didn't want a girl who would have anything to do with his other half.

And then it happened, like it always happened. He felt it first in his stomach, a nauseating heaviness as though he'd swallowed a hot stone.

The heat from the stone rose up through him, boiling as it went, until he was so weak with anger that he didn't know which arm to lash out first. This was the worst, and he knew it: the urge for sex was uncontrollable but ultimately nothing compared to this insane rage, this desire to beat the living crap out of anything and everything, for no reason whatsoever.

Eugene felt like screaming until his throat bled. Felt like he'd been boxed, nailed inside his own coffin. His breath grew ragged, his heart hurt. How much pressure would it take for his skull to explode, for his blood and brains to blend into the loops and comet tails of oil and paint? Very Pollock, he thought, very Pollock. He looked down and realized he was still holding the green glass bottle with the blue velvet inside. He hurled it to the floor.

It broke with a tender pop: like a raw egg, cushioned in its fall by the velvet. Eugene stared at the tiny pile of green and blue rubble and felt some of the anger leave him, draining from his limbs and leaving him rubbery. So this was the cure for anger: smashing velvet-filled bottles. He sat on the floor of his father's office and scooped the debris together with his bare hands. He felt woozy and weak. He felt terrible that he had broken what would have made, really, a perfect gift for Oneida, who he suspected could benefit from smashing it just as much as he had. That was probably why he liked her. Thank God there were more bottles in the case.

9 ❧ New Blood

A nna was the first to notice.

"Something's up, kid." She rustled the sports section. "You've got your panties in a serious twist."

Mona wrinkled her nose and poured two cups of coffee. She hated the word *panties*. Just something about it. She set the coffee on the kitchen table and Anna tipped the paper forward, the better to seek aggressive eye contact.

"I'm a vet, Mona. That means I know without having to be told."

"That one of the courses at the Cornell vet school, *Psychic Bonds with Quadrupeds*? Taught by adjunct professor Dionne Warwick?"

"Ha ha. Come on, *I know you*."

Not as well as you think you do. Mona frowned into her cup of coffee. But Anna was right, she was blocking out the world with lame jokes. Overly ambitious wedding cakes. If she actually saw the world and smelled the world and told the world what she knew—that Amy Henderson was dead, that Amy Henderson met her end with the help of a hundred volts or more (and hadn't they both learned, as lab partners in junior high physics, that it wasn't the volts that mattered, it was the current?)—Mona didn't know what it would all mean. She only knew she feared it, and the only thing she wanted to do now was talk to Arthur Rook about a girl she had been a girl with. Arthur wasn't part of the real world and, when they were together, neither was Mona. They could bring Amy back to life between them and pretend their suspended animation was a sustainable state.

The last thing she wanted to do was tell Anna—anything at all. Strike that: the *last* thing she wanted to do was talk to Oneida. Her heart ached at the thought of her daughter, that after every hour, every day, every year they'd spent growing up together, Mona couldn't explain herself to her. Didn't want to. Wondered if she would ever be able to, and prayed, like a coward, that she would never have to.

But today was Wednesday, and here was Anna, being Anna. On Wednesdays, Anna didn't go into the clinic until eleven, and she and Mona would pore over the local paper, drinking coffee and chatting, both of them procrastinating like champs. It had been a ritual for as long as Anna had lived at the Darby-Jones, and despite knowing, deep down, that Anna was a good person and probably her only real adult friend, Mona secretly enjoyed Wednesday mornings less and less. Anna was something of an emotional vampire, and in this new unprecedented age (the Second Age Without Amy), she was far too nosy for comfort.

When Anna first came to the Darby-Jones, fresh from her divorce, she was a friendly stray, looking for a place to curl up. The house needed new blood: Sherman and Bert were fundamentally uninteresting to Mona as friends and companions, and Oneida, despite being the one person in the world Mona wanted to be stranded on a desert island with, was still a little girl. There were certain conversations, certain subjects, that Mona wanted to talk about with a grown-up.

Enter Anna DeGroot, with her severe ponytail, her constant cloud of dog hair, her chatty ease, and her penchant for gossip. Anna knew everything about everyone in Ruby Falls. The veterinary clinic, she said, was ground zero for gossip; when people brought in their pets, they brought in their problems. It was like reading tea leaves—a dog with a shedding problem bespoke owners who fought; a cat spraying all over the house was reacting to his owner's infidelity. Compounded by the wagging tongues of the assistants and receptionists, not a shred of information remained private. It was through Anna that Mona first heard about Tim Acres, who'd been two years ahead of her in high school, cheating on his wife with one of the seniors on the varsity football team. Anna tipped her off about the quarterly key parties that took place on the dairy farms (swinging milkers, she called them). And even though there was no way to prove it, because she had heard it from Anna, Mona was inclined to believe that the old maid who lived alone on the Blicker farm really had killed a Jehovah's Witness who came to her door, salting his corpse like a pork shank and feeding it to wild dogs.

When someone offered her such rare ridiculous pearls, Mona couldn't help but respond in kind, so she shared what she felt she could and Anna swore due secrecy. It was the kind of friendship she had never had with Amy, one of exchange rather than lopsided revelation. But after several years of greedy gossiping, they started running out of other people to talk about, and Mona began to fret about Anna's inability to keep her mouth shut. Anna had managed to convince Mona that Mona was different, her secrets were safe, she was special, and Anna would take care of her. Far too late, Mona realized Anna's ability to instill abject confidence was also what allowed her to keep animals calm right up until she administered that lethal dose of phenobarbital. You didn't think Anna DeGroot could ever do you any harm, so—of course—you exposed your pale pink belly to the sky.

"Is it what Bert said last week at dinner, about you flirting with the new guy? God forbid, right? That old crone needs to get laid." Anna blew across the top of her coffee. "I told Sherm he should pay her a visit."

Mona grimaced. "Too early," she said. "Too early to think about Sherman and Bert doing . . . anything together."

"I truly believe she could benefit from that man's ministrations."

That was another thing about Anna: she and Sherman had been screwing for years, three or four times a month, whenever one or both of them would get drunk and/or lonely. Mona suspected the easy-access affair was part of what kept Anna from moving out, despite the fact that there were more comfortable apartments all over Ruby Falls. Sherman, like Bert, would live and eventually die in his room, less so from any particular love of the house or Mona's proprietorship than from an inability to imagine an alternative. Anna complained about the drafts and the moodiness of the plumbing, the antiquated fixtures, the rolling, warped wood floors—but never left.

Mona could tell the lady vet, who was almost ten years her senior, thought of the Darby-Jones as her own personal coed sorority. And while Mona had never technically been to college (outside of a handful of culinary courses at the community college) or pledged a house, she didn't think the Darby-Jones was exactly Greek material. She regarded

Anna DeGroot's insistence on her inalienable right to get drunk and get laid as a little desperate, a little pathetic. It made Mona feel sad and odd, like an uncool little sister. She wanted Anna to want more out of her life. But then, Mona couldn't say with conviction that there *was* more to want. Not in Ruby Falls.

"It might do you good, too, kid," Anna said, and Mona spat hot coffee back into her mug.

"Egh!" she said. "Sherman was my tech ed teacher. The man gave me a B-plus when I was fourteen years old."

"What if he'd given you an A-plus?" Anna said, and chuckled.

"Gross. No offense." A breeze blew through the kitchen, carrying with it the musty odors of early fall: wet leaves, mud, and hay. The smell always reminded Mona of being in school.

"None taken." Anna folded the paper and pushed it aside. "Not who I was talking about, anyway."

Mona wrapped her hands around her mug and stared into the dark brown pool of coffee. Her arms prickled.

"The new guy—what's his name?"

"Arthur," Mona said, and sighed in spite of herself.

"Whoa! What was *that*?" Anna leaned across the kitchen table, the better to conspire. "How long has it been, honestly? Your sexual peak is right around the corner, Mona—it's thirty feet straight up—no. Wait. Which part of the house are his rooms over?" Anna poked a finger at the ceiling. "It's biologically imperative. Go get him, honey."

"I'm categorically not in the mood to have this conversation."

Anna cackled. "How long ago were you going out with—what was his name? The UPS guy?"

"That wasn't me. That was *Legally Blonde*." It had been a FedEx guy, anyway. And he had been nice and sweet—and unprofessional, considering he asked her out when he dropped off a package. Ron something. They went out for an unimaginative steak dinner, and Mona spent the evening wishing she were with someone smarter and funnier, and feeling bad because she knew he would try to kiss her, which he did, and which was predictably, slobberingly awkward. Her heart wasn't in it. Only once had her heart been in it—really *in it*, all the way—but that one time had been marvelous enough to convince her that it was worth holding out for, that everything else would pale by comparison. It had been disastrous timing, a critical distraction at a time and a place when Amy had needed her, and the broken heart that followed had hurt like hell. But still.

It had been worth it.

Anna giggled.

"Don't you have kittens to spay?" Mona said. Her coffee was already getting cold.

"Don't you have mysterious strangers to screw?"

"Arthur."

"Oh, excuse me. Don't you have *Arthur* to—"

"*Hi, Arthur!*" Mona slammed her mug on the table, which finally shut Anna up. "Nice to see you up and among the living." But it wasn't nice, Mona thought. *Go back, go back to your room, Arthur. Go back, so I can join you there. So we can hide from the rest of the world.* She'd spent the last two days sitting with Arthur in his room, telling him stories about Amy. Feeding him the scraps of her own memories: a food Amy liked (scallops); a book she loved (*It*); a shirt she always wore (a ratty Syracuse T, with the Saltine Warrior, the politically incorrect pre-Orangeman mascot). Stories about Amy making monsters out of pipe cleaners and molding clay and the two of them shooting movies, one painstaking shot at a time: Mona manning the trusty Super 8 Amy had found at a flea market, Amy moving her creature's limbs a fraction of a fraction of an inch at a time.

He looked better every day. Mona liked to flatter herself by thinking the stories she told him, the stories about Amy, were what brought focus back to his muddy bluish-brown eyes and sense to his mind. He had shaved and was wearing one of her father's button-down shirts again. There was a tiny blotch of old blood above the breast pocket, but otherwise Arthur Rook could have been showered and dressed and ready to go to work.

Then he opened his mouth. "Can you tell me anything about this?" he said. Pinched between his thumb and first finger was a postcard of the New York City skyline, the words *Wish you were here* in flowing script across the top.

No. Someone had cut the word *we* out of a magazine and pasted it over *you.*

Mona sucked in her cheeks.

Arthur pulled out a chair and sat down. "Look—on the back." He slid the postcard across the table toward Mona. Mona could barely bring herself to press a fingertip to the card. She was never meant to read it. "It's young, all big and loopy—but that's definitely her handwriting."

"Her handwriting?" Anna said.

Don't say her name, Arthur, Mona thought. Please, please don't say her name. Anna knew plenty about Amy and Mona: she knew they had been friends, that they had run away together—and that there was more to it than Mona had ever told her. Anna was probably under the impression that Amy was the love of Mona's life, and that Mona had sequestered herself in Ruby Falls as some sort of self-punishing act of repressed teenage lesbianism. Hell. Half of Ruby Falls—the half that didn't think Mona embodied the slatternly fall of the house of Darby-Jones—probably thought the same thing. If only it were that simple. And if Anna knew that Arthur, however obliquely, was somehow connected to the same Amy—

She wouldn't let it get that far.

"Arthur, can I talk—" Mona slipped the card into her back pocket. "Oh, Arthur, you're bleeding."

Arthur looked down at his chest. The spot over his breast pocket had grown to the size of a half dollar and grew even larger when he pawed at it. "Did I pop a stitch?" he said, his voice high and worried.

Anna laughed. It was the perfect excuse for Mona to glare at her.

"Excuse us, Anna." And then, pointedly: "Have a good day at work." Mona abandoned her cold coffee and steered Arthur out of the kitchen and up the stairs. Every step she took, she felt lighter. She felt freer. Free from what would have been an epic interrogation from Anna (and probably still would be, tonight, when they were washing dishes after dinner), free from the truth that Arthur would die to know, and free from every responsibility of her adult life. Free from the cake she really ought to be working on for Carrie Waters-soon-to-be-Kessler. Free from the vague certainty that Oneida was troubled by something, and free from the lingering fear that she and Arthur were precisely what troubled her.

Arthur walked ahead of her into his apartment, and when Mona shut the door behind her, she could have dissolved from relief. Here, in

Arthur's rooms, she had only to remember and tell stories, and she was loved for it.

And he *did* love her for it, she knew; he loved her baldly, desperately. In his eyes, Mona held all the answers to all the questions it broke his heart to ask; where Anna used her for information, Arthur revered her for it. He needed her, and Mona, who loved to be needed, found she was unable to care that Amy's widower had tracked her down (how, she still didn't know), frightened her terribly, lost his mind, and necessitated medical attention. All without her consent—in her house, in her life. Once again, Mona was desperate for new blood, and Arthur, bleeding all over the place, left her feeling sanguine with the promise of the first new friend she'd made in years.

She still knew very little about Arthur Rook himself, other than that he had married Amy and couldn't let her go. But what she could see of him, the parts of Arthur that registered in her peripheral vision, charmed the hell out of her. When Mona took him dinner on Monday night, Arthur had apologized for the mess he'd made and revealed that it was all Amy's fault, just as she'd suspected; the bric-a-brac belonged to her. He didn't offer to clean anything up and Mona didn't ask, and when she returned Tuesday morning to change his bandages and feed him more tales of Amy with a side of breakfast, it was clear he had been at work all night, organizing, straightening, building. Arthur had transformed his little part of the Darby-Jones into a walk-in work of art. Mobiles dripping Crackerjack prizes and postcard cutouts dangled from the overhead light; a line of tiny plastic dinosaurs wielding SweetTarts like tambourines marched across the fireplace mantel. The clothesline was still strung from wall to wall, and there were vignettes arranged on every available flat surface, tiny sets for miniature plays made of jacks and pins and movie stubs, behind curtains of accordion-folded magazine pages. A forest of paper drink parasols sheltered cat's-eye marbles, lined up like ducklings, from a looming photograph of Nikita Khrushchev.

Mona poked at the picture. It was glued to the wall.

"You glued Khrushchev to my wall, Arthur," she said, unsure whether she was amused or pissed.

"I . . . honestly . . . didn't think about it before I stuck it up there.

Sorry." He was sitting on the sofa, digging through a huge pink shoebox that, after closer inspection, Mona recognized as having once contained those ridiculous black stiletto-heeled boots that were moldering in her coat closet. At the time, she'd packed the boots by themselves in her suitcase but Amy must have kept the box—for herself, for more than ten years. Mona found this fact oddly moving.

There were plenty of stories she didn't tell Arthur. Amy having her heart broken by Ben, for one—she would have to make something up about that damned New York postcard, if Arthur remembered to ask her about it again. And running away to Ocean City—she hadn't decided yet whether she would tell him about that summer. She hadn't decided whether it would do any good for him, or for anyone, to know. But Mona was low on stories to tell and random factoids to share (the bulk of their friendship was sixteen years old, after all; her memory was excellent, but it wasn't perfect), and still Arthur asked for more. What else did she remember about Amy? What else had Amy been like—as a little kid, as a teenager? It was strange. If Arthur hadn't been so obviously damaged, so starved for the ghost of his wife, Mona would swear she was being shamelessly pumped for information. It wasn't as satisfying, for Mona, to field Arthur's questions; and it was also more dangerous. The more Arthur prodded her, the closer he brought her to the edge of what she was prepared to share with him. The danger existed that she would let the tiniest detail slip—and the tiniest detail, subjected to Arthur's endless prompts for more information, could lead to land mines.

"So—you didn't answer my question." Arthur came out of his bedroom with a roll of athletic tape and a square of gauze. "Did that postcard mean anything to you?"

Mona reached into her back pocket. It was message-side up in her palm. *Fine, fate,* she thought, *fine, I'll read it.*

All it said, in Amy's hand, was *I really do wish. . . .*

"I don't know," Mona said. She swallowed. "You want to lie down?"

Arthur, unbuttoning his shirt, sat on one end of the couch. Harryhausen bounded into the room, ran three tight circles around the coffee table, and sprang up off the couch to the back of the chair nearby, where he froze, four legs tensed, tail straight up and thick as a bottlebrush.

"Is he normally like this?" Mona sat beside Arthur. She spun the athletic tape around her finger.

"No." Arthur pulled his shirt back behind one shoulder. "He's usually cranky. Or depressed." He leaned back against the pillows, and Mona, looking at his shredded body in full daylight, felt like crying. Arthur was plastered with tiny intersecting cuts, but had three deep lacerations: one crossing from his left collarbone to his breastbone, one across the top of his belly, and a third zigzagging between them. Almost like a lightning bolt—the Harry Potter of torso mutilation. She frowned and then laughed at herself, and was glad she hadn't said that out loud.

"You look like a jigsaw puzzle," she said. She leaned closer and lifted the bloody gauze over his heart. "I think the stitch held. You probably just stressed it when you showered. So tell me, Arthur"—he *had* showered; she smelled soap—"what do you do?"

"What do I do?" His voice was loud, this close. She heard it echo in his chest. "When I'm not terrorizing my wife's old friends?"

Your dead wife's old friends, Mona thought. She nodded. "There can't be much money in that."

"I'm a photographer."

She folded a piece of gauze in two and pressed it against the fresh blood. "Let's get a little clot going," she said, because she thought it would be good to explain why she was holding it there, leaning over him, for longer than a second. "A photographer living in Los Angeles. Are you a soulless paparazzo?"

She sensed his head, above her own, shaking in the negative. "School pictures and head shots, mostly."

"When you're taking the head shots, can you tell if they're going to be famous? Is there some kind of phantom image, like a shining orb around their heads?"

"Not exactly," Arthur said. Mona resisted the urge to lift the gauze and check the clot. His chest rose and fell as he spoke. "But, in a way, with all of them, every—every time I looked through my lens, I could tell how much they wanted me to like them. Not just me, I guess. How much they wanted the world to like them. It's almost like their . . . desperation. Their hope. It glowed."

"Are we talking spirit photography? Very New Agey." She smiled to let him know she was teasing and then realized he couldn't see her smiling at his chest.

"It only happened with actors. Any of the crew guys I took pictures of, they just looked like normal people. Kind of nerdy but normal. I took a series at the shop where Amy worked, not for commission but just, for, you know—"

"In the name of art."

"Yes," he said. "I'm Dorothea Lange gone Hollywood. Photojournalist documenting the downtrodden practical-effects Techies, living hand-to-mouth in their Lucasvilles."

Mona laughed. "So you *are* a dork. Amy was dork catnip."

"Dorknip?"

Mona smiled. "Technically."

"So dorks loved her?" Mona heard a hesitation in Arthur's voice that wasn't there a moment before. Arthur didn't like to hear anything about Amy that contradicted what he already believed or could imagine about her, Mona had noticed. It was like he couldn't stand to be reminded of the things he didn't know about her, things he couldn't even guess. Yet another reason to exercise caution in telling him everything she knew. "Like who?"

She lifted the gauze and replaced it with a fresh piece. "No one, really. She didn't love them back, that's for sure. Oh, I'm sorry. I didn't mean—I didn't mean anything by that." She smoothed two strips of athletic tape over the gauze as quickly and gently as possible. "All set." Mona sat back on the couch. "Don't listen to a word I say. Seriously. It's like, open mouth, insert foot, never remove foot from mouth."

Arthur threw his shirt back over his shoulder but didn't rebutton it. He reached for the giant pink shoebox on the coffee table, source of all Amy's garbage, and pulled out a green plastic key chain. Heart-shaped. Cracked, a white plastic fissure clouding the center like an old scar.

"Can you tell me a story about this?" He dangled it on his finger.

Mona bit the inside of her mouth. She saw this exact chain with two keys on the ring, lying in her open palm; she smelled the ocean and felt the sun burning the skin between her shoulder blades.

She shook her head. "No idea."

Mona hooked the shoebox with her finger and pulled it closer. She drew out a playing card: an ace of hearts with the word YES written in black block letters across its face.

Arthur smiled. "That card," he said, "is the reason we got married."

"Tell me," Mona said. She tucked her feet beneath her.

"We went to Vegas." He blinked rapidly. "For the weekend, just for the hell of it. We're both terrible, terrible gamblers—not like we have an addiction: we just suck at it. It's embarrassing. Statistically speaking, I am a worse gambler than probability allows for. A monkey will play better blackjack than me." Arthur scratched at his chest absently. "We go out for a nice dinner, we wander around and look at how insane everything is—I'd never been before—and somehow we ended up at this disgusting dive of a casino. There are all these sad, sad people, overweight and pale and really unhappy-looking, and I remember turning to Amy and saying, *Why are they so sad?* And she said"—he cleared his throat—"*They're unhappy because they never fell in love. But I did once, and I can never be unhappy, no matter what, because you never forget what that feels like.*

"And I—I still can't believe this was my idea, but I'd like to thank Jose Cuervo, Jack Daniel's, and Captain Morgan for their invaluable contributions. We went to this tacky-as-shit gift shop on the strip, picked up a deck of cards and a marker, and I wrote YES on the ace of hearts and NO on the ace of clubs and MAYBE on both jokers. And I shuffled them all back into the deck and told Amy to pick one. To just—pick one. So we stood on the sidewalk in Vegas and she closed her eyes and she picked a card—"

"She actually picked the ace of hearts?" Mona, sitting with her legs crossed like a little kid, rocked forward.

"She picked the eight of spades."

Mona snorted.

"But this is—this is the part of the story that's really the story. She threw the eight of spades over her shoulder and kept picking. I forget what she picked next, but she definitely got one of the MAYBE jokers at one point, and"—Arthur started to laugh—"we're standing on the sidewalk in Las Vegas, a couple of drunk idiots playing cards, and Amy's shouting, *That one doesn't count! That one doesn't count either! That was practice!* And she just kept picking and flicking them away and we're definitely drawing a crowd at this point, but she still hasn't picked the card she wants. Until we're down to one card. Just one card left in my hand, and we're dying laughing, someone's calling security, and Amy says, *Oh, screw it, I don't care what the card says. Just marry me already.*"

"And you did."

"And we did. Stood in line with a crowd of drunken fools at one of those twenty-four-hour chapels. And it was the YES card, the last card in my hand. She held it up when the officiant asked if she did take me, Arthur Rook, to be her lawfully wedded husband. I didn't know she kept it until I found it in this box."

"How long had you been together before that?"

Arthur shrugged. "Six months, maybe. They're right: when you know, you know. Amy knew; and when Amy knew something, I knew it too. She made believers out of everyone she met."

"She did." Believers and fools, Mona thought: because there was something unsettlingly singular and past-tense about her initial confession, that she fell in love *once*. She had to give Amy more credit than that, though; no one *really* falls in love when they're a teenager. What Amy felt for Ben Tennant was an isolated incident of average teenage lust, the kind everyone grows out of. If only Amy could be classified as an average teenager.

Arthur flapped the card between his fingers and inhaled. He pitched it neatly back into the box.

"So, Mona," he said, "what do *you* do?"

"When I'm not patching up widowers?"

"Oh, no." Arthur turned pale. "I'm a widower."

"No! God, didn't I tell you to stop listening to me? I mean, you *are* a widower, but you don't have to think about it, yet. Or ever. I bake wedding cakes."

"What?" Arthur whipped his head back.

"That's what I do. I bake. Wedding cakes. I started my own business about ten years ago and I run it through word of mouth and the Internet. I own the house, so there's just taxes and upkeep, and between the rent I collect, my inheritance, and the cakes—that's how I live. That's what I do. When I'm not mothering."

Arthur was still a little stunned. He thought for a moment, blinked, and leaned forward, his elbows on his knees. "Why aren't you married?" he asked.

It stung and Mona couldn't pretend it hadn't. Her brow wrinkled.

"I'm sorry," Arthur said. "It's none of my business, I just thought—maybe you were like me. The other side of me, now—you know."

"What, orphaned by Amy?"

"A widow."

Mona took a deep breath. She could tell he had meant no harm, was embarrassed to think he had hurt her, and didn't understand what to apologize for, or how; and after almost sixteen years of fielding similar questions, Mona couldn't have helped him. She couldn't vocalize the way she felt about the path she'd chosen, had never found the precise words. She decided that if anyone ever asked, flat out, without pretense and with an honest desire to know how she felt about her life, she would hand them half a ripe cold grapefruit and tell them to sink their front teeth into the soft flesh. They'd shiver at the cold ache in their teeth and the bitterness on their tongue, but she'd tell them to keep sucking at the pulp, keep sucking until the juice became sweet and refreshing, until all you wanted was the other half, even though you knew how much that first bite would hurt.

"We're a matched set," she told him, because it was easier and not quite a lie.

"I'm a social oaf. Always have been." Arthur rubbed his eyes. "And I can't remember the last time I made a new friend." It was a shrewd apology, and Mona accepted it with a smile she hoped looked sincere. She had a problem taking her own smiles seriously.

"Me neither," she said.

"So you bake!"

Mona laughed. "Yes, I bake. I make sculptures out of sugar. I play with fondant."

"Well, if you bake as well as you cook—"

"Suck-up," Mona said, and then cupped her palm around her ear. "What's that? You'd like to go downstairs and help me make this insane cake I have to put together for Saturday? You're good with your hands," she said. "And you've got an eye for detail. You'd be a lot of help, if you're willing."

Arthur considered for a moment. "Sure," he said.

They smiled at each other for a beat longer than they probably should have. Arthur was the first to blink.

"Did Amy know that you baked cakes?" he asked.

Mona thought. "I don't know," she said. "She knew I could bake, that I liked to bake. She was there when I first learned."

"Where did you learn?" he asked.

"Jersey," she answered.

Just like that, the gate was open. He'd done it without meaning to, as she'd known he would; Arthur had found the point of entry to the stories and the secrets she didn't want to tell. But who was she protecting anyway? Amy's memory? Arthur's heart?

Arthur looked at her expectantly.

"I haven't told you about that summer," Mona said. "Amy and I . . . when we were sixteen. We ran away."

"Are you—" Arthur sat up straight. His eyes narrowed. "Are you serious? You ran away from home? God, that's huge. Why haven't you— have you been hiding this? Why?" There was panic in his voice that Mona hadn't expected, panic and concern.

"More like . . . saving it," Mona said.

Her heart had finally realized what was going on and was thumping painfully. So the real world was going to intrude on this perfect, imaginary one after all; she would be accountable. She would have to know and to tell. The time to float, suspended in memories, was abruptly over. "It's the best part of her I have left." The words stuck in her throat, came out thick. She uncrossed her legs.

"Mona, wait." Arthur, more alert than she had ever seen him, reached across the couch and grabbed both her hands. She was ashamed that her first instinct was to pull away, to retreat, to protect herself, but Arthur reached for her hands again and held on. "You don't owe me a thing."

"I know," she said.

"Thank you," he said.

"For what?" *Oh, shit, Mona,* she thought; *your heart could be in this one. Your heart could really be in it. This is so—so unfair, so screwed up, that the first new blood in your life in years is tainted. This is Amy's fault. Everything—everything in your life—is because of Amy.*

"For not calling the cops?" Arthur tilted his head. "For feeding me? For letting me sleep here?"

"You paid for the last two." Mona turned her hands over so that she and Arthur were palm to palm. She rubbed the outside of his pinkie with her thumb. She thought of pinkie swears with Amy, of her shaky little finger. She felt horrible and happy. "Unless your check bounces. It's not going to bounce, is it?"

"It shouldn't."

"Good."

"I have to tell you something." He sniffed. "It seems important."

"Go ahead."

He licked his lips and looked up at her. "No one knows I'm here."

"What do you mean?"

"No one knows Amy is dead. No one on this coast; you're the first. I couldn't—I couldn't tell anyone. Before you."

"You mean your family thinks you're still in LA? And that Amy is still—that everything is normal?"

"I have to call them, don't I?" He wanted to take his hands out of hers but Mona instinctively held on, pulled him back. "How do I explain—this?"

"You don't," Mona said. His palms were sweating. "You stay as long as you need to, Arthur. You hide. Amy broke your heart and your brain. I'm not blaming her; she didn't wake up and say, *Today I am going to die and take Arthur's whole world with me*—but she did. So you just—call your family if you want to, pretend you're home and everything's hunky-dory, I don't care. They'll forgive you. But take the time."

"I can't ask you to do that. I'm not that person; at least, I don't want to be."

"Arthur." She steadied her voice. "Let me tell you about grief. It's a sneaky son of a bitch with no heart and no conscience and absolutely no sense of timing. My parents had me when they were both older and they both died relatively young of heart disease, only a few months apart, a long time ago now. But you know when I finally realized they were gone? *Two years after they were dead*." Mona inhaled.

"It was Oneida's first day of fourth grade. She came home with a split lip because some jerk at school tripped her on the playground.

She's crying and clinging to me—clinging, Arthur, like I can save her life—and I squeeze back, but the whole time I'm thinking; *I want my mom. I want my dad.* And it hurts all over again, worse than before, because I never took the time to realize that they weren't coming back.

"So don't be in such a hurry. Stay. Stay for the weekend, Arthur; stay for the week. For the month. Stay here as long as it takes for you to realize what it means that Amy is never coming back."

She almost kissed him. She was close enough to, and she wanted to—she wanted to so much that it frightened her. But she couldn't tell if she was being supportive or pushy, selfish or insane; if her intentions were pure or if she was a manipulative head case. She didn't know why she'd said any of that to Arthur. She'd never said any of that to anyone.

"I'll tell you about that summer," she said. "I *want* to tell you. Now, why the hell do you think that is, Arthur?"

Arthur laughed nervously.

"Your breakdown might be catching," Mona said. Arthur looked at her steadily, silently. He had dark half-moons under his eyes; he was still exhausted, still hurt. He didn't have the strength to run away again.

"Promise," he said. "Promise to kick me out if I stay too long."

"Pinkie swear," she said. "The most sacred oath there is."

She hooked her pinkie with Arthur Rook's and they smiled at each other. Mona felt light-headed—light-headed but oddly excited—and a kind of awake that had nothing to do with her morning coffee. Possibility, newness: they were things she thought she had learned to live without. She hadn't known the lengths to which she'd go to keep them in her life, hadn't known her own desperation.

Don't ever take my picture, Arthur, she thought. *I'd blind you.*

10 ∾ WWPTD?

What, thought Eugene, would Robert Plant do?

"He would dance around in tight pants," he said to his empty bedroom. It didn't seem like spectacular advice, given his present situation. He doubted his crushing failure with Oneida—what had he been *thinking*, luring her to his lair?—could be forgotten by writhing around in uncomfortably low jeans.

What would David Byrne do, then? "Dance around in a huge puppet suit," he said, and sighed. He needed to find some new heroes, heroes who did more than dance.

"Let's go, Gene!" *Tap tap tap tap tappity tap tap.* His mother was tapping her drumsticks on his bedroom door. "You're gonna miss the bus, and you don't want to have to wake your sister for a lift."

Eugene stared at the poster tacked above his bed, one corner drooping free, wishing, for the millionth time in the three days that had passed since Sunday, that he could melt into the landscape with Dalí's clocks. He could feel his limbs going soft and warm, oozing over his mattress like the crayons he once left on the stove. He hated himself for scaring her like that, hated himself for telling the truth, hated the truth for being so—so dumb-jockish. Now Oneida thought he was just another horny teenage guy.

Maybe he was.

"No," he said, sitting up and balling his fists. The last thing Eugene Wendell was was some average teenage asshole. He was an artist, a surrealist, an anarchist. He was himself, unique, and he was better than the rest. And he chose Oneida, not because she was a girl, but because she was a weird girl, a specific girl. He needed her to know she was chosen. He needed to tell her so, if not to change her mind, if not to buy himself another chance, then to let her know she was wrong to think of him as another asshole ruled by an indiscriminate dick. It made him sick to imagine Oneida Jones running home that day, freaked the hell out, under the total delusion that his dick wasn't discriminate (which it was, it *was*—his dick was a frickin' chick sommelier, comparatively speaking).

And if she did change her mind, if she did give him another chance— the thought was too goddamned awesome to contemplate. She had tasted like lemonade.

He grabbed a mostly clean T-shirt from his floor and pulled it over his head. Ran his fingers through his hair. Looked in the streaky mirror over his dresser. Eugene frowned at the zit that had sprung up overnight (on his chin, bright red—how the hell did that happen?), and, instead of his usual morning glower, he flashed a grin. It looked a little frightening, a little wolfish. He brought his lips closer together to cover his teeth, and said to his reflection, "I am not Wendy." Eugene was ready to go to school.

But it was Wendy who got off the bus at Ruby Falls High. He hadn't realized, until that moment, just how used he was to playing the part. It was second nature to lurch and swagger everywhere, to slit his eyes and grimace, to grin when a seventh-grader, staring, looked away nervously. Then again, maybe this was some kind of bizarre female voodoo; if Oneida believed he was Wendy, believed he was capable of Cro-Magnon violence and no more, he *became* Wendy. Changing her mind took on an even greater importance.

It had been easy to avoid her thus far. They had only a handful of classes together: second-period gym, but they were separated while the girls did aerobics and the boys lifted weights; fifth-period lunch; and seventh-period U.S. history. Dreyer hadn't made their groups meet during class all week, so there'd been no reason for them to speak or even look at each other. Of course, there was a good chance today, Wednesday, would be the day for group work—and that meant Eugene had six periods, approximately five hours, to prepare himself for a tearful confrontation. Or a cold shoulder. Or a knee in the groin.

First period: tech ed. Eugene spent the entire fifty minutes sanding a block of wood, grinding the corners against the sand belt until it was smooth and round, mind wandering to the composition of his opening lines. Should he say her name? Give her a nickname? Or stick with a classic like "Hi." Eugene worried briefly that Oneida would rat him out to Andrew Lu and Dani, how he'd fake-canceled the meeting, but then thought she might be too embarrassed to bring it up at all, which both relieved and made him feel like an even bigger jerk. Second period (gym) he spent in the nurse's office with an upset stomach, which was real for once. By fourth period—geometry—he was seriously considering skipping the rest of the day. He managed half a piece of pizza for lunch and spent the rest of the period staring at a wall, trying not to think at all. By the time Eugene arrived in sixth-period study hall, he was so anxious he could barely blink.

And then the bell rang and there was nothing to do but go to history class. He took his normal seat at the back of the room, underneath a laminated poster of the Declaration of Independence. Dani came in first, chewing a piece of gum so hard her jaw was spasming. Oneida was next, paler and weirder and more beautiful than ever. Eugene's stomach fell out like a trap door.

In the flurry of people arriving just before the bell, he didn't notice Andrew Lu—that is, until he saw someone out of the corner of his eye hoisting an acoustic guitar case down the narrow rows of desks. Andrew set the case—flat black, new, nothing like Patricia's bedraggled one, which was peppered with stickers and odd stains—on the floor and sat down, looking around expectantly. He caught Oneida's eye and gave her a thumbs-up, and Oneida, a beat late, waved awkwardly.

Holy shit.

Eugene barely had time to register that something was going on between Oneida and the Lu kid before Dreyer closed the classroom door and announced that they were going to spend the entire class working in their groups.

"Yes," she said. "Because I had better things to do last night than put together a lesson plan." She sat at her desk and began to call roll.

Shit, thought Eugene. Shit shit shit. So there was a chance that Andrew Lu already knew what he'd done, there was a chance Oneida had run to him, spilled the beans, and—what then? It wasn't as though his image could be ruined; it was already awful. His heart sank a little. He'd never intended to actually live up to his own reputation.

The classroom was plunged into controlled chaos as people spun their desks to face one another, recombining rows into circles and horseshoes. Dani tossed her bag against the wall and sat next to Eugene. Oneida and Andrew Lu came over next, side by side, and turned in two vacant desks. Andrew had brought the guitar.

"What's in the case, secret weapon?" Dani asked. Eugene could see her gum, a flash of purple between white teeth.

Andrew Lu smiled. "Sort of, yeah," he said. "We can get to that in a minute. First we should go over what we were supposed to do on Sunday." He looked at Eugene but Eugene saw no accusation or anger in his face. Well, that was something.

Oneida cleared her throat and Eugene, for the first time at this close distance, looked at her. It was an involuntary reaction, his head had only turned toward sound, but their eyes skittered and locked for a fraction of a second. Just long enough for Eugene to see Oneida blush from her chin to the tips of her ears. He wanted to crawl under his desk and die.

"Have we decided what we're actually going to do for this stupid project?" Dani's voice, for once, was a merciful distraction. "I thought we decided when we met, like, forever ago, but I don't know. The more I think about using the Beatles, the dumber it seems. I mean, this is *American* history, right? Shouldn't we do a report on an *American* band?"

"The Beatles *were* practically an American band," Eugene said. Jesus, she was dumb.

"Oh, right, because Americans get all crazy about something, it automatically makes it American? We have to co-opt it to—to legitimize it?" Dani was wearing silver earrings like tiny chandeliers. They made a jingling noise as she bobbed her head.

Andrew Lu shrugged. "That's a good point," he said. "But I think it's fair to include the Beatles as part of American history. I did some research online this weekend, and it sounds like they were a huge part of the sixties, in America and everywhere."

Eugene was torn. Andrew Lu wasn't dumb, and he wasn't wrong; but Oneida, now that Eugene was paying attention, clearly hung on his every word. He had never felt real jealousy but this had to be it, burning in his chest like he'd swallowed a hot potato whole. It wasn't unfamiliar. It felt, horrifyingly, like the inexplicable anger he couldn't control. He gripped the edge of his desk. Took a deep breath.

"I'm not arguing that," Dani continued. She shook her head. "Of course they were huge. Which also makes them totally obvious, you know? Everybody already knows how they influenced the world, so it's just—" Her brow furrowed. "It feels too easy."

"Well, *duh*," said Oneida under her breath.

"*Well, duh* what, Jones?" Dani bristled.

"You've got me curious, Group Three." Dreyer appeared out of nowhere, looming above their desks, hands clasped behind her back and head cocked to the side. Eugene couldn't help liking Dreyer. The way she strode around her classroom, going on and on about the Swamp Fox and the Boston Tea Party, reminded him of a general preparing her troops on the eve of battle.

"What's with the ax?" she asked, and nudged the guitar case with her foot.

"Yeah, Andrew, what's with the ax?" Dani asked, and snorted.

"I'll show you," he said, and ducked down to open the case. He had to stand; the seats in Dreyer's classroom were hybrid desk chairs that wouldn't allow him to sit and hold the guitar at the same time. The effect, as Eugene couldn't help thinking the Lu kid knew, was that everyone stopped what they were doing and paid attention to him.

"I was thinking," he said, tightening the strings. *Fucking show-off*, Eugene thought, and the anger, the uncontrollable rage, flared in him like a gust of hot dry wind. "I was thinking the exact same thing, Dani: that just talking about the Beatles is too easy. So maybe it would be cool to play a Beatles song. You know, make it a little more interesting."

Dreyer nodded appreciatively.

"They can't be hard to learn. Especially the earlier stuff; those songs were all simple chord progressions." He strummed a G chord that was out of tune sixteen different ways. *Doesn't even know what he's doing.* How could he? The guitar was brand new, had barely been played.

"Not to rain on your parade, Mr. Lu," Dreyer said. "But where's the group element?"

"Oh, we'd all play." Andrew Lu was addressing the whole classroom now, lapping up the attention like a total whore. "You have a guitar, don't you, Dani?"

Dani's eyes darted back and forth, clearly confused that this was public knowledge, or, at least, knowledge to the likes of Andrew Lu. "Yeah. I've got a bass."

"Oneida can take drums." Andrew looked down at her for a second before tossing a glance at Eugene. "And Wendy can play tambourine or something."

People laughed. Not loud. More like a ripple. Eugene knew they would (hell, it wasn't *unfunny*), and he didn't blame the laughers. He'd been laughed at before—admittedly, never when the anger was rising and close to boiling, but it wasn't the laughter that bothered him. It wasn't the laughter that pushed him over.

It was Oneida.

As the ripple flattened to static chatter, Eugene looked over at Oneida. She was staring at Andrew Lu in shock. He was still talking with Dreyer; they were discussing the easiest Beatles songs to learn in time for the project deadline, and when Dreyer said, "Looking forward to it— great idea, Mr. Lu!" Oneida's chin crumpled. It flattened out half a second later, but Eugene saw it, and in that half-second, whatever higher power guides and protects the would-be sex lives of horny teenage boys awarded him a flash of divine telepathy: *The band idea was Oneida's.* For whatever reason, she'd told Andrew Lu, and Andrew Lu had taken all the credit.

Oneida, looking utterly dejected now, turned back to the center of their little circle of desks. And then she did something extraordinary: she looked at Eugene directly, without blinking or turning to break the gaze. Her eyes were tiny, defeated behind her glasses. She'd been betrayed and a part of her didn't care that Eugene knew it. A part of her *wanted* Eugene to know it.

Eugene was instantly full, so happy and so angry he couldn't keep still. He stood. Andrew Lu, still fussing with the gear heads, tightening when he should have been loosening, raised his head. He shrugged.

"Sorry, man, I didn't mean anything by that." He smiled. He had no idea. How could he have no idea? Did he understand anything about honor among band mates, honor among history project groups? Honor, period?

"S'cool." Eugene felt Oneida watching him and it made the anger feel less wrathful and more righteous. "I can play." He held out his hand for the guitar. "C'mon, I won't hurt it."

Eugene and Andrew Lu faced each other from opposite shores on their island of desks. *He thinks this is a showdown*, Eugene thought, and smiled. *He thinks he can still beat me.*

Andrew raised the guitar over his head, the strap catching for a moment on one of his ears. "Show me what you got," he said.

Eugene slipped into the strap, adjusted the guitar so that it rested comfortably, and tuned the poor thing, *finally*. As he'd hoped, most of the class had noticed that something a thousand times more interesting than their particular history project was transpiring and had turned in their chairs to watch. Even Dreyer, on the other side of the room, was glancing in his direction.

He didn't know too many songs. The only complete lick he could play relatively well was "Blister in the Sun." He could remember Patricia teaching it to him, years ago, before Brooklyn—remembered how at first she'd hunched over him from behind, moving his fingers on the strings, then stood in front of him and sang and clapped and jumped up and down on her bed, more screaming than singing the lyrics.

He'd played it for hours, for days, for months; and now, in seventh-period U.S. history, muscle memory served him well. If he had to know only one lick, it was a great lick to know—the kind everyone recognizes even if they don't know the song, and half the class joined in on the hand claps. Eugene could still feel Oneida watching him, her gaze warming the back of his neck like the sun. Andrew Lu was nodding, blinking, pretending he knew something about music or what he was hearing or how to treat people.

Or how to treat a guitar, Eugene thought sadly. It was a good guitar, he could tell; a little stiff, very new, but it had a nice warm sound. And Andrew Lu would screw with its soul until it was a sad, hollow, broken box. What Eugene had planned for the guitar, then, was really an act of pity.

What, Eugene thought, *would Pete Townshend do?*

As the class quick-clapped at the end of the phrase, he grabbed the guitar by the neck with both hands, lifted it, and swung it into the floor with all the force he could muster.

It rang, splintering with a sound like a dropped cartoon piano. Then Andrew Lu swung his fist into Eugene's right eye and Eugene went down, into the heap of nylon and tinder from the first guitar mercy killing ever to take place at Ruby Falls High. There was some yelling, a lot of loud talking. He heard Dreyer's major-general voice telling them all to pull themselves together, to *shut up,* while she called the front office. Eugene lifted his head—oh his *head,* his head felt like a bag of wet sand—and saw Oneida watching him, fingers curled over the edge of her desk, her eyes enormous. As he watched, a tiny smile spread across her lips.

"Hi," he said to her. He raised one spindly arm in triumph.

I am Wendy, he thought; *hear me roar.*

"Since when have I ever been grounded?" Eugene poked at the pile of green beans on his dinner plate. "Since when did you ever ground Patricia?"

"Patricia never pulled a Hendrix in her history class." His mother cleared her throat. Maggie Wendell was having a hard time keeping a straight face.

"So what's this kid's deal? He some kind of douchebag?" Patricia, still wearing her McDonald's uniform, stank of grease. Her hair was wound in two white-blond braids over her ears. She inhaled sharply. "Is he your competition?"

Eugene shrugged. How did his sister know this shit? Was it a girl thing, or was his sister uniquely psychic?

"Don't tell me this is about a girl." His mother put her utensils down with a click.

"What?" Eugene's voice jumped an octave. "How do you—how do you know this shit?"

"I had a feeling." Maggie resumed eating, and said through a full mouth, "You're a fifteen-year-old boy, Eugene. Everything is about girls. Am I right?"

Eugene felt his cheeks and forehead getting warm. Wendy wouldn't get embarrassed so easily, he thought; but of course, at home, Wendy didn't exist.

Astor came back from the kitchen with two bottles of beer and handed one to Maggie before sitting down. He had barely spoken since they showed up at the principal's office. Eugene and Andrew Lu had waited side by side in those crappy plastic chairs outside Middleton's door while both sets of parents discussed with the principal what, precisely, had happened and what, precisely, ought to be done about it. Eugene had stopped trying to figure out what they were saying and was staring instead at his reflection in the glass partition that separated them from the front hall. He adored his black eye. The nurse had given him an ice pack but he hated to obscure the amazing eggplant-colored bruise that was spreading from his brow to the side of his nose.

Andrew kept exhaling violently, like he wanted to say something but his anger, too great to verbalize, would only come out in gusts of air.

"Thanks for the shiner, Lu." Eugene couldn't help himself.

Andrew Lu hated him. Eugene could feel it, physically, and it amazed him; no one, to his knowledge, had ever felt this strongly about him for any reason, good or bad. He wanted to say to Andrew: *Dude, what are you so angry about? So I broke your guitar. You deserved it. Let's remember who was a total dick in this situation first.* But Andrew Lu didn't look like he was in any mood to discuss his crimes—and their punishments—rationally, so Eugene slumped in his crappy plastic chair and grinned at his reflection.

They weren't called into the office until the terms of penance had been agreed upon, which seemed insanely undemocratic to Eugene. He would pay the Lus for the guitar, he would apologize to Dreyer for disrupting her class, and he would apologize to Andrew Lu, right then and there.

Andrew's parents were both wearing suits and vaguely confused, angry expressions. Andrew's mother, with her short spiky hair, looked a lot like her son.

"Make it good, Gene," Eugene's mother said, poking him gently in the ribs. He looked at Astor, whose eyes were narrowed. Next to the Lus, his parents—in their jeans and T-shirts, their sandals, his mother's tattoo peeking under her shirtsleeve—looked like teenagers. Pride fluttered in Eugene's chest.

"I'm sorry I smashed your guitar," he said. He flicked his eyes up to meet Andrew's on the last word and was surprised to feel a stab of true guilt in his heart. Well, it *had* been a nice guitar.

"But why?" Mr. Lu leaned forward and Eugene flinched. "Why did you smash his guitar? What did my son ever do to you?"

Eugene's hands found their way into his pockets and he shrugged, staring at Middleton's ugly ass carpet. "Nothing," he said, and thought, *To me. He didn't do anything to me.*

"Nothing," was Astor's first word to Eugene on the entire subject. He sat down at the head of the dinner table across from his wife and took a long pull of beer. "Andrew Lu did nothing to you. You pulverized a three-hundred-dollar guitar over—and I quote—*nothing.*"

Eugene screwed up his face. The tone of his father's voice had brought an instant pricking warmth to his eyes.

"No shit, kid," Astor said.

"Dude," said Patricia. "You are so dead."

"Not necessarily," Maggie said, and Eugene looked up to see a combative, fleeting look pass between his parents.

"You want to tell me why you really did it? Don't think you're not grounded. You're not going to get out of jail free, but you might get parole for good behavior." Astor stabbed at the beans on his plate with his fork. Eugene had never seen his father act quite so authoritatively. It was frightening, disturbing—since when had the Wendell household become a place where people were *so dead*?

"I—" Eugene coughed, his voice catching. "I smashed his guitar because it was clear that he didn't know how to treat it with respect."

Patricia laughed out loud.

"Can you believe this kid?" she said, addressing Astor. Astor gave her a short, withering glare and she turned back to her plate, raising her eyebrows.

"There's more," Eugene said. "He *betrayed* this . . . girl. The girl who was here last Sunday. He stole her idea, told the teacher it was his, and then took all the credit. And she was really—I could tell she was really upset—so when the opportunity to knock this *douchebag* down a peg came—yeah, I took it. And I'm not sorry at all." He crossed his arms and stared defiantly down at his mostly full plate.

"Oh my God," said Patricia, and laughed again.

Eugene dared to look over at his mother first, who was struggling even harder to keep from laughing. Her dark eyes were shining. He followed her gaze when she focused from Eugene to Astor, and *thank God*, Astor was smiling too, smiling the large, toothy grin Eugene had inherited from him.

"Grounded until next weekend," he said, and took another swig of beer. "And you owe me three hundred bucks."

11 ∽ Real Boys and Girl Friends

"Fondant, meet Arthur." Mona scooped a warm ball of shortening and powdered sugar together and dropped it in Arthur's open hands. "Arthur, this is fondant. Now shake."

Arthur squeezed his fingers into the warm white putty. "That's . . . different," he said. "How much do we have to make?"

Mona spun her sketchbook on the kitchen table. Carrie Waters-soon-to-be-Kessler had been explicit about her ideal wedding cake: "Cover it with daisies—daisies with happy yellow centers. Hundreds of them. I want it to look like you rolled the whole cake in a field of white sugar daisies." When Mona had shown Carrie her sketch—three tiers carpeted with fat fondant flowers—it had occasioned a double high-five.

She'd approached the task mathematically, calculating the number of daisies it would take to carpet the top of the smallest tier, multiplying that by the percentage each subsequent layer grew larger, subtracting from that the area covered under each stacked layer, and finally concluding that she'd forgotten everything she ever learned about math and would need, precisely, a buttload of sugar daisies.

"A buttload, Arthur," she said. "We need a buttload of these things."

"Is that metric?"

"I've been working on these for a few days by myself, but now that you're helping we're going to Henry Ford this sucker." Mona grabbed her own hunk of fondant and began kneading it. "I've got two daisy-shaped cookie cutters, a whole stack of trays, an empty table out on the back porch. We knead the fondant, we roll it, we cut and shape daisies, we knead, we roll, we cut daisies—"

"That's not a true assembly line. I'd have to knead the fondant and you'd have to roll it and then I'd have to cut it for it to be a true—"

"Was I unclear? I asked for assistance, not sass." Mona grinned and leaned her full weight forward on her palms, into the fondant, spreading it flat on the table.

Arthur, facing her, did the same. His hands were larger than hers, and stronger; his fondant already looked pearly and smooth. They both leaned forward, Mona lifting herself off the ground half a foot. She flopped the fondant over, set her palms again, pushed, and lifted with a small grunt.

Mona, balancing in the air, wiggled her bare feet. Arthur locked his arms and pushed himself up and into his fondant. They teetered on opposite sides of the table.

"Who taught you how to do this?" he asked, wobbling. "Circus folk?"

Mona touched down and smoothed the fondant with her fingertips. "My first real boyfriend. The only one who counted, really," she said. "In Ocean City."

⁂

Mona learned to bake in a pizza place on an old section of New Jersey boardwalk, a hundred yards from the ocean, nestled between a decrepit video game arcade and a souvenir shop that sold hemp bracelets and tiny personalized license plates. The pizza place was wide open to boardwalk traffic and all the smells of the beach, so that each gust teasing hair from her ponytail brought with it a touch of coconut Coppertone, mustard and hotdog, sand and salt. She worked from five until closing, Tuesday through Saturday, downing her free slice of cheese pizza as daylight faded over her dinner break. Between serving house pies to families with matching plastic flip-flops and individual slices to bikinied girls who seemed younger than her but probably weren't, Mona experimented with cakes and cookies and pastries—and the owner's son—in the shadow of the great Vulcan oven.

His name was David Danger, she told Arthur sixteen years later.

David Danger. He was shifting slices and pies around in the belly of the Vulcan when she first saw him, wielding the big wooden pizza paddle with a finesse that took Mona's breath away. He was older, she guessed, but not much—seventeen, maybe eighteen. He was laughing with someone else behind the counter, someone she couldn't see. His teeth were white and perfect, his hair was dark, long in front and a little floppy, his skin smooth and tanned. There was a five-pointed red smear on his white shirt, like he'd adjusted his collar with saucy hands. He leaned against the counter with the lazy confidence of a boy who owns his place in the world—which he would one day, he told her, when his father died and left the pizzeria to him.

But Mona didn't know that the first time she walked into the House of D'Angier. Mona didn't know anything about the boy behind the counter, other than he was beautiful and she wanted him.

She was glad Amy wasn't there. Amy would march up, ask if they were hiring, and march right back out. Amy had no patience whatsoever for flirting, and Mona intended to give her prey both barrels.

She wasn't even sure where Amy was. Amy had passed over the House of D'Angier as being too fast-food, too kid-friendly—not a place she could make serious tips. Ever since they'd arrived at the minia-ture Ocean City bus depot, Amy had been a mess of nerves about money or, rather, their relative lack of it. They didn't have the money to waste on a cab; they could walk. They didn't have enough money for a real restaurant; they'd grab some snacks or order Domino's. Mona tried to calm her down (it wasn't like money was the thing she needed to worry about most), but Amy was silent and stoic, which meant she was freaked right the hell out. Mona didn't blame her. She was freaked right the hell out herself. She had never imagined she was the kind of kid who ran away from home, but she couldn't let Amy do it alone.

They'd paid cash for a room at the pink-stucco Seahorse Motel, which was practically rotting but insanely cheap and only a few blocks back from the boardwalk. Their room smelled stale, last year's sun-screen and beer and sand permanently bonded to the bed linens and the woolly shag carpeting. Amy dropped her backpack on the closer bed and ran to the bathroom to throw up.

"Let me in." Mona leaned her shoulder against the bathroom door, painted a sickly pink. The whole room was a symphony on the theme of Pepto-Bismol: faded pink drapes, pink-and-teal striped blankets, a pink-shaded lamp overhanging a wobbly-looking table and two painted-pink chairs. Even the television was supported by a pink rattan cart. "Come on, Amy, you have to let me in if I'm going to help you at all."

The door creaked open. Amy was curled around the toilet, her head and knees on either side of the U-bend.

"The floor feels good," she said. "Tile's cold."

"Probably hasn't been mopped since last summer." Mona flushed the toilet and dropped the lid. She sat on it, tenting her legs over Amy's wraparound body. "Who knows what you're going to catch down there. Hepatitis. Syphilis. Leprosy."

Amy choked or laughed, she couldn't tell which.

"I ordered a pizza," Mona said. "Just cheese. Cheapest they had."

"'K."

The silence and stillness after eight hours on a roaring Greyhound was disorienting. Mona's butt hurt from sitting for so long and her head was killing her. It was past five o'clock—her parents, wondering why she hadn't come home from school, would have found the note by now, propped on her pillow, not hiding. She didn't want them to think she'd left because of anything *they* did. The whole time she was trying to write it, Mona thought of that Beatles song about the girl leaving home— about how the note she ended up writing was a note she'd hoped would say more. What could she have said, though, other than the barest truth? *Hi, Mom, Hi, Dad, Amy is running away from Ruby Falls, and she's scared so I'm going with her. We'll be careful. I love you. Don't worry about me and please don't come looking. I'll be back. Desdemona.*

Her mother would be hysterical. Her father would be irate. Maybe in the evening, when her father was putting away his pocket watch and his tie clip, he'd notice the empty space in the valet on his dresser—the space where William Fitchburg Jones's red jasper and diamond cuff links usually sat. Now they were secreted in the bottom of Mona's backpack, an insurance policy wrapped in a tube sock. It would break her father's heart. She felt like throwing up.

When she woke the next morning, sweaty and sticky from damp summer sheets, Mona's stomach rumbled unhappily. She lay in bed and studied the water-stained ceiling, trying to find a sign or a signal or anything, anything at all, in the irregular brown and yellow eddies. She saw a cat, maybe: a big fat cat.

"Hey, Amy," she said. "You awake?"

Amy's voice sounded stronger. "Everything's going to be fine."

Mona winced. "Well that's a relief," she said. "I was a little worried last night, when I went to sleep and you were still one with the toilet." She rolled over. Amy was sitting cross-legged on her bed, already showered and dressed, her brow creased in concentration. It made a huge difference to see Amy back to her normal self—well, close to her normal self. Maybe this wasn't the most asinine thing they'd ever done after all.

"Today," Amy said, springing out of bed and whipping Mona's sheets off, "today we get jobs."

Today we meet boys, Mona thought, as she drew up to the counter at the House of D'Angier.

"Plain cheese slice," she said. "And a large Mountain Dew."

The boy pushed his hair out of his eyes with the back of his hand and smiled at her. He was sweaty. She could feel the heat from the oven on the other side of the counter.

"That all?" he asked.

She propped her elbows on the red Formica. "Actually," she said. "I'm looking for a job. For the summer."

The boy tilted his head and smiled at her funny, like she'd said something monumentally insane. Mona bristled.

"What?" she said. "You think 'cause I'm cute I can't fling a pie?"

It worked. The boy grinned and called over his shoulder to the invisible other, and a sandy-haired man with a stomach like a beach ball waddled into view. A terrible sunburn was peeling across the bridge of his nose beneath a large pair of Ray-Bans.

"Uncle Roof, we have an applicant," the boy said, tipping his head at Mona.

"Darling," said Uncle Roof, and Mona couldn't tell if he was addressing the boy or her, "you're too adorable. Also, you're hired. I'll leave David in charge of your training. I'm gonna go smoke a bowl." He untied an apron stained with brown and red smears (tomato sauce? chocolate? blood?) and flung it over his shoulder as he lifted a section of countertop and maneuvered his girth out. "What should I call you?" he asked, as he squeezed by her.

"Desdemona," Mona said, a second before realizing it might be safer not to use her real name.

Uncle Roof clapped a ruddy balloon of a hand to his heart. "Sweet Jesus, what kind of hippie assholes named you? Never mind, I'm sure they were well-meaning hippie assholes. I'll be back in an hour."

"Come on." The boy was holding the counter up and motioning her in. "I can show you the basics before the lunch crowd shows up. I'm David Danger." He shook her hand and Mona felt a charge, bigger, better, than she'd ever felt before, leap between their warm palms. She smiled at him and said hello. Then she realized what he'd just said.

"Wait, no, I can't—work—you know, *today*." He closed the countertop behind her and she had no choice but to step forward into the bubble of oven-dry heat. The space behind the counter was no longer than thirty feet, no wider than ten, with two doors leading off each end, one marked OFFICE, the other propped open by a bucket and mop. In between was a wooden table spattered with sauce and shriveled toppings that had slid off their intended pizzas long ago, abandoned to the horrors of mummification.

"It's easy, don't worry." David propped his hands on his hips. "Pies are already baking. I'm just going to need you to take orders and money. Have you worked a cash register before?"

Oh, crap, this was a mistake.

"You've made change, right?" David's voice dropped. The overpowering miasma of melting cheese, of salt and grease, in the roiling heat made her feel fuzzy. She was too hot. She should have worn shorts instead of jeans; she was going to faint. Whose fault was this? Amy's, she thought; I am here because of Amy *Freakin'* Henderson, because for the second time in her life she told me a secret, and for the first time in her life she asked for my help. I couldn't say no. I didn't want to say no.

For the first time ever, Amy needed her.

"I can make change, David Danger," she said. "Just watch me."

Amy found her right after the dinner rush. Mona had just finished ringing up two cheese and one pepperoni for a huge family roosting in the rear booths, flapping and preening like a flock of seagulls in fluorescent sunglasses. Amy casually approached the counter.

"I'd like a slice of pepperoni, and make it free?" she said. There was a looseness to her that Mona hadn't seen in weeks, not since the Ocean City plan was hatched.

"Hey, David?" Mona called. Uncle Roof had not returned in an hour; had not returned, in fact, all day. That frantic afternoon and evening had taught her that the quickest path to undying love was to slave and stand, side by side, between overweight vacationers and their precious slices of pizza. She felt comfortable with David Danger, easy, free to tease. Giddy. "My friend Amy's here, can I steal some inventory for her?"

David was washing utensils in the second room, the one not marked office, and she knew he couldn't hear her over the roar of the dishwasher.

She grinned at Amy. "Guess that's a yes," she said, and slid an already-plated slice across the counter. Amy folded it in half and bit off the point.

"I can see *you* had a good day," Amy said. She wasn't really paying attention or expecting a response, Mona could tell; she was scouting the location, eyes wide and unblinking, taking it all in: the bright red counter and tabletops, the smudged murals of Venice, Rome, maybe Tuscany that covered the two walls that weren't the counter or open to the boardwalk. Amy sniffed.

"Pizza's not bad," she said. She licked a drop of brilliant orange pepperoni grease from the corner of her mouth. "God, I was starving. I would've eaten cardboard with a little mayo on it."

"You didn't eat all day?" Mona leaned against the cash register. Her cash register. That she'd mastered in less than twenty minutes. She felt so stupidly proud of herself.

"I was busy," Amy said. "Got a job. Good one! Waiting tables at this sit-down place close to the condos up the beach, other end of the boardwalk. Trained with this funny little woman who's been working there since she was our age, I'm sure." She folded the rest of the crust into a pizza origami and stuffed it in her mouth. "Ev'thin' gon' 'e fine, li' I tol' you."

David Danger chose that moment to appear with two fistfuls of clean shiny knives and spatulas. Mona watched Amy's eyes bug—an involuntary reaction she held just long enough for Mona to anticipate the conversation they'd have that night back at the motel. Amy swallowed, the lump of pizza visible as it disappeared down her long throat. They both watched David replacing the cutlery around the prep board, white shirtsleeves glowing as they exposed his tanned and sculpted arms. He kept brushing his hair back with the back of his hand—he'd done it all afternoon—shaking it out of his eyes. His eyes were blue, as Mona had discovered when he was explaining the cash register: blue and deep as the ocean on the other side of the boardwalk.

"Mona," Amy said. Her voice sounded so far away. "Please don't do anything stupid."

⁂

She still didn't tell Arthur everything. She hit the high points—running away, the motel, meeting David Danger—and focused on her fondant daisies, steeling herself for the questions to come.

"Why?" Arthur began. He held a sugar daisy in each palm like he was suffering from pastry stigmata. "Why there? Ocean City, New Jersey?"

Mona pressed a neat row of daisy shapes into her sheet of sugar.

"The summer before her parents died, they went there as a family. On vacation. Her parents met on the Jersey shore, actually, when they were kids. Amy had a picture of the two of them as teenagers, standing in the ocean holding hands."

Arthur gasped. "I've seen it," he said. He smiled wide. "It's in her shoebox. They look like—"

"An **M**," Mona finished for him. It was the only sentimental object Amy took when she ran away. She'd taped it to the spotted mirror in their hotel room, in the upper right corner, so that every time Mona smoothed her hair in anticipation of David Danger mussing it up all over again, she'd see Amy's parents watching over her. She thought they would approve. They looked too happy together to disapprove of anyone else who had found someone to love—and make out with.

"Why run away at all? Why that summer?" Arthur asked.

"It was as good a summer as any," Mona said. "She'd had it with this town. It was time for her to start her life, time to get out and get on with it, and finally making that decision? Made her so happy," she lied. She raised her eyebrows. Careful there, Mona. "How many flowers we got so far?"

Arthur collected his scraps of fondant and began rolling them into another ball.

"She never talked about Ruby Falls," he said. "Never."

"There's a shocker."

"I met her grandfather once. He seemed like a nice enough man— very quiet. Stuck in his ways."

"I think he said a total of five words to me the whole time Amy and I were friends." Mona carefully pinched one of the flat daisy shapes at the base of each petal. It bloomed in her hand. "Hello. Good-bye. How's school? Be careful."

"That's six words," Arthur said. "And good advice."

"A little too general to mean much to a teenager," Mona said. She pinched another flower.

"I don't understand why she never mentioned you," Arthur said.

This had never occurred to Mona.

Not that she had spent the past sixteen years of her own life telling everyone about her friend Amy Henderson—but she *had* told a few people, because Amy was part of her story. Amy was part of her life. And Amy hadn't mentioned to the man she ended up marrying that Desdemona Jones even *existed*?

"Are you kidding?" she said. It hurt—it hurt terribly, because she'd never seen it coming. But of course, it made sense. *Amy never told anyone anything.* And Mona was just another anything, just a person Amy had known, had been a kid with. In a life and a world that didn't matter once Amy got what she wanted: once she got to Los Angeles and started her real life. It could only have hurt more if Amy had actually stabbed her in the chest.

Arthur seemed to have realized, too late, what he'd done. "I only meant—you're—great." He set his fondant down. "Sorry."

Mona shook her head. "It's not your fault, Arthur. Don't apologize."

"Can you hand me the rolling pin?" he asked quietly.

"So basically—if I had died instead of Amy, if my nonexistent husband lost his marbles, traveled across the freaking country to harass her, would she have *anything* to say to him?" She squashed a daisy in her hand. "It's not important. It doesn't matter anymore."

She felt ridiculous. *So Amy made a fool of me too,* she thought, *me and everything I ever did for her. Everything I might have ever meant to her, which couldn't have been much.* Mona was pissed at Amy—actually *pissed*, over a decade too late, at a dead woman. What kind of loyalty did she owe a corpse that hadn't even thought to mention her *name* while it was living?

Mona flattened the fondant before her with her fist. Arthur flinched. She'd actually felt privileged to share her childhood with Amy, who, for all her faults, had changed Mona's life in ways she would never be able to quantify. And there was nothing, absolutely nothing, in the world that would convince Mona that she hadn't meant anything to Amy. Would it have killed her to admit it? Would it have killed her to say *I remember you? You were there? We were there together?*

She was so tired of fighting with Amy's nature. Because it was Amy's nature to be unknown and unknowable, just as it was Mona's nature to want more than people ever seemed to be able to give her.

"I really don't get it," Arthur said. "Why she didn't keep in touch."

"Then you didn't know Amy Henderson," Mona said.

Arthur recoiled, slapped harder by her words than by any hand. And there were other things she could have said—other things that could have hurt him more. It was tempting to tell him all those other things about his enchanting, enchanted wife; tempting to cross the field of fondant daisies between them. But Mona didn't get beyond an open mouth. She was stopped by the realization that she wanted to hurt him—really hurt him. Shake him. Smack him. She was sick of all this bullshit, she was tired, and she wanted Arthur to grow up and get over it and realize that Amy Henderson had been a human being after all: a human being who could be mean and cowardly and inscrutable and not the essence of eccentric perfection, lost forever. But on the heels of that came another, more disturbing, revelation: she wasn't really mad at Arthur, she was mad at Amy, and Arthur was just her hapless undeserving patsy.

But was she actually mad at Amy? It hadn't been for Amy that she'd been keeping secrets all those years; it never had been, really, and she knew it. *Let's not think you're so special,* she reminded herself. *Let's not think you've been so very betrayed, or that what you felt was loyalty.*

"That wasn't fair," she told Arthur, catching his eye and holding it, "but it was true."

They made fifty more fondant daisies in silence. After he'd helped her wipe down the kitchen table, Arthur went up to his rooms and didn't come down until dinner, and when he spoke, all he asked was for her to pass the mashed potatoes.

⁊

Mona, exhausted, spat toothpaste into the sink. It was only nine o'clock, but it felt like she'd been up for days. The face that stared out of the bathroom mirror looked older than the one she'd seen that morning: the skin around the eyes was looser, baggier. Mona had never given much thought to aging. Her body had always been an indestructible marvel, flexible and pliant to her wishes. She was both aware and not aware that, in this regard, she was lucky—she read enough magazines to know that the campaign against crow's feet was a major battle for most women, and yet it was a battle she had never taken up. She still got carded at the liquor store. Getting old—specifically, having her body change—was something she thought she wouldn't have to deal with for years. But apparently that wasn't true. The proof was matching her every move in mirror image, looking old and tired and reaching for dental floss.

She hated herself tonight. It was an unusual state of mind for Mona. She hated how angry she was at Amy, and how hurt. She hated caring so much, so many years later. She hated herself for being the kind of friend that Amy could put on a shelf, or in a shoebox, and forget.

But she trusted me once, she thought, sliding the floss between her top molars. She trusted Mona enough to run away with her.

Or maybe she didn't trust Mona to stay behind and not tell anyone where she went.

She'd flossed too hard and spat a ruby polka dot on the toothpaste in the basin.

Oneida entered from her connecting bedroom door, index finger marking her place in a yellowed school copy of *The Scarlet Letter.* She one-handedly squirted a drop of toothpaste on her brush. Then she sighed and caught Mona's eye in the mirror.

"What's up?" Mona asked. Oneida had been quiet and withdrawn all night, but no more so than she'd been for the past week or so. She'd decided to let her daughter come to her in her own time, and her heart fluttered at the possibility of having made precisely the right decision. Mona had terrible instincts for motherhood, despite years of ostensible practice. Each tiny victory seemed more a product of dumb luck than skill. "Something's bothering you, huh?"

Oneida nodded. She dropped *The Scarlet Letter* on the counter.

"Is it the book?" Mona asked. "I remember being forced to read it. Certainly sapped *my* will to live."

A smile skipped over Oneida's face and just as quickly disappeared. She frowned, as though she suddenly remembered to be upset about something else entirely. Mona tensed; there were tiger traps everywhere these days.

"It's not the book," Oneida said.

Still watching her daughter's reflection, Mona could see her brain working, her eyes narrowing, and her furry eyebrows drawing closer together than they already were. It was the face she made whenever she couldn't figure something out—a face Mona saw seldom enough for it to be an immediate cause for concern. She was wearing an old flannel nightgown Mona remembered buying on sale at JC Penney's years ago. It was threadbare in the elbows, and the hem that had once been floor-length was skirting her knees and coming undone, threads floating like fringe around her calves.

Mona felt even older.

"There's a . . . guy," Oneida said. "Today at school, he did—it's hard to describe, actually, what he did." She frowned again and pushed her glasses up her nose.

"Do I know who this guy is?" Mona asked. She was painfully aware this was the first conversation, practically speaking, she had ever had with Oneida about real boys. Not abstract boys, and the mechanics of abstract sex: real boys, who would be interested in real sex. She set her toothbrush down with a clack of plastic on tile.

Oneida shrugged. "That's not the point," she said.

Mona's skin prickled. "What did he do?" she said.

"No, that's not what—" Oneida crossed her arms and looked from the mirror to the countertop, focusing on the harmless, less judgmental witnesses: the stack of paper cups, the chipped plastic bowl of cotton balls. A foot brush shaped like a big toe. "It's not what he did, it's why he did it," she said. "He did it for me, to show off. Like, I know he likes me, you know what I mean? I *know* he likes me."

"What did he do?" Mona asked. She crossed her arms too, and shifted from foot to foot.

"No, Mom, that's not the point. The point is, I don't know how I feel about what he did. I—there's a part of me that absolutely loved it, and there's a part of me that thinks I should call the cops on him. You know?"

Mona's heart rate rose so high, so fast, she thought she might black out. "I *don't* know, Oneida," she said, and put her hand on her daughter's arm as much to control her as steady herself. "I don't know what you're talking about, and I need to. You need to tell me what you did."

Oneida gaped. "I didn't *do* anything," she said. "God, Mom!"

"What did *he* do?"

Oneida shook her off and stomped into her bedroom. Mona followed. Her palms were warm and tacky and her head was buzzing. She hated this, she hated every second of it. Why couldn't Oneida be six years old, or eight, or ten; why couldn't she fit in that nightgown like she used to, and look at Mona like she used to, and be the person she used to be?

Oneida jumped into bed and pulled the covers up over her head.

"I didn't do anything *stupid*, you know, I'm not a complete moron." Her words were muffled through her blankets. "You really don't know me anymore at all, do you?"

Mona, shaking, sat down on the edge of the mattress and curled her bare toes in the carpet nervously. Her limbs felt too large, floppy and cartoonish.

"That's not true," she said. "I'm sorry, I didn't mean—I'm only trying to help. But you have to talk to me. You have to tell me things, OK?"

"You have to tell me things too, *OK*?" Oneida said. "Like—I don't know, let's start small."

"Fine. What do you want to know?" Just posing the question produced an unpleasant dizziness. Answering it felt impossible.

"Am I named after a spoon?"

Mona paused half a beat too long. Her daughter had always been too quick for her.

"Oh my God," Oneida said, her voice shocked and small. "I knew it."

"Oneida—of *course* you aren't named after a spoon, I've told you this story a thousand times. *Oneida* is the name of a whole county, a lake, a tribe of people. I read about it in those old encyclopedias downstairs, the ones you love. I chose it for you because it was different and pretty, and I liked that it meant People of the—"

"Standing Stone. I know. I know all the stories you ever told me." The lump that was Oneida shifted. "I know all the lies you ever told me," she said.

Mona was too tired to be a grown-up. "What about the stories you tell me?" she said. "Huh? Stories like, *This boy at school did something that might be illegal, but I liked it, and for no good reason I don't want to tell you about it.* You want to tell me how that story ends?"

"Forget it. You don't have to worry about me making your mistakes."

"How many times do I have to tell you?" Oneida had pushed the big red button. "What have I ever done to make you think you weren't wanted? I chose you. I kept you. *You are not my mistake.*" She wanted to rip that stupid blanket off her daughter's head, drag her upright. Look her in the eye. Pick her up and feel her daughter's arms wrap around her neck the way they had when she was six, warm and soft and just looking for someone to hold on to.

Oneida's silence was painful. The lump in the bed rose and fell as she sucked in harsh, audible breaths, and Mona felt a cold dread when she realized she'd brought her daughter to tears. This was her life, over and over again: a place she'd never intended to be, arrived at through no one's fault but her own.

"Please just tell me what he did," she said. She rubbed her daughter's back through the blankets.

"I thought you were my friend." Oneida's voice was high and wobbly. "I thought *friends* weren't bullies."

Mona stopped rubbing. "I'm not a very good friend," she said.

Oneida rolled away, hiccuping back sobs. Mona had never felt older, or more exhausted, or less like herself. She didn't have anything to blame on Amy, not anymore; she had secrets of her own to tell, and she had to tell them soon.

She brought Oneida a paper cup of water and left it on her nightstand. Without another word, she crossed the bathroom and closed her connecting door, undressed, and climbed into bed. Before she fell into a blank, motionless sleep, she wondered if she'd be herself again when she woke up. But then, she probably hadn't been herself for quite a while. This feeling—this raw, pulsing vertigo—was probably how it felt to finally be awake.

12 ❧ Boobs

Oneida announced her intentions on the first day of Eugene's grounding. As stipulated, Eugene had gone directly home after school. His brain was humming with a million preoccupations: news of his guitar homicide had traveled with a speed and ferocity the Wendy Project could never have anticipated. The antiestablishment badasses and JD fuckups (the *real* Wendys) glared at him, obviously considering recruitment. The majority of Ruby Falls High, however, thought he was completely, violently insane, and their combined animus—token disapproval with a strong current of perverse excitement—was a physical presence.

All day long, Eugene bore the sickening sensation of being scrutinized and gossiped about. It wasn't at all like when the Wendy Project first took off: then the sheep had been every bit as ridiculous, entertaining, and manipulated as the rumors they were spreading. This was . . . different. Everybody knew: teachers knew, seventh-graders knew, seniors knew. The lunch lady, when she looked up from the scoop of mashed potatoes she flopped on his tray, flinched at his magnificent black eye. There was an implicit understanding that Wendy had finally done the something they'd always known he would, and their moral and social superiority was at long last confirmed.

On top of the subzero atmosphere were three very specific, very troublesome facts:

One: Andrew Lu wanted to end him. Everywhere Eugene went, Andrew followed: he was drinking from the water fountain next to his locker, shuffling three feet back in the lunch line, glaring at him the instant Eugene stepped into geometry, into biology, into bio lab. Eugene had never noticed how many classes they shared. But then again, Andrew Lu had never had any cause, before yesterday, to blast him with a double-barrel glare that clearly meant *I hate you and I want you to die.* If his life had been a prison movie, Eugene would have been shivved before second period.

Two: He had no clue where he'd find the $300 he owed Astor. He'd woken to a pink Post-it note on his bedroom door with the words *EW: U O Me 300* followed by a cartoon clam sweating giant drops of what Eugene assumed must be salt water. He thought he'd been saving at least half of his allowance for the past six months, but the holey green sock where he normally kept his money yielded a whopping twenty dollars and a fuzzy piece of old gum that kind of grossed him out.

And three: Oneida didn't look at him once all day.

Of Eugene's many reasons to be unhappy, the last was by far the most painful.

He was in the middle of constructing a peanut butter and bologna sandwich he didn't think he had the heart to eat when the doorbell chimed. And chimed again. It rang three more times before he answered it.

At school she'd been wearing her typical uniform—jeans and a T-shirt—but she had changed into a pleated blue skirt with tiny white polka dots. Her sweater was short-sleeved and fuzzy and tight; her hair was pulled back and fell around her shoulders. At first Eugene didn't recognize her, though that had less to do with the improbability of Oneida Jones delivering herself to his doorstep than with her lack of glasses.

She squinted.

"Crap," she said, and reached into a bedraggled purple purse. "Sorry, I really can't see anything without, but I thought I might look, you know, better—" She widened the opening of the bag and scrambled furtively. "Where the hell—?"

Eugene was exploding all over. This was happening. *This was really happening.*

"Ah!" Oneida pulled out her glasses but immediately fumbled them.

They landed on the mud mat and Eugene dove. Oneida stepped back, frightened, probably; he had gone after her glasses like a cobra striking. He straightened and held them out to her.

"You look better with glasses," he said. "I don't mean you don't look, you know, good. I just—I mean, you look like you. When you wear them."

She took her glasses from his hand silently and slid them on her face. Despite ostensibly being able to see, Oneida didn't look at him. She stared at her feet.

"Do you want to come in?" he said.

"I—" She cleared her throat. "I'm ready to make out with you now."

So Eugene was dead. He was dead, and it was official: the afterlife both existed and was awesome. Had Andrew Lu jumped him on his way home? He didn't remember a fight, but Andrew was smart enough to attack from behind.

Oneida was looking directly at him. "Are you OK? Your mouth is open."

His teeth clicked as he snapped his jaw shut.

They stared at each other.

"I . . . thank you," Oneida finally said. "How did you know?"

Eugene's voice rose higher than it had in almost two years. "Know what?"

"About Andrew. That jerk stole my idea. You knew that, right?" She hugged her arms against her stomach, under her boobs. Boobs, Eugene thought, unable to take his eyes away. What a wonderful, wonderful concept: Oneida's boobs.

"How did you know that?" she was asking. And then, "Are you staring at my boobs?"

He snapped back.

"I guess it's all right," she said, and sighed. "I figured boobs would be part of the deal. Can I come in? It's cold out here."

"Yeah, sure, definitely, come in." Eugene's pulse thrummed in his temple.

"You're blocking the door," she said.

"Right," said Eugene.

Oneida, on his doorstep, reminded him of a page in the illustrated history of religious painting Astor kept on the bottom of his bookshelf, laid flat because it was too tall to fit upright. She was symmetrical, framed by the late-afternoon sunlight filtering through her hair; and her face was pale and severely featured and enigmatic. He heard himself laugh, a short, weird bark, and then the icon that was Oneida did something unprecedented for a painting: a corner of her wide mouth twitched up in a confused grin.

"I've never actually done this before," she said, taking a step closer. Eugene felt the hair on the back of his neck rise. "Well, except for the time you kind of . . . jumped me in your kitchen. I don't think that counts." When she put her hand on his bare arm, it was warm.

"Am I dead?" Eugene asked.

Oneida paused long enough to say, "No," before she kissed him. She had to stand on her toes and lean into him for balance, and Eugene, who had never been more excited to not be dead, propped her up and bent down. She didn't taste like lemonade today; today she tasted like—like butterscotch. Warm, soft butterscotch. With tongue.

The fuck?

"Sorry!" she said, covering her mouth with her hand. "Did I do that wrong?"

"No!" Eugene said. He laughed again, jittery. "I'm sorry, I don't know, it just—it was a—a surprise."

"Oh," she said, and glared at her feet again.

"Come in." He finally stepped out of the doorway. "Please, please come in. Good surprise! Not a bad surprise." He was on the verge of uncontrollable laughter, and the only viable solution was to attach Oneida to his mouth again as soon as possible. He held the door, and she stepped into the long hallway, heading in the direction she already knew, toward the door to the living room staircase.

"Wait!" he shouted. She twitched. "Wait, I know someplace else we can go that's more comfortable." *Where my sister won't interrupt us, or my mother, or my father, or Terry, or the FedEx guy.* He grabbed her hand, which was a little damp, and led her down the other side of the hallway, toward Astor's office.

"Isn't this the garage?" Oneida wrinkled her nose as Eugene fumbled with the doorknob. "I assumed from the outside—I guess I don't really care where we go, but I'd like at least . . . a couch?"

"There's a couch," he said. "It's really squishy."

"Good." She let out a shaky breath. The primitive part of Eugene's brain that had taken control when Oneida's lips came within ten inches of his own took a moment to collect itself. It was just enough time for him to register the reality of his current situation: he was going to take Oneida Jones into Astor's office. He was going to let a stranger—but she wasn't a stranger, *she was Oneida Jones and she was going to make out with him*—see what his father really did for a living. Astor had never explicitly told Eugene to never tell anyone about the forgeries. It was one of the natural assumptions of the Wendell household: of course you didn't tell anyone about it. The secrecy, the subterfuge, was all part of Astor's superhero identity, and Eugene didn't need to be told to protect his dad. Then again, maybe betraying Astor's secret had never been a problem before now because there had never been anyone Eugene wanted to tell.

And he wanted to tell Oneida Jones. He wanted to do all sorts of stuff with Oneida Jones, but the first thing he wanted to do was tell her Astor's secret.

He put his back to the door and grabbed her fluttering hands.

"Can you keep a secret?" he asked.

She smiled an enormous smile, which was good enough for Eugene. He turned the knob behind his back and reached inside to flip on a bank of lights. Oneida's head swiveled madly in the still murky office, but she made a beeline for the drying rack. The landscape Astor had been working on last week was nowhere to be seen and neither was its original.

"What is this place?" Oneida asked. There were only a few canvases in the rack, and none of them were of anything recognizable. Eugene frowned, disappointed. "Is your mom or dad an artist or something?"

He walked up behind her, unsure if or where he should touch her. He made a grab for her waist but she darted past to Astor's desk. "Why is that a secret?" she asked. She traced her finger across the spines of Astor's books and adjusted her glasses. The battered suitcase full of yellowed clippings and random bits of junk was still on the desktop, and Oneida dragged a lazy finger under the latch. Then she opened it.

Eugene approached as quietly as he could, considering his heart was shrieking. They stood side by side in front of the open case. He had crossed a distance of five feet at most, but by the time Oneida's hair was brushing his shoulder, Eugene had no idea where he was anymore, how he'd gotten here, or how to get back. It seemed the past two weeks of his life had been leading to this particular moment, in this particular place with Oneida, but whether he was now Eugene or Wendy, or some other person entirely, was a complete mystery to him.

In one hand Oneida held a small green bottle with a fat corked neck. He had smashed a bottle just like it in this very office, had hung another outside her window. He felt the fingers of her other hand weaving between his own.

"Thank you," she said.

"You're welcome."

For a moment Eugene was sure she was going to let fly with a torrent of questions: her lips parted on the verge of a what, a why, or possibly a where. *Ask*, he thought; *ask me*. He wanted her to ask and he wanted to tell. He wanted to see her eyes grow wider with each revelation, to see understanding dawn in her face—understanding of what he had done, what he was responsible for, and who he was, really, truly, who he was. Then she closed her lips, her eyes darting. Maybe there were too many questions, Eugene thought. Maybe she just didn't know where to start.

She replaced the bottle and shut the case with a dusty *plop*. Oneida pulled him away from the desk. But before they reached the logical conclusion of the couch, she wrapped herself around him, slowly and completely, locking her arms around his back and burying her head into the hollow of his shoulder. He could smell the fruity soap of her shampoo. The fuzz of her sweater tickled the underside of his arms. She didn't cry, which he half expected. She breathed—huge inhalations and exhalations that ballooned her entire body, until Eugene found his own lungs matching her breath for breath. After a while, she raised her head to look at him.

"I feel weird," he said.

"Me too."

She prodded the edge of his black eye with two fingers, and he winced. "Ow."

"You can see my boobs now," she said. "If you want."

Eugene couldn't have heard that right.

"I'm not going to take off my bra," she said, loosening her grip on his torso. "And no touching, not yet."

She backed away and grabbed the bottom of her sweater with both hands. Eugene thought if he moved at all, he'd fall in a heap of useless arms and legs.

"You ready?" she said, grinning.

He nodded. She pulled her sweater up and over her boobs, and there they were, right there, in a bra: *real girl boobs.* They were the first real girl boobs Eugene had ever seen up close—and the contrast between a real girl boob and the thousands and thousands of boobs he'd seen on television, in movies, and in the lurid film loops that played constantly in his mind was astounding. He adored how very real they were.

She was still holding her sweater up. This was no mere flash, and Eugene felt a rush of abject gratitude even as his hands, slightly more base, floated up toward her.

Her sweater came down like a curtain. Oneida had a smiling face, and Eugene smiled back and lunged. Their teeth clicked audibly. She made a noise halfway between a yelp and a nervous giggle, and kissed him back, a hard full kiss she broke a half-second before his knees liquefied. And then she was gone; he heard the front door slam behind her, the crunch of her shoes on the gravel driveway. There was nothing in the world but the lingering taste of butterscotch on his tongue, a promise and a secret waiting to be kept.

⁊

Eugene woke up at 3:00, 4:00, and 5:00 in the morning, rolling over in bed to check the blinking red digits of his alarm clock each time, even though he knew it would only be an hour later. It felt like Christmas morning. Christmas in October—and out in the world, not under any specific tree, a present was waiting that had already shown itself willing and able to unwrap itself. Eugene was too elated to stop grinning and fall asleep.

He bounced out of bed at 6:45 before his mother even had a chance to hassle him, and was showered and fed so early he didn't have to run for the bus for the first time in weeks. His mother gave him a knowing look when he kissed her good-bye, and even in his hormone-addled state, sloshed on residual pheromones, Eugene could see why. He'd shaved, washed his hair, brushed his teeth, and put on jeans and a

T-shirt that had only been worn once or twice since their most recent laundering, none of which were exactly prerequisites for leaving the house. The jeans were stiff. He hop-skipped down the long driveway to loosen them up.

Would Oneida walk up to him in the hall and stick her hands in his back pockets? Would she pretend it had never happened? His forty-five-minute bus ride allowed Eugene plenty of time to consider the complexities of all possible outcomes. It was possible that, given the time to digest what she'd done, Oneida would become so disgusted with herself for flashing him that she would stay home sick. It was also possible that she would follow him around like a lost puppy. He doubted it—she seemed far too cool, too prickly, for that—but you never knew; it wasn't impossible, and it was very troubling. To make their . . . whatever it was that they were doing a matter of public knowledge wasn't something he thought Ruby Falls High—or he—was quite ready for. They were both marginal freaks. He had a bad feeling that they wouldn't cancel each other out but that, instead, their social stigma would be concentrated, focused. Mutated something dreadful.

It wasn't until second-period gym that he caught a glimpse of her: a cloud of dark hair disappearing into the girls' locker room. All of the possibilities where Oneida had to stay home sick, full of self-loathing and regret, mercifully dissolved. The girls and the guys were still separated, so he didn't see her again until the period ended, and then only from thirty feet away, turning a corner on her way to the science wing. Eugene felt a not-entirely-unpleasant mixture of frustration and thrill, like he was a big cat stalking a particularly elusive gazelle.

She pounced first. Too absorbed in plumbing the pockets of his still too-stiff jeans for lunch money, he didn't notice she was following until she slid into step beside him.

"Hey," she said. "Where are you going?"

"Hey, yourself." She smelled wonderful, like cinnamon and something toasted. He sniffed the air and smiled.

"It's not me, it's the hallway," she said. "Someone burned cinnamon buns in home ec. I guess they were on fire and everything. You want to go to the drama club prop loft?"

This had not been one of Eugene's many possibilities. "What?"

"I brought us lunch," she said.

Eugene had never been anywhere near the drama club's prop loft (or the drama club's anything, for that matter), both because of a vague discomfort with musicals in general and a hatred of most of the key players in the drama club clique. It didn't make sense for Oneida to have the inside track on the prop loft either, until they had crossed the silent auditorium's sea of half-lit chairs and were standing in the wings of the stage, musty curtains solid and warm around them. He felt safe, insulated from the rest of the school, alone in the world with her. Oneida was a girl who knew how to hide out.

"This is the hard part," she said. He followed the tilt of her head to a metal ladder bolted into the wall, the bottom rungs hanging six feet off the ground. "I usually just stand on something and jump up, but I thought maybe you could give me a boost. You're so tall."

He wrapped his hands around her hips and lifted. She wavered a little, surprised, but soon rebalanced enough to grab the bottom rung. He felt her lift her own weight out of his hands. *If only you'd worn a skirt*, he thought, watching her butt undulate as she climbed up the ladder.

The prop loft was a high open landing, adjacent to the stage, which Eugene discovered after jumping to the bottom rung from a rickety chair and ascending. Weights and ropes and pulleys hung, dark and heavy, above their heads. Meager light came from the auditorium below; the farther from the edge he went, Eugene could only make out simple shapes and colors. Oneida was sitting on one of two beanbag chairs, unpacking a paper grocery bag she must have brought up earlier. So it had been planned; it had all been planned.

"I just discovered this place last spring," Oneida said. She flattened the paper bag and set it like a table: two sandwiches and two apples on a paper plate, and (weird) two pieces of fancy-looking cake in plastic take-out containers. "They only do one show a year, so it's pretty abandoned for the rest of the time. Come on, it's OK. You can sit down." She patted the other beanbag. In the darkness, her teeth flashed in a nervous smile. "Are you afraid of heights?"

"What? No." Eugene turned to look over his shoulder and, yes, he was a little afraid of heights. The loft had a very short railing, which would do absolutely nothing to prevent him, should he slip, from falling twenty feet down and breaking his neck. He moved toward her but the darkness was disorienting. She'd clearly been up here often enough to have her sea legs, but Eugene felt completely undone by his body. He didn't know how or where to move without falling.

"One sec," she said, and disappeared into the dark behind the beanbags.

There was a moment of indeterminate scuffling and then a Christmas tree burned itself onto Eugene's retinas. Several blinks later, the tree—and Oneida, sitting on the beanbag in front of it—came into full candy-colored focus.

"I think they did *White Christmas* a few years ago. . . . Please . . . say something."

Eugene hadn't realized how long he'd been standing there, not moving, not speaking, just staring at Oneida—her skin a stained-glass patchwork of light—and feeling something so far beyond anything he had ever felt before that he could only understand it in parts. He felt safe. He felt stunned and awake. He felt cold and electric and terrified of what would happen next. He didn't want to move. He didn't want the world to burst.

Oneida shifted on the beanbag, tugging the neck of her T-shirt.

"I love you," he said.

She looked up, stricken. "I made you a sandwich," she said.

Eugene had to sit, immediately. To her credit, Oneida didn't recoil when he collapsed into the beanbag next to her.

"You showed me your boobs," he explained.

She blinked.

"You do that when you're nervous," he said, pointing at her hands, which were fluttering like jellyfish. "Please don't be nervous."

"I'll be nervous if I want." She shifted again and tucked her hands beneath her thighs.

The fact that she hadn't slapped him or flung herself off the edge gave Eugene the courage to reach down the side of her beanbag, under her leg, and pull out one of her hands. He held it in both of his own until she turned to face him.

"Please don't take it personally," he said.

Oneida's eyes were hiding somewhere behind the multicolored reflections dancing across her glasses. He wished he could see them, instead of the only thing he could see: his face, looming as he moved closer to kiss her, a reflection too large and too colorful to be his own.

13 ↝ *Missing Persons on Vacation*

Arthur felt good.

Sure, his chest ached and itched and would occasionally weep blood through his shirts—or, rather, Mona's father's shirts, which were smooth and cool and crisp; far nicer than he, Arthur, had ever dreamed of purchasing. He had a black bruise the size of a bocce ball on his hip from tumbling down the stairs, and he must have wrenched his neck because he couldn't look over his right shoulder without a sharp twinge. But his days now were full and different and he felt better than good, actually. He felt *great*.

He hadn't taken a vacation—a real vacation, not a long weekend or a trip home for the holidays—in years, and he saw now that all the usual excuses (they couldn't get time off work, they didn't have the money) had been just that: excuses. Vacations were *worth* it. This sensation of escape, of relief: it was *worth* it. When he slept at night, he slept deeply and long; and when he woke in the morning, he woke to Mona. A small voice in the back of his head would occasionally chirp *Amy's not here!* and Arthur would hear the voice but not understand why it sounded so concerned. Yes: Amy wasn't here. But *here* wasn't anyplace he had ever known Amy to be; she wasn't missing, and Arthur wasn't missing her, in this place. If anything, he was discovering her—as she'd been in this house and this town, and as she'd been to Mona.

He had the greatest vacationing companion in Mona Jones. He adored her, so easily it would have shocked him, had he the wherewithal to notice or to care. She brought Amy to life because she had so much of her own to spare. She was the first person Arthur had been able to see clearly in weeks, since he left Los Angeles; he saw that she was tough and tenacious and sarcastic. She was talented and young. He saw that she had no idea how beautiful she was—as he'd told Amy the last time he saw her, moments after his trip down the stairs. Amy had acted a little surprised; he hoped she hadn't taken it the wrong way. But he couldn't help seeing Mona when she was right in front of him.

"You watch all these cake-decorating shows on television," Mona said, handing him a carton of eggs, "and it's all about the concept and sculpting and rolling the fondant and air-brushing it and—you know. How it looks." She ducked back into the refrigerator. "Which is perfect for television—it *works* for TV, since TV can only engage two of the five senses." She passed him butter and a large bunch of carrots, green tops feathery and ticklish, and propped her elbows on the top of the open fridge door. "But it drives me nuts, because nobody ever seems to care how the cake *tastes*."

It was Thursday. Mona had knocked on his door and asked if he wanted to help her bake, neither of them acknowledging the awkward conclusion of the previous day: how Arthur had hurt her without thinking, and how Mona had hurt him in return. He felt both deserving and guiltless, because it was Amy's fault, really. And today, when he thought of Amy, he realized he didn't want to.

"And isn't that the whole *point*—the *cake*?" Mona heaved a giant silver KitchenAid mixer from her counter to the kitchen table and wiped her forehead with the back of her hand. "The frosting is just the, like—well, it's *the frosting*. If the frosting were the point, it wouldn't be called cake."

"You've got a whole philosophy here."

"I'm an existential baker," she said, and grinned at him. "Metaphysical mistress of pastry." She shrugged. "Was going to name my company that but it sounded too much like an escort service."

"The most delicious escort service *ever*," he said, which made her laugh. She handed him a bristle brush and asked him to scrub and grate the carrots while she separated egg whites. Carrie had ordered her most popular cake, she explained, the four-tiered Stairway to Heaven, which started in the ground with carrot cake, then chocolate, then lemon, and finally ascended to angel food.

"It doesn't get ordered much, but my personal favorite is Dante's

Nine Circles," she said. "Eight layers, nine different kinds of chocolate. I count the ganache on the top as Limbo."

A silence fell. Mona broke it with the crack of an egg into a big blue mixing bowl. Any other day, this would have been the moment when Arthur induced Mona to tell stories, asking a leading question or showing her some mysterious artifact he'd pulled from the depths of the pink shoebox. But he hadn't brought anything to show her this morning, and he couldn't think of anything else to ask about Amy; he was no closer to understanding her will and had, if he was being honest with himself, stopped believing that *his* scrutiny of each and every detail would be the pathway to the revelation he was seeking. The cuff links had already done what they could for him: had made his introductions to Mona, broken the ice (and his body), and brought him into her confidence. Now he knew: it was through Mona that Arthur would find what Amy left behind.

He set his jaw. He was annoyed with Amy, irritated with Amy, for not sharing Mona with him. He didn't understand what Mona could have done or said to make Amy scoop her out of her life, to deny Arthur this part of her history, of her self. It was just as big a mystery as the postcard, but it was a mystery he felt he had a better chance of solving.

"How about some music?" Mona asked.

"What *does* one listen to while baking a Stairway to Heaven cake?" He accidentally skimmed his knuckles against the grater and winced.

"This part of the country is the undisputed adult contemporary radio station capital of the world. I'm not kidding. You haven't heard easy listening until you've heard it in upstate New York." Mona flicked on an ancient combination cassette player/radio on top of the microwave. Other voices, fuzzy with static, echoed between them.

"What's it like, running your own business?" he asked.

"Parts are difficult. That I have to cover my own insurance is a bitch, and so are taxes; but there's very little overhead, now that I own so much equipment." Arthur could watch her crack eggs all day—she did it smoothly, cleanly, one-handedly. "And I'm the only lonely little employee, which means if I screw up, *I* have to deal with the consequences. But I also don't have to cover anyone else's ass, I don't have to deal with a shitty boss, I make my own hours and my own decisions about the jobs I take. I can do eighty percent of it in my PJs"—she pointed at her pants, which were bright green with tiny yellow shooting stars—"while listening to Lite FM. What's not to love?"

"The Lite FM?"

"It's my kryptonite. I'd wager many persons born in the mid to late nineteen seventies share the same affliction. Like, whatever radio waves were wafting through the air at the moment of your conception inexorably bonded themselves to your disposition. Ergo: my parents were really into Lionel Ritchie and the Commodores." She gathered the eggshells in her hands and joined him beside the sink. "C'mon. Everyone has a musical weakness. Even you."

"Um." She smiled up at him and he wondered, with something like distant shock, whether this was something he had ever told Amy. Had it ever come up? He couldn't remember. It seemed like she would have teased him about it, had she known. "My parents had a greatest hits of the Bee Gees album that they played constantly. I'd dance in front of the stereo until I fell over."

"Do you still?" Mona jammed the eggshells down the garbage disposal. "I bet that makes family gatherings kind of fun."

"My parents—" Arthur's voice caught. His parents. He hadn't thought of his family in days, in a week. In *weeks*, maybe—how long had he been on this vacation, anyway?

"Did you call home?" Mona asked.

He shook his head. The carrot he was shredding was down to a rounded nub and the tips of his fingers brushed against the surface of the grater. His mind was curiously still. He couldn't imagine what he would say to his mother, to his brother. To his father. And since he couldn't imagine the act of doing anything about it—of calling them and telling them and dealing with whatever happened next—it didn't feel like anything he had to worry about. It was unthinkable. It was undoable. It was unimportant.

"I bet you're a missing person by now." Mona sloshed the egg whites into the silver bowl on the big mixer.

"I don't know who would have reported me," he said. "Unless— maybe Max Morris."

"Brother of Zack?"

"Max is a guy I worked with. He's probably the only one who'd miss me." And for a small sharp moment, he missed Max too—missed his company, his quiet humor, the little donuts from his boyfriend—and then the world became very clear and very bright, and Arthur Rook snapped upright and understood everything that was happening was happening to *him*: Amy was gone and Arthur had run and nothing was going to be the way it had been, or the way he had wanted it to be for the rest of his life. All the air left him and he leaned forward to catch the counter.

And then the moment was over and Mona, her voice small but growing, like she was walking toward him from far away, asked if he was all right, did he want to lie down or—

"No." He straightened and faced her with a plateful of grated carrots. "I'm fine."

"You don't look fine."

"I've looked worse," he said.

"While true, not comforting. Tell me more about Max."

His brain sputtered and refused to give up any more detail beyond coworker, carpool, donuts. The subject of Max was tagged in his mind as dangerous, uncharted territory: *Here there be memories.*

"Like I said, we worked together," he said. "Taking school pictures."

"Sounds like you had a raging social life out there."

He shook his head. "I didn't . . . we didn't go out much. We went to dinner sometimes, but—I worked a lot. Amy worked all the time."

Arthur was profoundly unsettled by this conversation and couldn't quite say why. Perhaps it was the perspective of the vacationer—remote from his everyday life, he sees it for what it really is and finds it lacking. But he had loved his everyday life while he was living it, hadn't he? He thought he remembered *feeling* as though he did. He pressed the heel of his hand to his eyebrow to ease a sudden stab of pain.

"Hey, I have an idea," Mona said. "Later, let's look you up online. Let's see if anyone has reported your missing ass—"

"No," he said—harshly. Mona froze and he softened.

"I'm not trying to get rid of you," she said. "I just think it might be . . . funny to—"

"See proof that no one noticed? I vanished, left my whole life behind, and the world didn't bat an eye?"

Mona didn't speak for a while. She turned on the mixer. "I know the feeling," she said.

The mixer whirred methodically and Arthur felt better. The sound wrapped around his head. It made him think of wind through the trees or the pounding of the ocean: the music of vacation elemental and static, calm, and filling.

⁂

Mona knocked on his door.

He knew it was Mona before he answered, and not just because she was the only person in the house he had any tangible connection with: he knew it was Mona because she was knocking on his door with both fists to the rhythm of the Bee Gees' "Jive Talkin'."

"Are you dancing yet?" Her voice was muffled.

"No," he called, though in a manner of speaking, that's exactly what he'd been doing for the past hour, for the past day, and the past weeks: dancing with the idea of Amy, with the fact of Amy, around the strange small things she'd left behind. He'd been nose-deep in the shoebox since dinner, amusing himself—and Harryhausen—with a penny racer he half-remembered Amy playing with: a bright blue Volkswagen Beetle he could picture her pulling back and letting fly across their dresser. Or was it his brother he remembered, playing with his own bright blue Volkswagen Beetle penny racer?

"I'm your landlord, Arthur. I can let myself in if I want to."

He blinked. Time was slipperier every day. He placed the tiny car back in the shoebox and slid it beneath the coffee table. He had cursorily explained to Mona that the box and its assorted contents had belonged to Amy, but he felt odd about giving Mona unrestricted access, about letting her paw through it without his careful supervision. For one, she'd find Amy's will, addressed to her. He wasn't ready to tell her about that yet, at least not until he understood more about why Amy had never sent it.

Mona was standing in the hall with a box of her own under her arm: long and flat and maroon in color.

"Scrabble?" she said.

Harryhausen watched as they scrambled the letter tiles in the box top and unfolded the board and then decided, as Arthur knew he would, that this was a perfect time for a nap. It was a perfect time, period; the night was cool but not cold, and it was already dark outside even though it was barely past seven. Mona sat to his left in the old easy chair and examined her letter tiles intently, switching two back and forth and chewing her bottom lip. Arthur eased back into the couch cushions.

"We should drink some warm milk, watch *Matlock*, and call it a night," he said.

"I bet that works on all the ladies at the old folks' home." She didn't look up from her tiles. "You go first," she said.

The game of Scrabble, as Arthur had always played it—and he had *always* played it; all Rooks had, at the insistence of his mother, who lived and breathed for crosswords and acrostics and anything having to do with the ingenious placement of letters and words—was a battlefield that said more about the players than the tiles they'd been dealt. His imagination-challenged brother never played a word longer than three or four letters, frequently pluralizing tiles already in play; his father, who felt the need to justify every action he ever took, played with one thumb in the official Scrabble rule book, ready to riffle to his defense. Since her cancer, his mother had taken to playing fast and loose with rules she had once considered unimpeachable and would occasionally accept a proper name, depending on how cleverly it was employed. But Arthur's weakness had always been playing words that occurred naturally on his tile bench, that didn't have any definition that he knew of but that were too funny not to use: MURDLET, QUINK, DOXEN. *Choose your words carefully,* his mother would say, sitting across from him. *Make sure they're real.*

RUN was his first word, which, considering his recent history of flight—and the history of his present company—seemed plenty real enough.

"Do you mind if we don't keep score?" Mona asked. "I just like playing with the words."

Arthur nodded. "Sure," he said. "But how will we know when I beat the pants off you?"

"When I am no longer wearing pants," she said, and played the word NYMPH off the N.

He nodded again, appreciatively, and frowned at his own tiles. Mona sat back, stretching her arms over her head, and Harryhausen yawned and stretched sympathetically.

"Ha. I made your cat yawn."

She inhaled. Harry rolled on his back and began to clean his bib.

"Amy's cat," she murmured.

"Tell me something," Arthur said—not too abruptly, he hoped. He was weary of Amy at the moment; it was so much more fun to understand his wife through Mona. "Word association. With the word." He laid down TIPS.

"Frosted."

"Right." He spun toward her. "*What?*"

"You know. Prominent among boy bands of the early aughts," she said. "I once had a thing for Lance Bass. Don't judge." She played MATCH.

"Us," Arthur said, without thinking.

Mona froze, her hand still over the board. "Did this just get weird?" she said.

"No—I mean." He looked over at Harry, who had paused mid-lick to throw him a stone cold glare that clearly meant *Don't be a pussy*. "I just thought—we're a set. A widower and a widow. That's what I meant."

"Oh," she said.

They both looked at the board and, when they spoke, talked over each other.

"I'm—you go," said Arthur.

"I'm not a widow."

Arthur hadn't realized until that moment how much of what he knew about Mona Jones he didn't actually know. Until very recently, in fact, all they had talked about was Amy, and all he had learned about Mona was *relative* to Amy. This feeling that he knew her, then, was only an illusion, perhaps a residual of his concussion or a substage of grief. But he *did* feel as though he knew her: he could see her, couldn't he? He tried to remember why he thought she was a widow, and stirred up a dim memory of a conversation several days ago; all conversations, it seemed, slipped behind a curtain of fuzz these days. Had it been purely his own assumption that the only reason Mona was alone—Mona, who had once been with someone seriously enough to produce a child that she then raised with love—was on account of that same someone's untimely death?

"I'm—" His brain skipped ahead to the logical conclusion. "So is Oneida's father still—" God, he didn't even know how to say he was sorry.

Mona looked down at the board and puffed out her cheeks. "I believe so," she said. "Yes."

Harryhausen sighed audibly.

Arthur watched Mona blink, silently, at the board. She pushed her hair out of her face and over her ears and he thought, *Mona has big ears.* Large rounded ears, the tops neatly folded over; with two small piercings in the lobes but no earrings. He hadn't noticed that before. He would have to look even closer than usual, apparently, to know her.

It was his turn. Around the T in MATCH, he built PLZTELMI.

"That's not a—oh." She smiled halfheartedly and said, "Nice use of all your tiles."

"You don't have to if you don't want to."

"You ever write songs for Prince?"

"Mona," he said, trying not to laugh, "you don't have to be so serious all the time."

She chewed her lip again and rearranged several of her tiles. "His name was Ben," she said. "Tennant. He rented a room in this house when I was in high school. He was a teacher, a drama teacher. A director and an actor." She still hadn't looked at him.

"He was . . . I don't think he was a bad person." Her brow furrowed, as though she were reevaluating truths she had long held to be self-evident, reassessing them in new contexts. "He was young. Talented. People *loved* him.

"I don't think he knows . . . about his daughter." Her brow furrowed deeper. "I told my mother, years after, and she wanted to press charges, skin him alive, roast him over a hot pit, you know, really make him suffer—until I convinced her that there was no point. There would be no purpose. It was done, and Oneida was here, and she was healthy, and she was mine. I don't know where he is now because I don't want to. I believe that he cared. That's enough."

"You cared," he said.

She bobbed her head.

"I think you loved him."

Finally she looked at him, through sad, squinted eyes. She held her thumb and index finger half an inch apart. "I loved him a little," she said, "about this much." And she didn't look away when she said, "Amy loved him more."

Arthur didn't hear it at first. Well, he *heard* it, but he didn't immediately grasp it for what it was: the reason he'd been looking for, the solution to the mysterious disappearance of Desdemona Jones from the life of his wife. It snuck into his brain gradually, so that when it finally arrived, all Arthur could do was open his mouth. "Oh," he said.

Mona crossed her arms over her chest.

"I—" His throat was dry and he swallowed. "I see."

Mona leaned forward, clearly intending to dump all her tiles in the box top. "Sorry," she said. "This got weird." She paused. "Weirder."

Arthur's brain was doing curious things. It was accepting and understanding information, but it wasn't sending any signals to any other part of his body that might give him some indication as to how he *felt* about all this. What it meant that Mona—as a girl—had had a child by a man that Amy had loved, also as a girl. What it meant that Amy had never told him anything about this. Not that he was numb, far from it; he felt plenty. He was at home on this couch in the light autumn chill, his stomach was full and happy—Thursday was meat loaf night—and even the scrape on his knuckle from the vegetable grater didn't hurt so much as remind him, pleasantly, of good work he had done. *It's only information,* his brain said. *The important thing is just that you have it. Deal with it later. You're on vacation.*

"Don't apologize," he said to Mona. "Tell me more."

"What makes you think there's more to tell?"

"There's always more," he said. "And we're not finished with the game. I can tell because you're still wearing pants."

Mona wrinkled her nose. She set her tile tray back on the table in front of her. "This isn't weird," she said. "Not one little bit. Totally normal."

Arthur felt so good, sitting next to Mona. "What are you trying to say?" he said, and smiled.

"Oh, nothing," she said, and played STRANGER, off the R in RUN.

"Nice use of all your letters," he said.

14 ✑ Marriage and Love

Mona's attitude toward weddings was complicated. She didn't dislike them, though it would probably be a lie to say that the opposite was true. She'd baked two hundred cakes over the past ten years, and while the majority had been received by happy, smiling, gracious people, she had seen enough sobbing brides, disgruntled caterers, and hideous bridesmaid gowns to have a disproportionate fear of weddings-gone-wild: of a simple happy ceremony's propensity to metastasize into the equivalent of a hydrogen bomb with taffeta. She'd had a piece of her own perfectly delicious cake mashed into her hair. She'd been stiffed, insulted, and, once, contacted by a lawyer for her "flagrant disregard of her client's color palette."

There were plenty of valid reasons for her to dump her cakes, snatch payment, and get out before the DJ ever had a chance to cue the Electric Slide. She never stayed, even though she was occasionally invited to do so. The invitations were always verbal and came at the last minute, as though they had been contingent on her showing up with a dessert that didn't look like crap. Mona would decline, tuck her payment away safely in her back pocket, and drive home, her meticulously constructed cake forever whole in her memory.

She didn't get into cakes for the proximity to ceremonial wedded bliss: she liked baking and she needed money, and weddings were more lucrative than bake sales. Her mother, who knew everyone in Ruby Falls (and everyone's sons and daughters), was instrumental in spreading the word that Mona was now a baker for hire—and not only could everyone in Ruby Falls show their social solidarity by contracting with the fallen daughter of the house of Darby-Jones, her cakes were good.

Magnificent, really. Baking was a talent she'd never suspected she possessed, a talent that, once discovered, completely overhauled Mona's
idea of herself. She had never thought of any of her personality traits as
useful before; they had just been parts of a whole that did homework,
hung out with Amy, and daydreamed about making out with her juve-
nile delinquent *du jour*. To have a talent, though—a skill, a gift—was
thrilling. It was like discovering she'd had an invisible arm stuck to her
side her entire life, just waiting for her to figure out how to use it. Despite
everything, she felt ridiculously lucky to have gone to Ocean City, to
have met David Danger. If she hadn't, she might never have known all
the pieces of who she was: Mona Jones, Funny Girl, Baker. Mom.

Her feelings about love—which, beyond the party line, had very
little to do with weddings—were no less complicated. Mona had never
seen her own parents while they were in love with each other. By the
time she was old enough to notice, they had reached a sort of static fond-
ness that would characterize the mid to late years of their marriage and
their lives. They were like brother and sister, Mona used to think, listening to them talk over dinner about repairing the eaves of the Darby-
Jones or fixing the broken chain in Bert's toilet. They never held hands;
they never kissed—really kissed, beyond a quick peck that usually meant
drive safe or *thank you for my Christmas presents*; and God knows,
they'd only had one child. Surely, that wasn't love. Mona, at sixteen,
didn't want it to be.

Mona, at sixteen, only knew the joys of the crush: the giddy highs of
unexpected meetings; the delights of flirting, teasing, tickling each other's minds; the hours of pining with a smile on her face, imagining how
and why and where and when that very first kiss would come to pass.
Her follow-through was terrible—she would lose interest in the object
of her crush as soon as he proved to be less than imagined or someone
better rolled around—but Mona thrived on the search for Great Love.
She was absolutely certain there was a person in the world who would
never disappoint her or be one-upped by someone else, who would be
an alpha-and-omega deal: an eternal crush, that incandescent high captured forever in the space between two specific people.

She had made few concessions to reality by the time she met David
Danger. Logically, she understood dependability and companionship

were good things—but wasn't that why you had friends? Wasn't your boyfriend supposed to be something a little better, a little bigger, a little more magical? She'd kissed Eric Cole at the sixth-grade dinner dance, and she'd let Tony Littleton, who was suspended for lighting a music stand on fire with breath spray, get to second base during a basketball game in eighth grade. But neither Eric nor Tony held a candle to David Danger, whose casual, constant flirtation kept Mona delirious with fantasy, visualizing the moment when she and David would reach to fill the same empty shaker with red pepper flakes and end up with their tongues tied instead—which was precisely the way it happened, one night after closing.

That June on the Jersey shore was one of the best months of her entire life, though David Danger was only a part of it. She remembered everything with a clarity that was almost painful, as though those thirty days had flared bright enough to scorch her, leaving a permanent sunburn in her mind. Beyond her attraction to boys who weren't necessarily nice and/or sane, Mona had never been particularly willful or rebellious, probably because she had never had to be. Her parents had expectations about her grades, but she had no strict curfews or irrational edicts, which Mona realized in hindsight had less to do with their faith in her than the dearth of available trouble in Ruby Falls. In Ocean City, drunk on independence, Mona felt the incalculable folly of her tiny life. There was a whole world that stayed up late and served you whatever you asked for, so long as you could pay for it; and Amy, who had somehow known this the whole time, shared Mona's delight at discovering it for herself.

Every night, after their respective shifts ended, they would meet at the amusement park at the far end of the boardwalk, eat blue Italian ice, and connive their way into extra turns on the Ferris wheel from the operator, an eager, chubby boy who came to the House of D'Angier every afternoon, blushed at Mona, and only said three words: "Cheese pizza. Thanks." The wheel would lift them high into the dark sky, its blinking red and yellow and purple bulbs manic beneath the looming white moon, and they'd talk about the minutiae of their days—which, by virtue of being utterly and completely their own, were nothing short of miraculous.

The Ferris wheel was enormous, the kind with circular banquettes instead of two-person swings. Each car could seat eight to ten people, but Chubby Cheese Pizza let them have one all to themselves. Amy liked to prop her aching bare feet on the railing and Mona would lie down and follow the curve of the basket with her body.

"Hey, guess what happened to *me* today," Mona would say.

"Wait wait wait, let me guess." Amy tapped her forehead and furrowed her brow. "*You* made out with David Danger?"

Mona laughed. "Yes," she said. "It's really slow in the afternoons. What else are we supposed to do?"

"Mother, may I sleep with Danger?" Amy's voice squeaked. It always squeaked when she rushed to speak, trying to get the words out before she was laughing too hard to talk.

Mona cracked up. "Oh, *may* I?" she drawled, and she and Amy both hooted into the dark night air.

Their conversations danced neatly around the truth of their situation and were full of gossip and jokes and laughter without ever addressing anything serious, anything with repercussions, anything (God forbid) grown up. But at the time, neither of them realized it; neither of them cared. They were friends at the top of the dark world, held aloft in an electric basket, and though they must have known the wheel would turn and bring them back to the ground, for that month the ocean wind ruffled their hair and they swung, weightless.

Through the end of June and into July, whenever Mona would start to feel despondent that her parents had read her note and *taken it at face value*, that they *weren't* moving heaven and earth to find her, David Danger kept her doped and ecstatic. Instead of sitting alone in her room at the Pink Seahorse while Amy pulled another double shift at Maggione's—picking up the pink plastic phone, dialing home, slamming the receiver down before it had a chance to ring—Mona went to the House of D'Angier just to hang out, to flirt with David and learn, from his Uncle Rufus, how to bake.

Uncle Roof had a penchant for humming the Beach Boys and a constant tang of pot; he reminded Mona of a hippie walrus. He was also a trained pastry chef and only ran the pizza place out of filial duty. The room marked OFFICE was his laboratory, a cramped windowless closet with just enough space for a table, a giant KitchenAid mixer, and three people, standing, if two of those people (and Mona and David didn't mind) stood right on top of each other. Deflated pastry bags and enigmatic implements hung on the pegboard walls; powdered sugar drifts filled the crevices and gaps in the floor tiles. They spent hours sculpting cakes, shaving and rounding the corners into obscene and surreal shapes; one night, they covered stuffed animals with fondant and left them on the beach to freak out the gulls. David stayed at his uncle's beach house for the summer, and Mona developed her taste for beer on his rickety porch, watching the surf break and pull against the sand, break and pull. At the end of July, instead of feeling terrible and selfish and that this whole thing had gone on far too long, Mona and David slept together—just slept (after rounding a few bases), but still. Mona woke up first and watched David sleep for a long time. *So this*, thought Mona, fascinated by the movement of his eyes beneath closed lids, *this is love. I knew it.*

The next morning she snuck back into the motel, grinning so hard her face hurt, but Amy was already awake, sitting upright in a nest of bed linens and reading the newspaper.

"Guess what." The way Amy said it, it wasn't a question. "It's August."

"August already?" Mona kicked off her flip-flops.

"Watch it. You're getting sand everywhere."

"What do you care? Someone comes in and cleans this place every day."

Amy glared at her. She had purple shadows around her eyes and her hair looked dull and unwashed.

"What's the matter?" Mona bit her tongue. What a stupid question.

"Other than the really fucking obvious?" Amy wadded up the newspaper and threw it at her. "Where are you?"

"I was at David's, I told you—"

"No, where *are* you." Amy covered her face with her hands, and Mona's heart leaped. She hadn't seen Amy this upset since the afternoon she confessed her crush on Ben Tennant—she hadn't even cried when she first laid out the Ocean City plan, which had been a fairly upsetting afternoon. Before Mona could even move closer, Amy began sobbing, violently, and this time Mona knew exactly what she wanted to do: she wanted to run. She wanted to run back to David and Uncle Roof immediately. She knew that Amy had been working hard, working all the damn time, in fact, which had made spending her free hours with David easy. Natural. If she'd even suspected Amy was this close to breaking down, she would never have left her side.

That's such a lie, she thought; *you lie you lie you lie.*

"Haven't you wondered?" Amy hiccuped and pulled the comforter closer around herself, tighter, until she was completely tucked in, immobile. Only her head was visible, a disheveled cherry on a blanket sundae. "Where I am when I'm not here? I'm never here, Mona, I'm only here when I'm asleep, and sometimes not even then. Sometimes I sleep in the break room at one job for two hours and then get up and go to the next."

Mona's stomach hovered and dropped. "How much money do we have left?"

"Oh, that's not the problem," Amy said. She rolled her head back. "I have plenty of money. I could leave tomorrow. I could fly to LA first class—"

Mona burned. "If you have plenty of money, why did you hock the cuff links last week?" Last Tuesday, Amy had been nervy and short about ordering a huge fish fry dinner that neither of them could finish, which Amy had pronounced a disgusting waste of money.

"Take the cuff links," Mona had said. She couldn't bear to hock them herself. "If it'll make you feel better, take the cuff links, take the money." She'd tried to feel noble, like her sacrifice was precisely what Amy needed at the moment she needed it most. But when the cuff links, cool and heavy, tumbled out of her sock and into her palm, and then passed from her palm to Amy's, Mona mostly felt like dying.

And now—to find out Amy hadn't even needed them and had accepted them anyway—she felt worse than sick. She felt stupid and used.

Amy shut her eyes and shook her head. "There's no such thing as enough money," she said. "I've been cleaning other rooms before my shift at Maggione's every day. I get tips and we get to stay in this room for free."

"I thought you took double shifts—"

"I did. I did both. And then Maggione's fired me last night. They decided they just didn't need my help anymore. I wonder why." Two twisted blooms appeared on the comforter as Amy clenched her fists inside her pink cocoon. "Those stupid assholes. I was the best waitress they had and they threw me away like a piece of garbage. And of course I'm still scared that there's not enough money. There isn't, ever, enough—what happens if the Seahorse fires me next; will they kick us out? I don't know what to do. I don't know what to do next. I want to give up and I know it's too late, but if I can't work—if I can't work, I don't know what to do. I'm so—scared of everything that's going to happen next."

Mona was standing by the door, her flip-flops less than two feet away. Her brain blazed white with an image: she saw herself grabbing her shoes, looping her fingertips through the purple plastic thongs, and running. *Amy Henderson has made her own bed*, she thought, *Amy Henderson must lie in it. This has nothing to do with you. Amy Henderson has used you to make herself feel better about doing the stupidest thing she could possibly have done in her situation, and you need to get away, get away, get away. Save yourself.*

Part of Amy gave up. Mona saw it happen: Amy stopped crying and deflated inside her tepee of blankets, her eyes glazed and unblinking. A terrible calm settled over the room. Mona, who had only understood love as something that burned bright and then out, was forced to consider that love was something you didn't really understand, ever, at all. Because it must have been love that made her kick her flip-flops under the bed and bring Amy a cup of cold water. It must have been love that reminded her, in that tacky room so far from home, that Amy was her best friend, and had been her best friend for as long as she had memories; that Amy was selfish but had her own kind of magic; that Amy, who never needed anyone, needed her and needed her now. So it was love that pushed Amy's sweaty bangs back from her forehead and tucked her in. And it was love that made Mona walk into the Pink Seahorse office and tell Ralph the night manager, just coming off his shift, that she would be taking over Amy's cleaning duties for the foreseeable future.

৯৯

But it wasn't love that made her want Amy's widower. It couldn't be, because she barely knew him. It couldn't be, because he barely knew her. And it couldn't be, because if it were, then love was even more inexplicable than Mona was prepared to accept.

They finished the Waters-Kessler wedding cake on Friday evening. Despite Arthur's presenting himself as willing to talk about the circumstances of Oneida's conception—and what it had meant to Amy—Mona hadn't pursued the matter further. She was both relieved he hadn't pressed and thrilled that he wanted to hear at all; because he did want to hear, and not just because of the Amy factor, she thought. And she did want to tell him, though she just couldn't figure out how.

Or *did* she want to tell him? She didn't know. She hadn't told anyone in so long, she didn't think she still knew how to say the words. She had tried whispering them to herself in front of the bathroom mirror, and her entire throat had constricted. The fact that Oneida was twenty feet away, silent but most definitely in the room next door, probably had something to do with it.

It was easier to focus on assembling the Waters-Kessler cake.

"My daisies are too dense," Arthur said.

"So spread them apart. Start from the center of the layer and fan out." Mona was painting the requested happy yellow centers on each daisy with food coloring. She held two finished flowers up over her eyes. "Does this look as terrifying as I think it does?" she said.

"Yes," Arthur said, and laughed. It was a nice laugh. She thought if she ever heard it when he was really, truly happy, it would be a wonderful laugh.

They were through at eleven o'clock and toasted their success with hastily mixed screwdrivers. "To your health," she said, and clinked her juice glass against Arthur's mug. And after she went to bed and fell asleep, she had an astonishingly powerful dream about her able assistant that was as surreal as it was pornographic: about the two of them, lying in a field of rippling fondant daisies, powdered sugar blowing on the wind. It stuck to their skin, collecting in the hollows of their collarbones and frosting their bodies.

Apparently her feelings for Arthur had moved beyond the contact high of novelty and the allure of friendship to something more elemental. She didn't quite know what to do with it, other than explain it in terms like *biological imperative*, and *last adolescent gasp*, and *Jesus, woman, it's not like you didn't* know *you need to get laid*. She hadn't had a crush—a real crush—in years. *Years.* She had had sex with Eric Cole, yes; she had gone out with the FedEx guy. Forever ago, when Oneida was still a toddler, she dated the son of one of her mother's bridge club friends. She couldn't even remember his name. He had been the first boy she kissed after David Danger, and the comparison was so pathetic that it broke her heart all over again. It reminded her that David Danger existed, that he was somewhere in the world—somewhere else. She hadn't spoken to him since she came home from Jersey, back to Ruby Falls. She had been too embarrassed after her parents threatened to press charges against the House of D'Angier for hiring and sheltering a runaway minor, which she didn't think was even actionable or provable (she'd never been on the books) but had been the only concrete action they could think to take.

And there was Oneida. Whom she had no explanation for—at least, no explanation that would make sense to David. As Oneida became a larger part of her life, a greater responsibility and a greater joy, so David Danger began to fade, until Mona could only think of him fondly, remotely. He was crystallized with that summer, like Amy: kept whole and perfect and still as a photograph in her mind.

God, she thought; what if David Danger reared his head again? Amy (via Arthur) proved it was possible. Best not to think about it; best to concentrate on what was in front of her: Carrie's cake. Oneida. And Arthur.

She must have given up hope a little, she realized—only because her desire for the interloper in her life, once admitted to herself, was so irrationally virulent. But she wanted Arthur and she loved it. Whenever she saw him, or felt him near her, or made him laugh, she had to swallow giggles. She'd forgotten how wonderful this felt: how exciting, how childish and thrilling.

"Why are you grinning like that?" he asked.

"Because it's wedding day!" Mona said, which was true but not why she was smiling. It was Saturday morning. They were driving to Syracuse in the pouring rain to deliver Carrie's cake.

"Are you sure the cake's safe?" He kept glancing in the back of her station wagon, where she had removed the seats to make room for a plywood base and cake brace.

"Yes, I'm sure it's safe. Safe as houses."

"Why do they say that?"

"Because houses are safe."

"Compared to what?"

"Guns. Knives. Matches."

Arthur turned to look back again.

"Would you relax?" she said.

"I can't. It's like this giant baby made of sugar. It's too quiet. I have to check on it to make sure it's still OK."

"God help you if you ever have human children." Mona bit her lip. She shouldn't have said that; she just . . . shouldn't have. Arthur stared ahead at the straight gray road disappearing beneath them.

Mona's tongue felt clumsier every day, ever since that horrible conversation with Oneida about the boy at school, a conversation that had rendered her daughter effectively mute. Oneida didn't say hello when she came home in the afternoon, she did all her homework in her bedroom with the door shut—and locked; Mona had tried the knob—and ate dinner and breakfast in complete silence. Everyone at the Darby-Jones had noticed. Even Sherman, normally as sensitive as an old boot, asked Mona if her daughter was having trouble in school and, if so, was there anything she wanted him to keep an eye out for?

"I know things. I see things," he said, bristling his mustache. "These kids today are such boneheads. It's not hard to figure out what's really going on."

She was touched (and a little weirded out) by the offer, but declined. Spying on her daughter—she hoped it didn't come to that.

"I'm sorry," she said to Arthur. "That was thoughtless."

Arthur stared straight ahead. His voice was flat when he spoke.

"We didn't talk about kids, Amy and I," he said. "We should have before we got married, but I guess it turned out not to matter. She already had kids, anyway. Before she ever met me." Arthur looked out his window. "They were covered in fur and teeth and scales, and that's the way she loved them."

Mona chewed her lip.

"Kids," Arthur said, "always felt like something that would never happen to me."

"Tell me about it," Mona said, and they both laughed. She flicked on her windshield wipers to clear a few drops of rain.

"So where are we going?" Arthur asked.

"Landmark Hotel. Look in my bag." Mona jerked her head toward the well at his feet. "Big white envelope. When I accepted this job she handed me a bound, precisely detailed itinerary of who she needs to meet with and when, so that she personally inspects every single moving part of her wedding day *on* her wedding day. She gave me this a year ago. I shit you not."

Arthur flipped through the binder. The plastic slip-sheeted pages made a soft rustling sound that reminded Mona of high school, of research projects and science labs. Carrie was the kind of girl who thought no problem was so messy it couldn't be solved with the judicious application of Contact paper.

"There we are," he said, pointing at a line of text. "*10:45: Meet with representative of baking company to confirm receipt and approval of cake,* right between *10:40: Confirm via cell phone that caterers are en route* and *10:55: Inspect reception hall for appropriate placement of flowers relative to tables, chairs, serving stations, DJ booth, gift table, and wall sconces.*" He looked up. "Does she bring her own director's chair to the set?"

"Oh, she's definitely nuts. But a very organized and effective nuts—which means she's actually quite calm."

Thirty minutes later, when Arthur and Mona arrived at the once grand but now gothic and shabbily chic Landmark Hotel, Carrie Waters-soon-to-be-Kessler was many things.

Calm was not one of them.

Carrie was barely five feet tall with long black hair and a turned-up nose she had probably spent her entire life living down. She undercut her inherent adorableness with a borderline-obsessive, no-bullshit demeanor, and had endeared herself to Mona forever with her very first e-mail. *Ms. Mona Jones,* it said.

> *I'm getting married in October of next year. WhiteWedding-BakingCompany.com is the only website I have visited that did not have an embedded sound file playing "Here Comes the Bride" or some hideous clip-art of two doves drinking champagne. Let's talk about cake.*

She drove a converted hearse (she came from a family of funeral home owners) and brought both her fiancé and her basset hound to their first meeting. But on the morning of her meticulously thought-out and pre-planned wedding, Carrie Waters was sitting on the dais at the edge of the grand ballroom's dance floor in nothing but a sports bra and sweatpants, drinking a 40 of Miller High Life.

Mona knocked on the ballroom door even though she could see Carrie quite clearly, nursing her giant bottle of beer, which looked even bigger in her tiny hands. Her hair had already been done up in a high, heavy bun that tipped her head back thirty degrees. "Carrie?" Mona called. "Your cake has arrived."

"Fantastic!" Carrie shouted. She set the bottle down with a clunk. "Now if only the flowers and the photographer and my grandmother from Des Moines would get here, life would be *peaches.*"

The heavily gilded ballroom was fully decorated, with swags of goldenrod and blood orange across the head table, maple leaf and acorn centerpieces dotting the rest. She hadn't realized Carrie was going to go with an autumnal theme; it made the daisies on her cake seem out of season. Maybe that was the point. "I'm curious, Carrie—why daisies?" she said. "And where do you want them?"

"Mortician humor. As in, we're all pushing them up. Eventually. But you can push *those* daisies over to the right of the buffet table."

"Did you say the photographer's not here?" Arthur stepped past her. Carrie raised her head. "And you are?" she asked.

Arthur tugged on his black White Wedding Baking Company T-shirt. "Arthur. I belong, don't worry," he said.

"He's my assistant," Mona said. She rolled the cake forward on the room service cart the hotel had lent her. "I've gone big-time. Is here good, Carrie?" She had a strong, strong instinct for flight on this one, for many reasons: just because there weren't tears yet didn't mean there wouldn't be soon. Beer before noon was never a good sign, especially when one's wedding service was scheduled for twelve-thirty.

And there was also the element of location; she had delivered many cakes to the Landmark Hotel and every time it made her uncomfortable. The hotel was built in the early twentieth century and retained much of its original ornamentation; it was a registered historical landmark, and while Mona could appreciate the art deco details, the rich red woods and gold leaf, there were far too many ghosts lurking on the edge of her vision: of the hundreds of thousands of people who'd worked and slept and cried and danced here.

She was one of those ghosts. So was Amy.

Six months before they ran away to Ocean City, in December of their sophomore year, the Ruby Falls High winter semiformal was held at the Landmark Hotel. Mona made Amy come with her because she wanted to go and nobody had asked her, and a lot of people were going with their friends without dates. And Amy, miraculously, said *Sure, why not*? Every time she came back to the Landmark, she had to train her brain to keep quiet, not to think or remember too vividly, lest she lose herself: when she walked into the lobby, and into the ballroom, and back and forth across the majestically threadbare carpets, Mona couldn't help but imagine the myriad other directions her life might have taken, had she and Amy not come to the dance that night. Her memories were thicker than cold fog, in stereo and Technicolor; her other futures hid in the shadows, the ghosts of lives she hadn't lived.

Carrie Waters stood and walked to Arthur, holding out her hand for him to shake.

"Carrie," she said. "Pleased to meet you. And yes, I am drinking very cheap beer, very early on my wedding day. And I have forbidden anyone to come talk to me because the flowers are going to be late and my Nonna is stuck at motherfucking O'Hare and the photographer actually had the stones to call me this morning—*this morning*—and tell me he couldn't make it and his normal pinch hitter is already booked. The one thing I didn't think to plan for. No backup for my photographer. *No backup*." She shook her tiny fist at the sky.

Mona spun the cake to face her. "But you have daisies!" she said.

Carrie closed her eyes and sighed. "It's lovely, Mona," she said. "It's the one thing that's perfect today. Thank you."

"You're welcome," Mona said, and thought, *So that means you can pay me. Anytime!* She clasped her hands and grinned at Arthur, who appeared deep in thought. She should have discussed exit strategies with him in the car; she should have explained that cakes were to be dropped off and bakers were to flee before the chaos. She rolled her eyes toward the door.

Arthur shook his head.

What do you mean, no? she mouthed.

"I think I can help," he said. "I'm a photographer."

Carrie, who'd been staring dreamily at the cake, choked. "Get *out*," she said.

"My cameras are in the car. I brought them thinking I might—or rather, *you* might—let me take some pictures for my portfolio. And now that your other photographer has left you in the lurch—"

"Mona." Carrie handed her the beer. "Could you take this please?"

"Sure," Mona said, stunned numb. The nagging urge to leave, to leave quickly, stilled long enough for her to pay full attention to what was going on. What the hell did Arthur think he was doing? This wasn't his responsibility, this wasn't his—job. Though Carrie would probably pay him for it—but why would he—were people really this thoughtful? Was *Arthur* this thoughtful?

"I'm sorry I don't have my portfolio or anything, but I've shot a few weddings for family members. I have my digital, but I also have my old school camera with film, too, which I think takes nicer pictures, frankly—whatever you're comfortable paying me, even if it's just dinner. Or cake." Arthur was rambling.

Mona's heart flickered in her chest, as if warmer than it had been a moment ago. Arthur was good. Arthur was decent. Arthur wanted to help. This was what Amy must have seen in him and loved; she was happy that Amy had had someone like this in her life, someone kind, if only for a while.

Carrie, beaming, stood before a towering Arthur with her tiny hands on her tiny hips. She crooked her finger. "Come closer," she said. "Bring it down to earth, Bird."

Arthur laughed awkwardly. Then he bent forward, arms out for what Mona assumed would be a grateful hug.

But it wasn't. Carrie shot up on her toes and plastered her mouth over Arthur's and kissed him so deeply that Mona felt a rush of heat ten feet away. The rush was quickly followed by a surge of jealousy that nearly knocked her off her feet—because Arthur kissed her back. Only a little, once he'd apparently gotten over the shock—and here Mona wondered if he felt it was only polite—but his chin tipped down as she pulled away like he wasn't ready for her to go.

"Name your price," Carrie said, and wobbled to the exit. "I've got a dress to pour myself into. I'll send a bridesmaid when I'm ready for my close-up."

The ballroom door swung shut behind her. Arthur and Mona, alone, saw one another for what felt like the first time. Mona couldn't imagine what she looked like to him, only knew that her eyes were wide and she still clutched a giant bottle of High Life in one hand. Arthur was bright pink, his hair, usually parted and pushed back, was mussed across his forehead. She saw panic and pleasure on his face. She was even more aware of his body than she had been during her tenure as Florence Nightingale—painfully aware of the shattered chest beneath his shirt. The soft curve of his jaw arcing up toward his ears, which were a little big and stuck out; the sloping bulb of his nose and the leonine trough leading to his lips, now parted for breath. She wondered if it was tasteless to want him. She decided she didn't care. Amy wouldn't have cared, she told herself. If Mona were the dead one, Amy wouldn't have given it a second thought.

But I'm not Amy.

Mona tipped the bottle straight up against her lips and polished it off in one long, violent gulp.

15 ❧ Junk

Eugene had achieved awesome. Lost his effing mind and never wanted it back. When he peeled off his too-tight jeans before falling into bed late Friday night, he discovered a folded piece of paper in one of his pockets—a note from Oneida, a college-ruled reminder of places her hands had been.

The note said:

> Hey—
> I think the rest of our history group is out, but you should come over tomorrow to work on our project. 10 a.m. My mom will be gone by then.
>
> O

He read it a few times until he was absolutely sure he knew what she meant when she said *work on our project*, and then, instead of going to sleep like every part of his body save for a few choice bits was insisting, Eugene raided his parents' music collection. The pressure of selecting the perfect make-out score focused his attention to a fine white edge, which immediately blurred and gravitated toward the greatest hits of Journey and Chicago—and Foreigner. Foreigner was one of those bands he didn't know much about, other than that they were cheesy. Mockable. But there was something about the *idea* of Foreigner that spoke to him, something intriguing. The track list was enticing. Yes, he thought, it *is* Urgent. I *have* been Waiting for a Girl Like You.

He rode his bike over to the Darby-Jones Saturday morning in the pouring rain. It wasn't explicitly stated in Oneida's note that he wait for her mother to leave, but Eugene hid in the trees until a blue station wagon creaked down the drive. He recognized the woman behind the wheel from their first group meeting, however many weeks ago, as her mother. Did that make the guy in the passenger seat her father? He'd gotten the impression that Oneida didn't have a father, other than in the biological sense.

His curiosity, mixed with lethal levels of anticipation, made him impervious to the cold and wet, so that when he stepped inside the Darby-Jones, he barely noticed the lake dripping out of his hair, off his sweatshirt, weighing his jeans down, spreading across the checked tile floor, and making his sneakers squeak. All he saw was Oneida, wearing jeans and a blue and green striped shirt with a V-neck that didn't plunge quite as low as he would have liked, telling him to take off his shoes and come back to the kitchen.

His shoeless feet were freezing. The kitchen, thank God, was much warmer than the front hall, but the items spread neatly across the kitchen table made his gut ice over: a stack of CDs and an old boom box, several large coffee table books about John Lennon and the Beatles, and two notebooks open to clean white pages, a blue uncapped pen laid neatly beside each one. Eugene didn't understand. He had been positive, *positive*, that he knew what she was talking about. Was he crazy? How was he *supposed* to interpret a note jammed down the front of his jeans?

"Have a seat," Oneida said cheerily. She tipped a teakettle over two mismatched mugs, and the smell of hot chocolate hit his nostrils a second later.

"I—sure." Eugene sat in one of the chairs and picked up the blue pen, defeated. He started to shiver, and curled his ice-cube toes. Oneida plunked a mug in front of him that said ASK ME ABOUT MY SMALL BUSINESS LOAN FROM CAYUGA COUNTY BANK, LLC in slanted blue letters.

"Marshmallow?" she asked, settling into the chair opposite him.

It wouldn't have been so painful, Eugene decided, if Oneida didn't look so damn gorgeous. She'd pulled her hair back in a ponytail, and it framed her face the way it had that day she came over unannounced;

her cheeks were flushed, though how she could be warm enough to flush in this godforsaken tomb of a house, Eugene couldn't fathom. She pulled open the top of a bag of giant marshmallows.

"Ever play chubby bunnies?"

"What?" he asked.

"Chubby bunnies," she said. "It's a game."

A . . . game? *Oh, here we go*, he thought. *Yes, please.*

"I learned how to do it in Brownies," she said, and handed him a single marshmallow.

"Dirty bitches," he said, and Oneida looked up, confused, and he stuffed the marshmallow in his mouth before she could ask him to explain what he meant by that.

"Don't chew it!" she said. "Hold it in your mouth and try to say *chubby bunnies.*"

"Wha?" He swallowed some spit. "Hubby unnies."

Oneida giggled. She passed him another marshmallow and he popped it in his mouth.

"Ubby unnies," he said, and rolled his eyes, because his mouth was full of sugar and spit and it was kind of disgusting but it was also kind of hysterical. "Oo ry it!" he said, pointing at Oneida, who understood, if not his actual words, that he'd thrown down his gauntlet. She popped three marshmallows between her lips and said, quite clearly, "Chubby bunnies."

"Ur eating," he said.

"Not cheating," she said, and added another marshmallow.

"Ess oo ar."

Oneida was giggling so hard she was rocking back and forth in her chair, shoulders shaking, not making a sound. Eugene, beginning to grasp the reassuring truth of the situation—that Oneida had just as much interest in working on their history project as he did—felt warm again.

And then, for no apparent reason, Oneida whipped a marshmallow at him. It caromed off his forehead with a powdery *fwop* and plonked into his hot chocolate.

Eugene stared at the bobbing marshmallow for a stunned second and swallowed his mouthful of marshmallow. Oneida's face, when he looked up, stunned him anew. She was far too happy to be the result of looking at him: smiling with her entire face, glasses winking in the light, glowing like a tiny sun. It was impossible, Eugene thought, unless Oneida was some kind of mirror, one that reflected the nameless warm knot that had lodged in his chest, gave it a nose and eyes and a wide crescent of a mouth, so that he could see what he felt like, albeit on the face of another person. She swallowed her mouthful of marshmallow neatly.

He placed both palms flat on his side of the table and leaned forward; as his dutiful reflection, Oneida followed suit. They met in the middle. He heard, quite clearly and almost certainly only in his own head, the slow synth intro of a Foreigner song, sweet, warm, and sonorous, and not at all ironic.

⁂

Heaven was a couch at the Darby-Jones. It was old and ratty, with more than a few unruly springs and worn patches; wide enough and long enough for two people to lie side by side or some variation thereof, provided those two people were Eugene Wendell and Oneida Jones. It was less than three feet from the stereo speakers gently oozing "Waiting for a Girl Like You" on single-track repeat, secluded in the den at the rear of the house. It was a world unto itself, and Eugene, who generally found the concept of eternity terrifying, finally understood the appeal of life without end.

The first thing Oneida said, after they'd relocated from the secular kitchen to the divine couch, was that he was the only person she'd ever kissed. "With tongue, I mean. And with specific, you know, *intent*," she said. Eugene was getting a little better at recovering from the various curveballs Oneida pitched at him: he blinked, nodded, and said that he had technically first-kissed a girl at a family reunion, but he was five so it didn't count.

"Also, you were related to her," Oneida said, brows raised.

"No! No, I mean, I was at a family reunion, but it was in a big park and she was with another group at the pavilion next to ours."

"Yeah, sure." And she took off her shirt.

She took off her shirt and put it back on several times during the afternoon, though the only reason she put it back on, she admitted, was so she could take it off again. "Your eyes get so huge," she said. "A little bigger every time."

They spent a cursory thirty minutes devising a plan for their group project presentation, which was due the following Thursday. It involved two index cards' worth of biographical information on their respective Beatles, all taken from the same book, and a willful decision to crash and burn in all other aspects of the assignment, grades be damned.

"Dreyer can't *really* expect us to regroup after the hurt I put on Lu's guitar," he said.

"That was awesome," she said.

"You're welcome."

She snuggled in closer to his side, tangling her cold bare feet with his own. The sun was setting, filling the room with harsh rays alive with dust. The Darby-Jones, the house itself, ate time. How long had he been here? Long enough for the rain to stop and the sun to come out, cross the sky, and begin to set; long enough to forget he was ever anyone other than Oneida Jones's boyfriend Eugene. Wendy, who had truly only existed long enough to murder a guitar, was dead.

"Where did the bottle come from?"

"Hm?"

"The green bottle. That you hung outside my window."

"Oh, that." He swallowed. "Estate sale. My dad likes to go to estate auctions and buy cool junk."

"He's the painter, right?"

Sort of. A tiny chill tickled his spine. He considered the lie of omission he was about to tell. The intense desire, felt so strongly the other day, to tell her the truth—to tell her everything—was gone, leaving nothing but a faint, terrifying memory of having ever been that close to spilling the Wendell guts. After last night—after what Astor told him—

God, *especially* after last night.

"It's a hobby," he said.

"So who died?"

"What?"

She tented her elbows across his chest and propped her chin on her hands. "Who died so that your dad could buy the bottle?"

"Some old guy named Joe."

"And Joe was a big bottle collector?"

"Joe collected . . . all kinds of crap."

"So what else did your dad get from Joe?"

Eugene hated this conversation profoundly. He didn't think she was consciously badgering him—she was grinning, and her questions were chirps more than anything—but it felt like an interrogation. Then again, everything felt like an interrogation when you had something to hide. He shifted beneath her, tried to get comfortable, but what had felt warm and thrilling earlier was now only a dead weight pressing against his rib cage. He was afraid to lie to her. He was more afraid of the complicated half-truths he knew he would tell her instead.

The night before, when Eugene had been in the happy fog of early Christmas in October, but before he found the note and before his thoughts turned to Foreigner, Astor had asked him to help move boxes out of the studio. Once inside, he'd nudged his son, pointed to the battered suitcase on his desk, and asked if he could guess what all that junk was for.

"Uh . . . what junk?" Eugene asked, reminding himself that he'd never seen the suitcase before in his life.

"Open it." Astor propped his hands on his hips and grinned. "Tell me what you think."

So he opened it and was greeted by the familiar nest of paper and plastic and glass: tiny ceramic cups and pipes, curlicues of metal, and stacked folios, funky and musty with age.

"This is it, Gene."

Astor walked over to his bookshelf while Eugene gamely poked through random crap he'd already poked through several times before. He rubbed his index finger against the blue velvet and thought of Oneida and smiled.

"This is beyond forgery. This is creation, authentic creation and misdirection. This could be my masterpiece. Look at this." He thrust a book in Eugene's face, pages splayed with his thumb and first finger, open to a picture of a small wooden box that looked like a much fancier version of the shitty dioramas Eugene had made for book reports in third grade: a paper cutout of a hotel, under glass, amid a forest of spindly trees. There was a lot of glitter.

He didn't quite know what to do with his father, who had never been this excited about any of the forgeries before; had never told Eugene so much before, never shown him anything in such an early stage. He felt honored and, frankly, more than a little freaked out to see Astor, King of Cool, flip his shit.

"This guy, Joseph Cornell—total wackjob, antisocial—kind of bounced from the surrealists to the abstract expressionists until the pop artists figured out he'd scooped them by about thirty years. Strange, strange guy. Lived with his mother his whole life in the same house in Queens, worked on everything in the basement, which was just . . . Christ, it must have been *packed* with shit just like this. He made intricate shadow boxes and collected every tiny bit of junk he could get his hands on, thinking someday he'd use it. Major obsessive-compulsive. Loved ballerinas and kids and perfect pretty girls he couldn't touch."

Eugene stepped back, clear of Astor's pinwheeling gesticulations.

"This suitcase—all this junk—this belonged to him."

"How do you—" Eugene started to ask.

"Terry found it. *At a flea market.* Downstate. The schmuck seller didn't have a clue what it was, but Terry knew right away. C'mere, look." Astor hustled Eugene over and closed the lid of the suitcase, revealing a tarnished brass plate that read J. CORNELL. "Seller thought the case was the find; you know, what with the lucrative antique-luggage-enthusiast market today." Astor crowed. "Cornell never *went* anywhere in his life, so the case is in perfect condition, of course. There's an entire folder in there, photographs, clippings, all devoted to Rose Hobart, who was this obscure silent movie actress Cornell adored. There's only so much I'm prepared to take on coincidence, you know, before I start calling it evidence." Astor actually giggled, and Eugene, swept up now, followed suit. "It's perfect—it's pure profit, minus the thirty bucks Terry already paid; and Cornell's famous enough to fetch cash but obscure enough to avoid major scrutiny, I mean, I'm not passing off an undiscovered *Rembrandt*, right? It's going to be a challenge, for sure; I'm not the most skilled collagist in the world, but really, how hard can it be? To hit the right notes, to make people see what they want to see?"

Astor took a deep breath and let it out slowly, looking sideways at his son and smiling.

"I'm a little excited," he said.

"So you're going to—"

"Make a real fake."

Eugene felt like he was airborne. He didn't know what to say. "That's so cool," when he finally managed to get it out, was embarrassingly inadequate.

"It's so *fucking* cool, is what it is," Astor said, eyes bright. "I might get something *into* a museum instead of *out*." He laughed again, closed his eyes, and shook his head, and Eugene wondered, for the very first time, if his father was sick and tired of his life's work; if he saw this as his final score, his last chance to make a mark before getting out and going legit. The explosion of excitement came from nowhere and vanished just as quickly, and in the too-quiet studio left behind, Eugene felt his father's fatigue, his worry, and his hope for an end. Astor didn't see himself as a superhero, or at least he didn't anymore, and he wanted Eugene to know.

"I know your life . . . our life, really"—Astor inhaled—"has been odd."

And amazing. It has been so amazing, Eugene wanted to say, but couldn't make himself.

"It wasn't fair, to you or to Patricia. You know . . . I worry—I worry about the damage—the stress it must have put on you. I want you to understand that I—"

Eugene's throat tickled. "Is this about the guitar?" he said. "Because that had nothing to do with—anything, really, and I won't do it again. I have too much respect for guitars. It was just, in that one instance, I was probably doing the guitar a fav—"

Astor held up his hand. "It's time," he said. "To bow out with a bang."

Then I won't ruin it, Eugene had thought, even though a part of him died right then, in the studio with his father. *I won't ruin it for you, I won't I won't I won't.*

To Oneida, he said, "Just junk. Nothing too exciting."

"Well . . . I thought the bottle was neat." She turned her head, pressing her ear to his sternum. "It's gotta be an antique, right? Kind of reminded me of the weird glass stuff Bert has. She collects these little glass slippers, like, fancy heels and boots made of bright purple and blue and green glass. Makes her place look like the closet of a gnome drag queen."

Eugene laughed a little too hard, he was so relieved to be heading toward another conversation entirely.

"Who's Bert?" he asked.

"An old crone." She sighed. "She's lived in the attic my entire life. My mom's whole life too."

"No way. The Darby-Jones has a crazy lady in the attic? She's gonna burn this mother down if you don't treat her right."

Oneida didn't laugh.

She sat upright, her face still and her eyes slightly narrowed, and stared at the dark television across from the couch. She opened her mouth once, thought better about whatever she was about to say, and closed it again. The relief Eugene had felt upon leaving the subject of the green glass bottle receded slightly.

"Do you want to . . . tell me about it?"

She turned toward him sharply. "Tell you what?"

"Bert freaks you out." Eugene pulled himself up on his elbows. "It's kind of obvious. Does she, like, lure kids up there with sweets and leave the bones?"

Again, she didn't laugh. It may have been the result of hours of investigating the inside of her mouth, but Eugene felt a strange possessiveness overcome him: why didn't she want to tell him? It was his right to know, after all, as her boyfriend, what made her worry her lower lip like that. "Hey," he said. "Tell me."

"Do you want a blow job?" she asked.

At first Eugene thought he'd had a stroke, because the words that he thought came out of Oneida's mouth were *do you* followed by *want a blow job,* something he didn't think he'd ever hear issue from an actual girl's mouth when he was the only male in the room. Then Oneida laughed at him, said something about how his eyes were the biggest she'd seen all afternoon, and Eugene regained partial control of his speech.

"Yes, please," he squeaked.

Oneida, thank God, didn't laugh at that; but she did slide down the couch *(oh God this was going to happen)* and push up the bottom of his shirt (*oh shit oh shit*) and kiss him right below his belly button, a tiny pressure like a damp fingertip, surprisingly cool against his warm skin, which effectively curtailed all cogent higher-level thought on Eugene's part. Which was probably a good thing, considering Oneida's mother chose that moment to enter the room.

16 ⁓ Past and Present

Mona broke.

Information crashed into her in waves—music—couch—above the back, Oneida's head—a face, the face of a boy, slightly recognizable—in her kitchen, weeks ago—and then she broke: broke like a glass jar full of beads, a crack and explosion of glass, her innards pouring out like colored sand, too fast and too various to scoop back together before they were everywhere, irretrievable, lost under furniture and baseboards forever.

All this, Mona processed in less than a second. Her mouth couldn't keep up.

"*Foreigner*?" she shouted.

Oneida flew back and clutched the arm of the couch, rigid and redder than Mona had ever seen her. The boy (pants still fastened, thank God for that) gave an inarticulate cry and spun to the floor, cracking his skull on the coffee table in the process. He popped up, an adrenalized gopher, and just as suddenly went down again, clutching his head in mute pain. Mona would have laughed if she had been outside her body, if she had been watching this from the ceiling or on television: if it had been a pretend life in a story. But it was hers. It was her only life.

"I think I'm bleeding," said the boy on the floor. His voice cracked.

"Arthur," Mona said. "Please help."

Arthur put his hand on her shoulder, and she remembered how it had felt, earlier, at Carrie now-Kessler's reception, when Arthur touched her. "I'll take him upstairs," he whispered. "For a bandage." Her mouth and brain were still in the process of syncing, so she nodded, and Arthur went to the boy's side and helped him up and out of the room.

Oneida hadn't moved. She crouched, tense as a rabbit, and blinked rapidly.

Mona's throat filled. "I'm going to turn off the music."

She coughed. Oneida didn't speak.

Mona pressed the power button on the stereo and Foreigner died mid-warble. The silence that followed was flat and cold.

"I'm not mad at you," Mona said.

Oneida still didn't speak, or move, or do anything other than blink.

"I'm not mad at you at all," she repeated. This can't be right, she thought; this can't be how to have this conversation. There must be a better way. Maybe if she sat down on the couch beside her daughter, her brilliant daughter, and held her hand and spoke perfect platitudes in gentle tones; that would be the way. She tried to remember how her mother had talked to her. What had she said? How had she said it? Had they ever sat down over tea and cookies and talked about—men? Sex? She didn't think so. Everything she remembered learning, she'd learned from magazines. Television. Or Amy.

"I'm afraid for you," Mona said again, and covered her mouth with her hand.

"The hell is that supposed to mean?" Oneida's little-kid voice wobbled.

Mona tried sitting beside her on the couch. Her daughter leaned away.

"It means I'm afraid of what you don't understand." She swallowed. "I'm worried—about what you don't know and how you'll come to know it."

Oneida shook her head slowly and rolled her eyes like this was the most ludicrous conversation she'd ever been forced to have.

"I don't want you to get hurt," Mona said. Finally, words that felt right. "Life hurts, and I want you to know how to protect yourself." From all the ways there are to *be* hurt, she thought, but couldn't quite say. *The people you love will hurt you worst of all.*

Oneida was still shaking her head. "I am not *you.*"

The crack through Mona's heart widened. "What do you mean?"

"A, I'm not stupid. And B, I'm not a slut."

Mona raised her hand.

She was as shocked to see it hovering in the air as Oneida was—palm out, flat and tilted and aimed for her daughter's cheek—and it stayed there, in the air between them, frozen in space by the realization of everything that it implied. Mona would have cried in shame if her mouth hadn't been so dry. Oneida looked at her with fear and pain and regret. She drew back against the couch, deeper into the cushions.

Mona tucked both hands against her sides.

"If that's what you think of me"—she inhaled—"that's your problem. I have done nothing but love you your entire life."

Oneida stood up.

"Good for you," she said, and walked out of the den.

Mona sat and listened to Oneida's feet pounding up the stairs, and finally she rose and followed, heavy and slow—because she did *not* want to talk to her daughter anymore. Not about this. Not today. Today had been a day of visions from the past and from strange, impossible futures; she had swum in the latter and dreamed selfish dreams. She had seen Arthur at work, happy. They had shared a piece of cake.

But now Oneida was reminding her of other things—things that had been more present to her today than in years—things Mona would have preferred to forget. Things she had concealed from her daughter for a lifetime. How much Oneida suspected, Mona couldn't say, but she did know she resented Oneida's desire for the truth. She resented it the way she resented Oneida's having to grow up at all, as a force beyond her control and a reminder that she had yet to accept the only unmitigated truth in life: that everything changes and everything ends.

Why today? Why any day? she thought. She was close enough to the top of the stairs to see her daughter disappear into her bedroom and slam the door behind her.

"Oneida!" Mona called.

Silence bounced back.

"Apologize to me," Mona said.

Still: silence. Mona tried the doorknob but it was immobile in her hand. Out of sheer frustration and unhappiness, she slammed her fist against the door and it rattled and she hated herself for having done it but she had to. She had to feel an object move beneath her.

"Pardon me," said a voice she didn't recognize. "May I talk to you for a moment?"

It was the boy from downstairs. She remembered a few weeks ago—when Oneida had had that group meeting—he had been there. He was very tall and very thin and his hair was dark. There was nothing about him that made sense to Mona. He was too young. He was too average. Boring, even. He had a strange little scar running through his eyebrow, but other than that—*Why this one, Oneida? Why this boy?* Did she have *no* idea how special she was?

He held out his hand. "My name is Eugene," he said. He didn't look at her when he spoke. "I'm sorry we had to meet under such—uh, awkward circumstances. So I'm thinking, How can I make it up to Oneida's mother? You know?"

Mona shook his hand cautiously. "I don't know," she said. "How can you?" She saw Arthur down the hall, in his doorway, watching. He caught her eye.

"Oneida and me, we have this—project. School project. We have to, like, make a piece of art in the style of a famous artist and write an essay or something about it, and our guy is this weirdo named Joseph"—he looked back at Arthur, who nodded—"Joseph Cornell. He made freaky little collages and, like, Arthur here, I think he could be a tremendous help."

"How does that make up for what happened here?" Mona asked.

"It would give you a chance to spend some time with me and I can prove I'm, like . . . not an asshole."

Mona had to hand it to him; he had cojones. Too young, too average, but no shortage of confidence or ego. He grinned at her—no shortage of teeth, either. Her heart skipped in her chest. She could dictate the terms of the afternoon; she would be present. It would be a peace offering, if Oneida could be bothered to recognize it as such. And Mona knew she couldn't protect her daughter forever, from the world outside or the secrets within. Was it wrong to use the outside world as a distraction—to buy Mona a little time and a few of her daughter's good graces? *Have your boyfriend today, Oneida,* she thought, *and tomorrow I'll tell you what you really want to know.*

Maybe not tomorrow. Maybe next week.

"That would be OK with me," she said. "Oneida, what do you think?" She nodded at the closed door, which opened violently.

"What the hell are you doing?" Oneida thrust her head out.

"Me?" Mona asked.

"*Him.*" Oneida jerked her thumb at the boy and hissed, "Are you freaking insane?"

"No," he said. "I'd really like to get to know your mom and her boyfriend."

"We're not—" Mona started, before realizing she didn't really know how to finish that sentence.

"Sorry." Eugene held up his hands. "Didn't mean to presume."

Mona's head ached. "I think you should go now," she said.

The boy nodded, reminding Mona of a pubescent ostrich. She examined him again, tried to imagine what Oneida was drawn to: his bare, bony feet; his clothes, yards of extra fabric flapping around limbs like Tinker Toys; that little scar over his eyebrow? From a past piercing gone horribly awry? His eyes were almost black and thickly lashed. She had known boys like him in high school: boys whose bodies grew too fast for their brains, who spent the bulk of their teenage years masturbating because they hadn't yet figured out how to love someone else as much as they loved themselves. Eric Cole had been like that. He had never figured it out, but not because Mona hadn't tried to help.

"Come by tomorrow at noon," Mona told him.

"This is going to be fun," Oneida said. Then she shut her door with a thud.

⁂

Had this all been the same day? Had everything that just happened occurred in the space of the same twenty-four hours?

Some days expand, Mona thought; their seams stretch and they hold more than a day's worth of time. More than a day's worth of memories old and new. Falling into a time warp would explain why she was so exhausted; why she was so nervous about what was going to happen next. Why she was so excited. She thought about pouring herself a cup of coffee but realized she was nuts, today had *not* been a coffee day, and poured herself a juice glass of gin instead.

The kitchen was dark and claustrophobic and Mona didn't think she'd survive if Anna should show up and ask what the hell was going on, she heard shouting earlier—so she took her gin into the den and curled up on the couch. She turned on the stereo for the company of sound and sipped her drink in the dark, and remembered both the recent and the distant past, which had overlapped today in ways Mona didn't think were strictly kosher with the space-time continuum. Different pieces of her life folded and bent back, reached across time and touched like origami.

She didn't think the weddings of people you didn't really know should be fun at all, let alone *that* fun. Maybe it was the fact that every one of Carrie now-Kessler's guests seemed to know the story of the Magical Photographer Savior and that Mona was responsible for delivering both the cake *and* him. Maybe it was because Carrie and her husband, Charlie, a funeral director in training (apparently the industry had a high rate of intermarriage), adored each other plainly and perfectly. Maybe it was the food (delicious), maybe it was the cake (not to be overly pleased with herself but: divine), and maybe it was the music (a live nine-piece funk band that practically tore the gilt off the walls).

Don't kid yourself, kiddo. It was the company.

Arthur Rook was alive again. Mona, who had really only known him two weeks, had been unprepared to meet this version of him. He smiled easily and laughed often and gave of himself in a way that was absolute and charming. He listened to Carrie's ideas, orchestrated formal photos that were extremely well composed, and wove in and out of the day's activities, cautious not to miss a single moment, no matter how small. In the words of his thesis adviser, *photojournalistically interesting yet formally sound,* Arthur told her, one brow arched, when she complimented him on his style later. He was professional and accessible and involved, and Mona, who wasn't a bad businesswoman herself, saw an opportunity to align more than their bodies.

"Arthur," she said, handing him a plate of food from the buffet, "would you go into business with me?"

He took the plate and balanced it on his knees. They were alone in the ballroom lobby, in a small sitting area to the right of the grand staircase. He smiled at her and took a bite of roast beef.

"I'm going to take that as a yes," she said.

The volume of the band spiked as a guest opened the ballroom door.

"You'd have to change the name on the shirts."

"White Wedding stays. It weeds out the humorless couples."

Arthur swallowed. "White Wedding Baking and Photography is a bit . . . cumbersome. It's a lot to say—or to print on a business card or T-shirt."

"I'm serious," Mona said. "Not about the name—well, I *am* serious about the name—but I meant the offer. Think about it."

Arthur speared another piece of roast on his fork. He jiggled it over the plate and then set it back down. He turned to Mona. "Do you want to dance?" he said.

Arthur couldn't have known that Ben Tennant, chaperoning the Ruby Falls Winter Semiformal, had sat in that exact same chair sixteen years earlier and asked her the same question, or that Mona would respond to both of the men Amy loved, sixteen years apart, with the same words.

"Are you sure?"

Arthur cocked his head toward the ballroom. "It's the Bee Gees," he said. "I'm going to dance regardless. But I'll look like less of an idiot if you're dancing with me."

Ben had answered *Of course—for old times' sake!* So history isn't repeating itself, Mona thought, relieved. *Not completely.* She remembered wondering, at fifteen, if Ben was being irreverent or if he actually *was* referring to the old times they'd shared: when she was thirteen and he was nearly twenty-five, when he made her popular just by living in her house, and when her best friend thought she loved him. And in these new times, when her best friend probably *still* loved him. Mona wasn't in the Drama Club, but Amy was, head of the tech crew, and Mona knew she interacted with Ben Tennant all the time: director to head of tech, going over set changes and lighting and sound cues. The less Amy talked about something, the more important it was to her, and, since that one afternoon years ago, she had never mentioned Ben Tennant again.

Ever.

Screw it, Mona thought. She took Arthur's hand, and they stepped on the parquet dance floor together, as the band played a funked-up version of "How Can You Mend a Broken Heart?" And Arthur was right: he danced like he couldn't help himself. He put one hand on her back and she wrapped both of hers around his neck. While she faced him, the happy photographer was all Mona knew. But when he spun her out the length of his arm, she saw ghosts in the dark corners of the ballroom. In the corner by the chocolate fountain she saw the other Arthur, blank-eyed and bleeding grief. Beyond the last row of dining tables she saw Amy—fifteen, wearing a plain black dress, her hair in a messy ponytail like she'd just pulled it back—her head turning as she searched for someone. Mona saw a much older Amy with another Arthur as they danced close together, as they surely must have. And there, to the right of the band, was an Amy Mona had never known, reaching for a wire live with electrons, moments before the thoughtless touch that would make her body dance for the last time.

She held Arthur closer because she was afraid of what she would see the next time he let her go. So they danced and Mona almost forgot everything. Everything that had happened since the night Ben Tennant asked her to dance. Everything she had done. Everyone she had lost. And gained—and when Mona realized she had almost forgotten her daughter, she stumbled. Arthur caught her.

"You're a slippery one," he said, and she thought, *Everything could still happen. Every choice could still be made. Every future could still come to pass.*

They had talked about the future, she and Ben—sixteen years ago, right before he asked her to dance, Ben and Mona were talking, just talking, out in the lobby. Mona had been bored silly by the semiformal—the food was disgusting, and the music was lame, and Amy was bitching with Chuck Wozniak about all the sets they'd need for *Mame*—so she had left the ballroom and was sitting by herself in a deep blue velvet high-backed chair in the ballroom lobby to the right of the grand staircase, the exact same chair she would sit in with Arthur Rook half a lifetime later. She was wearing a kelly green dress that made her feel like she was sixteen, at least. Her shoes were off, but her toes still hurt. She rubbed her bare feet together and sighed because she was utterly, inescapably, soul-crushingly bored.

And then Ben passed by, a short glass filled with amber liquid in one hand. He must have run over to the bar on the other side of the lobby. "Desdemona Jones!" he hailed. "How are things at the old Darby-J?"

Her conversation with Ben replayed for Mona in fuzzy loops of spectral audio for the rest of the Waters-Kessler reception. No matter how hard she tried to lose herself in the present, she heard herself gossiping in the past with Ben: about his life, about the other tenants he'd known when he still lived at the Darby-Jones.

Ben had asked, *How are you?*

Honestly?

Carrie and Charlie hugged her and Arthur before rushing out to start the rest of their lives.

Honestly.

Arthur passed her a small paper plate with a slice of cake on it. "I grabbed us a piece for the road," he said. "They're packing everything up, closing it down. This is now an ex-wedding."

I'm bored, she had said. *I'm bored as shit, Ben.*

Ben had smiled his beautiful smile at her and said *I promise you it gets so much better than this. I promise you the future—your future—will be interesting.*

She had believed him. Mona, at fifteen, believed him absolutely—believed him enough to blush and grin, flattered beyond words that Ben Tennant—the famous, the talented and brilliant and Hollywood- and Broadway-bound Ben Tennant, who could come and go from Ruby Falls as he pleased, who had seen other parts of the world and would see more—could see into her future. Could see that it was interesting.

Then he asked her to dance.

Are you sure?

Of course—for old times' sake!

And then Amy—who Mona hadn't even noticed approaching across the lobby—hurled her purse at Mona's head, opened her mouth to say something but didn't, and ran away. Actually *ran*, staggering on her heels so badly that Mona thought she was going to snap her ankle or wipe out face-first—but no: Amy's will was iron, no matter how wildly she pinwheeled her arms, she would right herself or be damned. Ben Tennant dropped his empty glass on the carpet and followed, calling out for her to slow down, Amy, calm down—wait.

And Mona just sat there and watched Ben Tennant run after her friend, around the corner, down the hall of the Landmark Hotel. She looked down at her hands and knew, intuitively, that the futures of other people were solidifying all around her. Her presence was neither required nor wanted. She picked up Amy's purse and went back into the ballroom, where she half-listened to Chuck and his nerd buddies quote lines from *Wayne's World* at each other for about an hour. When Amy returned, her cheeks were pink with tears. She took her purse when Mona handed it to her and she said, *I'm so ready to get out of here*, and Mona couldn't agree more, so they left.

Amy Henderson had made all the choices she was ever going to make. There were no more futures available to her. But for Mona, everything could still happen. Every choice could still be made, and every future could still come to pass.

And here Mona sat. She tossed back the last of the gin and realized that Arthur was standing in the doorway.

"Foreigner?" He smiled.

Mona had turned on the stereo just so she didn't have to sit in the dark, in the quiet, alone. She hadn't even been listening before now, but sure enough, "Cold as Ice" was oozing out of the giant speakers that had been in the den her entire life, that were older than Mona.

"The kid must not have taken his CD when he left," she said. "Pretty sure I don't own any Foreigner." She blinked. "I'm drinking gin alone in the dark, listening to Foreigner. How . . . did I get here?"

You know exactly how you got here, Jones, she thought. *Where you go* from *here . . . that's the question worth asking.*

"I hope you don't mind," Arthur said, "that I offered to help them."

She shook her head. "You're a good person." She raised her empty glass. "Cheers."

He sat on one end of the couch and patted the tops of his thighs. Grinning, she stretched her legs out across his lap.

"My feet might smell."

"I thought female feet didn't smell."

"That's a myth."

"Myth? Oh, myth!"

"Yeth?" Mona laughed. "Sweet mother, you *are* a dork."

"And you're not alone," Arthur said, cupping her bare feet in his hand.

"Well." Mona wiggled her toes. "Not *anymore*."

She felt the world tilt and caught her breath. Until she said the words, she hadn't known—despite Anna and Sherman and Bert, despite her daughter—how very alone she'd been; or how very frightened she was now of the moment, closer than ever, when she would have to be alone again.

17 ⌒ *Untitled (Satellite)*

"Like this," Eugene said, holding Astor's book like a kindergarten teacher, one hand propping the pages open, the other pointing at the sparkly castle diorama captioned *Untitled (Pink Palace)*. Eugene never got that—calling a work *untitled* and then giving it a title anyway. It seemed so pointlessly timid. But then, from what the book said about the lame little life of Joseph Cornell, *pointlessly timid* sounded about right. "Kind of, like, half collage, half . . . stuff in a box."

Arthur took the book from Eugene and leafed through it. "One of my studio requirements was a mixed-media overview, and the grad student teaching my section was into Cornell. I'd forgotten all about him, honestly."

Holy shit, it was hard not to laugh maniacally. "Thanks, man," Eugene said, and sat back down opposite Arthur, rubbing his scar. Eugene had given the performance of a lifetime yesterday. In no more than the thirty seconds it took Arthur to find a bandage, Eugene had assessed his room (*full of collage*), formulated a plan (*Arthur could make the real fake*), and set the scene: he hauled a massive, comatose cat into his lap and began to pet him (*use props, cute props*).

"Are you an artist?" Eugene had called.

"Photographer." Arthur had reappeared with a gauze pad. "You look like Dr. Evil," he said.

Eugene's hand froze mid-stroke. The cat growled or sighed or farted, he couldn't tell. "Ever hear of Joseph Cornell?" he asked.

It had played perfectly. He made up the specs of the assignment on the spot, asked for Arthur's help, and Arthur had been intrigued enough to defer to Oneida's mother rather than refuse outright. And now

Eugene was sitting in the Darby-Jones dining room in the light of day, so excited, so pleased with himself, he thought he might pop.

The dining room table had been covered with brown butcher paper, and someone had set out a plastic basket of markers, poster paint, and glue sticks prior to his arrival. Oneida, at the head of the table, was playing with a shiny pair of scissors, opening and closing and spinning them lazily on their point. He shot a glance in her direction. She didn't smile and snapped the shears shut.

Still, all things considered, Saturday had been something like the greatest day of his life.

He'd made out with a girl for *hours*; he'd gotten his first offer of a blow job, which, even in the offer stage, was significant; and he'd discovered a solution to his $300 dollar debt. Not to mention stumbling headfirst into his *third* great work, after the Wendy Project (complete) and the Oneida Project (concurrent). Eugene wasn't one to require constant validation, but every once in a while it *was* gratifying for the universe to remind him how much of a prodigy he was.

"What's the assignment, exactly?" Arthur asked.

Eugene reached into his backpack and came up with a faked assignment sheet, appropriately bedraggled by his own hand: he'd made a ring on it last night with a glass of orange juice, a touch of genius he was particularly proud of. Arthur smoothed it out on the table and, while he read, Eugene dared another quick glance at Oneida. She held the scissors still, tensed *en pointe*.

What are you doing? she mouthed.

Art, he mouthed back, but she still looked confused. He wasn't sure if she couldn't figure out what he was trying to say, or could and just didn't get it. *Art,* he mouthed again, pulling his lips back and punching a silent *t*. Oneida shook her head.

"*Art,*" he whispered.

"What?" Arthur looked up.

"Nothing. What? Nothing." Eugene wrinkled his nose. "So I brought a bunch of junk we had lying around the house."

"I'm not going to do this project for you. To be clear." Arthur pushed the fake assignment across the table and leaned back in his chair. "I agreed to help out, but it has to be yours. So you guys ought to pick the pieces you want to use, and start working, and I'll step in if and when you need advice."

"But it's a group project, and our group bailed on us." Oneida put the scissors down with a clunk. "Anyway, group projects aren't really about everyone pitching in. One person always ends up doing most of the work, and it's usually me, so it would be kind of nice to get a break."

"Good point," Arthur said.

Oneida looked shocked, but Eugene couldn't tell if she was stunned by adult solidarity or solidarity from Arthur specifically. Assumptions aside, he knew the barest details about Arthur's presence at the Darby-Jones (gleaned from their conversations yesterday, they amounted to his being *a tenant my mom wants to bone* and *grade-A freak meat*), and he was fascinated. The concept of sharing a living space with people who weren't related to you, who paid you, was completely alien to Eugene. The practical possibilities were both mesmerizing and terrifying. What would you learn about strangers, and what would they learn about you? How could you possibly keep secrets from each other when you shared the same bathroom, the same cereal bowls and sofas? He knew that the Wendell family, by necessity, was more secretive than most; that his family bubble was designed to be impenetrable, but still—it was thrilling, and a little horrifying, to imagine what life was like for Oneida every day. No wonder she was so high-strung.

"Let's see what you brought," Arthur said.

Eugene grinned. Arthur's circumstances may have been mysterious, but the man himself—as Eugene knew, cold, the second he entered Arthur's room—was completely naked: he had a peculiarly obsessive talent with random objects, at just the moment in Eugene's life when a peculiarly obsessive talent with random objects was most useful. Also, Arthur Rook was totally nuts—albeit in a gentle, nonviolent way—and Eugene, quick to identify the more malleable human natures, intended to play him like a Fender Stratocaster.

Eugene opened a paper bag and spilled selections from the Cornell suitcase across Oneida's dining room table. And just as Eugene knew he would, Arthur Rook went bye-bye.

"*Wow!*" Arthur stood. "Where did you get all this—this is old, antique, maybe, not valuable per se, but this is—so cool. Where did you get this?"

"Estate sale," Eugene said. "My dad goes to estate sales. Like a hobby."

Oneida stretched her pale arms across the table and snagged a page ripped from a magazine decades ago: a yellowed advertisement for an indoor icebox.

"Does he know you're using this for a school project?"

Eugene nodded. Of all the lies he was telling today, it was the only one that made him nervous. He wanted to believe Astor would have faith in him, would back the plan two hundred percent, but Eugene couldn't afford to take the chance; he was going to do this, period. Who was Eugene Wendell to ignore a gigantic glowing message from the jumbotron of the universe? It was too important, and he was too sure of himself, to waffle. Plus, if everything went well (which it would), it would be all the more amazing if Astor never saw it coming.

"I brought a box, here—" He plumbed his backpack for the cereal box he'd carefully cut the front panel out of. "I figured we could build the thing in here and maybe cover it with plastic wrap or something. Tah-dah! Instant Cornell."

"How's it going in here?" Mona's voice yanked Eugene to attention. She'd answered the door when he arrived, and despite a totally normal greeting ("Hello, Eugene") it was clear she was every bit as thrilled with his existence today as she had been yesterday. "Suffering for your art yet?"

It was not Eugene's imagination that she looked directly at him when she said *yet*.

"What's all this?" She crossed behind Arthur and approached the table.

Arthur was too engrossed in a dead guy's garbage to respond, and Oneida didn't say anything either; so Eugene said, "I got it from my dad. We're going to use it for the project."

Mona picked out the leftover blue velvet Eugene hadn't been able to resist bringing. He heard Oneida squeak in recognition.

Wrapping the velvet around her fingers, rubbing it with her thumb, Mona read from the assignment sheet. " 'The Sincerest Form of Flattery.

For the creative portion of your assignment, your group will produce a piece of art in the style of your assigned artist. You may not copy a famous work. You must create something new while keeping faithful to that artist's style.' Whose class is this for?"

"Dreyer's," Oneida mumbled. She was doing her best not to look at her mother at all, Eugene noticed.

"That's weird. I thought she taught history. This seems more like an art project."

"She does teach history." Eugene had prepared for this. "It's one of those interdisciplinary things—you know, history and art. Art history." He swallowed. Mona was incredibly distracting, which he had noticed last night but had been too terrified to truly process. She was far too young—far too hot—to be his girlfriend's mother. Where Oneida was harsh and enigmatic, Mona was all curves and cheerful colors: a bright blue shirt, ponytail, faded jeans. Next to her mother, Oneida looked bloodless, transparent: a vampire in dire need of a transfusion, glaring at a mother with blood to spare.

"This isn't quite . . . this isn't quite enough," Arthur muttered, loud enough for the three of them to notice he'd spoken, though they clearly weren't his intended audience. "There's no . . . there needs to be an *object*." He'd made several small piles on the butcher paper: an assortment of one-inch-square mirrors and blue glass tiles. Four tiny jars made of clear glass. Several pages from what must have been an astronomy textbook: moons and planets and constellations, green-haloed where their garish yellow and blue inks bled together. Two bottles, stoppered with black rubber, one filled with small black stones and the other with a kind of white sand.

Eugene's heart thrummed. Holy shit, this was going to work. This was really going to work.

"Cornell was a worshipper." Arthur stepped back from the table. "He worshipped film stars, like Lauren Bacall. There was some ballerina that he loved. He loved—from a distance. . . . I'll be right back," Arthur told no one in particular, and bolted from the dining room.

Mona turned to Eugene. "He does that," she said. "It's nothing personal."

Eugene licked his lips, which were cracked and dry. He was thirsty.

If only Mona would stop looking at him, or standing there and smelling—God, so good, she smelled like icing, like a cake. He coughed and hoped it didn't sound as fake as it was.

"How'd you get that black eye?" Mona asked, and then she actually took a step closer. He twitched and hoped she didn't notice, because it wasn't fake in the least. "Yesterday?"

He shook his head.

"He got beat up at school," Oneida sniped. "For me."

Mona tilted her head. Her mouth pulled into a slight frown, but her eyes flashed as if she was about to laugh. A lock of hair, shiny as a ribbon, swung away from her temple, and she tucked it behind her ear.

"At first I didn't know how to feel about it, but I've decided it was awesome." Oneida was still talking, and what she was saying, Eugene's brain dimly realized, was pertinent. But he couldn't break Mona's gaze, couldn't pull himself out of the depth of her eyes, couldn't stop imagining her prowling the hallway at school, a graduating senior, the Prom Queen–Head Cheerleader–Lead in the Play whose wake was littered with the stunned bodies of easily aroused underclassmen. He felt a familiar, terrifying warmth in his lower gut. In approximately thirty seconds, this was going to be a severe problem.

"What's for dinner?" Oneida's voice was high and thin and far away.

"I don't know if Oneida has told you, Eugene, but you're welcome to stay for dinner. We're having roast beef and mashed potatoes." Was it his imagination, or had Mona not broken eye contact with him this whole time? Had she even blinked? "Carrots. You know the drill."

Carrots, Eugene thought desperately. *Drills.* Thank God he was sitting down, but still. This . . . was . . . a problem. He leaned forward, elbows on the table, and drummed his fingers.

"Thanks," he said. "But I think my parents are expecting me. Sunday dinner is always, like, a thing. At my house." *Lie.*

"That's nice," Mona said. "What do your parents do?"

"My dad's a security guard and my mom stays home. She does some freelance design stuff, like brochures. Letterheads. Business cards." *Keep listing office supplies. No one gets hot for office supplies. Post-its. Paper clips. Scissors.*

Mona sat in Arthur's recently vacated chair and focused on the

Cornell pile. The only sounds in the room were the light thudding of Eugene's fingertips on the table, Cornell's trinkets clinking and papers shuffling, and the cold metallic grind of metal on metal as Oneida opened and closed her shears with a methodical rhythm that Eugene, even in his current state, realized was some sort of message. He was too far gone to understand precisely what that message was, but it had a quality about it—threatening, promissory—that was its own kind of messed-up hot. He was certain of one thing: the Jones women were going to be the end of him, and he was going to love it.

"Got it!" Arthur barged back in, startling Eugene into squawking like a strangled chipmunk. Arthur was holding a giant pink box under one arm and a photograph in the other. When he set both down, Mona recoiled. Violently.

Oneida didn't see it. She was leaning forward to look at the picture, and asking "Who is she?"

The photograph was black-and-white and showed a woman, her face turned away from the camera, lying naked on a beach at the edge of the water. Her body, like her face, was twisted away, hips turned, one leg thrown over the other. She didn't look dead, even though you couldn't see her eyes to tell if they were open or closed; every line of her was alive, Eugene thought, like a mermaid washed up and resting for a moment before she regrew her tail and headed for home. The angle of her jaw. The bend of her elbow, lying across her chest. The long curving muscles of her thighs. A foot curled over her calf, toes like tiny pearls. Her hair trailed above her as the water lapped it out to sea.

"My wife," Arthur said.

Oneida's mouth opened in a circle.

"I took this picture at Zuma Beach," he said. "She loved tequila. We were celebrating. I don't even remember what—she'd probably solved some insurmountable problem at work. We drove down to Malibu and smuggled the bottle under our coats and hid in the dunes and drank and—" Arthur smiled and shrugged. "You get the picture. I took it."

Mona wasn't looking at the picture. At all. She was looking at her hands, and then the other side of the room, and then at Eugene, who by this time was looking right back at her. She jerked her gaze away. *The hell*, Eugene thought; *the hell is going on here?* If Oneida was right and Mona was into Arthur, was this the first she was hearing of Arthur's wife? And where *was* Arthur's wife, beyond naked on a beach in a picture?

Eugene let out a long breath. "She's hot, man," he said.

"Uh . . . thanks." Arthur rubbed his face.

Oneida picked up the photograph and examined it, eyes narrowed. "What's her name?"

"Amy," Arthur said.

Oneida slid the picture back across the table without comment.

Eugene, watching Mona now out of curiosity more than lust, saw her body slacken when Oneida handed the photo over. His curiosity raged. He opened his mouth to ask Arthur another question—anything to keep him talking about this mysterious Amy, and where the hell she was—but Mona gave him such a sharp spike of a look that the words died in his throat. Jesus, she had an issue and a half about this broad. Eugene, knowing it was best, for a host of reasons, to stay on his girlfriend's mother's good side, shut the hell up.

Arthur pushed the unwanted Cornell bits to the side, clearing the center of the dining room table for the photo of his missing wife, and cracked his knuckles. Mona hugged herself like she was freezing cold, and Oneida crossed her arms on the table and propped her chin on them.

"Pass the glue," Arthur said. "And the scissors. And the box."

⚜

Their history project was a disaster.

They never had another group meeting. On Thursday, when Dreyer called them to the front of the classroom to present their project, Eugene, Oneida, and Dani stood in a line and read from index cards about Ringo, John, and Paul, respectively, to a sea of snickers and shifty eyes. Andrew Lu refused even to stand up and casually drew a finger across his throat when Eugene began to speak.

Dani came out looking the best.

"Paul," she said, "was desperate for the whole world to like him. Because of his innate dependence on others for happiness and validation, fostered by the codependent nature of the group, he never developed a solid sense of self. When he no longer had John Lennon to prop him up, Paul wrote dumb songs about love, racial harmony, and his dog and then sold the entire Beatles catalog to Michael Jackson. In conclusion, we should all be learning to be independent, so that we never make the same unfortunate choices."

Eugene applauded, as did a few of the authentic Wendys sitting in the back of the room. Dreyer shook her head and said, "Thank you, group four, for that illuminating editorial."

It didn't matter, and Eugene knew it. The project didn't matter. High school didn't matter one stupid bit. Three things mattered. One: the look on Astor's face—astonishment passing to gratitude and finally beaming with admiration—when Eugene showed him Arthur's real fake. Two: the way his stomach soared when Astor drove up in a bottle-green vintage Impala a day later, shouting over the roaring engine, "You like? It's yours, Gene!" And three: the warm weight of Oneida's hand in his, in front of Dreyer and Andrew Lu and everyone, in the hallway, in the cafeteria, walking to the student parking lot at the end of the day. Eugene knew he wasn't the type to peak in high school—yet to think it would get any better than this was dizzying.

⁊

It was fair to say he was drunk on good fortune when he told Oneida what his father really did for a living.

They were parked in the field behind his house. The Wendells owned several acres, and Astor had suggested that Eugene learn to drive by barreling around on their own land, where there were no errant telephone poles or mailboxes, pedestrians or police. He had his driving permit and had taken the required five-hour course; he parked in the far corner of the student lot and had pasted a fake parking tag to the inside of his windshield. The sheer awesomeness of Vlad the Impala (as he had dubbed his ride) more than made up for what he lacked in legal licensure.

But what Eugene was practicing that Thursday afternoon in the car with Oneida wasn't parallel parking or three-point turns. He was honing his skills as the most naturally adept maker-outer in the history of teenagers: guru of the grope! Inexhaustible, inventive! Surely, no one had ever thought to move his tongue quite in that manner before! If only Oneida weren't so grave the whole time—she matched him for stamina but she hardly ever smiled, and she only laughed if he tickled her. Which he was doing when she accidentally kicked him in the shin and he rolled away across the Impala's backseat, laughing and gasping.

"Oh my God, I'm sorry," she said, a leftover giggle leaking out like a sigh. "Please don't tickle me again, OK? I kind of have to pee."

"I have a strict no-peeing-in-the-Impala policy," he said.

She coughed and popped her elbow out the open window. It was a perfect October day, the sun low and setting the trees on fire. The high grass of the field rustled in the breeze.

"Are you afraid your dad's going to take the car away after what happened in history?" she asked.

The question puzzled Eugene, it was so foolish, so beside the point, so . . . nothing Astor would ever do.

"No," he said, a little harshly, because she stiffened and crossed her arms. "He would never do that. He's not a dick."

"I didn't say he was a dick."

"He gave me this car as a reward for something a thousand times more important than that stupid project."

She blasted him with a glare. "Does this mean you're finally going to tell me what the hell that was all about on Sunday?"

It was the first time she'd asked for an explanation, and she was unreasonably pissed about it, Eugene thought, considering it was also the first time they'd really been alone together since he kissed her good-bye after they (or, rather, Arthur) finished their project—furtively, on the porch of the Darby-Jones. It wasn't like he was keeping it from her; it wasn't as though she could never know. He had always planned on telling her, it just . . . hadn't come up. He'd been too excited about the car, and too excited about what Astor had said to him when Eugene went home on Sunday, sweaty, heart pumping not from the bike ride but because of the treasure strapped to his back. Racing home not for Sunday dinner but to show off his brilliance to the one person in the world whose opinion mattered most.

Astor was reading a book at the kitchen table, sipping a beer, turning the pages in the afternoon light. Eugene unzipped his backpack and slid the cereal-boxed Cornell across the table without a word of greeting.

"I read that Cornell built and painted his own shadow boxes and then baked them in the oven to get that crispy antique look. So I thought, why not cut out the back panel and remount it and how would anyone know the difference?" Eugene had spent the bike ride home crafting those lines and was disappointed that they still came out sounding so clunky, so rehearsed.

"You did this." Astor's voice was a whisper as he gingerly righted the box. His eyes flicked back and forth, scanning the whole—which Arthur, surpassing Eugene's greatest expectations, had put his entire self into. He'd papered half the box with a page from the astronomy text—a constellation, Eugene wasn't sure which one, whose curving form mirrored that of his missing wife, pasted opposite, her hair carried not out to sea but into space. Her body was half-obscured by some wire netting that Arthur had trimmed down like a hedge and painted white, which faded into the swath of white he'd daubed across the bottom. Against the white he'd lined up the four tiny glass jars, open, empty, ready to catch anything that might fall from the heavens—or already full with something that couldn't be seen. At the base of his wife's neck, Arthur had pasted a single silver star, a pendant and a distant world.

"You did this?" Astor's voice was stronger, more excited.

"More or less." Eugene shrugged. "Does this cover the money I owe you?"

Astor put the box down carefully, stood, and crushed Eugene in his arms. Eugene folded into his father completely and was at first frightened, then amazed, to feel a tear roll down the side of his nose. "You really are my boy," Astor said, and then they both laughed, just the two of them, in the citrus green and yellow Wendell kitchen. Eugene replayed it in his mind, reliving it exactly as it had happened: his own art, his own triumph, his own father, and his own father's love, whole and perfect and his.

His to share, to do with as he chose. To tell whomever he chose. Evidence to prove his worth to the world—starting with his wide-eyed girlfriend, sitting at the other end of the Impala's backseat.

He told Oneida, "I didn't lie when I said my father was an art forger. He borrows real paintings and copies them, and his friend helps him sell them all around the world to private collectors. I tricked Arthur into making a new fake, a real fake that nobody knows exists, that my dad's going to pretend to discover."

Oneida didn't say anything. She sat very still and stared at him without blinking.

Eugene shook with a cold flood of adrenaline.

Oneida, who still hadn't blinked, said, "You're telling me the truth."

Eugene nodded. If he opened his mouth, he was sure he would throw up all over her.

Oneida pressed the door handle and ran out and around the car, shouting and laughing. "Oh my *God*," she screamed. "That's the most *amazing thing I've ever heard!*"

Eugene flew out of the car after her, spaghetti-legged and close to fainting. "Shhhhh!" he said, his voice hoarse. "Don't shout, it's a secret! It's a huge secret, you can't tell anyone ever!"

"I know, I know!" She braced one arm against the hood of the car and laughed hysterically. Eugene had no idea what to do—what her reaction meant or how he was supposed to handle it. If it was possible, he had to convince her it had been a lie—he had lied, it wasn't true. There had to be a way to get her to stop knowing it, there had to be. Oh, God, it was too dangerous. He saw that now: he understood with a clarity that stung like acid. And everything he'd felt or thought about Oneida Jones shifted beneath him like a landslide, an earthquake, a sinkhole: uncontrollable and unknowable and terrifyingly out of his hands, forever.

She stood upright and wiped her eyes (was she laughing so hard she was crying? Good God, what did that *mean*?). Then she grabbed his hands and said, *Don't worry, don't worry, I won't ever tell anyone, ever; I think it's amazing!*

Stay very still, Eugene thought: *be cool. Act like you don't care. Act like you never said a word.* He kissed her and prayed it would make them both forget what they knew.

18 ❧ Glad I'm Not There

Mona decided on Sunday—after Eugene went home and they ate dinner and Oneida, unasked, helped clean up. She even said, "Thanks, Mom" in a gravelly whisper, barely audible over the slosh of the dishwater, which Mona acknowledged with a nod that stood in for the relieved whoop she would have rather expressed. The last dish dried and put away, Oneida retreated to do homework and Mona went looking for Arthur, who'd said a few positive words about the roast, pushed himself away from the dinner table, and promptly disappeared.

She found him sitting on the back porch, keeping company with Oneida's old friends—the badminton racquets, the folding lawn chairs, and the mangled rakes. She sat beside him on a wobbly picnic bench (the picnic table long since lost to dry rot), and they didn't speak for a long time.

"Where . . . am I?" Arthur finally asked.

Mona's heart quickened. "You're in my house," she said. "The Darby-Jones. In Ruby Falls."

Arthur blinked rapidly. He turned to her. "That's what I thought," he said. "But I don't . . . I remember how I got here, but none of this feels—real. I don't know what—it means."

He swallowed.

"I think something about that—what I did today. That collage. Something about it."

"You helped two impressionable kids cheat. Maybe it's your conscience." *Shut up*, she told herself. *Just shut up and let him think this through.* But she couldn't. "I wouldn't worry about it. It was *way* too good for Dreyer to be fooled into thinking they did it by themselves."

Arthur nudged her with his knee. "Would you kiss me?" he asked.

This close, it was impossible to ignore the black crescents under Arthur's eyes or the hungry confusion in them. Mona's stomach fell away. So the person she'd gotten to know these past couple of weeks wasn't real, after all—had only ever been a waking dream.

Oh, Amy, she thought. *You almost killed him.*

"Please," he said. "Please, I think . . . I think I want to wake up."

Mona looked out the porch windows. Every day it was getting darker earlier. The long shadow of the house stretched out across the grass, all the way to the trees.

Everything you want and everybody you love, you lose: whether through waking or dying, you always lose the past to the future.

Arthur sniffed. "I'm sorry," he said, "I don't know what I'm asking. You know how things are in dreams: they make sense, but they don't. Not when you really think about them."

Mona licked her lips. She thought of the last man she kissed—the FedEx guy or the UPS guy. (How horrible was that? She couldn't even remember what express mail service he worked for.) It had been on her front porch, not this back one, but still. That's your lot in life, Jones: always kissing strangers on porches.

"This is Walt Disney's fault." Arthur shook his head. "Who the hell gets woken up by a—"

Mona turned his face with her fingertips. "Wake up, Arthur," she said, and kissed him on the mouth.

She scared him; she could tell. He pulled back, but only for a second, and when he kissed her back, briefly and gently, she felt warmth in her throat. A tickle in all four chambers of her heart that could have been electricity. And something more: she felt that all the different Monas that ever were and ever would be could be shown to this person. Would be safe with him.

Arthur sat back. He turned his palms over and shook out his arms.

"I'm still here," he said.

Mona nodded. "Must not have been true love's kiss."

Arthur tried to smile.

"I assure you," Mona said, "this place is very real. And you are very real and very here."

"If you say so," Arthur said.

"Fuckin'-A, I say so."

He smiled. "You kiss your daughter with that mouth?"

No, Mona thought. *I kiss Amy's daughter with this mouth.*

"I think it'll just—take a minute. Or two. Kiss me again?"

Mona smiled at him and wanted to cry. "One at a time. I think your system can only handle so many shocks." *And I've got a good one for you. Oh, Arthur, I've got a nice big shock for you. Guaranteed to wake you right the hell up.*

She had decided. It wouldn't be easy, but it would be right: she would tell Arthur everything he wanted to know, even if it meant he woke all the way up and left this dream behind. She would tell him that Amy was pregnant when they ran away. She would tell him that she had kept and raised Amy's baby as her own.

⁂

Mona woke up on Monday morning with the words heavy on her tongue, poised to spring forward as soon as she mustered enough breath, but Arthur was so invested in wanting to develop the Waters-Kessler wedding pictures he'd taken on film that her breath shifted like the wind.

"How much room do you need to do that?" she asked. "How many square feet?"

"Not many. I need space for basins, for a drip line. If there's a water hookup, all the better."

"We can use the broom closet on the third floor. If you don't scare easily."

Arthur mumbled around the piece of strawberry-rhubarb-covered toast in his mouth. "Whyz tha'?"

"Some chick drowned herself in the third-floor broom closet in the nineteen-tens. Dunked her head in the mop basin and didn't come up for air."

"So you're saying there's a water hookup."

"You sick bastard, that's exactly what I'm saying."

They drove back to Syracuse, to the art supply warehouse on Erie Boulevard. Mona amused herself by juggling blocks of polymer clay while Arthur selected chemicals and papers and other assorted supplies. They ate lunch at the neighborhood Italian place Mona's parents used to go to on special occasions—anniversaries, birthdays, and her graduation from high school, when an infant Oneida had painted herself, her booster seat, and the majority of the booth in marinara sauce. Mona hadn't been back since they died, but nothing about the restaurant had changed. She made Arthur inspect the mural of Sicily on the rear wall, and there they were, in black ballpoint, hidden in the scraggly leaves of an olive tree: her initials and the date.

"I had to do it quick, while my mom went to the bathroom. There was no way she would have ever let me get away with defacing property like a delinquent." Mona, full of pasta and cheese, which always made her feel overwhelmingly content, poked at her handiwork. "It was my dad's idea."

Arthur reached across the table and took her hand. Mona was past caring whether it was wrong or right or selfish or delusional. She adored him, and that was that.

And she didn't want to see him torn apart, fully woken before he was ready, broken and disconnected and all because of Amy (or what was left of her). She convinced herself that this was why she didn't tell him on Tuesday, when he developed the negatives; or Wednesday, when he made so many prints he had to string extra drip lines over her bathtub; or Thursday, when he presented her with a photograph he'd taken when she didn't think anyone was looking. She'd been trying to be inconspicuous while the bridal party arranged itself up one of the grand staircases of the Landmark Hotel. Arthur had caught her leaning below one side of the sides, black pant cuffs and sky blue dress hems rising step by step above her head. She was smiling a Mona Lisa smile, sure with one glance and faint with another, hair falling over her eyes and arms crossed over her stomach.

"Very mysterious," Arthur said.

"Not as much as you might think," Mona said.

She went to bed on Thursday night with a knot in the back of her head that ached all the way down her shoulders and pulsed in her temple. She had never told this secret to anyone. Yes: she had told Anna who Oneida's father was, thinking it would prepare her for a conversation with her daughter that seemed necessary in the abstract. Halfway through the revelation, Mona realized she had nothing to say about Ben Tennant but his name. She didn't know anything else, and couldn't say more without revealing the other secret: the secret that had been hers and hers alone for years. She didn't even know how to begin telling it, so she didn't. It was safer that way.

So where did the story start, exactly?

Did it start the afternoon they watched Godzilla ravage Tokyo, when Amy first cried over Ben Tennant, when she told Mona about the postcard and her broken heart?

Did it start the night of the winter semiformal, when Mona talked with Ben in the lobby of the Landmark, Amy threw a purse at her head and ran, and Ben followed?

No: all that was backstory. Supporting evidence, details of the case. The story Arthur came to Ruby Falls to hear—the story Mona hadn't told a soul except her mother, in the year before she died—started in Amy's bedroom on a spring day in 1993.

᯽

When Mona opened her eyes on Friday morning, there were no more costs and no more benefits to analyze. There was only an attack to plan and a liquor cabinet to assess. The vodka was lower than Mona remembered from the last time she checked, which was probably months ago. She would have to talk to Sherman, who loved his afternoon cocktail, about replacing his share of the booze.

There was an almost-full bottle of tequila, and Mona added *pick up lemons* to her mental to-do list. She left a menu for the Milky Way Bar and Grill on the kitchen table with her usual Friday night take-out note (*All tenants: write down what you want, leave your $, dinner by 7*) and left the Darby-Jones. She didn't wait for Arthur to wake up. She didn't want to see him yet, not today.

Mona drove into town, picked up three lemons and a box of tissues at the convenience mart, and then drove out to Route 12 with all the windows down. She passed a bus rattling on its way to the high school.

The only indication that anyone had ever lived on this particular desolate lot in the woods was a mailbox by the side of the road, listing to the right, door lolling open like a rusty tongue. Mona pulled off the road and walked the overgrown driveway on foot, until she was standing in the middle of a flat treeless patch. Not much was left of Amy Henderson's house. Mona didn't know what, legally, became of the property after Amy's grandfather died, but whoever owned it had razed the squat box that had started its life as a double-wide trailer, that had kept Amy dry and mostly warm.

Mona faced the direction she'd come from and turned to the right, toward what would have been the front corner of the house. She walked over the earth to the former site of Amy's bedroom.

She thought she would feel something other than cold, but at first she didn't. She closed her eyes and tried to remember everything about that afternoon after school, when Amy kicked off her sneakers, threw herself down on her bed, and said, "So I'm pregnant," the way one might say, "So I'm hungry."

That was how this story began: *Once upon a time, Amy Henderson kicked off her sneakers and said "So I'm pregnant" to her best friend.*

Mona hadn't known if she was allowed to ask questions, had barely been able to grasp what those questions might be. She remembered hugging herself and saying, "I'm so sorry." It had been spring, late April, sunny, warm, and damp, and Amy tucked her legs beneath her and said, "Don't be sorry. It's OK. I mean, it's not OK, but it will be."

Mona, thirty-one and freezing in the ghost of Amy's house, suddenly felt cool linoleum floors beneath her bare teenage feet. Smelled the musty damp that clung to the shabby rugs and orange curtains. Behind her, she could sense Amy's looming bookcase, shelves sagging under the weight of too many books about movies and monsters and creatures and the various methods of making them. Mona was always terrified the bookshelf would tip in the night, crushing her in her sleeping bag on Amy's cold floor. She never slept when she slept over at Amy's.

"What do you mean *it will be*—are you going to, you know—um, abort?" Mona was blushing so deeply she felt her head would burst into flame.

"No." Amy blinked rapidly. "No, I don't want—I don't want to. I want to see what happens. Plus it costs money I don't have to spare. I need everything we can get—everything, between the two of us. We need money to get out of here."

"Oh my God, Amy, it's—what are you—"

"This is what we're doing." Amy cleared her throat. "I'm running away to the shore, to Jersey. Ocean City. It's easy to get to and it's big but not too big, and it's not runaway central, like New York. I won't get lost but I won't be found either. And I can make a ton of money waiting tables while I get bigger—" She circled her hands over her belly, which, now that Mona was looking at it, was larger than normal. And Amy had been wearing baggier clothes lately, oh *God*, how had she not seen— how had she not noticed—how *dare* she call herself a best friend?

"Then I'll have enough money to go to LA. And that's it."

Mona's mouth was so dry she couldn't swallow. "But what are you going to do with the baby?"

Amy cocked her head. "What do you mean?"

"I mean . . . if you're not going to get an abortion—Amy—you're going to have a *baby*. A baby. It's going to need you—"

"Do you think I'm stupid? I'm not going to keep it. Someone else can raise the thing," Amy said. "I'm not *completely* nuts."

"Have you been to a—you know, the doctor? To make sure every-thing's—"

"Jones." Amy patted her bed for Mona to sit. "After all the creatures I've made on my own, without instructions, you think I'm not going to know *exactly* how to make one more?"

Mona collapsed on the bed next to Amy, quaking under the weight of too much information. It felt like her entire body, not just her brain, was processing this. "OK," she said. She cleared her throat. "Can I ask . . . who—?"

"Who do you think?" Amy said, and it was the only time that day Mona thought Amy might cry. But she didn't: she got angry instead. "We were always careful, always used those mythical little things they can't teach us about in health class. Except for one time. Remember when I threw my purse at your head?"

"At the—at the dance? What, was something in your purse?"

It seemed like such a childish question, stupid and naïve, and when

Amy didn't answer, it seemed even more so. Mona blushed again, and covered her eyes with her hands, and when Amy said, *So in a way, this is kind of your fault,* Mona, at sixteen, didn't stop to realize Amy was too terrified by her circumstances to accept responsibility and trust that, when asked for, a friend's help would be given. All she could think to do was guilt Mona into sharing the burden of consequence.

Everything about this was wrong. They sat on the bed in silence.

"So you're coming with me," Amy said, her voice thin. "It's a good chance to get out of Ruby Falls, anyway. You know we don't belong here. We're meant to go places. Faraway places. We're supposed to send postcards *back* to Ruby Falls."

"*Wish you were here,*" Mona said, more jauntily than she felt. "*Glad I'm not there.*" She swallowed. "When? How?"

"I have a plan," Amy said, exactly as Mona knew she would. "I've saved up about five hundred dollars." Amy leaned over and pulled a fat envelope from between her mattress and box spring. "I sold the camcorder my grandpa gave me for my birthday and that brought in another one-fifty. We can hitch a ride with one of the semis on their way into Syracuse and pick up a bus there. The Greyhound one-way is fifty bucks apiece, and we're going to have to stay somewhere, but it's off-season for motels right now and we can find someplace cheap once we're down there. And food—we'll figure that out later. But we need to go with eight or nine hundred, at least; otherwise we're not going to be making any bank once we start working, we'll just be treading water."

"I have a college fund, but I can't get to it without my parents," Mona said. "Sorry, that wasn't helpful. I'm thinking out loud."

"Do you have anything else saved?"

"Maybe a hundred in cash. Babysitting jobs. Did some extra stuff around the house, and my parents paid me for it."

"Do you have anything you can sell?" Amy's eyes were large, her gaze sharp. She was getting at something specific, and suddenly Mona knew what it was: the cuff links. Amy wanted her to sell the diamond and gemstone cuff links that had belonged to William Fitchburg Jones himself; that had been given to him by Daniel Darby and been passed all the way down the Jones lineage to Mona's father, and, as her parents had told her all her life, would one day belong to Mona. And to Mona's kids, and so on, and so on. It wasn't that they were insanely valuable, even: though they were beautiful, made of red jasper with small diamond chips. They'd probably fetch a few hundred dollars at a pawnshop, which apparently was all Amy needed. It was just—God, they belonged to the *house*.

"They're basically yours already," Amy said quietly.

She wasn't wrong. Mona's ears rang. This was too much to decide in one afternoon, this was too much to learn, too much to have to handle, too much to—

"I just can't—I can't stay in Ruby Falls and be pregnant. It would be too depressing," Amy said, in a voice Mona had never heard before but would hear from time to time that summer in New Jersey and, as an echo in her mind, on and off for the rest of her life: hollow and colorless and utterly convinced that there was no other choice but this. There was no other future but this. "I think I would kill myself, Mona."

"What's in Ocean City?" she asked.

Amy blinked. "A boardwalk, a beach, an amusement park. Movie theaters. Seagulls. Funnel cake."

"Pawnshops?"

She smiled. "I'm sure. Somewhere."

Mona was shivering but she stuck out her hand and Amy shook it—because Amy needed her help badly enough to ask for it. And because Mona knew, even then, that Amy didn't have a clue what she was really getting into; not that Mona knew any better, but she hoped she did. Or she hoped she would, when the time came.

Mona opened her eyes and saw the woods that had been outside Amy Henderson's window for the majority of her very short life. She felt even colder than before, and when she got back into her car she rolled all the windows up and blasted the heat.

⚘

Mona spent the rest of Friday at the Darby-Jones, sketching designs for a client (Rebecca Applewhite-soon-to-be-Gretsch) she was meeting the following week. She made herself grilled cheese and tomato soup for lunch, discovered she had no appetite whatsoever, and took it upstairs to Arthur, who was so engrossed in assembling the Waters-Kessler proofs in an album he would have skipped lunch otherwise. Oneida came home at 3:00 and stuck her head in the den, where Mona was sketching and half-watching an old Kate Hepburn movie on cable, to ask for a ride back to the high school at 6:30.

"Halloween carnival. Dance," she said when Mona asked her why. "Eugene asked me. I can show you the flyer if you want."

"I trust you," Mona said.

They'd barely spoken since Sunday night, since that *sotto voce* "thank you." Mona didn't think they were purposely avoiding each other— which was some improvement, at least. Their lives were just running parallel where once they'd been on the exact same track. Mona wished she didn't care as much as she did—she knew it was perfectly normal, that this was what happened when children (and parents) grew up—but she dreaded what it might mean if she ever told Oneida the truth: if her daughter would veer off her parallel course completely and irreparably. She couldn't do anything about it now, other than choose her moments carefully and hope. And be grateful and excited that, for the first time since puberty, Oneida—her Oneida, her weird, wonderful, borderline-outcast of a daughter—was going to a social event at school. With a boyfriend. It was a miniature miracle, but a miracle nonetheless.

At 6:30, Mona and Oneida left the house, Mona with money for take-out and Oneida in her long winter coat. The coat seemed odd to Mona (it wasn't that cold outside) but not odd enough to mention. During the car ride, Mona learned that Eugene's older sister's band was playing at the carnival and that Oneida was planning on getting a ride home from Eugene's parents. Mona bit her lip.

"I'd prefer to pick you up myself," she said.

"God, Mom, they're not *morons*. They know the difference between the gas and the brake and everything."

"I don't appreciate that tone."

There was a beat of silence and then mother and daughter laughed desperately.

"Oh my *God*, when did I become Bert?" Mona hooted. Oneida giggled and rubbed her right eye. They were both smiling when Mona pulled the station wagon into the circular drive of the high school.

"Just . . . call me if you need a ride, or if you don't feel safe getting into a car with someone," Mona said to Oneida, who already had one leg on the pavement. Oneida turned back and nodded, lips pressed together. "Aye-aye, Mom," she said, and slipped out of the car. Mona watched her daughter walk up the concrete path to the gymnasium entrance. From the back, Oneida was indistinguishable from a grown-up. Or a stranger.

She drove to the Milky Way Bar and Grill, picked up the food, and was back standing in her kitchen before she even knew time was passing. Anna, not bothering with a plate and tucking into the Styrofoam container, paused mid-bite to comment that Mona was acting weird. And was she just eating cereal for dinner?

"Not that hungry," Mona said. "I think I might be coming down with a bug."

She rinsed her cereal bowl, grabbed lemons, tequila, a knife, and a cutting board, and went up to her bedroom and closed the door. This was the only thing left to do: dull the edge and knock on Arthur's door. She set the cutting board on the bathroom counter and cut up all three lemons before she realized she hadn't remembered to bring a glass.

"Guess I'm drinking it straight," she said, and sat down on the closed toilet lid. She tipped the bottle to her lips. It was full and heavy, and she hit her teeth on the first swig.

She'd also forgotten to bring up a salt shaker. *Well, this was poorly planned*, Mona thought, and laughed stupidly, even though she wasn't even close to drunk yet. She took another swig, a long, gulping pull, set the bottle down, and jammed two slices of lemon into her teeth.

She shouldn't be doing this in a bathroom. It was too easy to see that other bathroom, the bathroom in the Seahorse Motel, when she was a little buzzed. She grabbed a handful of lemons and took the bottle by the neck and sat cross-legged on her bed. Mona took another swig and sucked on a lemon; and another swig and another lemon. She held the bottle at arm's length and estimated that, in less than five minutes, she'd reduced the level of liquid by about four inches.

"So why don't I feel more drunk?" she said, fishing lemon pulp from between her teeth with her tongue. *I must be broken*, she thought, and took another deep gulp.

And then Mona was *astonishingly* drunk.

It hit like a brick. And it didn't matter if she was standing in her own bathroom or not: she saw the bathroom at the Seahorse. Saw the streak of brown blood drying on the pink tile. Red blood glowing against the white porcelain tub.

Someone knocked on her door.

"Who?" she called.

"Arthur."

Of course, she thought, and took another gulp of tequila. This was perfect. Also: she wasn't sure when she'd gotten a waterbed, but her mattress felt incredibly buoyant. "Come in!"

The sight of Arthur passing through her bedroom door made her extraordinarily happy and then extraordinarily sad. She felt her face brighten and crumple in the space of a single expression, which might've accounted for Arthur's reaction.

"There's something I should—tell you. What?" He quickly shut the door behind him. "What are you doing?"

"I have to tell *you*." She slopped a little tequila on her quilt and muttered, "Fuckshitballs." She had a fleeting sober thought: *This is so undignified. This is the wimp's way out.*

"What's wrong?" Arthur came closer but didn't make any attempt to take away the bottle. She wasn't sure if she had the capacity to share at this point anyway. He was carrying—he was carrying the pink shoebox. Amy's shoebox. Oh *God*. "Mona, this is—what is this?" And he kind of laughed.

"This is . . . the story of my life," she said after a long pause, wherein her mind wandered far enough to realize that, even if Oneida did telephone (improbable), Mona would be too drunk to drive. Poorly planned, all around. "Lemon?" She threw a slice of fruit at him.

He caught it one-handed.

"That was *hot*," Mona said. "Sorry, that's not what I had to tell you. I have to tell you." She thrust the bottle of tequila at him. "You can take this. I'm brave enough, I don't need any more. I have to tell you."

"What do you have to tell me?" Arthur took the bottle and put it safely on her dresser. Next to the picture of Mona and Oneida, wrapped up together in that blue blanket, right after they came home from New Jersey. Standing on the steps of the Darby-Jones, just daring the world to say something. Anything. It was taken two weeks before Mona's parents adopted Oneida.

"She's legally my sister," Mona said. It was as good a place to start as any. "Sit." She pointed at the bed next to her, damp with tequila. "Please sit. I have to tell you."

Arthur sat and Mona opened her mouth but made the mistake of eye contact.

"Don't be scared," she said. "It's not a terrible thing. It's just a difficult thing."

She grabbed his hands, which were cool. "I'm telling you this," she said, "because you want to wake up."

"I *have*—I think I have—that's what I was coming here to—"

"You're not all the way awake yet." Mona inhaled. "You can't be, because you don't know what I'm about to tell you—even though I think it's why you came here. To know this."

"In August, in Ocean City," she started to say, but her throat closed and her eyes stung.

> She was coming home from spending the night with David Danger, which she did more often than not these days. But last night she'd been spending the night in the most euphemistic sense of the words—she'd had sex, for the first time, and it was so strange and thrilling and she didn't know what to do with herself. It was nothing like she expected. It was awkward and it hurt and she didn't think she came. At least, she had expected orgasm to be more exciting than—that. It seemed the kind of thing you wouldn't doubt occurring, if, in fact, it had occurred. David had been kind and she didn't feel used or embarrassed or like she had done anything wrong, but there was a nagging feeling, a fuzzy feeling, like her brain and her body had stopped talking to each other. She didn't feel entirely solid. She was tired and a little hungry. It was six in the morning, and she wanted to go to sleep.
>
> The door was open.
>
> Mona shouldn't have, but she went into the motel room. Mona shouldn't have, but she called for Amy. Mona shouldn't

have, *after she saw the bloody sheets on what had been Amy's bed, but she kept walking, past her own bed, to the bathroom.*

There was a streak of dried brown blood on the pink tile. Red blood glowing against the white porcelain tub.

In the tub.

It didn't move.

It didn't look like anything. It was wrinkled, and purple, and it didn't move.

Oh, Jesus Christ, Amy, she thought. Oh, Amy. Oh, Jesus.

Last night—she called last night from David's place, to let Amy know where she was and tell her not to worry—Amy had sounded like Amy, normal Amy. Amy said she was going to watch ER and go to bed, and she'd see Mona in the morning. Since Mona had picked up Amy's housekeeping shift at the Seahorse, Amy barely left the motel room, but she didn't seem more or less happy than usual. She watched a lot of television. She sucked on ice cubes out of the pink plastic ice bucket, refilling it at least three times a day. Mona made sure she ate, bringing home pizza and salads and pastries from the House of D'Angier. Mona made sure she got up and walked around. "Confinement isn't so bad," Amy said one night, when they were watching reruns of Saturday Night Live *and eating chicken wings. "Except for how I'm so freaking fat."*

Had she been planning this the whole time? Mona had been spending the night frequently at David's, but had Amy deliberately waited for a night she wasn't around—could you do that? Could you control your labor like that? How had she done this—how had she gotten this baby out without waking anyone up, without passing out, without dying? Because she was Amy, Mona thought. Because she was Amy Henderson, and she did whatever the hell she needed to do. But there was a monstrousness to this act that chilled her; Mona couldn't fathom how Amy was capable of doing this. Of squirting it out and leaving it behind. Mona couldn't breathe.

It was so small. It was too small.

Mona really couldn't breathe. She was going to pass out. She grabbed the bathroom sink and forced her breath to leave her lungs. It came out high-pitched, at first no more than a whine, and it slowly, slowly built into something like a high howl.

The baby opened a mouth round and dark as a grape and screamed back.

Mona and the baby screamed at each other. The baby, who was a girl, opened her eyes and stared at Mona. Mona had never been more terrified. She had never felt more alive or been more certain that someday she would die. She had never felt more necessary to another living creature as she did to the baby girl in the tub, tiny, wrinkled, purple, abandoned. Mona ripped one of the coarse white towels, bleached stiff, from the towel rod and wrapped up the screaming baby, who screamed louder when the rough nap touched her skin.

Mona stumbled out of the bathroom, slamming the door back on its hinges and staggering into what would become the rest of her life. The baby was warm and impossible in her arms and she hated and loved it. She looked around the room for more signs of Amy and only found conclusive evidence of her absence—a missing suitcase, an empty open drawer. On top of the television, where the picture of Amy and her parents used to be, was a leftover pizza box, full of grease and dried red pepper flakes. There was no note. The baby was the note.

Oneida wouldn't have a name until a week later, when Mona was back in Ruby Falls, sitting in her parents' kitchen and ladling sugar into her Rice Krispies. The words would jump out at her from the shining back of her spoon and strike her with their toughness and their strangeness: Oneida Stainless. But named or not, she was Mona's from the moment Mona stepped out of the motel room. Oneida was Mona's when the EMT crew rolled up, called by a hysterical guest who'd seen Mona, shivering and clinging to a bloody towel that didn't look empty, rocking back and forth on the motel's concrete steps. Oneida was Mona's even when the doctor at the Ocean City Medical Center, brows raised knowingly, challenged her refusal to be examined. And Oneida was Mona's when her parents

came to the hospital in New Jersey to collect their daughter and
their new granddaughter alike. The lawyers recommended they
formally adopt Oneida as their own, which they did—but
Oneida was always Mona's.

And Mona, the blurry daughter of the Darby-Jones, who
thought she might one day be a funny girl or a baker, discovered
the person she was meant to be: the mother of Oneida Jones.

To Arthur, she said, "Oneida is Amy's. Amy ran away because she
was pregnant, and she ran away again after—after she gave birth somewhere between a bed and a bathtub in a motel in Ocean City." Arthur's
mouth opened but Mona held up her hand. "I kept her. I wanted her
because she gave me—she gave me a future. Amy wasn't just my best
friend, Arthur, she was my *only* friend, and she was going to take herself away. Amy was wonderful and terrible. Terrible. She didn't want her
daughter, she left her behind, in a bathtub, Arthur—she had her alone,
she had her all by herself, and once the baby was out of her body Amy
just left her behind. She was the only thing Amy left behind, and I kept
her."

Mona didn't feel the least bit drunk anymore. She felt like she
was falling, fast and straight, and the bottom would never rise up to
meet her.

Arthur was white. He shook his head once, twice.

"Come *on*, Arthur," Mona said. The tequila rolled her eyes for her.
"She doesn't look anything *like* me."

The truth of her own words came in like the tide and pulled her
under. She felt it flood the deepest hollows of her heart—her liar's heart,
her coward's heart, her weak and utterly delusional heart—and all the
years of lying to herself bowed inward under the weight of water, the
walls she'd built around the truth flimsy and porous as paper. And
Mona Jones, who had spent the past sixteen years of her life believing
she was a mother, remembered that first she had been a thief.

19 ⁓ *Revelations*

Eugene Wendell had lost his mind. He would have done anything in the world to get it back, but it wouldn't come. It was gone.

What he had in place of a mind was a high whining fear, occasionally spiked with panic, cold bursts of anxiety, and bouts of intestinal distress. He didn't know who he was anymore (other than a stupid kid who'd blown his father's cover, who'd told on his father, who'd opened his big fat mouth, for reasons he couldn't even remember having). This wasn't like a project. This wasn't art. He was unmoored and floating and nameless.

And then somehow he was hauling his mother's drum kit into his high school gymnasium. One more thing, on top of everything else, that felt categorically wrong. But he had to believe that, even if he'd never said anything to anyone, it would still feel weird to see his mother on the makeshift stage beneath the basketball hoop, pulling her hair back in a ponytail and discussing the sound system with John LoCosta, senior class president, King of the Douchebags.

And Halloween had always been his favorite holiday.

"Pick it up, Donnie!" Patricia, arms wrapped around a tom-tom, passed him on the right.

What's that supposed to mean? Eugene had such a feeling of impending doom, it was amazing he could put one foot in front of the other, let alone traverse the entire gym lugging a kick drum. *Oh, Patricia,* he thought, sick to his stomach, watching her quickstep ahead of him, *you were right, you were so right.* He'd ridden a tidal wave of anxiety into the early hours of the morning, researching art forgery on the Internet, which his sleep-deprived mind had condensed into a series of abstractly terrifying propositions: fraud—grand larceny—incarceration—flight—and Elmyr de Hory, who was, according to Wikipedia, something of a rock star when it came to forgery, and who'd spent his final years in Ibiza before committing suicide on the eve of his extradition to stand trial for crimes relating to something like eight million counts of intentional fraud. *What Astor did was stupid. What Astor did was illegal. What Astor did would tear his family apart.*

What Oneida knew would tear his family apart.

He had had a chance to realize it, long ago; Patricia had been trying to help him. Patricia had been trying to wake him up, and he'd chosen to stick his head deeper in the sand. He'd gone so far as to make his own piece of fraudulent art. He'd entrapped Arthur, who was a nice guy, who Eugene actually liked—this was so bad, he could barely wrap his brain around all the levels of bad this was. The Wendells were so screwed up, they couldn't possibly be saved. It was only a matter of time, and Eugene had lit the fuse.

Patricia set the tom-tom on the stage and cocked her head. "Donnie," she said. "Nice costume." She pointed at his shirt. He was wearing jeans, sneakers, a gray hooded sweatshirt, and a black T-shirt with a glowing white rib cage on it. He'd thought it was a decent effort, considering his strict policy on dressing up (only conceptual/ironic costumes allowed after the age of twelve). But Patricia's intimation that this was, in fact, some sort of identifiable character costume was another sign that forces were at work behind the scenes, and they were forces that hated him.

"Oy, kid," Patricia said, "I thought you were supposed to be hip." She vaulted onto the stage and it shivered beneath her. They hoisted the kick drum between the two of them, and when Patricia took it off his hands, Eugene hopped up behind it.

The Ruby Falls Halloween Carnival was always held at the high school. It was the only place in town big enough to host a dance at the same time as a bunch of dippy booths and games for the elementary school kids. There'd been a lot of town meetings about whether it was better or worse to cram all the kids of Ruby Falls, ages five to eighteen, into one building on the Friday before Halloween, but Eugene didn't see what the problem was. Did the school board actually think seven-year-olds were going to score weed off some junior and then go smoke up together in the bathroom? The little kids stuck to the games in the cafeteria and toured the Haunted Home Ec Room, and the dance was so locked down, chaperoned to within an inch of its life, that the two groups hardly crossed paths. At most, high-schoolers with younger siblings hurried them through everything, drove them home, and came back to the dance, which lasted until midnight.

"Or until they kick us off the stage," Patricia had said, when she announced that Insane Armhole, her hastily composed band, would be making its debut in the very room where she'd once refused to play volleyball on the grounds that it violated her constitutional right to pursue happiness. She'd found a guitarist: a very short coworker at McD's named Chas, who had a shaved head and thought it was funny to ask existential questions to no one on the drive-thru intercom. Eugene had had the pleasure of driving up in Vlad the Impala, Oneida in the passenger seat, the PLACE YOUR ORDER HERE box in the middle of a rant about the myth of objective truth as co-opted by a capitalist society.

Patricia said the drummer she'd lined up fell through, but Eugene guessed the truth: she hadn't even tried to find one. Their mother was a far better drummer than anyone Patricia would find on the Internet or the bulletin boards at the community college. And Maggie said, "Sure, why not?" like she'd actually been asked, when they all knew if she didn't agree to help, her daughter would throw an atomic conniption fit.

And now here they were, after their CD of creepy Halloween-appropriate covers was approved by the senior class and the Ruby Falls Rotary club, Halloween carnival co-sponsors. Eugene hadn't heard them practice—he'd been too much in his own world, or trying to collide worlds with Oneida—but he could vouch for two-thirds of the band. Insane Armhole couldn't be any worse than the other bands Eugene had heard at the Halloween carnival, which were always local and tended to be hairy and paunchy, old enough to be everyone's dads and restricted to the greatest hits of Crosby, Stills, Nash and Young and The Doors. Patricia, in her own words, wanted to go Carrie White. "I want ears to explode," she told him. "I want screaming. I want to bring that gym down in sonic flames."

You'll get your wish, Eugene thought. The air was full of doom. It mixed with the ghostly funk of the thousands of sweaty teenagers who had run and danced and smacked shuttlecocks in this very room, days and months and years before Eugene Wendell leaned against a shaky stage and wanted to throw up. He'd asked Oneida earlier in the week if she wanted to go to the dance with him, and there was no way he could cancel now without looking like—well, without looking like he was having a panic attack. Which he would then have to explain; because if he didn't explain, he'd end up pushing her away. Armed. It was scary to be close to her, to tell her things, but it was a thousand times more terrifying to send her on her way with the equivalent of an information bazooka and, once scorned, a reason to use it.

He'd seen her in a few classes but hadn't spoken to her much all day; there was no reason to assume she wasn't coming, even though he really wished she wouldn't. Inertia, Eugene thought; inertia would save the day. She'd show up; they'd dance; they'd make out. It would be fine. Maybe he'd take her out to his car in the parking lot and try to go down on her. Another chilling prospect, yet slightly less chilling than the inevitable conclusion of his family torn apart, his mother on the lam, his father in jail, all because he'd opened his stupid mouth.

Chas was tuning his guitar, the amplifier fuzzing and growling and hurting Eugene's head. He jumped down from the stage and wandered out of the gym, across the hallway to the cafeteria, bustling with costumed kids and their parents and teachers. The lights were too bright, too fluorescent. Eugene felt required to slink away.

The hallway by the Haunted Home Ec Room was quieter. It was just seven o'clock, almost time for the packs of middle-schoolers that were its primary audience to start showing up. To his surprise, Dani Drake was standing at the door of the home ec room, hair coiffed in shining curls, bright red lips parted in a maniacal smile. She was wearing an old-fashioned dress, high-heeled shoes, and a white apron, all splattered with blood, and there was a string of pearls and a gummy-looking red slash across her throat.

"Canapé?" she chirped, holding up a tray of eyeballs and ears and noses, neatly arranged in concentric circles.

Eugene's natural instinct was to continue slinking by, glued to the lockers on the far wall, but there was something unmistakably awe-some about what Dani was doing. He hadn't expected such a thing from her, though that may have been a side effect of Oneida's vocal dis-like of her, which Eugene felt obliged to echo.

"The blue eyes taste the best," she said. "Raspberry or something." She stuck out a lurid blue tongue.

Eugene silently chose the proffered candy and looked over Dani's shoulder, but the rest of the home ec room was shrouded in darkness. A recording of creaks and rattles played nearby, and he heard a familiar voice—maybe Heather Atkins?—saying *Oh my God, he did* not.

"It's pretty lame inside," Dani muttered out of the side of her mouth. "I feel like a false advertisement."

"You saying this is as good as it gets?" Eugene pointed to her cos-tume.

"As far as the Haunted Home Ec Room is concerned, hell, yes."

"I heard that, Dani!" It *was* Heather Atkins. "That doesn't sound like sophomore spirit to me!"

"Suck it, Heather!" Dani shouted back. To Eugene, she said, "I kind of . . . had a run-in with the local authorities." She grinned, showing all her teeth. "This is what community service looks like at Ruby Falls High."

"It looks good," Eugene said, and then caught his breath, because he couldn't quite believe he'd said it. He coughed. "I have to get back to the—the band, my sister—my sister's band?"

Dani nodded. "Later, Donnie."

Eugene blinked and half-waved good-bye before skulking back to the foyer between the gym and the cafeteria. He chewed the blue eye (Dani was right, it was tasty) and sighed. Nothing was normal and noth-ing was right, and it was only going to get weirder. And worse.

Because Oneida was standing in the foyer, waiting for him. Dis-tracted by the little-kid rabble emanating from the cafeteria, the very promising sounds of Insane Armhole warming up, and the sour blue thrill of Dani's eyeball on his tongue, Eugene didn't recognize her at first. She was wearing black leggings and a tight black shirt with a shiny silver zipper down the front, unzipped an inch or three. The zipper pull, dangling and round as an aluminum pop-top, glinted hypnotically, crying out for him to loop his index finger through and give a yank. She caught his eye and shrugged, holding out her arms and spinning to present the full effect. The leggings ended in high black boots, and there was a wide leather belt around her waist, a waist that was much smaller than even Eugene, who ought to know, knew.

"You're"—his brain clicked—"You're, uh, you're Elizabeth Hurley in *Austin Powers*." Oh, Jesus, his girlfriend was hotter and stranger than hell and scared the living shit out of him. Eugene actually felt his heart flutter, and not in a good way.

"What are you talking about?" She smiled and reached into her coat.

"Aren't you supposed to be a spy, a British spy?"

He swallowed past a dry patch in his throat.

"I'm a cat," she said, and slipped two black ears on a headband over her hair.

"Oh! You're Catwoman!"

She shrugged. "I guess so. I mean, I'm a cat and I'm a girl, so I suppose it could be interpreted that way. But I"—she fluttered her hands—"I don't know. I'm just a black cat. I thought you'd—"

"I do! I like! I very much like!" Eugene said, his voice a little too high. He tried to smile to show her he was happy, when he was really something else entirely, something that didn't have a name but that he could vaguely begin to understand as insane and self-defeating, with a side of retarded. *Why don't I like? Why am I such a stupid asshole?* A girl who lets me stick my tongue in her mouth shows up in a black bodysuit, and I don't love it the way I'm supposed to love it. And it can't be because she doesn't look insanely hot, because she does look insanely hot—and it's not because I'm gay, because I'm not—it's just—

He thought of Dani as Dead Donna Reed and immediately grabbed Oneida's hand to lead her into the gym. Oneida Jones, revealed: ordinary and artless—who, he suddenly realized, barely knew anything about him, except for the biggest secret he'd ever had and had been unable to keep.

In the war for Eugene Wendell's soul, his penis lost to his brain exactly one day too late.

❧

"I'd like to dedicate the next song to my little brother." Patricia covered the mike with her hand and coughed. "You all know I have a little brother who goes to school here?"

The crowd, which clearly thought Insane Armhole was the greatest thing to happen in the gym since Annie Holmes fell face-first off a cheerleading pyramid, roared.

It was an unusually well-attended Halloween carnival. Eugene allowed himself a moment of pride-by-association, knowing the crowd had doubled after the first few songs brought out cell phones and calls of "Get down here, they don't suck!" Patricia had changed into a truly righteous costume, a light pink nothing of a dress, skewed tiara on her head and floppy corsage on her wrist, her arms pale as bone under the harsh lights set high in the makeshift stage scaffolding, where, Eugene knew, a bucket of fake blood teetered, waiting patiently to be poured over his sister's head at the conclusion of the first set. He loved his sister; of course he did. How could he not? She was crazy. She was talented. She could play the shit out of that bass. He tried to be as happy for her as he could tell, from the wide grin she couldn't suppress, that she felt herself. But where once he'd been afraid *of,* now he was afraid *for* her—afraid this would be it. This would be her debut and swan song together. Whether because their parents got sent to jail or ran away or they were orphaned, their lives ripped apart—or if none of that happened, if Patricia simply never Made It Big. Eugene almost wished, for his sister's sake, that she'd be able to blame it on her little brother if it never happened for her. *This must be what it feels like to love someone*, he thought, and felt both very big and very small. He squeezed Oneida, clenched in his arms, a little tighter.

Eugene thought Chas was stalling by strumming a repetitive riff that sounded like the whirring of an industrial fan motor. Then Patricia growled the word *Beetlebum* into the microphone.

Eugene's body went rigid. This song. *This* song. It was the kind of thing they played at the prom in hell. His sister's voice flew over everyone else's heads but pierced Eugene's brain: *what you done*, she sang.

What you done?

"Who sings this?" Oneida asked his shoulder, where her face was pressed. "It's creepy."

"I'm thirsty." Eugene coughed. "You want a drink?" At great peril, he removed his arms from Oneida. Someone jostled him from behind and he walked. He didn't care if she followed or not, he needed to get away from this crowd of swaying morons, and this horrible song, this horrible horrible dirge of a song that knew too much, that asked perfectly awful questions in his sister's voice.

A lunch table had been set up with punch and plastic cups, and when it came into view, Eugene was so desperate to get to it that he elbowed someone hard in the back of his head. He didn't realize who he'd knocked until Oneida, following close behind, said, "Andrew Lu"—as though she were shocked to see him; as though he didn't go to the same school they went to; as though the cosmic forces that hated Eugene Wendell *wouldn't* put his archenemy between him and the salvation of punch, directly in line with the point of his elbow.

Eugene kept walking. Lori Whitman, unpopular, dull, pathetically eager to ingratiate herself, had been given the job of punch ladler, Eugene suspected, because she could be easily convinced to look the other way while some senior dumped a quart of cheap vodka in the punch bowl. Eugene tossed back three tiny cups, which were disgusting but not yet spiked. The song droned on, its refrain repetitive, monotonous, "Hey, Jude" but a thousand times more evil. There was no way Patricia could possibly know how apt that dedication was. There was no way. Chalk it up as a moment of prophecy. His brain burned and he felt like crying.

Then he saw Oneida and Andrew, standing a few feet clear of the crowd. Talking. Just talking. She was smiling, just a little, but he wasn't. What were they talking about? Andrew Lu rubbed the back of his head and Oneida said something, and shrugged, and then Andrew Lu smiled at her, and the music was loud again, different, a new song. The punch warmed Eugene's stomach; maybe it had alcohol in it after all, and he'd just sucked it down too quickly to taste it.

But no—no, it wasn't the punch—oh, it wasn't the punch—it was anger. It was rage, and Eugene hadn't felt it in so long, he'd forgotten how to recognize it at first. A hot stone. Brilliant pain. A helpless, mindless thing that built upon itself until it took him, took him over and took him under—and here it was again, it was self-destruction, self-immolation, and it was going to happen, here and now. There were no velvet-filled bottles to smash. There were no projects, no works of art in the making, no distractions—there was only Oneida, the uncontrollable variable, and Andrew Lu, who hated him, and this was the way it started. This was the start of something bad, the beginning of his end.

All those feelings of doom, those precognitions of destruction, had been about this moment—this moment when he could choose either to let the end come on its own or be an active agent of the apocalypse. And Christ, he needed to do something.

The anger lit him like neon. It drove him across the floor and squared his shoulders. He swung at Andrew Lu with more fury than he'd ever mustered in his life. But Andrew, athletic, deflected, ducked, and clocked Eugene, this time in his left eye. Insane Armhole had moved on to something with a nefarious disco beat, and Eugene, who loved to move to music, jabbed at Andrew once, twice, three times on the beat. Nothing landed. Andrew swept his legs out from under him. Eugene, on his back, kicked Andrew in the stomach with both feet and rolled out of the way. He felt large hands on either side of his shoulders, felt himself lifted off the floor and pulled out of the way, out the gym doors, down the hallway past the locker rooms, and pushed against the crash bar on the door to the student parking lot. He stumbled down the short flight of steps and spun around to see Harrison, fat, lazy—of course, the PE teacher—pointing and yelling for him to stay the hell away from the dance for the rest of the night, you screwup!

"I mean it, you stay the hell—"

"I'm with the band!"

"You little piece of—" Harrison was jostled as someone came up behind him and pushed him out of the way. She ran down the steps, the silver zipper pull on her shirt jangling with each bounce of her boobs.

"Onei—*ow*." Eugene's head hurt. Andrew Lu had fucking walloped him.

"He's all yours, honey!" Harrison called, and shut the door, leaving them alone in the cold, dimly lit parking lot, loose gravel scraping under their feet.

Oneida was hugging herself to stay warm and not looking at him. Whatever had propelled her so dramatically out of the gym after him had evaporated, shrunk with cold, and she looked around nervously, like she'd made a really stupid, really rash decision. Eugene didn't blame her. She had. But so had he, and he didn't know yet if he would live to regret it or if it wouldn't mean a thing in the grand scheme. He'd only known how good it felt when his Chucks connected with Andrew Lu's stomach, how he'd pushed and Andrew Lu had given. Maybe he had some power after all.

"Where's your car?" She rubbed her nose.

They slid into the car's front seat from opposite sides. There was no question of trying out a few tricks in the backseat, no question of whether either one was interested in sucking a little face. Eugene turned the ignition and cranked the heat as high as it would go.

"What do you want?"

The question was so abrupt, and Oneida's voice so dimmed by the roar of the heaters, Eugene thought he could reasonably pretend he hadn't heard it.

"What do you want, Eugene?" she asked again.

"I don't know," he said. "What do *you* want? 'Cause I don't think it's me."

She looked really hurt, and Eugene wished he hadn't said it, even though the answer to that question was, in fact, exactly what he wanted. Along with a blood oath assurance that she'd never tell his secret to another living soul.

"You really want to know?" she asked.

"Yes, I really want to know."

"I want you to tell me what you want."

"I already told you, *I don't know*." His voice squeaked on *don't*.

"You're lying, dumb-ass. Everybody wants something, and I asked you first." She crossed her arms over her chest again, got tangled in her zipper pull, and spastically zipped it all the way up her throat.

His head was killing him. He thought Andrew Lu might have given him a concussion. Speak of the devil: out of the corner of his eye he saw a figure on a bike pedaling furiously down the school's driveway and away up the road. At least both of them had been bounced. *Crash, jerk,* he thought. *Crash your bike in a ditch.*

"Fine," he said. "I want to know your biggest secret. I already told you mine." Even mentioning it, however obliquely, made his gut hurt.

She dug her front teeth into her lower lip and inhaled. "Why do you want to know that?" she asked, prickly.

"Because I just want to. You didn't ask me to explain why I wanted to kiss you in the first place, did you?"

"Actually, I did, and you did explain," she said, and then blushed so bright Eugene could see it, even in the faint glow of the floodlights mounted above the gym door. "You told me I might be the only person in our whole school who might be worth getting to know, and that if you didn't have sex soon you would probably die."

"Oh. Right." Eugene sat back in his seat.

They stared ahead in silence for what felt like forever. The view from the student parking lot was of the football practice field, muddy with leaves and autumn runoff. In the dark, Eugene could just make out the outlines of that stupid thing with the pads and the wheels that the football team used to practice tackling. He exhaled slowly. The only thing left to do, the only thing he could do, it seemed, was to put the car in drive and take Oneida home, and—

Then what.

"I want to know your secret," Eugene said. "Because I'm afraid, now that you know mine."

"Afraid?" Oneida's voice was small. "What do you think I'm going to do?"

He shrugged. "It's a big secret," he said. "And it really wasn't mine to tell."

"My secret isn't mine either," she said.

Voltage skittered up his spine. "Whose is it?"

"My mom's."

"Does it have to do with Arthur?" He hoped not. Despite the whole duping incident, he really liked Arthur, and from the way Oneida's eyes were widening, staring straight ahead, it didn't sound like this secret was particularly good.

"Could be. I don't know who my father is." She swallowed. "I guess it could be Arthur."

"Your mom never told you?" Eugene couldn't imagine not knowing. Not being at home, being away all the time, being divorced—that he could imagine. But not having a clue who your dad or your mom was, not knowing? He shivered.

"Oh, God." Her mouth turned down. "I guess it really could be Arthur, couldn't it? Mom really likes him, and she won't talk to me about him, but—I've been so mean about him. Oh my God." She took off her glasses and wiped at her eyes, and Eugene realized, with horror, that she was crying, and had been, silently, maybe this whole time. Her face was too wet to be the product of this moment of realization alone.

"It's OK."

"No, it isn't," she said. "It's all different. I've been such a jerk. I miss my mom, I miss—I miss not caring that I didn't know. If I could understand a little, it might be better, I don't know—but maybe it's horrible, you know? There has to be a reason she didn't tell me, like my father was married, or he's in jail, or she was—r-raped." She snuffled wetly, and Eugene, who had no idea what to do, was at least able to hand her a fast food napkin from the pocket in the door. She blew her nose.

"It's like—it's like this question just gets bigger and bigger inside of me, and the bigger it gets, the more I forget who I thought I was, or used to be, or am. It's—it's—"

"Totally assy," Eugene said, out of panic more than empathy, and Oneida, mid-sniffle, laughed out loud. It was a beautiful sound. It was a sound of salvation. Of reprieve.

"Can you talk to your mom about it? Can you ask her?"

"I know I should. I know it would be the right thing to do, but I don't think I can trust her to tell me the truth. The whole truth, all of it. But—do you remember Bert? I told you about her that day you came over?"

"Lives in the attic, going to burn your house down?"

Oneida nodded. "She knows. She almost told us all at the dinner table one night. I've been working up the courage to ask her for, like, weeks."

"Ask her tonight," Eugene said. "Imagine how good it's going to feel once you know. Even if it's bad, it can't be as bad as all the horrible things you've imagined, because, I mean, reasonably, it can only be one horrible thing. If it is, in fact, horrible. And you'll know. You'll know, and you won't have to wonder, and you won't have to not feel like yourself anymore."

Oneida dabbed at her nose with the napkin. "I know," she said. "I should."

Eugene felt grand. Magnanimous, even. Not only did this revelation make them even, it made them equal. He had never liked her better than he did right then, half in shadows, half lit from the school floodlights, wiping her face with a McDonald's napkin, very real and very sad. And he could save her—it wouldn't be hard at all. And then she'd be in his debt, and he'd feel safer, feel better, about everything she knew.

"I'm taking you home," he said, leaning across the seat. "I'll drop you off and you have to promise that you'll talk to either the creepy old bat or your mom tonight. And call me tomorrow about what you find out."

"OK." She pushed her hair behind her ears and put her glasses back on. "And *you* have to promise to stop beating up Andrew Lu."

Eugene, hand on the gearshift, grinned from the tips of his toes. "Don't you mean getting beat up *by* Andrew Lu?"

They smiled at each other—really smiled at each other, with their eyes and their teeth and their noses and their whole damn faces.

"You know, black eyes are sort of hot," she said. And then, unzipping her shirt: "Can you drive with one hand?"

So it was that Eugene drove home from the Ruby Falls Halloween Carnival with one hand on the steering wheel and the other inside his girlfriend's shirt, resting comfortably on her boob—his girlfriend Oneida Jones, who was bizarre, unhappy, and maybe unknowable, but still a girl and a friend who let him touch her boobs, and even at the age of fifteen, Eugene had the wherewithal to realize it might not get much better. The Milky Way Bar and Grill parking lot was full, muffled country music dopplering in the still air as they drove past. The world hadn't ended, and Eugene felt fine. The heater roared. The car hummed.

His only regret that night, as he hurtled through the dark back roads of Ruby Falls, was that he hadn't seen his sister showered in gore, hadn't heard her banshee wail; that he wasn't able to share that moment with the women in his brilliantly screwed little family—the women, he suspected, who knew what was really going on the whole time. An old Zeppelin song came on the radio. Patricia had played it for him once—when they were very young, little kids, not grown-ups, which it felt like he was becoming a little more every day. It was the kind of song that played at the end of movies, right before the black screen and the roll credits, designed to trick you into feeling good right before you had to make that final concession to reality, pick up your empty popcorn boxes and shuffle back to your life. It made him think of Astor, of the world he'd known before he told Oneida his secret, a world where his father was a superhero. But now a door he'd never believed existed had opened: he'd stepped through and the way back was shut, sealed, locked forever. The lost world made him a little sad, more than a little anxious, and glad that Led Zeppelin existed—that all music, all movies, all art existed—to make him feel a little better about the real world. Which seemed a terribly poignant and grown-up insight, and he smiled to himself in the dark. Then he drove under the old trestle overpass on Bleeker Road and the rock smashed into his windshield from above, and the last conscious thought in Eugene Wendell's brain was

Oh fuck me.

Part III

20 ～ Oneida Underwater

The song was still playing on the radio.

Oneida didn't know who sang it or what it was called, only that it was still playing on the radio, which seemed ridiculous—that after the windshield splintered and the car swerved and rocketed over and down and the seat belt dug into her chest and stomach and the edge of her neck—that after all that, once she stopped moving forward and her body had paid the price, the song was still playing. Like nothing had happened.

Oneida blinked. Looking out was like looking up from the underside of a ripple in a pond. Like opening your eyes underwater. She was underwater; she felt slow, pressurized. Dislocated and unable to breathe. Her stomach and her chest hurt, so she reached down and released the buckle and then she could breathe again. Once, in; again, out. She made fists with her hands and wriggled her toes and bent her legs at the knee and knew she was going to throw up, immediately, so she opened her door and vomited into the soft dirt lining the ditch where Eugene's car lay dead.

Eugene.

"Eugene," she said. "Eugene, wake up, we had an accident. Something—fell, Eugene."

Eugene's head was resting on the steering wheel. He'd been wearing his seat belt, but something must have happened, he must have hit his head on the wheel or—she didn't know, she couldn't remember anything other than the web of glass and the swerve and the seat belt and the song.

There was blood. She could see it now, a tiny drop rolling from his lips. She watched the red drop trace a line from the corner of his mouth down his chin, giving him a ventriloquist dummy's jaw; she watched the blood pool in a droplet, dangle, grow fat, and finally drop.

She couldn't wait for it to land.

The door wouldn't open all the way, but it opened far enough. She scrambled out of the ditch. Narrowly avoided planting her foot in her own puke. Where were they? Just past the bridge on Bleeker. She scanned the road in both directions, but it was deserted. It was always deserted. Who lived around here? Could she just start shouting, would someone show up? Did Eugene have a cell phone? She didn't; the reception wasn't that great out here to begin with, and anyway she didn't have any friends and she never went anywhere, so there was never any need for her to call home—

Oh, God, she did have a friend and he was unconscious.

"Somebody, *help*!" she screamed. It sounded so stupid, so lame, to actually shout the word *help*. Her voice was so puny.

The song was still playing. She could hear it through her door, which was open; how long was this taking? How long had it been since the—whatever—had hit them? She wobbled up the road, eyes jerking back and forth, looking for—what? A rock? A soda can?

What was she supposed to do? Where could she run? There were woods beyond the ditch to her left, and there were more woods beyond the road to her left. She had no idea how close any houses were, she had no time to waste, she couldn't move him to search for a cell phone without being afraid she'd break his back—

"I'm so sorry," said a voice behind her, a very familiar voice—and she turned and it was Andrew Lu, his face red, eyes full of fear, hands cupped over his mouth and nose like he was terrified of the sounds he was making. "I was aiming for the roof, not the windshield, I just wanted to scare him, I just wanted to scare him, I swear to you—"

Andrew Lu, standing in the middle of the dark road, now starting to cry.

Andrew Lu, whom she had dreamed of; who was so beautifully different and worthy, her worthy soul, who would know her and save her—

Who had stolen her idea like a cheap bastard and had only been trying to scare Eugene Wendell, had been aiming for the roof. He was still talking. Actually trying to explain himself—*Wendy destroyed my guitar and screwed up my GPA; you know you need a 3.2 to be on the cross-country team, and he screwed it up, and I hated him*—but Oneida had stopped listening. She thought of Eugene sitting in her kitchen, so obviously horny it was kind of hysterical, and his beautiful, wonderful secrets—and she thought of Eugene sitting on the beanbag chair beside her in the prop loft, telling her he loved her, which was so stupid it was almost certainly the truth.

"Do you have a cell phone?" she asked Andrew Lu, who was still babbling and quivering, a pile of human Jell-O. He reached in his pocket and handed her a small silver phone.

"Thank you." She punched 9-1-1 across the glowing yellow-green buttons, and congratulated herself for not punching him, or tearing out his throat, or throwing a rock at his head, but only saying, "You are a piece of shit, Andrew Lu."

"You can't tell anyone," he said, and grabbed her, hard; grabbed her by both arms and stared into her eyes. "You cannot tell anyone. If you tell on me, you're going to ruin my life."

The cell phone was warm against her ear. The line to 9-1-1 was ringing.

"I'll do whatever you want, tell me, just—tell me, whatever you want me to do, I'll do it, I swear to God—" His grip tightened.

"Let go," she said, just as a voice said, "Nine-one-one dispatch, what is your emergency?"

"I've been in a car accident on Bleeker Road in Ruby Falls, just past the bridge overpass."

Andrew loosened his hold but didn't let go. She could feel him searching to hold her gaze, even as she looked off, trying to concentrate.

"Are you hurt?" It was a woman's voice, low and professional. Calm. Like she'd done this a million times before; how weird was that?

"I don't think I'm hurt, I got out of the car fine. My friend was driving and is unconscious. There was blood coming out of his mouth, I think he bit his lip or something—"

"Have you tried to speak to him or move him?"

"No." She swallowed. A huge lump had grown in her throat. She couldn't even swallow her own spit. "I said his name but he didn't wake up. I think he hit his head on the steering wheel."

"Is he breathing?"

"Oh my God." She didn't know where she'd been but apparently she was coming back, right now—back to a place where her body felt pain (all over, *God*, she hurt *all over*) and her eyes had tears and her voice wasn't her own. "I think so," she said. "How can I tell? Oh—mirror, I can use a mirror, I have to find a mirror."

"Please remain calm, miss. Help is on the way and should be there very soon. Is there anyone else there with you?"

Andrew's hands tightened, harder than before. He loomed close enough to hear every word the dispatcher said. She could smell something sweet and fruity on his breath—punch, maybe, or a Starburst. Even this close, where Oneida assumed most people became a lunar landscape of pores and blemishes, Andrew Lu was absolutely stunning: skin milky and bluish in the moonlight, eyes large and dark and beautifully lashed. She felt a twinge, a memory ache, the ghost of her not-quite-forgotten desire passing through her. He was near enough to kiss her, and for a moment she wondered if that would have made her answer differently. Not that it would have mattered. By using his cell phone, Oneida had already connected Andrew Lu to the scene—which actually had not occurred to her until that moment.

"I'm not alone. I'm with a student at Ruby Falls High named Andrew Lu who is both the cause of the accident and a complete piece of shit."

"What was that, miss?"

Andrew Lu pushed her and spun away, running his hands through his hair, that beautiful inky hair that Oneida doubted she would ever get over.

"I'm not sure what happened exactly, but I believe Andrew Lu dropped an object from the overpass which struck the car I was riding in, causing it to go off the road and into the ditch. I am bruised but otherwise fine, but my friend, who was driving, is still unconscious and bleeding from his mouth, and I'm about to go check if he's still breathing, but the thing is—"

"Miss, calm down. I need you to calm down and check on your friend. Do you have a mirror?"

"I will save you, Eugene," Oneida promised the empty road. She could hear gravel crunching behind her, fast, as Andrew Lu ran away—actually *ran away*, that wuss. That bastard. Oneida wobbled back to the car. What had she been thinking when she put on these boots, other than that they would make Eugene's eyes do that hysterical cartoon-animal bugging-out thing. She'd found them in the back of the hall closet and they'd surprised the hell out of her. She couldn't fathom Mona ever wearing them, and it looked like she never had; they were old but hardly worn, the leather still tight and stiff. The inside tag that she remembered because it was shocking pink—Gumballs, that was the brand; what a stupid name for a company that made shoes—was rubbing the top of her calf raw.

"Have you found a mirror, miss?"

"Just a sec," Oneida said, and plopped straight down in the road to rip off the boots. The simple act of standing up again took everything she had. Her body wasn't going to last very long, she knew; she must have been running on pure adrenaline.

She didn't have a mirror in her bag. She vowed to care more about makeup from now on, if only because it would always keep a mirror in her purse. There wasn't any mirror in the car, either, that wasn't attached to something or that she could remove without breaking. "I can't find a mirror!" she told the woman on the phone. "I'm such a crap girl, I don't even have a compact."

"It's all right, miss, it's going to be fine."

Then Oneida remembered what she did have in her possession, tucked into the pocket lining of her winter coat: a flask, half full of vodka, shiny and silver.

"I have a flask!" she said, and the woman on the phone made a confused noise, and the faint whine of a siren grew louder, like someone was turning up the volume on their television. Oneida, who had taken her first taste of vodka earlier that afternoon, unscrewed the cap and took her second. It had seemed the thing to do, when going to a lame school function; she had planned on shocking (and eventually sharing with) Eugene. Why anyone would drink this stuff for any reason other than to get drunk was totally beyond her.

Shaking, she crawled back into the passenger seat and held the flask as close to Eugene's nose as she could manage, but it was too dark in the car to see if his breath was fogging the silver. He was too awkwardly bent, too close to the steering wheel, for her to get the flask properly under his nose or his mouth.

A different song was playing on the radio now, an old song but one she recognized, something chipper and electronic-sounding from the eighties. It was too fast, too cheerful, to be real. It made Oneida feel like shouting at the radio. She told the woman on the 9-1-1 dispatch that she couldn't get the flask close enough to Eugene's face to be able to tell if he was breathing, and the woman on the dispatch told her to sit tight and wait. The siren was getting louder and louder. Oneida unscrewed the flask again and took her third and fourth slugs of vodka. The alcohol stung her throat, which was already raw from throwing up.

Oneida's hands began to shake. Eugene wasn't waking up, Eugene wasn't moving, and it may have been the fifth and sixth slugs of vodka talking, but Oneida was gripped with the sudden terror of the truth— she actually liked him. *Liked him* liked him. She'd begun to suspect it approximately twenty minutes ago, when they'd smiled at each other in the student parking lot. It had reminded her of that day in Dreyer's class when he'd slain Andrew Lu's guitar, how they'd known each other with only a look, the two of them an island in a sea of meaningless sound. That one moment had shocked Oneida into going over to his house, into venturing toward what frightened but grew to fascinate her.

But everything she'd done with him since had been—what had it been? It had been easy. He had been obvious, and surprisingly easy, and it had felt so nice to have that much control over someone when everything else in her life was going to shit. It had been nice to play with Eugene Wendell.

And now he was broken.

The blackness of Bleeker Road was perforated by flashing white and red, and the siren was louder than ever. Oneida took slugs seven, eight, and nine and reached for Eugene's hand, which was a little cool and didn't come to life in her own. "Wake up, Eugene," she whispered into his big pink seashell of an ear. "Please wake up."

A hand knocked on her window, three sharp raps. Three reminders of the world that existed outside of Eugene's underwater car, that had no business existing, that Oneida had never felt like being a part of anyway.

⁂

Arthur came for her. He stepped through the revolving door of the emergency room. He looked like hell, and only half because of the sick fluorescent lighting. He hadn't looked like hell in weeks, which made the backslide—shirt untucked, face unshaven and pale, eyes red-rimmed and glassy—all the more disturbing. Oneida couldn't help searching him for parts of herself, now that the possibility that he could be her father had occurred to her. Is that what her nose would grow into, someday? Were those her ears, her arms; did she walk like that? She thanked God she was drunk. There was no way in hell she would have been able to deal with this sober.

"Hi, Arthur," she said.

"Have—have you been drinking?" Arthur waved the air between them, which must have been a tiny cloud of vodka.

"Maybe." She rubbed her nose with the back of her hand. "Where's Mom?"

"Like mother like daught—" Arthur mumbled cryptically, before losing his voice and turning the color of skim milk. "She's—she's checking you out. At reception."

The waiting room teemed. A little kid holding a bag of ice in a baseball mitt against his knee was hiccuping, great violent hiccups that shook his body like sobs (or maybe they were sobs, what did she know, she could barely feel her brain). Nurses and doctors and people, so many people, were walking and hustling and hobbling, crisscrossing, narrowly avoiding collisions, between the check-in desk and the waiting area and the hallway with all the little half-curtained alcoves, where they'd sat her on a table, blinded her with a tiny flashlight, and pronounced her a little drunk but whole. Someone had called her mom— she thought she remembered filling out a form with her name and her telephone number. Friday night, full moon, *Halloween*—so it wasn't a myth that emergency rooms went nuts like this. Or maybe it was the vodka that made everything seem louder and brighter and made her, in the center of it all, feel slow and exhausted and like she didn't give a rat's ass about any of these stupid people flitting around like guppies. She didn't know for sure if what she was feeling was buzzed or shock. She'd never felt either before tonight.

And then there was Mona.

Looking even worse than Arthur, which Oneida wouldn't have thought humanly possible until it was staring her in the face, in plaid pajama pants and sandals, hair a shambles, puffy and red and eyes leaking tears. *I did this,* Oneida thought. *I have brought Mona to this state.*

Oneida almost barfed again, right on the floor of the ER.

"Mom," she said. Mona started to cry. Actually, to *cry.* Then she wobbled on her feet and slammed into Arthur's side and Oneida understood what he'd meant when he said *like mother, like daughter:* Mona was drunk. Mona wasn't devastated with worry, she was *drunk.* Oneida needed her mother, and her mother was *drunk,* and Oneida was too buzzed herself to see the irony in the situation. She was only ashamed and embarrassed. For both of them. She shut her eyes.

Then she stood from the sticky blue vinyl seat and swayed on legs like warm bubblegum. Arthur darted forward and caught her under one elbow to steady her, and she pitched forward, her face smashing against his chest and her arms whipping around his back, where she clung, because Arthur was real and Arthur didn't move. She remembered Arthur's bristly chest wounds and hoped they were healed or, at the very least, that her head butt had missed them.

She closed her eyes and buried her face in Arthur's shirt. "What the hell happened to my mom?" she asked him.

"She's fine." Arthur sounded like he was halfway to crying himself. What the hell was this all about? What the *hell.* "She's right here. Your mom is fine."

Oneida rolled her head to the side against Arthur and watched Mona watching her, blinking but lacking the capacity for speech. She hugged Arthur tighter. Mona swallowed but didn't say a word.

"Come on," Arthur said quietly as he maneuvered her to face forward, propped her with an arm around her back, and led her through the emergency room, away from the guppies in lab coats, the wounded Little Leaguer; and somewhere, hidden from her, Eugene Wendell—Eugene Wendell, whose cool hand she'd held in the ambulance and, once they arrived at the hospital, who'd been borne away on the human tide. She'd noticed a very tall, very thin man with a beaky nose swim by that she thought might have been Eugene's father. That was long before Arthur and Mona showed up. Before they showed up, but after they blinded her with the little flashlight, and a man in a dark blue uniform with watery eyes had asked her to describe what she remembered. She told him everything, which wasn't much, but which included numerous repetitions of the name *Andrew Lu Andrew Lu Andrew Lu.*

Everything was swimming.

"Come on," Arthur was saying. "Just a little farther."

She didn't even look to see if Mona followed.

The automatic doors whooshed apart. Cold October air smacked her in the face.

"I'm sorry," she said. She wanted to specify—*I'm sorry that I can't walk like a human being*—but it seemed like too much work.

They crossed the street, approached a parking garage, got into an elevator. "Come on," Arthur said again, and shifted his arm around her. Is this what having a father felt like? Did dads haul their drunk-ass daughters out of emergency rooms so calmly, so steadily? Arthur was warm. He smelled like soap and something she couldn't quite place, something harsh and chemical, and, on top of that, sweet. Sugary. He smelled like her mother. She squeezed her arm around his middle and opened her eyes to see that Mona had, in fact, followed them from the emergency room and was pressing a button on the elevator panel.

They rode to the rooftop level. Oneida summoned the last of her mental energy to appreciate that the ambulance had driven them to one of the hospitals in Syracuse instead of the local clinic. *You know what that means,* she tried not to think but couldn't help herself: *Eugene needed more than an Ace bandage or a sling or a booster shot or a lollipop.* There was a city six stories down, all around; traffic lights blinking from red to green. Streetlamps glowing. There was so much—sound.

The station wagon was parked a few spaces over from the elevator, and Oneida let Arthur guide her the rest of the way, the last few steps to the car and into the front passenger seat. The seat belt hurt where it rested against the bruises she'd gotten earlier that evening.

Arthur dropped into the driver's seat and started the engine. She heard a third door slam as Mona got inside.

"What happened to Mom?" Oneida asked. Everything was slipping away. She couldn't keep her eyes open, couldn't be aware any longer. Not today. She just needed an answer to this last question, she told her brain; just hang on for this one answer.

Arthur didn't respond. Oneida felt the car back out of its space and slowly corkscrew through the parking garage, slaloming down to street level. She heard Arthur talking to the parking attendant.

"What happened." The car floated down a curb, turned right, stopped at a traffic light. Oneida's eyes opened blearily. Round red stoplights swayed in the blue darkness.

"It was an accident," Arthur said.

21 ⌐ *Arthur's Accident*

Everything in Arthur's life was because of an accident.

All of it. Absolutely all of it, Arthur thought: all of my life is because of *one accident*. Because of one moment that was never supposed to happen—one moment that bred a maelstrom of cause and effect and randomized happenstance—that's the only explanation. That's the only explanation for how he—Arthur Rook, photographer, husband, born in Somerville, Massachusetts, and transplanted to the City and County of Los Angeles—could find himself the sole sober person in a car hurtling through Syracuse, New York, at midnight on a Friday night, in the position to explain to the daughter of the creator of his world—*Amy, Creator of Worlds*—that he, Arthur, had come to destroy hers.

It was an accident.

"Nobody gets drunk by accident," Oneida said.

Arthur tried to catch Mona's eye in the rearview but Mona was staring out the window.

"Go to sleep," Arthur told them both. He didn't know which had a stronger hold over them, alcohol or exhaustion, but sleep was the solution. He looked sideways at Oneida, at the streetlights rippling over her pale face as he drove beneath them. *God, she looked like Amy.* He could see it now—it was so plain, so clear. That long face, her jaw, her nose, her eyes; the timbre of her voice; and the way she stood, the way she walked, all strange angles and flat planes. Architectural brutalism in the form of a girl. This is what Amy must have looked like, back when Mona knew her—a collection of parts, of pieces, that by the time she met Arthur had learned what they meant in relation to one another, how to move as one.

How had he not seen this? How had he, Arthur, not *seen* what was physically in front of him—the best parts that Amy left behind? Her brain, her blood, her heart?

Arthur Rook was awake. He had been awake for three hours and fifteen minutes, give or take. In that time he had thrown up once. He had eaten one slice of lemon, because it was in his hand and he wanted to taste something cold and sour and real. He had held Mona until she stopped crying. He had answered the telephone and handed it to Mona when the anonymous voice asked to speak to the mother of Oneida Jones; that was when he threw up. The mother of Oneida Jones was Amy.

His Amy.

Who was *dead*.

Arthur merged into traffic heading south on the Route 81 overpass. The wagon's tires whined on the high bridge surface. He could theoretically understand why it had been easier to keep Oneida in the dark. He couldn't imagine how you prepare for a conversation like that, let alone what it would feel like to be on the receiving end of that news—but wouldn't it have been easier to tell her the truth from the beginning? Not to lie to her, ever? Not that anything could be done about the choices Mona had made years ago—and not that they had anything to do with *him*.

Choices she made when she was a kid, choices she lived with for half her life. Choices she loved. There wasn't a doubt in his mind that she loved Amy's daughter (the same way she'd loved Amy, he thought) with an intensity that defined her entire existence, a sort of paralysis of love. Which, if he was being honest with himself, was also how he loved Amy: blindly. What had Amy been to him if not his entire world in Los Angeles?

Amy was *dead*.

Arthur's stitched-together chest pulsed like a toothache. His mouth tasted metallic. He rolled down his window, and the cold night air stung. He felt each hair on his body rise, his skin pucker; he felt like throwing up again, thrilled to be so near what was left of Amy in this world. He wanted to tell her everything and was terrified he would actually do it.

And there was so much—so much to *tell*. To everyone. He thought of his brother, David, and his sister-in-law, of his father and mother. He remembered Max and Manny and realized he had probably been fired. He tried to remember the last thing he ever said to Amy, and she to him. He couldn't.

He tried to imagine his Amy—his wife—leaving a baby, *her* baby, behind in a bathtub. He couldn't reconcile the Amy that Mona described with the Amy he had known for years, who was a little intense, a little nuts, but whom he loved so much he just didn't care. She fell asleep to *The Late Show* with her head on his shoulder. She kept a can of olives in the refrigerator and ate them off her fingers as a snack. She blasted Depeche Mode on the stereo and danced around in a T-shirt and a pair of his boxers. She was warm against him as they lay side by side, their backs against the cooler, green woolen blanket scratchy beneath their legs on the lawn of the Hollywood Forever Cemetery, where movies were screened on the side of a mausoleum on hot summer nights. Just last year they'd gone to see *Rosemary's Baby*—had watched Ruth Gordon kill Mia Farrow with kindness and a little Tanis root—and now, Amy lay. . . .

Amy's body.

Arthur's hands went numb on the steering wheel. What had he told them to do with Amy's body? He remembered being asked the question and not knowing. Had he answered?

He was struck with a sudden image of his cell phone in his palm, and in the middle of its tiny blue screen, a picture of an envelope. Flashing. Ten missed calls. From Bill (Stantz), one message saying, more or less, *There's been an accident, Arthur, where are you?* And where was his cell phone now? What had he done with it? He hadn't seen it in days, in weeks, and he had never felt its absence before this moment.

How many messages would be on it now?

He exhaled slowly. How the *fuck* had he done this to himself?

That wasn't quite true: Amy did this. The accident did this. His entire life was made in the image of one accident.

No.

Two accidents. For he was sure Oneida's conception had been an accident—not her birth, but what Mona told him about Amy and the tenant sounded too simple to deny. An avowed *inappropriate* relationship, a stupid risk: an accident. So which accident was it, then, that made Arthur's life, the one that brought Amy to Los Angeles or the one that sent him back into her past?

Oneida turned away from the center console to rest her forehead against the passenger-side window. She breathed mindlessly, contentedly. It horrified Arthur to think she had begun her life on a bed of cold white porcelain by her mother's hand. He could barely accept Amy had done it—*his* Amy wouldn't have—but acceptance wouldn't change the fact that he had loved her. That he *still* loved her. And that he loved Mona, too—for keeping the pieces of Amy she hadn't wanted but were hers: for keeping them and loving them and letting them grow up, until they were old enough to have catastrophes of their own.

Thank God she was safe: drunk but basically unhurt. He would remember how she had looked in the emergency room forever. He'd made a point of leaving Mona at reception so he could see Oneida alone. Well-meaning curator though Mona was, Arthur needed to see the girl he now knew to be Amy's daughter and feel however he was going to feel that first time without interference. He wanted no context, no filter, no descriptive placard mounted unobtrusively on Oneida's lower right side, bearing the mark of this particular work's creators:

> Amy Henderson & Ben Tennant
> *Oneida Jones*
> Circa 1992
> Skin and blood on bones

And so he saw her: a ghost dressed entirely in black. A collapsed star in the center of a bustling Friday-night emergency room, Amy-shaped without being Amy, worn and woozy. A baby half grown. Now she was fast asleep beside him, a companionable comet streaking down Route 81 in the dark. In every art theory requirement Arthur had ever taken, at the heart of every essay about experience and subjectivity he'd ever wrung out of his typewriter at three in the morning, Arthur had regurgitated the usual theories about the untrained eye: the gaze, the myth of impartiality; about how you could never see something without seeing yourself through it.

Which is probably why he looked at Oneida and thought, *I could have been your dad.*

How, in what possible world? he wondered. But still—any world was possible. Any accident could happen.

🙢

His vacation was over. He woke up early on Saturday and considered the terrifying option of calling his parents but decided to clean his room instead. His room—more like his disease. Harryhausen approved of the exorcism, and perched on top of the loveseat in a shaft of sunlight, bulk spilling in furry flaps over the sides, blissed out and purring. Arthur untacked the clothesline and the paper-clipped cards and the beaded runners. He disassembled the dioramas and at last regretted gluing Khrushchev to Mona's wall. Each tiny work was a sketch, he realized, a cartoon made in preparation for the only real work of art he'd made in years, that he'd ever made, period: the collage of Amy taken out to sea and out to space. The best thing he'd ever done, and two high school sophomores had used it to cheat on their history project.

He'd helped Amy's daughter cheat.

Amy would have loved the hell out of *that.*

He understood now what had happened when he put the collage together, could name the trigger in his brain that made him ask Mona for a kiss. With the collage, he was burying Amy the way he'd buried goldfish as a kid: in a paper box with a few trinkets to keep her company. And the pink shoebox—it was just another vessel for her corpse, more mausoleum than museum. It had reminded Arthur that Amy was more than a series of anecdotes and memories, that she had had a body, and that he would have to go back to it. He would have to deal with it as intimately as he had dealt with the pieces of her that were made of paper and plastic and tin.

"I need to know, Harry." He scratched at his chest. "Shit, Harry. I need to know what they did with her body." He felt queasy and he gagged. Waking up to the world again was murder—every part of him pounded, every piece was heavy as lead. He put the bits of Amy back in her shoebox: the pink monkey, the green Lucite key chain, the ruby-red cuff links, the pictures from Zuma Beach. And the postcard that had led him to the Darby-Jones, that he'd intended to finally deliver to Mona on Friday night when she ended up delivering the news of Amy's daughter instead.

He reread his wife's loopy handwriting:

> *Mona, I'm sorry. I should have told you. You knew me better*
> *than anyone—I think you knew me better than me. Don't worry,*
> *I swear I'm happier dead. Anyway, I left you the best parts of*
> *myself. You know where to look.*

Wait.

Arthur's brain caught like a gear and stalled, then turned. Amy never sent this postcard. Amy had sixteen years to send this postcard and she didn't, and *that had to mean something.* It had to mean she had kept this postcard because it was an important memory. She had left this postcard to be discovered upon the occasion of her death, discovered by someone who would know where to look. Someone like Arthur, with the hope, perhaps, that it would lead him to Ruby Falls—as it had—so that Arthur could name her heir—

"Oh!" He stood up so fast Harryhausen hissed and bounded away.

Mona wasn't Amy's heir. Oneida was. Her *daughter* was.

Amy wanted Arthur to tell Oneida the truth.

"Oh, *shit*," Arthur said, because in his new, wholly awake state, the power of this realization gave him an instant skull-splitting headache. He leaned against the sofa for balance. "Oh, shit," he repeated softly. So this was what he came here to do. This was what he could do for Amy: he could tell her child about the woman her mother had grown up to be. The talented and driven woman, whom he had loved with all his heart; who had been Mona's friend but not a very good one; who checked herself out at the age of sixteen, chose a new life on the other side of the country, and died again, sixteen years later, by accident.

But *this*. This was no accident. This was what Arthur was meant to do. This was the one thing that only Arthur—only Arthur Rook—could do for Amy.

He had to do it now. He had to do it today. It was too late to wait a second longer.

Arthur flung open his door, and there was Oneida, fidgeting in the hallway.

"Hi," she said.

"Oneida." Arthur pitched forward with lost momentum. "How are you feeling today?"

She shrugged. "My head kind of hurts." She was nervous—he could tell from the way her hands were fluttering—but she was looking at him with a concentration that made him wonder, for just a second, if she already knew. She didn't blink.

"Would you help me—do something?" she asked. "I could use some company."

She *did* know. Or she suspected, at the very least. Arthur smiled and felt a twinge of pride in Amy's stead: she was smart as hell.

"Of course," he said. "Whatever you need."

She let out a long breath and nodded. "OK," she said. "Please don't say anything yet, until—just let me handle it. OK?"

Arthur nodded. Oneida about-faced and marched away. But they didn't go downstairs, to the kitchen where Arthur knew Mona could have been grinding coffee; and they didn't knock on Mona's bedroom door, where she might have still been sleeping it off. Instead, Oneida climbed up two flights to the top floor of the Darby-Jones, where Arthur had never even set foot, and knocked on a heavy wooden door. Her knock was answered by a methodical tapping: the slow and steady approach of a cane.

"Hi, Bert," Oneida said, when the ancient woman finally opened the door. Bert squinted at Arthur, scowled, and addressed Oneida.

"What's the trouble?"

"Can we come in?"

"Can't keep you out, can I?" Bert turned and clomped away.

Bert's rooms resembled not so much an apartment as a belfry. The ceilings were pitched at odd angles to follow the eaves of the house, which was perfect for a stooped old woman like Bert but treacherous for Arthur, who felt unsteady and off-kilter. Oneida must have been having similar difficulties—she was fairly tall (like her mother)—but no: either Oneida was familiar with the terrain or she was naturally more nimble, because she was already sitting on a red settee that was pink with dust.

Bert settled into a rigid-looking leather chair opposite her guest, and both women looked back, gauging his progress. He knocked over a stack of tabloid magazines and Bert clucked her tongue.

"Sorry," he said. He sat beside Oneida and she bobbed up on her end of the old cushion.

"Don't bother. For the record, Mr. Rook, I would never have let you in if you hadn't been accompanied by this young lady. I don't like you and I don't trust you and I want you to know precisely where you stand."

So that dinner—with the vet and the shop teacher and this old woman—had actually happened. Arthur was still sorting his memories of the past four weeks to determine which had been real occurrences and which hadn't. They had all felt real enough at the time, but so did dreams while you were still dreaming them. The only memories he trusted were of Mona: Mona talking to him about Amy. Mona teaching him to knead fondant. Mona at the wedding. And Mona on the porch, trying to wake him with a kiss.

"That's fair," Arthur said. "I was an insolent little shit."

"I'll thank you not to swear. But yes, you were insolent."

"Actually—Bert. Why I came here, it's about"—Oneida's voice wobbled—"it's about something you said at that dinner."

"Should have known you wouldn't pop by for a nice chat and tea." She crossed her gnarled hands over the top of her cane. "What do you want?"

Oneida adjusted her glasses. "You know an awful lot about this house. And the people in it. You said you knew—everything."

"I do know everything." A television from another room suddenly went to commercial, the volume spiking. "I know that big oaf who teaches at your school is going to get his heart broken by the divorcée, and I know you"—she pointed at Arthur—"*you* are going to leave just as suddenly as you came."

Oneida frowned and turned to Arthur, who hadn't known that about himself until Bert said it—hadn't known it but knew it now. It was absolutely true. He would have to leave: suddenly, and soon. This wasn't his life, it wasn't his world, and it wasn't his dream or his vacation anymore. Loneliness licked at his heart.

"Bert, what do you know about—my mom?" Oneida's voice was so small, Arthur could barely hear it. Bert definitely didn't, and continued to rant.

"I know you, missy, are also going to leave and not come back other than for Christmas and maybe your mother's birthday, and it's going to break *her* heart. I know Roger Beers used to grow marijuana by the third post in the split rail fence on the northeast corner of the property. And I even know why that poor girl drowned herself in the broom closet. Your mother ever tell you about her?"

Oneida shook her head. "I only know that it happened. Bert—"

"That woman never tells you anything, does she?" Bert, again, didn't notice, but Arthur saw Oneida's cheeks color. "It was Mrs. William Fitchburg Jones. Killed herself—dunked her head in a basin and held herself under—because she just couldn't go on living anymore. And why do you think that was? That's right, she'd been lied to. For years. And she learned the truth and couldn't go on living that lie. Now what do you suppose that lie was, and who told it to her?"

Oneida cocked her head to the side.

"Her husband. Mr. William Fitchburg Jones, who gave you your last name, who built this house—he lied to her for as long as they were married. And the lie he told her was that he loved her."

"Bert—" Oneida tried to interrupt, but Bert had been waiting her entire life to tell his secret. The opportunity took twenty years off her face.

"That's *right*—he didn't love her. Never did! But he married her anyway, because it was the proper thing to do, it was then and it's still the proper thing now, when you get a girl in trouble—not that your mother would know anything about that."

Oneida's hand darted across the settee toward Arthur's, wrapping around his like a fierce, cold little claw.

"The truth is"—Bert cleared her throat—"all his life, Mr. William Fitchburg Jones only really loved one person. Loved that person until the day he died, and they lived here together, in this house—and do you want to guess who that person was?"

Arthur and Oneida, hands clasped on the ragged and rotting settee, leaned forward. Bert grinned, exposing a partial bridge that shone silver in the dim light.

"His portrait's in the front hall."

Oneida started, crushing Athur's hand in a spasmodic squeeze.

"They were lovers!" Bert whispered. She cackled with glee. "William Fitchburg Jones and Daniel Darby—their entire lives, they were lovers. It's the God's honest truth, as passed to me from Beth Carrington, she was their cook for fifty years and was still in the kitchen when I was a young thing and first moved into the house—oh, now *she* knew *everything*."

"Bert!" Oneida squawked. "Bert, is Arthur my father?"

Bert's face froze, lips pursed to a point.

And then Arthur realized what Oneida had asked.

So *that's* what she thought, *that's* what she suspected. It made sense, of course; she didn't even know her mother was a mystery to be solved. "Oneida," he said gently, "why didn't you just ask me? Why go through Bert?"

Oneida pressed her eyes shut tight. "I wanted to make it impossible for you to lie to me."

"What the devil are you talking about?" Bert asked.

"Is he my father?" Oneida asked Bert. And then, turned to Arthur: "Are you?" She didn't open her eyes.

"No," Arthur said. Just saying the word, he felt the loss of the past and the future alike. "No, I'm not." *But I could have been.*

"Nobody knows who got your mother into trouble, dear," Bert said. "No one but your mother. And the boy, I suppose, though who knows if she ever told him. I wouldn't have put it past her to lie to him. She's always been a bit selfish."

"Hey." Oneida bristled. "That's my *mom* you're talking about."

No, it's not.

A raw silence filled the air. Arthur put his other hand over Oneida's and said, "I'd have been honored."

It caught her completely off guard and she pulled away. "You don't know anything, Bert," she said, her voice low. "I have to go." And she pushed herself off the settee, sending up a plume of dust.

Bert, flustered, craned her neck to watch Oneida leave. Arthur stood and followed, kicking over another stack of magazines.

Oneida was sitting on the fourth floor landing, perched high over the sunny center of the house. She'd pushed her glasses up into her hair and pressed both palms against her face. Arthur sat beside her.

"I meant that," he said.

"Thanks." She sighed. "Hypothetical Dad."

She wasn't crying. If she had been, or if she'd been any other person in the world besides Amy's daughter, and therefore a stoic to the core, Arthur wouldn't have told her. He would have left the revelations of the day stand with the anonymity of her father (who even he, Arthur, knew more about than Bert). But Amy wanted her daughter to know. Amy sent him to Ruby Falls to tell her daughter the truth.

"I could have been your step-dad," he said.

Oneida dropped her hands and her glasses plopped back down over her eyes. "What do you mean?"

"I was married to your mother."

Oneida's mouth pulled tight at the corners. "What do you mean?" she said.

"Her name," Arthur said, "was Amy."

They sat in silence at the top of the house, suspended: Oneida with her arms propped on her knees, her hands limp, and Arthur, next to her, wishing he could see her eyes for the glare off her glasses. If he could only see her eyes, he thought. If he could see them, he'd see that he'd done the right thing. This was what Amy wanted. He'd faithfully carried out her final will, made her final testament.

But Oneida hid, her lenses pools of white, reflecting the dim hallway bulb above them and all the ambient sunshine from a November day that had dawned too bright—light like an ocean wave, crashing through the first floor, pooling in the front hall and rising up through the empty core of the house; until the house was full and there were no shadows, no dark corners, no places for the truth to hide. A whole world, drowned in light.

22 ⁓ Bottle, Broken

Oneida thought, *Huh.*

Then she felt a bone—tiny, fragile as a bird's—in her throat. She swallowed against it once, twice, but it was stuck.

"What"—she whispered around the bone—"what do you mean?"

Arthur looked less sure of himself. Frightened, even. His eyes darted back and forth.

"Don't you dare," she said. "Tell me what you mean."

"Come down to my room," he said.

"No." Oneida swallowed again, and again. That stupid bone. "Tell me here, tell me now."

"Mona raised you," Arthur said. "Amy carried you."

The bone snapped, and when Oneida swallowed again it sank its jagged points into the soft flesh of her throat. "But that's . . . impossible," Oneida said. "Why would you tell me that?"

"Because it's true," Arthur said. "Please, come down to my room, I can show you—" He pulled on his face with his hands. "I don't know. I don't know how to prove—"

"Fuck you, Arthur."

Oneida ran downstairs.

Mona was sitting in the kitchen, drinking a giant mug of coffee like every other Saturday morning of Oneida's life. She looked up when Oneida appeared in the doorway.

"How are you feeling?" Mona asked.

I don't know. Like I'm choking on my own blood.

"Fine," Oneida answered. She tried to swallow.

"There's fresh coffee and some grapefruit in the fridge. The troopers called a while ago. They need a statement about last night." Mona's eyes shivered in their sockets. "I told them we'd be there at ten."

"Fine."

And it was fine. Oneida told the troopers everything she'd told the police in the ER the night before, though her speech was considerably less slurred.

"Is that true?" Mona asked when they got back in the car. "What you said about Andrew and Eugene?"

"Of course it is," Oneida said, and thought, *I told them the truth. I didn't tell them everything, but what I told them was true.* I told them Eugene broke Andrew's guitar; I didn't tell them he did it for me. I told them Eugene and Andrew got into a fight at the dance; I didn't tell them Eugene was freaked out and afraid I would spill his wonderful secret, his beautiful secret, which I will never tell, ever, to any soul on this planet or any other plane of existence I ever happen to reside upon. And I told them what Andrew Lu told me: that our group history project screwed up his GPA and he wanted revenge. I didn't tell them that I could have been nicer to Eugene Wendell when I had the chance. I didn't tell them Eugene Wendell was a worthy soul, finally: a worthy soul and a freak and my only friend.

"I'm so sorry." Mona sighed. "That you went through all that. And I'm so sorry you didn't feel like you could tell me about any of it until—now."

Oneida didn't respond.

Oneida didn't know what was happening. She sat next to her mother in the car and they didn't speak, and Oneida tried to imagine what it would be like for Mona to *not* be her mother.

"Honey," Mona finally said, "you know you can always come to me. You can always use me. That's what I'm here for."

Use me. It was an offer that didn't strike Oneida as particularly ironic until after dinner, when Arthur told her everything and she realized that Mona had used her first.

Dinner was awful. Bert was quiet and jittery, probably afraid that Oneida and/or Arthur would spill her gossip about Daniel Darby and William Fitchburg Jones (whether she would be more upset about her association with scandal or having been scooped, Oneida could only guess). It was the one piece of information gleaned in the past twenty-four hours that gave Oneida any of the old pleasure: the first time she walked up the main staircase and saw the photograph in the front hall (which now had a strange reddish stain all over it) with new eyes, she smiled. What better way to immortalize the meeting of worthy souls than side by side in a photograph, facing each other forever, in the house where they once lived. But then she saw old Mrs. Fitchburg Jones in the same photograph—grim, sad Mrs. Fitchburg Jones—and heard Bert's words in her head: *She'd been lied to. For years.*

Oneida hated to think she might know exactly how that felt.

Sherman and Anna must have been having a spat, because neither spoke a word to the other. Arthur was absent and Mona, usually able to make the most mundane conversation cheerfully, was in a funk. You could taste it in the food: colorless, bland, heavy with mood. Oneida excused herself before dessert.

She lay in bed, *The Scarlet Letter*, still unread, beside her head on the pillow. She couldn't even imagine what Arthur thought the truth of her life was. Oneida remembered one of the first things Mona had ever said about him—*Arthur Rook is not a well man*—and how she had then asked, *So why is he still here?* Mona acted like she had some sort of responsibility toward Arthur, for his general health and safety and sanity. It couldn't be human kindness: her mother was nice, but she wasn't *that* nice. God, everything had made more *sense* when Oneida thought Arthur was her father.

She snorted, because *that* was hysterical.

If Eugene were here, he would tell her to find out; she'd gone to see Bert for him, had gone looking for the truth in his honor. Mona had called the Wendells and was told, brusquely, that Eugene was still in the hospital, unconscious—stable, but out. Oneida half-imagined that the truth, whispered in his ear, would have the power to wake him; and if Arthur could arm her with an even larger truth than she'd ever imagined, there was no way Eugene could sleep through its revelation.

Oneida sat up straight. For Eugene, for herself, it was time to know. She would conduct an experiment with Arthur, she would gather data, she would draw conclusions, and she would have a hell of a story to share. A thought struck her: She could potentially exonerate Mona Jones.

What if Mona Jones had not had an illegitimate child at sixteen? What if she finally had proof that her mother—that Mona wasn't a waste, wasn't a screwup, wasn't what Ruby Falls thought she was? And what if disproving the rumors hurt worse than bearing them ever had or ever could?

Arthur was sitting on the green loveseat in his room when Oneida, who knocked but didn't wait, stepped inside. He turned at the sound. Oneida could see he was holding a postcard. A huge pink box sat on the coffee table in front of him.

"What the hell did you mean?" Oneida shut the door behind her with a hollow thud.

Arthur set the postcard down. "Are you sure you want to know?"

Last chance, Oneida thought. She bit the inside of her mouth and tasted pennies. She heard a soft tapping—claws on the tile in the bathroom, maybe—and Arthur's fat tabby rushed toward her, winding in and around her legs like a plume of furry smoke.

"Harryhausen used to do that to your mother," Arthur said. "He was her cat. This whole time—he knew."

Oneida slackened against the door. Arthur was right—this stupid cat had been pestering her ever since Mona gave him free run of the house. She had to keep her bedroom door shut all day to keep him out of her sheets and her closet and from rolling around on her shoes. She slid down and the cat rose on his back paws, sniffing the air wildly. Oneida couldn't bring herself to pet him. Not yet.

"Tell me," she said, and looked up to see Arthur watching her. Studying her. "Stop staring at me like that," she said.

"You look so much like her. Except for your hair . . . she was sort of blond."

Oneida rubbed her eyes. "I don't understand how this is possible," she said. "I don't—Mom—"

Arthur left the sofa and sat on the floor in front of her, Harryhausen between them. "What do you know already? What has Mona told you?"

Oneida shook her head. "No," she said. "*You* tell *me*. Then I'll tell you how wrong you are." *Or how right you are.* Her face burned. The world around her began to swim like it had in the emergency room.

"OK. Amy and Mona were friends in high school. Amy ran away

because she was pregnant. With you." Arthur rubbed his arms. "Then Amy—ran away again. And Mona brought you home and raised you."

Oneida felt a chill in her gut. "The hell does that mean, *Amy ran away again*? What, did she squeeze me out and skip town?" She almost laughed but caught it in time; it would have turned into a sob anyway. Harryhausen had crawled into Oneida's lap, and her hands involuntarily ran through his furry pelt. Her leg tickled with the vibration of his purr.

Arthur didn't want to say anymore. She could tell from the way he opened his mouth and held it open but didn't look her in the face.

"That part—all of that, you need to talk about with Mona." Arthur shook his head. "I only knew my Amy, and I loved her. I just"—his voice caught—"I adored her. She was magnificent. She made monsters, you know—"

"Monsters?" Oneida squeaked.

"In movies. Movie—oh, I didn't mean *you*." He grimaced. "She was a puppeteer and animator. She made monsters and creatures and fantastic—critters."

"Magnificent," Oneida sneered. "So where is she now? Did she dump your ass too?"

Arthur's eyes opened wide and he blinked. He was—

Arthur was crying.

The truth struck Oneida Jones in the face. Or maybe she had been the moving object all along, rushing headlong toward the truth like a crash-test dummy hurtling at a brick wall—the truth immobile, her own velocity the steadily increasing variable. Her boyfriend was in the hospital, unconscious. Her mother was not her mother. This stranger had been married to a woman named Amy, and it was because of Amy that Oneida was alive—

But Amy was no longer alive.

"Oh, screw *this*!" Oneida shouted. Harryhausen, spooked, hissed and leaped away. She felt his claws through the fabric of her jeans. "Are you kidding? First you tell me my mother's someone else, then you tell me she's *dead*?"

Arthur tried to reach for her hand but Oneida shoved him away. If she hadn't already had her back to the door with no place to go, she would have fled that instant. "You're *sick*, you know that? You're disgusting. *Why would you tell me this?*"

"It was an accident." Arthur seemed to be having trouble swallowing. *Choke on it,* Oneida thought. "She was electrocuted. At work. I promise you it's all true—"

"Give me one reason to believe you."

"I don't have any proof. I can't."

"This is—this can't *be.*" Oneida covered her face with her hands and prayed that it wasn't true—prayed that the sensation creeping over her wasn't real and wasn't to be trusted—because she *did* feel it, sense it, as the truth. Her truth. And whether it was because Arthur so utterly believed what he was telling her that his conviction was contagious, or something innate, something native to her own heart, was responding to the truth of its creation—she didn't know and she didn't care. She only knew that she believed him. She believed her biological mother was not Mona. She believed the woman who had given her her life was dead—never to be known, never to be seen, never to be thanked or blamed or cursed or communicated with in any form. Death was the price of life. That was mortality.

She was done. She had reached the end of her quest for knowledge. She now knew more than she ever wanted to know: she had learned that she didn't know who she was or where she came from. And she had learned that someday, without warning, she could die. *Would* die.

Arthur had succeeded in grasping one of her hands. Then he talked to her for another fifteen minutes. It was all about Ocean City, all about New Jersey—some of which Oneida knew (that Mona had worked at a pizza place) and some of which Oneida didn't want to know (that Amy hadn't even left a note). He asked if she was all right.

"Of course I'm not all right."

"If there's anything I know about your mother—"

"Which one?"

"Your mother. Mona." Arthur grimaced. "She loves you. As much as one human being can love another."

"She used me." Oneida's voice was dull and deep. It was someone else's. "Her best friend ditched her and she was afraid and alone. I *know* her, Arthur. She needs to be needed. She needs an audience.

Enter abandoned me: I needed a world and she needed to be one. She used me."

"No," Arthur said. "That's a gross oversimplification. Please, you have to talk to her about this."

"Thank you for telling me." Oneida untangled her legs and stood. Her knees were sore. "And don't worry. I'll be fine."

Arthur knew she was lying. She felt his worry, felt his concern, follow her back to her room. She didn't care if he told Mona; she imagined his conscience would force him to. If Mona came to talk to her about this, that was fine. Oneida didn't hate her. What she felt for Mona was something too complicated to go by a single name: for a moment she felt pity for a girl her age who had been left behind, who was probably still waiting for someone to come back for her. Then came a sure sense of awe for the woman who'd raised her, who'd had more of a choice in the matter than Oneida ever dreamed. But these were faint and, like her voice, the province of another person entirely. They were nothing compared to the swollen knot in her chest that crowded her heart, that was spreading—down to her stomach, up to her throat—numbing her body from the inside out.

I want to feel something good, she thought. I *have* to feel something good—right now, right now—

She grabbed the green glass bottle that Wendy had tied to her tree, the bottled blue velvet that would feel good between her fingers, that had been waiting patiently on her dresser to be broken in case of emergency.

It was an emergency.

She broke it.

23 ⌒ *Wake Up and Grow Up*

On Monday, Arthur packed. He folded his clothes, even the dirty ones, and stacked them neatly in the bottom of his giant backpack, which still gave off a faint feline musk and probably always would. He folded the striped button-down that had belonged to Mona's father and placed it on the dresser, and then reconsidered, since it had a smear of his own blood across the breast—a little more personal than a Lacoste logo. It wasn't right to leave it for Mona to deal with. Nothing wrong with a souvenir, anyway.

With every sock and T-shirt neatly stowed, he felt lonelier.

He had nowhere to go. Nowhere to be.

He could go back to Los Angeles. He would make amends to his boss and to Max, and he would go back to work. He would deal with the question of Amy's body. But Arthur would never be able to cook in his kitchen without remembering his wife sitting on the counter, swinging her legs; without feeling her knees pressing against his hips and tasting vanilla bean ice cream as she spooned it into his mouth. He would never be able to brush his teeth without seeing Amy reflected beside him in the mirror, gargling mouthwash. He would never sleep in his bed without hearing her sigh in her sleep, or snicker, which killed him. Los Angeles had always been a town of ghosts, of zombies and phantoms, and now they were in his apartment. It was a life too haunted for Arthur to fathom living.

He could go back to Boston, to Somerville. His parents—well, his mother—would welcome him with open arms and regular feedings, and his father would hand him a beer and they would watch the Red Sox on television. His brother, David, and his sister-in-law, Denise, would have him over for parties and introduce him to new, nice girls every weekend. They would never talk about Amy. They would never mention her name again. His family had been technically supportive of his marriage, though he did know his mother was hurt that he eloped (until David got married a year later with much fanfare, after which she didn't seem to mind). But Arthur knew none of them understood it—none of them understood *her*. She represented everything about Arthur that his family humored under the assumption that he would grow out of it. They would see his return as natural and a relief, and his life with Amy would pass into family apocrypha. Arthur would wake up in ten years married to a nice person and have several nice kids, and he would wonder if he had ever lived anywhere and any way other than this.

It wasn't such a bad future, he thought. He only wished it had a place for his past.

Harryhausen howled.

He could stay.

"No," he said out loud. He *couldn't* stay here. He'd already done more than enough damage to this world—this world that was barely real, that could blink out of existence, he thought, given the slightest provocation. Arthur followed the sound of Harry meowing into the cheery front room, slightly shabby but loved and cozy, and knew he wanted to stay and stay and stay. He had always been more at home in his dreams than his real life.

There was a knock on his door.

Mona was standing in the hallway, just as her adopted daughter—no, her *sister*—had stood the day before. He hadn't had an opportunity to be with Mona, to really see her—just the two of them alone—since he'd told Oneida the truth. Mona never made him swear, but Arthur knew she'd told him the truth about Oneida's birth in confidence, and now he saw Mona with the eyes of one who had betrayed her trust. She looked older. More breakable and more human. She appeared less an overgrown teenager and more the adult that overgrown teenager had been trying to become for the past sixteen years, with hints of the woman she would be for the next forty or fifty. Her eyes were clear and open, softened with lines that told Arthur she had laughed, had lived, and had lied; her jaw was firm and resolute. She was lit from behind with something warm that danced as it burned, the way a candle gives life to the paper skin of a lantern. He imagined her face framed with bright silver hair, the creases around her eyes and her mouth deeper and longer.

"Explain this." She thrust a folded paper at his chest and pushed him, hard, knowing that he was still a stitched-up mess. She wanted to hurt him, and he couldn't blame her.

She shoved him aside and walked into his room. Arthur shut the door behind her and unfolded a piece of three-hole-punched notebook paper, strafed with thin blue lines. *Mona*, it read.

> *I know about Amy. Arthur told me. I know that you love me but I don't know what that means. I'm going away until I figure it out. Don't worry and don't come looking. I'll find you when I'm ready.*

"Who do you think you are?" It wasn't quite an accusation; and Arthur, who had never been able to recognize a rhetorical question to save his life, thought he finally knew the right answer.

"I'm Amy's executor," he said.

Mona punched him. He hadn't been expecting it, had never been sucker-punched in his life (unless you counted the way that Amy died). Blood rushed to his nose. His skin flamed from his cheek to the edge of his nostril, which was warm and suddenly wet. He croaked with shock.

"Amy doesn't get a say here, Arthur. Amy gave up her right to have anything to do with my daughter when she dumped her in a tub."

"I don't—disagree—"

"Arthur, wake up." Mona held her hands in front of her, fingers splayed, trying to palm the truth like a basketball. "I—*Jesus*—Amy Henderson was a piece of work. She wasn't this brilliant, magical creature. That was an illusion, Arthur, it was make-believe, and I'm sorry that you loved it, but you *have* to see that now. *You have to see that now.*"

"I don't—"

"She left her *baby*!"

"What can't you forgive her for?" Arthur's face stung. "Abandoning her child or abandoning *you*?"

"I have to choose?" Mona shouted. "What can't you accept: that you loved a person who did a very bad thing, or that you loved a person you didn't really know?"

"Grow up, Mona," Arthur said. "No one's the same jerk they were at fifteen, thank God. You screw up and you figure life out. You change. Amy grew up and Amy changed into something fantastic. You didn't know her."

He thought of the postcard. *You knew me better than anyone. I think you knew me better than me.* And Arthur understood.

His Amy. *His* Amy—the same woman who looked at a pile of metal and wire and saw the blueprints for life, whose fingertips were soft, whose mind was single and absolute—had once been a young girl in an untenable situation. Had been a body with a desire, then a body in thrall to biology and curiosity, and finally a body in a position to make choices she had no precedent for surviving. His Amy created realities out of sheer will. His Amy had spent her waking life pretending. And his Amy had been a girl with the imagination and the will to plan her own escape and then to plan it again: she had her child and she left her child behind because she had to. To continue to pretend, to create the life she imagined for herself, she had to. He shuddered. Would she ever have told him? Would she have wanted him to know? Or would she have kept her secret her own, for the rest of the days she never had the chance to live?

He was so very weary of useless questions he would never know how to answer.

But she hadn't totally abandoned her child or her friend: she had left them with each other. And in doing so, she had also left her husband a trail of bread crumbs to find her again. To see her—to see *all* of her—for the first time.

"What did you *tell* her, Arthur?" Mona leaned against the back of the chair and hugged herself. She was furious and her voice warbled. "Did you tell her everything?"

"No. I just—I told her Amy carried her. *Had* her. That you found her and brought her home."

Mona shut her eyes.

"So she knows her mother abandoned her. You stupid bastard." Mona looked away and shrugged her shoulders melodramatically. "And you know what the funny thing is? You want to hear the punch line, Arthur? This morning I was feeling really awful about what *I* did to *you*."

"You didn't do anything." He sniffed, felt his nostril clog with blood, and pressed the sleeve of his shirt to his nose. Were you supposed to tip back or forward for a nosebleed? The pain felt good. Deserved. He almost wished she'd punch him again.

"I called Max Morris."

His legs buckled and he came down hard on the couch.

"Two days ago. The morning after I told you everything that happened in Jersey."

"But—"

Mona pointed at his half-filled backpack, leaning against the doorway to the bedroom. "Look at what you're doing. Look, you're packing. You know you can't stay here. You know you have to go home and finish your other life."

"But how did you even find—"

"Little thing called the Internet. Pardon my tween, but: *duh*. Nobody hides anymore. Nobody *can* hide anymore. I mean, how the hell did you find *me*?"

He wiped gently at the base of his nose and examined his sleeve, soaked through in a Rorschach blot that didn't look like anything at all: just his own cherry-red blood in a shapeless smear that defied reason or interpretation, that held no meaning or solution.

"I was going to tell you on Friday," he said. "When I came to your room with the shoebox, I was going to tell you how I got here." He pressed the bridge of his nose with his fingertip and was rewarded with a fresh stab of pain. "I can't believe you punched me."

"Tell me now, Arthur. Tell me what the hell that box has to do with any of this."

The shoebox was sitting on the coffee table, as it had for weeks, and now it loomed like a pink elephant between them. He removed the lid and pushed it closer to her, until one corner jutted over the edge of the table. The postcard was right on top.

"It was the closest thing to a will I could find." Mona, still standing, hovered over the open box expectantly until Arthur nodded and she reached in for the card. "I admit I—I wanted the parts she left behind for myself. I thought I could use your memories to discover them, to figure out what she was talking about."

Mona's lips moved as she read.

"I never dreamed," Arthur said, "she meant a daughter."

Mona's brow creased. "She didn't," she said.

"What do you mean?"

"She wrote this in nineteen ninety-three. Right after she left New Jersey. She had no idea I kept Oneida until years later. Four—five years later." Mona tucked in her lip. "This is why you told Oneida, isn't it. This postcard. You thought Amy would have wanted her to know that she was special. That Amy left her for me, to me. Like a bequest."

"Yes," said Arthur.

"Did it ever occur to you that Amy knew exactly where her daughter was and never tried to contact her? And never told you about it, and never once talked to me in all those years?" Mona flicked her thumb against the edge of the card, and the old paper bent. "She didn't want her to know. She didn't want to know *her*. And *I* didn't want Oneida to know that her mother—her mother"—Mona swallowed—"her mother threw her—"

She stopped speaking. And before Arthur even knew it was happening, Mona lunged hard on her left foot and swung the right up violently to kick the shoebox. She connected with the jutting edge and it launched, spinning, exploding in the air. Postcards and clippings and photographs flew up and sailed down lazily; mood rings and key chains and buttons caromed off the table and the couch, skittering like plastic shrapnel. Most of it landed on Arthur. He sat perfectly still, nose still bleeding, coated in the confetti of someone else's memories. Clues that had been intriguing, had inspired him and kept him company, but were themselves meaningless objects: that could point to places or to people but that would never tell him their secrets.

"She saved all this junk but she threw away her daughter." And Mona ripped the postcard in half three times and tossed the bits in the air.

Arthur didn't dare move.

"I'm not happy I punched you." She disappeared into the bathroom and came back with a tissue. "But I'm not sorry, either."

He accepted the tissue and dabbed at his nose but he wasn't paying attention to anything other than a strange new sensation in the very center of his body, which felt raw and unprotected. Open. He felt his ribs had cracked apart and his heart and guts lay exposed to the cold breezes of the world; and if he didn't wipe the pieces of Amy off of his body soon, they would crawl inside and congeal, and stopper him like a bottle, forever.

"Max just called from the road. He should be here in about two hours," Mona said. "Finish packing."

She closed the door behind her when she left.

꙰

Max brought Amy. In a brown parcel that he handed to Arthur—after enveloping him in a hug that made Arthur's eyes sting—in a small silver-plated tin, were the ashes of Amy Henderson Rook.

"Ashes?" Arthur said. He didn't like how heavy the tin was. Or rather, how heavy it wasn't.

Max tilted his head. He was sitting on Arthur's green loveseat, Harryhausen comatose in his lap. "Do you remember, at the funeral home?"

Arthur heard the sound of crystal vibrating and this time, instead of cutting away to a different scene, his brain rolled film of what happened after the morgue—when Max went with him to the funeral home. Stantz hadn't been able to stand it, had abandoned them to return to his own, still-living wife, but not before plying Arthur with an anecdote: that Amy always joked about having Viking ship burials for her creatures, about setting them on fire and floating them down the trickling LA river after their movies had wrapped. "I'm not sure she ever did it, though sometimes her critters would disappear. I don't know why I thought of that just now," Stantz said, and shook his head, because he knew exactly why he'd thought of that just now but couldn't say the words.

There had been a squat crystal vase—hardly a vase, low like a bowl—with a few white votives floating in three inches of water. It sat on an end table in the hall outside the empty viewing room, where Max was speaking quietly with a very large man in a dull suit. Arthur had dipped his fingertip in the water and ran it around the rim of the vase and it sang so low he thought he might have been making the sound up.

The sound rose, even though Arthur wasn't anywhere near the vase, when the man in the dull suit asked if he would prefer to have the remains embalmed or cremated. "I understand there is no will," he had said, "and no family." The man's eyes were the only part of him that weren't dull; they were small and mean and wanted to get on with it, and Arthur heard the crystal sing so high his ears ached and he thought *No family?*

No family.

"Viking funeral," he muttered.

The director made a notation on a peach-colored form and Arthur signed where Max pointed.

"I do. I do remember, Max." He felt winded and wobbly, as though his recovered memory had passed through every part of his body. Though he supposed cremation was perfectly fine, that Amy wouldn't have minded in either case. Like she had said about her grandfather when she didn't even go to his funeral: she was dead. She didn't care. His ears popped and he set the tin back on the table.

Max swallowed. "They called me when they couldn't get in touch with you, after they, you know, *after*. And the thought that she'd just sit there unclaimed was more than I—anyway. I thought you'd want them.

"I called the cops when I found your place all ripped to heck," Max went on, coloring, "and the police tracked your flight to New York City but you were just . . . *gone*. Your parents are freaking out, Rook. Completely." He smiled. "*Oh Max, you've got to find ahr Ahty. Weah so wurried.* How come you don't talk funny like them?"

"I do. When I'm with them."

"God bless Desdemona Jones," Max continued. "She called me out of the blue on Saturday, explained everything, said she'd even pay for my ticket out here to collect you. Said she didn't want you to go off wandering alone again when she sent you out the door."

When she sent you out the door. That hurt. All of this hurt—to think that he was being removed, systematically, from this life; that people he cared about were conspiring behind the scenes. Not that he blamed any of them. He didn't belong here. It didn't matter that it felt like home.

"So of course I call your parents again, I say you're fine, and that I'll take you to them."

"Max, you really didn't have to—I mean, I could have . . . I'm sure my brother would have come for me. You flew across the country to—what—drive me from New York to Massachusetts?"

"*Mona Jones* flew me across the country to drive you from New York to Massachusetts." Max grinned at him. "I'm sorry, I know I'm going on and on, I'm just so fucking *happy* to see you, Rook. To see that you're safe. That you're OK. You look pretty good—you look *great*, considering."

"If I took off my shirt," Arthur said, "you'd take that back."

Max reddened. "I have to be honest," he said. "Booking like that was a hell of a thing to do. A hell of a dick move. For weeks I've thought that if I had only stayed with you that night, none of this would have happened. You'd be going to work, Amy might not be—" He gestured to the silver box on the table, where a similar receptacle for Arthur's wife, only large and pink and cardboard, had so recently sat. Max cleared his throat. "Things would be different. You'd still be home, instead of . . . here. In this place, wherever it is. You know I can barely get cell reception? And what's with all the trees, are these people loggers? It's like freaking Twin Peaks out there. If you see a dwarf in a red suit, run."

"Home is a moving target," Arthur said. He sat on the couch beside Max. Harryhausen raised his head in languid greeting.

Max put his hand on Arthur's arm. "Hey," he said. "What's wrong? Other than—everything, I guess."

Arthur nodded and said thanks for coming, which he wasn't thankful for in the least. He was flattered that Max had come so far to be the first person from his old life to enter this half-life, now rapidly drawing to a close, and he was grateful that Mona had known enough to realize that Max, not someone from his family, would be best equipped to shepherd him back. But he wished he'd never been found at all.

What he really wanted to thank Max for was leaving him alone that first night, for effectively tipping the first domino. If Max had stayed, Arthur would never have come to Ruby Falls. Arthur would never have met Oneida or Mona and would never have known Amy for everything she truly was and had been all along: a mysterious, magnetic, and cruel creator.

After Mona left, he had brushed the pieces of the pink shoebox off his body like a man who believes himself covered in something unclean, something that crawls; but Amy was back, she was still there, on the coffee table, more herself than ever. He could hold Amy's ashes—her entire body—in his hands, and he couldn't pretend. He held Amy in his hands and thought: *So this is you. This is all that's left of you. The parts I loved. The parts that Mona knew and has a reason to hate. All the parts of you that ever were: no longer missing, waiting to be found, but all right here in my hands.*

He didn't know what to do with her, didn't know what she wanted. Not anymore. The certainty he'd felt when he found the postcard, and then when he'd known that Amy wanted him to name her heir, was gone. In its place was a dull, sonorous ache that made his breastbone thrum like a tuning fork. The ache was understanding: Amy was finite, and whether he loved her despite the things she'd done was irrelevant. Their time together was over. There was nothing he could do to change any of this. This was his life, and, except for an obese cat with a superiority complex, he was alone.

Though not quite alone, never alone, not in this house, as dinner—Max in Oneida's seat and Anna and Sherman sniping at each other more than usual and Bert staring both Max and Arthur down like a sharpshooter—reminded him. Mona had thrown together a massive pan of ziti. Now he wished he had the appetite to devour it with the proper gusto: gusto that said *I can't thank you for everything you've done, and I can't apologize for everything I've done, and that Amy did. But I feel that stuffing my face with this food might be a start.*

He shoved a forkful in his mouth and burned his tongue on hot cheese.

Mona wasn't even paying attention. She'd ignored him since Max arrived, preoccupied, Arthur could only guess, with worry for Oneida. Arthur assumed she had called the police, but he didn't know; she didn't tell him. When Bert asked whether Oneida would be joining them for dinner, Arthur heard a thickness in Mona's voice when she said her daughter was having dinner over at a friend's house.

"Oh, good for *her*," Anna said. "She's always had a hard time making friends." Her eyes narrowed. "Or is this *more* than a friend?"

"Just a friend," Mona said. She poked at her ziti.

"So tell me what you do, Anna—for a living," Max chirped. Arthur smiled, grateful. He'd already explained to Max about the missing daughter and confessed his role in her flight—and the story behind his swollen, purpling nose. When Arthur was done, an awed Max repeated, *God bless Desdemona Jones.*

Anna's cheeks plumped as she smiled. "I'm a vet. Country vet. Dogs, cats, horses, the occasionǎl guinea pig. I once treated a goat with asthma."

Max looked to Sherman.

"I teach shop," Sherman said. "At the high school. Pardon me— *technology education.*"

"Oh, so you must have known Amy."

Arthur could have killed him. Could have redirected his fork from his mouth straight into Max's chest. He'd told Max about Oneida, but he hadn't thought to mention that his connection to Ruby Falls was still a secret to everyone other than Mona—though, really, what was the point anymore? Oneida knew. There was no one left to protect.

Sherman's bushy brows rose in confusion and Max clarified. "Amy? Arthur's wife? I don't know what her name was before Rook."

"Her name was Henderson. Amy Henderson," Mona said. Both Anna and Sherman froze mid-chew.

"She must have been an amazing student. I saw some of the crazy stuff she built, that one time—Rook, remember, when we went on set to take pictures? And she was controlling that purple sea monster thing, with all the tentacles?"

"I haven't thought about her in years," Sherman said. "Not since the two of you ran off like a couple of jokers." He frowned at Mona.

"You're *married* to *Mona's* Amy?" Anna's face lit up like a pinball machine. She turned to Mona, laughing. "I can't believe you kept a secret this big for so long," she said. "I didn't think you had it in you!"

Mona smiled through tight lips.

"So tell us about the mysterious Amy, Arthur," Anna said. "How'd she turn out?"

Arthur looked at Mona, who shrugged, exhausted; then he looked at Bert, who was beaming, so overjoyed was she to see him prostrate himself on the altar of truth. And for the first time since the day Amy died and Arthur fled Los Angeles; since he came to the Darby-Jones, fell into a dream, and then fell down the stairs; since Mona Jones took him under her wing and to a wedding; since he discovered the truth about Amy, a horrible truth he hadn't been able to keep to himself, Arthur wanted to tell his side of Amy's story.

"She went to Hollywood," he said. "She made monsters. She met me. And she died."

His voice didn't shake. His throat didn't tighten.

"She died," he said again and shook his head because he could barely believe how good it felt to say the words—to say the words and understand the words and know that everything could still continue. Would go on from here.

"Bravo," Bert said, clapping softly, withered hands rustling like the beating of bird's wings. "Bravo, Mr. Rook."

Arthur Rook, lighter than a balloon, didn't hear Anna saying *I'm so sorry to hear that* and Sherman coughing gruffly, which he supposed meant he was also sorry. He didn't hear Max whispering *Was I not supposed to mention her?* and he didn't hear Ray Harryhausen galloping through the kitchen, his claws skittering across the tile as he tried to round a corner. Arthur Rook opened his eyes and saw the world again. The whole world. And he saw the people in it for what they really were: Anna, tired, a little lonely, and wishing that Sherman were a little kinder, a little more interesting, or, barring that, a little more likely to ever ask her to marry him. He saw Sherman's terrified old heart, terrified that Anna would leave him and that all he would have to show for the days of his life were a thousand lopsided spice racks and paper towel holders that didn't even hang in his own kitchen. He saw Bert, who had been beautiful in her youth—so beautiful—and who was enraged with herself for never leaving this town, for never finding a home of her own. He saw Max, in profile, sitting beside him, and saw that Max had a crush on him: a wistful, doomed little crush, and Max knew it, and when Max caught Arthur watching him, he smiled to see that Arthur knew it now too.

Arthur saw Mona and Mona saw him straight back. They both felt they'd already spent an entire lifetime with a person who'd left them, but there were still minutes and hours and days and years left to live.

These weeks, spent here, had been the time between ages. The transition was coming to a close; the bleed was staunching itself. So this must be the place, and this must be the time, Arthur thought; this is where and when the New Age begins.

And what would the New Age bring? Arthur saw his futures shimmer before him, saw all the possible places he could go from here: all the houses he could live in, all the jobs he could have, all the people he'd never met but could know for the rest of his life. He could work in an office in Portland, Oregon, selling customizable office supplies: staplers and rulers and coffee mugs in bright colors, their sides open and blank, yearning to be stamped with whatever the client desired. He could be the head of a portrait studio at a department store in Tallahassee, Florida, with a set of six-year-old triplets and a wife named Millie who worried too much. He could be Mona Jones's business partner, and Mona Jones's lover, and he could live right here in the Darby-Jones and go to Oneida's high school graduation; and one day, while playing a game of Scrabble in the still of the evening, when Mona laid out the letters MAR-RYME, he could play HELLYES in return.

Arthur felt his chest seal as the wound repaired itself.

Mona smiled at him across the table. She silently mouthed two words.

Hello, stranger, she said.

24 ⌁ Faith

Monday. Day two of the rest of her life.

Oneida said nothing to Mona. She didn't think Arthur had told Mona about his confession yet, which was a little surprising. Regardless, Oneida didn't know where to start—didn't know what to ask her, wasn't sure she wanted to hear Mona lie to her, as she surely would (why stop now?)—so there was no point in beginning. She'd spent all of Sunday in her room, stretched out on her window seat reading *The Scarlet Letter*. She finished it, a task that was more than a little cathartic. Hester, like Mona, had enough will, enough stubborn self-involvement, as Oneida saw it, to never tell a soul the biggest secret of her life. The secret that *was* her life. She didn't have to tell Dimmesdale (who just knew) and that creep Chillingworth figured it out on his own. Like Oneida figured it out on *her* own. Keep your damn secret, Mona, she thought; keep it for the rest of your life. Keep pretending that your secret is yours—that your secret isn't mine, and Amy's, and Arthur's, now—and my father's.

Whoever the hell *he* is.

She felt worse about not going to Eugene. Her secret discovered and ready to share, she'd had to admit to herself that she still didn't have the guts to call or to visit, to kneel by Eugene's bed and whisper the truth, discovered, in his pink shell of an ear. That she never had. So she put her head down on her desk and swallowed until she didn't feel like crying and allowed herself to obsess about the one thing she had no control over whatsoever.

I'm going to go, she thought.

Go where?

Where *would* she go, if she died? Her own mortality was something she had never thought of in such explicit terms; they didn't go to church. She half believed in ghosts (easy to do when you lived at the Darby-Jones). She wasn't an idiot; she didn't think she would die, as Amy had, of some freak accident tomorrow. It was simple as this: it wasn't until she learned of a woman named Amy Henderson Rook that Oneida Jones, who thought about everything, understood what it meant that she had to die.

It flooded her with dread. It froze her brain and goosed her heart and whenever she found herself imagining what it would be like to not *be*, Oneida would lose the ability to think. To breathe. To see. Until she talked herself down, until she drew the curtain back over what she knew and wished she didn't, she was useless. *Distract me,* she thought, glaring at Mr. Wasserman at the front of the classroom. *Show me a theorem. Give me a logic proof. Explain it to me. Take up the space in my brain that's thinking about what it would be like to not be. How it will feel to go.*

Distract me, she thought, watching Dani Drake make origami frogs from torn notebook paper. *Make those frogs hop across your history book. Launch one off your desk into Cassie Lowe's ponytail. Make it go away. Make me forget. Remind me that I can't do anything about it, that this fear is pointless.*

Because she couldn't know where she would go eternally, she was left with no option but to ponder, during math, during biology, during U.S. history—Eugene's empty desk burning a hole straight through her—where she would go *today*. Where *she* would take herself. Her two feet were hers to control, hers alone, for however much time she had left. And she would damn well tell them where to go while she still had a choice.

Of which there were many. Where first? Where would she go, say, if she skipped ninth period?

The answer came in the form of an origami frog. It landed on her notebook like a silent missile, fired across the chasm between her desk and Dani's. Oneida looked up, but Dani was watching Dreyer, chin in hand, the other hand doodling notes about the revolutionary war.

Oneida picked up the frog. DISSECT ME was written across its back in purple pen. She unfolded it.

> I heard what happened. Lu must pay. Meet me in the prop loft
> ninth period. Yes, I know you go there. You're not so great at
> keeping secrets. DD

There were too many shocking things contained in that one note for Oneida to decide which stunned her most. How had Dani found out (about Eugene *or* the prop closet)? What could she possibly want to talk about? Had the universe actually *heard* her plea and provided the most unlikely distraction possible in a world still bound by the laws of physics? And was she right to be slightly frightened to discover what Dani meant when she said *Lu must pay*?

U.S. history ended. Eighth-period study hall lurched from one minute to the next. Oneida was up and out before the first bell stopped ringing, but Dani, who must have come from a room closer to the auditorium, was already in the loft, waiting for her. She wore a black T-shirt with bright white letters that read ROCK THE CASBAH and skinny blue jeans that made her legs look like pipe cleaners. She was sitting on one of the beanbag chairs that Oneida and Wendy, no more than two weeks ago, had sat on and eaten lunch.

She was crying.

"I'm sorry," she said, her breathing ragged. "I'm sorry, let me just pull myself—hold on."

She tipped her head back and blinked rapidly, waving her hands in the air. Oneida took a seat on the other beanbag, her curiosity matched only by her discomfort. She thought maybe she should give Dani a hug, and then she thought, *I cannot believe you just thought that.* This was Dani Drake: know-it-all, show-off, mean, sarcastic, arrogant, nasty Dani Drake, sobbing and—in the middle of sobbing—trying to talk.

"I just—I found out this m-m-morning. My dad's on the school b-b-board and they're having a disciplinary hearing for that—that *asshole* L-L-L-L—"

"Hey . . . um?" Oneida held her arms out in an approximation of an open-ended hoop. Dani looked up, realized Oneida was trying to hug her from three feet away, and said, very softly, "You should know I have an insane crush on him. For a long, long time, and I—he wouldn't even look at me, but if he liked you, I mean, I hate you but you must be—sort of cool."

Oneida dropped her arms. "You like Andrew Lu?"

The suggestion so horrified her that Dani instantly reverted to her old self. "Oh, please, that's *ridonk*. I mean *Wendy*. He's the only p-person in this whole retarded school who's figured it out, who has a purpose, a fight, you know? With the guts to question and t-to *change* things. There's so much going on here that's just bullshit. Wendy stood for something different."

"You have no idea," Oneida said, rolling her eyes.

"Thanks. Real considerate, Jones."

Oneida blanched. "What?" she said. "I didn't say anything."

"Yes, you did. You said *I just learned you're desperately in love with my boyfriend, and I'm going to rub it in your face how much better I know him than you.*" Dani pressed her fingers over her eyes. "I'm sorry. I just—I thought you might be upset and want to talk. That's why I asked you up here."

"Upset?"

"Yes, *upset*, dumb-ass. Because of what happened?"

Oneida's stomach, which had been in suspense since the beginning of the conversation, plummeted to her toes. What happened. What *hadn't* happened in the past forty-eight hours?

Dani continued. "You're only his girlfriend. I thought you might—I thought you might be scared or, like, upset. I don't have to be here, you know, trying to comfort you." Her face crumpled pathetically, and fresh tears leaked down her cheeks.

"*Gah!*" she shouted, making Oneida's heart leap up her throat. "Why is it *so hard* to be nice to you?"

"I don't know. Why is it so hard," Oneida said, her voice rising, "for *you* to be nice to *me*?"

"*I don't know!*" Dani shouted back. "Look, I just—I should just go. I shouldn't have—" Dani nudged the plastic cake container left over from Oneida's picnic lunch with Eugene. A hunk of dried frosting broke free, and she ground it slowly into the floor with the heel of her sneaker.

"Thank you," Oneida said, after a long, frosting-pulverizing moment. "Thank you for being concerned. I am . . . pretty upset. About everything."

Dani snuffled. "So what do we do?"

"What do you mean?" Oneida asked.

"I mean . . . what do we *do*?"

"You mean, like . . . rent some movies and eat ice cream? I guess."

"God, you're so—"

"*What,* Dani? *What* am I that you cannot leave me alone?"

"All I *do* is leave you alone; what the hell are you talking about?"

"You are really, really unpleasant to be around sometimes, that's all. You're sarcastic and you're defensive and you think you know everything—"

"I'm *sorry* my personality traumatizes you. Get over it, cupcake." Dani kicked the plastic container. It skittered across the floor and flew over the edge of the loft. "And you're a ray of fucking sunshine to be around, you know—you're so friendly and accepting and cheerful all the time, and I can tell that you're *never* looking at the world and judging every last inch of it as not good enough for you."

"That's a perfect example of how sarcastic you are. And how defensive. And how you know everything about everyone. You don't know a *thing* about me, Dani—or about Eugene, for that matter."

Oneida hadn't a clue how any of this was happening, or was even possible, but wasn't that the way of the world these days? It felt so *good* to be saying all this, like she'd been saving it up for years. And maybe she had; she'd known Danielle Drake since the fourth grade, when Dani moved into the Ruby Falls central school district. There'd been a week or so when Oneida even thought they might become friends, but then Dani was adopted by the kids in the school play, and Oneida didn't truck with organized productions of any sort. And here they were, after five years of obliquely irritating the shit out of each other, yelling about how deficient the other was as a person, alone in the empty RFH auditorium, high above the stage, surrounded by props and flats and costumes, and Oneida, exhausted, didn't care anymore. Didn't want to fight anymore. Not even with her archenemy.

"Dani," she said, "just—stop. You don't have to comfort me, but thank you. For trying. And I'm sorry I said that about you not knowing Eugene. It was mean and I don't even know why I said it. I can't help it if I'm—"

She was too fractured. There were too many pieces, and she wasn't able to choose which she was above all.

I can't help it if I'm weird.

If I'm mean.

If I'm confused.

If I'm smart.

If I'm doomed.

Dani's smile was as flat as the horizon. "Me neither," she said.

They both sank back into their beanbags and stared out into the darkness.

"Anyway, what I meant was"—Dani grinned—"what are we going to do to Andrew Lu?"

⌖

I am a spy, Oneida thought. *I am undercover.*

"So this is my house," Dani said, jiggling her key free from her front door. "Home, sweet bourgeois pigpen."

I am in enemy territory.

Enemy territory had plush beige carpeting so thick Oneida felt like she was bouncing across it, and an old pair of sneakers, treads matted with grass clippings, floating on a plastic mat like survivors on a raft. Enemy territory had an antique gilt mirror and a small table covered with L.L. Bean catalogs, smelled faintly of chemical vanilla, and—oh dear God—enemy territory had three framed pictures on the wall opposite the mirror: school pictures, from second or third grade, of two boys who must have been her brothers and Dani Drake, missing a front tooth, wearing a pink ribbon in her hair and a sweatshirt with a cartoon Barbie on it.

"You have to understand the status quo if you're going to overthrow it," Dani said, tracking Oneida's gaze.

"Did someone force you to wear that?"

"Hell, no." Dani dumped her backpack on the floor and used one foot to pry the sneaker off the other. "I loved that bitch for real. Then I grew up, realized she's a tool of the patriarchy designed to mutate girls' conceptualizations of the feminine—and, by extension, themselves—into compliant, big-chested smilers with no genitalia."

Oneida didn't have any response to that.

"So then I had a Barbie bonfire in the backyard." Dani tossed her jacket across a small wooden chair that Oneida was pretty sure was intended only to be looked at, never sat in. "I took pictures, if you want to see. It's fucking rad what happens to plastic when you add an accelerant. Take off your shoes, OK? My dad'll shit twice. Hey, Dad," Dani called into the house. "I'm home. I brought my friend."

Oneida's throat caught and she shocked herself with a smile. Dani Drake had called her *my friend.* There were plenty of explanations, plenty of reasons for the choice of words; Oneida appreciated that it was just easier for Dani to call her a friend than to say *my mortal enemy, with whom I'm enjoying a sort of cease-fire while we enact revenge on the jerk who put the boy we both like in the hospital.* But she could have just as easily said "someone from my history group," and she didn't, and Oneida knew that what had started in the prop loft was responsible, the same way a plucked string kicks ripples of sound in all directions. In the prop loft, she'd felt one of those painful flashes of clarity that, before Eugene, before Arthur, before Amy Henderson, Oneida had assumed only happened in movies or in books, when characters were thrust into accepting circumstances that existed beyond their control or even their knowledge. The world really did slow to the point where it felt like her skull was a fishbowl, her brain sloshing inside; she noticed everything, from her shirt tag prickling the back of her neck to the scattered costume jewelry on the floor, looping around her feet like plastic seaweed in pink and green and purple. And when Dani Drake said *me neither,* Oneida heard the answer to a question she'd never bothered to ask: they hated each other because they were practically the same person.

"What are you doing home so early?" A male voice floated to them from around the corner. Oneida craned her neck, but all she could see beyond the vestibule was a brick archway, directly ahead, leading to the kitchen, and around to her right, a living room so clean, so sterile, you could perform open heart surgery on the coffee table.

"We skipped out early. We're miscreants."

"Don't tell your mom," came the reply. "And don't do it again."

"'K." She turned to Oneida. "Vengeance makes me hungry. Snack?"

The vengeance Dani spoke of, the revenge against Andrew Lu, made Oneida feel many things, though none of them were hunger. In the prop loft it had seemed a perfect act, its execution as thrilling as it was simple, requiring nothing more than a hall pass and a Sharpie marker. Dani kept extras of both in her backpack. Oneida took the upper corridor, Dani took the lower, and in less than twenty minutes every bathroom stall, in every single bathroom, was branded with the same epithet in faintly odorous, slick black ink: ANDREW IS A LU-SER. Her nose still itched from Sharpie fumes. Her gut churned, more from excitement than guilt. She wished she could see Andrew Lu's face when he realized what they'd done.

She wished she could see Eugene's face when *he* realized what they'd done.

She caught the peanut butter and chocolate chip granola bar Dani tossed at her with one hand and discovered she didn't have the stomach to eat it.

"Hey, what's wrong?" Dani closed the pantry door. The kitchen was full of shining stainless steel appliances and looked as spotless, as pristine as the living room. Oneida was momentarily distracted by Mona's voice in her head: *An all-stainless-steel kitchen reminds me too much of a morgue.*

And her own, in reply: *Isn't that what a kitchen is? Where food goes when it dies?*

No, food goes to Valhalla. Mona, throwing a pillow at her head. Sharing the couch, just watching television, just being friends. *Also known as my belly.*

"Seriously." Dani put down her own granola bar, package opened but no bite taken. "Are you OK? You look like you're going to, uh—oh, crap, don't cry."

Was she crying? Oneida tried to inhale and couldn't catch her breath. She hiccuped.

"Come on, let's go to my—my room's right down the hall. You can cry in there, my dad won't bother us, you can cry as much as you need to."

Dani gestured for her to follow down the hall, and Oneida went, still trying to breathe and only catching short breaths that filled her chest without going anywhere. Dani opened a door covered by a Che Guevara poster, and before Oneida had even crossed the threshold she was sobbing, her throat and her chest jerking up and down as her lungs struggled to fill and empty, fill and empty, and the rest of her body, hysterical with impulse, did the only thing any of its warring factions could agree upon: she stood in the middle of the room, her arms wrapped around her stomach, her eyes closed, and she shook and she cried. She was dimly aware that Dani, after shoving her inside, had fled; she was too upset by everything else to care if this meant the fledgling truce was off. She was thinking of Mona, only of Mona. She remembered dancing with her mother, dancing around the kitchen—Mona twirling her out the length of her very short five-year-old arms, spinning her like an ice-skater, dipping her over her knee, all the while singing that old Backstreet Boys song about wanting it that way, even though it ain't nothin' but a mistake. For the first time that stupid song, those inane lyrics, made a twisted sort of sense; Oneida didn't know if Mona had meant it at the time or not, but today—already dislocated by the strange clash of little girl and budding revolutionary that was Dani Drake's bedroom (canopy bed, piled deep with stuffed animals, the *Anarchist's Cookbook* peeking beneath a peach-colored dust ruffle)—Oneida heard her mother's confession: she was someone else's mistake. She was Mona's choice, made the way Mona wanted it. There was nothing for Oneida to apologize for. Nothing to feel guilty about. There was only the mystery of why Mona hadn't told her, the answer to which was contained in the question.

Mona hadn't told her the truth because she was Mona.

Her mother was afraid—of her. Her mother was a human being, a young one. Her mother, like her, would die one day. Her mother needed to be forgiven for her fuckups. And, perhaps most painful of all, Mona wasn't her friend, had never been her friend, really—had always been her mother. Would always be her mother, the only one she'd ever had and the only one she'd ever need.

"*Tell me why-ee,*" Oneida sang softly to herself, and laughed hysterically, which made her cry even harder.

"I brought you a paper bag." Dani had come back. How long had she been standing there, holding out a small brown lunch sack? "For you to breathe into. I used to hyperventilate when I cried, when I was little. I'd get so upset I couldn't stop myself. Here."

"Thanks." Oneida's breathing was still harsh, still beyond her control. Her glasses were smeary with tears, and she had a bad feeling there was snot and spit all over her face. She hitched her breath and pushed it out into the bag, which inflated with a satisfying crinkle.

"I think we should go see him," Dani said, and Oneida, focused on her breathing, at first wasn't sure who she was talking about.

"Oh, right." The bag swallowed her voice. "I—" Her eyes stung again.

"I thought that's—why you were—come on, sit down." Dani steered her over to the bed. "I think nonfamily visiting hours are only until seven o'clock, but I have a plan to get us past—oh, crap, there you go again." Dani's face folded and she sniffed loudly. "God, this is so effing girly. I hate this!" she said. "I hate everything about this, about . . . *feeling* . . . all this shit!"

"Me too," Oneida said, into her bag. She closed her eyes. "I wasn't crying about him before."

"What d'you mean?" Dani asked.

Oneida took the bag away from her face. "I was crying about my . . . because. Um."

She wanted to tell her everything.

It was terrifying. It was new. Dani Drake, unprecedented truce notwithstanding, was a stranger. Recently the enemy. She did not have to forgive Oneida anything or love her regardless—she was other, she was separate, she was an agent of her own desires and motives, and there was nothing Oneida could do to control what Dani would do with the information given to her. There was no protection from her. There was nothing that bound them to each other's interests, nothing that held them accountable to each other's feelings or reputations or ability to look in the mirror and like who she saw. There was only the promise and the hope that other people can be good, are good; that other people are the reason we are alive on Earth at all.

Friendship required more faith than any other kind of love, more faith than Oneida thought she was capable of having. But then she thought, *What the hell is the point of faith if you never take anything on it?*

"I was crying because I found out who my real mother is." She raised the paper bag a little, just in case another attack hit.

Dani blinked. "Wasn't that your mom—didn't I meet her at your house?"

"Functionally, yes." Oneida crossed her legs and sat back against the mound of stuffed animals. One of them let out a baleful squeak. "Biologically, no."

"No. Way." Dani crossed her legs opposite Oneida and reached for a large brown bear, loved so hard most of the fuzz had been rubbed from his hide. She folded him in half and propped her elbows on his head. "So where's your dad?"

Oneida blinked, not sure what to say. Dani took the silence for reticence.

"I'm sorry," she said. "You don't have to tell me. I don't mean to pry, it's just—you're dealing with this *on top* of what happened to—you know. I'm impressed."

"I don't know," Oneida said, "who my dad is." She smiled.

Dani's cheeks puffed out. She shook her head. "You're fucking hard-core, Jones."

Oneida smiled wider. She told her everything she knew.

⚘

It was Dani's plan, of course; and it was brilliant (of course).

"You'll feel better if you do something," Dani said. "Nothing big, nothing that's going to hurt anyone. This isn't revenge, this is restitution. This is you saying you're hurt and you're angry and you need some time. Also: screw you, Mom." Dani yanked open her desk drawer. "Just a little bit."

Dani handed her a sheet of notebook paper and a pen, and a large hardback copy of *How the Grinch Stole Christmas* that Oneida balanced across her lap to write on. Oneida took off her glasses and cleaned them on the edge of her shirt. Then she wrote a note to Mona that she hoped said just enough.

Dani drove her over to the Darby-Jones and idled at the foot of the driveway while Oneida snuck up the front porch and hand-delivered her letter—her fake runaway letter, just vague enough to freak Mona out but nothing, Dani said, that Oneida could actually get in trouble for. Even if Mona flipped enough to call the state troopers, to report her as a missing person, there was nothing concrete, nothing to hold against her. "Kids run away all the time, anyway," Dani said. "Nothing personal, but they wouldn't do anything to find you, I bet. At least, not in the first twenty-four hours." Dani's plan included Oneida sleeping over at her house, on a school night, which Dani's father—a self-employed designer who had a studio in the back of the house and brilliant blue eyes that Oneida couldn't stop staring at—said was fine, so long as Oneida's mother was OK with it too. Oneida called the movie theater at the mall in Syracuse, and the prerecorded movie times, predictably, thought it was *great* that she was staying over at a friend's.

When she hopped back in the car, she and Dani howled in triumph and sped away. She was giddy, drunk on insurrection—justified insurrection, which was even more intoxicating. But as soon as it was done, she made herself forget about it. She forced herself not to imagine Mona's face when she read the note, when she read between the words, and thought her thoughts and jumped to her conclusions. Oneida knew it would hurt Mona. She knew the implication that she'd run away would scare her. Hell—it was scary enough to *imagine* running away, let alone actually do it; and her mother knew precisely what there was to be afraid of. Which was what made this plan of Dani's so brilliant—it was perfectly tailored to exploit Mona's own fears, her own experiences: her own bed, once made, the covers drawn back by her own imagination.

Oneida told herself these things and tried to remember that Mona had brought it on herself. And then she imagined what it would feel like to go home after school tomorrow, the cool rush of relief as she hugged her mother, just wrapped her arms around her and smelled the vanilla in her hair and her skin, and then all this could end; and whatever happened after, whatever the world was going to be like from now on, could start happening.

Dani's mother, who was some sort of surgeon, came home at 6:30 and brought two large pizzas with her. She said she was so glad to finally meet Oneida, that Danielle had mentioned her frequently, and Oneida hoped nobody saw how that casual comment made her so happy she blushed. Dani had two younger brothers, Dylan and Duncan, twins in the sixth grade. They finished each other's sentences and ate an entire pizza all by themselves. Dani, around her family, was the quiet one—her mother told stories about the patients she'd seen at work, the brains she'd poked around in; and her father asked them all questions about their days, including Oneida, who surprised herself by answering honestly.

"I spent most of the day contemplating my mortality," she said.

Duncan Drake froze mid-chew.

"Then I took a geometry test."

Mr. Drake laughed. Then they all laughed, all the Drakes, and Oneida, who hadn't even been trying to be funny, saw that it *was* funny; saw that all of life was funny, precisely because it ended.

Dani was released from clearing the table because she had a friend over, and Oneida, again, felt a fresh burst of happiness, of pride, to be labeled so, especially by this clan of strange and brilliant people (Dani's father had used the word *pedagogical* and hadn't stopped to explain it, and nobody looked the least bit confused). "Your family is great," Oneida said, once they were back in Dani's room. "I really like your dad."

"He's OK." Dani knelt to dig through a pile of clothes. "They were all on guest behavior tonight. My mother is usually a raving hag."

"Oh." Oneida wasn't sure if that meant her initial assessment required an apology.

"Got 'em!" Dani triumphantly raised a bright orange plastic bag in one hand and a pair of wrinkled toothpaste-green scrubs in the other. "Are you ready for the plan?"

"I think so." Oneida sat on Dani's desk chair.

"This is how we're going to get in to see Eugene. It's just after Halloween, the hospital will still be nuts. No one's going to look twice at an intern and a nurse." Oneida guessed the scrubs were hand-me-downs from Dani's mother, but the white nurse's uniform that came out of the orange bag looked kind of short and still had tags from a costume shop. There was a heart, halved by a jagged crack, over one of the pockets. "Are you with me?"

Oneida chewed her lip.

"What?" Dani sounded impatient. "Come on, don't you want to see him? Don't you *miss* him?" The unspoken challenge, the barb—*do you love him enough, do you deserve him like I do?*—made Oneida feel queasy and guarded. Her faith teetered. "Look," Dani continued, "I'm going to see him tonight whether you come or not, I just—"

"I don't want to see his family. I don't know what to say to them."

"That's what the costumes are for. We'll just go in and, you know, check his vitals. Say hi."

"Can I wear the scrubs?" Oneida asked.

"They're my PJs."

"Does that mean I can't wear them?"

"I haven't washed them in, like, a week."

"I'd feel better in the scrubs."

"Suit yourself." Dani shrugged. "My boobs look great in the nurse outfit, just to warn you." She shook her head. "Sorry. Sorry—I didn't mean it like that. Wendy's your boyfriend, and I know that. I'll try to get better. I promise."

Oneida's faith buoyed. In this new world, in the second age of the life of Oneida Jones, a promise to try was enough.

Dani rolled her eyes and grinned, dipping her head sheepishly. "It's true, though, they look . . . friggin' *spectacular.*"

"How else would we snap him out of a coma?" Oneida deadpanned. Dani looked a little sad and a little hopeful, and smiled at her. Oneida would remember that moment, years later, when Dani called with the news that she was moving to Africa, to Zimbabwe—she'd gotten her Peace Corps assignment—and she would remember the seed of doubt that had hung in the air between them; that they were so similar, competition would be inevitable. Could preclude friendship. Then she would think of the time they tried to drive Dani's ancient Dodge Neon from Syracuse, where Dani was a sophomore, all the way down to New Orleans, but the car died before they got out of Pennsylvania and they spent spring break running around Pittsburgh, playing rummy, getting silly shitfaced in their motel. She would think of the time Dani came to visit her while she was studying abroad in England, eating fish and chips from a paper cone as they wandered along the Thames, and Dani confessing that she'd slept with her English professor, but only at the end of the semester, after he'd given her the B-plus they both knew she deserved. Dani was the first person Oneida called when she landed her internship at the Metropolitan Museum of Art; Oneida was the first person Dani called when her brother Duncan was killed in a car accident. She would picture Dani and her professor, Allen, eight years her senior but hiding his relative youth behind a mustache the color of carrots, showing up six hours early to help transform the Darby-Jones backyard into an appropriately festive venue—and she remembered Dani pulling her aside, asking her how she was doing; and Oneida remembered feeling so grateful that in all of the hustle, with all the responsibility of being both the daughter of the bride and the maid of honor, someone would think to ask—would think of her. She was doubly grateful the someone doing the asking was Dani Drake.

They were friends, good friends; had been for years.

25 ∽ Release the Kraken

Mona stood on her lawn and watched Arthur and Harryhausen and Max Morris (brother of Zack) drive away. She blew a kiss gently across her palm and lifted her hand in a high wave that chased the taillights of the rental car. As soon as the lights were gone, Mona turned away.

Her house had never felt so empty and Mona had never felt so full.

Full of anger. Of worry and love. Of ziti. This day, God—*this day*. This day when Oneida ran away, and someone came to take Arthur, and Mona hadn't known what the hell to do other than chop a zillion carrots and boil a pot of salted water and bake a shitload of ziti and wait and wait and wait for the revolving door of the Darby-Jones to spin, for the people she loved to come and go out of her life just like that, just like they always had and always would. But Amy coming back—as a ghost, in Arthur—proved that the door spun all the way around, if only you had the patience to wait for it. There was comfort to be found in that. In that, and in the small plastic bag she'd slipped in Arthur's pocket as they hugged good-bye, dried fondant petals sealed tight with a note that said *Leave a trail and find your way*.

She shut the front door. As if the clicking of the lock were a cue, Anna stuck her head out of the kitchen into the hall, eyes wild and greedy. "Oh my God," she said. "Mona. Spill."

"Shut up, Anna," Mona said, and climbed upstairs.

She put on a sweater—it was a little cool outside, and the auditorium wasn't very well insulated—and brushed her teeth. She grabbed her car keys and, from the broom closet, a screwdriver. When she passed Arthur's rooms (she would always think of them as Arthur's rooms now), she couldn't bring herself to shut the door he'd left slightly ajar. She supposed he might have left bits and pieces of himself behind—she'd punted that shoebox but good—so she'd need to thoroughly clean the space for the next tenant. But that wouldn't happen tonight. Tonight she finished her own business with Amy Henderson, and Amy Henderson alone.

Anna was washing dishes when Mona, wrapping a scarf around her neck, apologized for snapping at her. "I have my cell phone," she said. "If the police call, tell them to call me on that. If Oneida calls, tell her I'm on my way. Wherever she is. I'm coming for her."

"Where are you going?" Anna blew a puff of hair out of her eyes.

"To the school," she said.

Anna didn't ask why. She nodded and turned back to the dirty dishes.

The car radio offered her the company of Wilson Phillips. The high school was only a song's length away from the Darby-Jones, but Mona felt herself remember her entire friendship with Amy on the drive. Her friend. Her horrible friend, the best she'd ever had. She thought about Ocean City, about David Danger. The delirium of independence. She turned on her headlights and remembered Amy making her plans and canvassing the boardwalk—all legs and long pale arms and her belly, high and round, full of a life other than her own. She remembered Amy lying on her bed at the Seahorse, pillow under her knees and bare feet kicked high in the air, shirt hiked up over her hard melon of a stomach, poking it with a finger and saying to Mona, Can you believe it? Can you freakin' *believe* what my body is doing? Her face drawn and astounded, the terror of comprehension throwing shadows under her eyes, shadows that grew longer as the days passed. She remembered Amy in third grade, in fourth grade. She saw them eating Kraft cheese slices on round crackers after school at Amy's house, watching movies. Making movies, Amy and her Super 8 whirring away. Spending their high school study halls in shop building tiny wooden sets, and in home ec, stitching together furry sleeves for arms and legs and torsos. Building puppets. Making monsters.

And she thought of Oneida, of Amy's daughter who was *her* daughter. Of the infant she'd been. She thought of her parents, who had raised them both. Of Oneida as a toddler, a brilliant little brain, already old, wandering the same house Mona had wandered when she'd been that age. Playing with the grown-ups. Asking if anyone wanted in on a hand of Rook. A card game and the name of her real mother's widower—how funny was that. She heard Oneida crying with fever and stomachache: Mona's forearms burned from the memory of her daughter's hot little body, and then she laughed, remembering how Oneida had finally vomited, explosively, demonically, all over her bed; and Mona, smoothing her sweaty bangs away from her face and murmuring *The power of Christ compels you!*, had made her poor sick daughter smile without understanding what was so funny. She felt herself coming home from her parents' funerals, both times every bone in her body heavy and cold as granite, checking on Oneida in her room: folding down the old blue blanket to see her face, pink and warm, already looking like Mona's disappeared friend in miniature. Both times Mona whispered into her sleeping ear a promise: that she wouldn't leave her. That she belonged to Mona. *You are mine*, she'd said; *you are mine and I will always love you. I will never leave you. I will always need you.*

She had never prepared for the day when Oneida would cease to need *her*.

Not telling her the truth had been Mona's insurance policy. It was the one thing Oneida would always need, even if she didn't realize it. It was the one thing Mona would always have to give: the truth, the last trump card. And Arthur had played it, and Mona was livid and frightened and *relieved*, and so ashamed of herself for being too cowardly—always, too cowardly—to act. To choose. She had only known how to accept or resist a situation as she found herself in it. She had not known how to create a life for herself.

That was what Amy did.

A few cars were parked in the south lot, but the north lot, abutting the auditorium, was empty. Which was good, Mona thought; not that a witness would have stopped her from what she was about to do—what she had done, several times, many years ago. There was an old metal door with direct access to the back of the stage, a door that hadn't been replaced in a good thirty years, and whose lock yielded to a skillfully employed screwdriver just as easily as Mona remembered.

The smell—oh, the *smell*. Of dust and mildew and old upholstery, of teenagers and sugar and sweat. It was so powerful, so familiar, that Mona had to catch her breath. Her nose stung and her eyes teared, and when she closed the door behind her the smell was everything and everywhere. But the smell was nothing compared to the sight of a place Mona hadn't visited in half a lifetime: she'd come to the auditorium several times since her own graduation, for various school events of Oneida's, but she hadn't been back *here*, on the empty stage, with only the heavy curtains to witness her passing. It was different. It was so completely different, when you were alone in the dark on the stage—it was strange and exciting, yes, but it was also safe to be hidden among the shadows.

Up in the loft. High above the stage, like you're floating in the clouds, Amy used to say. *Away from the world.*

Mona turned on enough lights to see her way and hoisted herself up the metal ladder bolted into the wall. She'd only been in the loft a handful of times, but she *felt* that it hadn't changed a bit; it was still cluttered with necessary objects, with window dressing for imaginary places and people. There was an overstuffed cardboard box of costumes, dripping sleeves and pant legs, in the rear corner, and when she pushed it aside, underneath was the trap door—just where it should be—and inside—just where *they* should be—were Amy's movies. Nearly a dozen small reels nestled neatly beside Amy's trusty Super 8. Mona knelt in the dust, laid her hands on their cold metal canisters, and smiled. "They're still here, Amy," she called into the dark. "I've got them now. They're safe."

Mona had never known what became of the films after Amy left, and frankly she hadn't cared. After all, it was Amy, not her monsters, that Mona missed; and she'd forgotten all about this place, this safe high haven, until she read Amy's postcard. Then she'd known immediately: Amy was proudest of the monsters she created, the movies she made, and she kept those movies in the drama loft for safekeeping. She screened them against the large canvas flats—for herself, for Mona, and for Ben Tennant, Mona supposed—and Mona would, of course, know where to look. Despite knowing that the films were exactly what Arthur chased all the way to Ruby Falls, Mona knew they weren't for him to have. Amy meant them for Mona, even though she'd never bothered to tell her so directly. But that was Amy to the end: the girl who never told anyone anything at all. Who made you love her because you didn't know how she did the things she did; because you didn't really know her but thought one day, if you looked hard enough, if you waited, you might.

Arthur came for the best parts of the person he lost, for the pieces she had left behind when she disappeared. He'd found Oneida. And though Amy had never considered her daughter a part of her, let alone one of the *best* parts, Mona disagreed with her whole heart. Arthur had found exactly what he was looking for.

The Super 8 was even older now but still true to the name Amy had inscribed on its side in silver paint—*Trusty*. Mona selected a reel labeled *Steve the Seamonster* that she remembered filming in one of the Darby-Jones bathrooms, wound and set the film, and plugged the projector into the outlet set high on the wall.

She had to believe Oneida would come back to her. She had to believe that she'd forgive Amy, one day, for everything they'd given and taken from each other. But that night, in the loft above the world, all Mona wanted was to *be* with her friend again: to meet Amy halfway, a reunion of two, held between people who'd once been so close they'd lived the same life. Whose lives since had been their own, and who now saw each other across time and space as real and as distant as opposite sides of the grave. Mona would always see Amy in herself, in her memories. In the things Amy left behind.

They had been there, in that place, at that time, together.

Mona wanted to sit in the dark beside Amy and watch Oneida's siblings roar back to life. A beam of light shot out of the projector. The electric glow warmed her face and the movie began.

She would share this whole other family with her daughter, when her daughter came home.

⁂

"This is how you sneak out at night," Dani said. She put one hand on the front doorknob and turned it. "Did you see what I just did? There will be a test."

Oneida's heart thumped. This was too much revolution for one day—she was bone weary, and afraid that being caught would mean the loss of everything new and suddenly dear. It would be horrible to be seen in the eyes of the Drakes as anything other than welcome for dinner. Reminding herself why she was taking this risk—to atone, to find out, for Eugene, who deserved more than she'd given him—was imperative.

"Have you done this before?" she asked.

"Only all the freaking time," Dani said. The door opened soundlessly. Dani grinned. "OK, you got me; this is the first time."

"I'm not taking any blame for this." Oneida hugged her bag to her stomach. She was freezing; the scrubs were thin. "This isn't my idea. This is all your idea."

"And a mighty fine idea it is." Dani put her finger to her lips and jerked her head for Oneida to follow: low and bent, soft across the lawn, to the edge of the driveway where she'd parked her father's car after they dropped the runaway note at the Darby-Jones. It was a Camry, close to ten years old, Dani said. It smelled like her brothers' shin guards.

"You see how I parked it?" Dani was bursting with pride. She was bursting, period; the nurse costume made her boobs look frightening, Oneida thought. "I'm going to throw it in neutral, and it's at the perfect angle to just—push it. Back down the driveway."

"I thought you were kidding about having to push the car."

Dani shushed her again. "Why would I kid about that?" she whispered.

So Oneida set her feet against gravel and pushed the rear of the car. The hood *was* perfectly angled toward the base of the Drake driveway, and as soon as the Camry's front wheels coasted onto what was one of the few paved roads in all of Ruby Falls, Dani started the engine. It growled. Oneida leaped through the passenger door, praying nobody had heard; and also praying that someone *had*, and that that someone would run out of their house, brandishing a frying pan or a shotgun, and say, *You stupid kids, what are you doing? Go during normal visiting hours. Look his family in the face and say you're sorry for being the cause of all this. Like a grown-up. Like a grown-up, Oneida.*

But she wasn't a grown-up. Not yet, at least; she had to keep reminding herself that thinking she was a grown-up, and knowing more than most grown-ups, still didn't make her one. She wondered if she would ever be grown up enough to feel like one. She wondered if Mona felt like a grown-up (doubtful); if Arthur Rook did; if Sherman or Anna did; or even Bert. Or her mother, Amy.

To die before you grew up—Oneida could imagine no greater tragedy. No greater loss, no greater unfairness. She hoped Amy had grown up, all the way, before she died.

"I think we're safe," Dani said. She turned on the CD player. "Shoot," she said. "I don't have any CDs. I keep telling Dad he needs an iPod converter—"

But how would you know? What if you only knew whether you were a grown-up or not in the moment before you died? Oneida imagined— and it struck her that she could think of death, could imagine death now and not freeze from fear—that your last moments of consciousness would be a second that stretched forever, that brought you confirmation, that brought you an answer (good or bad) about the kind of person you had been. That brought you sight. Understanding. Clarity.

Oh, hell, she thought, and actually laughed at the grim humor of it all. *That would be nice, wouldn't it.*

She would have to ask Eugene. She would have to ask him what he had thought, what he'd felt, in that split second.

The drive to Syracuse was uneventful, silent, and companionable. Dani found the oldies station and they listened to a bunch of songs that were hits before they were born. The white orb of the Dome, the covered football field at the university, appeared on the horizon as a low-slung cloud of metal ribbing and fabric. Eugene's hospital was near the Dome, near the university, on the hill with all the others.

Dani took her ticket from the automated parking attendant at the same garage Oneida remembered walking toward with Arthur, on that night that already felt like a lifetime ago. The arm lifted and Dani drove beneath it, and she parked, crookedly, in the first empty spot she saw. Their footsteps echoed in the empty parking structure. Oneida, still freezing in her scrubs, felt she'd slipped sideways into an absurdly realistic dream. The air flowed around them like liquid, silent and heavy; it was too quiet to be a living city. It was barely midnight and they were close to the university—and wasn't Halloween just last weekend?

Weren't people supposed to be running around, making noise, being loud and stupid and a distraction from this horrible solid silence? They crossed above the street on a lighted glass walkway—like hamsters, Oneida thought, like rodents sneaking in. Fluorescent tubes hovering over the elevator lobby droned a fuzzy monotone, and here the silence had a faint chemical edge, an odor that reminded Oneida of adhesive tape, of plastic. They waited for the elevator that would take them up to the fourth floor. Dani had called the hospital earlier and found out Eugene was in room 420, which made her roll her eyes; Oneida felt like it was a joke she was supposed to get but didn't. The hair on her arms stood straight, charged.

The elevator arrived with a dead-sounding *donk*. The doors parted.

"Excuse me, visiting hours are past."

Oneida didn't think the voice was talking to them, didn't understand what was happening even when Dani pinched her forearm, hard, and she hopped jerkily into the elevator. She propped the already-closing doors with her hand. Dani glared at her. *Go now*, the glare said. *Go now, dumb ass.*

A man in a dark security uniform was walking toward them. The voice, which belonged to a woman behind a front desk Oneida hadn't even seen when she walked past it—it was beige, like the voice; they both blended into the liquid air—repeated itself. Asked for an explanation. Was now clearly addressing Dani alone.

The security guard was young. He had bright blue eyes, the kind of eyes babies have that are supposed to get darker.

"I'm going to have to ask you to leave," he said to Dani quietly. "This is a hospital, not a Halloween party."

Dani snorted, shouted, "Nice *manners*, babe!" Then she gave Oneida a steady gaze (*go go go*), and Oneida understood: Dani was too capable a planner of impossible missions to ever think she would get past security wearing the nurse's costume. The entire plan, as originally conceived, had been Dani's mission alone: she had intended to wear the scrubs, to breeze behind the cotton curtains and visit the boy she thought she loved, after hours (the better to prove that love, Oneida thought). And then today everything had changed, and Dani—who had given Oneida a choice of costume, a choice Oneida now saw as a sort of final test—sacrificed herself. Gave up her spot, gave up her plan, for a friend (the better to prove her love indeed). Wearing the nurse costume had been Dani's way of tricking Oneida, of goading her confidence, convincing her to go because she wouldn't be going alone. And whether she'd done it for Eugene or for Oneida, it didn't matter. She'd done it. She'd done it for them both.

"Th—" was all Oneida had time to say before the elevator doors closed between them.

She was near tears when the doors opened again on the fourth floor. She felt terrible: terribly alone, terribly grateful, terribly undeserving of such orchestrated kindness, and terribly guilty for having put Eugene Wendell in the hospital in the first place.

Why *did* she feel so damn guilty, she thought as she stepped into the dim white glow of the corridor. She didn't drop the rock. She didn't start the fight. The open doorways of patient rooms gaped like missing teeth, unseen occupants muttering and flopping and snoring and smelling faintly of menthol and bleach. What floor was this? Not intensive care, she thought; there was no sense of urgency here, only rest and watchfulness. Oneida passed by a nurse's station. The nurse, who acknowledged her with a nod and went back to reading her book, was wearing white scrubs with rainbow-colored balloons printed on them.

This was a kid's floor.

Eugene was just a kid. Just a kid, like her—just a kid, like her mother. And like Mona.

Oneida's feet moved faster. Room 420 was the second from the end, the doorway as dark and anonymous as every other she'd passed. She stepped inside Eugene's room and immediately pressed her back against the wall and closed her eyes, because she didn't know what she was going to do, hadn't really thought this far ahead. She sniffed. She smelled the harsh clean smells of the hospital and on top of that, something almost identifiable, something familiar. She opened her eyes and saw a boy she didn't know lying in a bed.

Oneida blinked. It wasn't a trick of the light or her imagination. She really didn't know this boy. He couldn't have been any older than nine or ten, with short light hair and a tiny snub nose, made snubber by a tube that ran beneath it and over his ears on either side. He was awake.

"Hi," he whispered.

"Hi," Oneida said. Her voice was high, embarrassed. She was frightened of the boy, frightened for him.

"Are you Ohn Ida?"

Oneida stared. She nodded.

"He talks about you in his sleep," the boy said. "It's really annoying. Listen." He faced the curtain on the right side of his bed; Oneida could see in the dark that it was striped like a circus tent. *What kind of sick bastards design children's hospital wings?* she thought, suddenly infuriated by the world. She was insulted on the little boy's behalf, insulted by the implication that a few cheerful stripes, a few rainbows, a few balloons, would camouflage the reality of whatever his situation was, would trick him into thinking everything was just fine. Life isn't a circus, she thought. Life is short and cruel and beautiful, and kids know it. It's the grown-ups who forget, and it's the grown-ups who need to lie to themselves, and to each other. The kids are quite aware of what they're going through.

Hell, she thought, her throat hitching. She looked at the little boy in the bed, at his round eyes, and she had the urge to tell him something: something true. Something honest. Something she'd learned.

"Growing up," she said, and her voice faltered as she wondered what the odds were, for this kid, on such a proposition. She swallowed. "Growing up . . ." What *had* she learned? Quick—she had to think—

"Listen. There he goes," the little boy said again, and this time Oneida heard Eugene, on the other side of the curtain, say *Oneida, please don't tell. It's a secret, Oneida. It's the truth.*

> He was sitting on the couch in Astor's study. He'd been sitting on the couch in Astor's study for a long time, he thought; his butt hurt in a vague, dreamy way, not enough to make him want to move but enough to make his butt cheeks feel numb, like flat pancakes of meat strapped to his tailbone. Ha ha ha. He laughed on Astor's couch, and then he realized he wasn't alone; there was a funny little man sitting on the other end. His hands were clasped over his knees. He was wearing a three-piece plaid suit and a bow tie and glasses, and he was mostly bald with little white tufts over his ears.

There were other people too—sitting on his left was Oneida's mother and on his right was Arthur Rook, and they were acting like he wasn't there between them. They were both staring straight ahead at the white open wall of Astor's study, where Astor had projected the movie about slicin' up eyeballs.

It was a different movie today. Wendy didn't know what it was or where it came from—it looked pretty old, but it was in color. There wasn't any sound, and there were scratchy lines all through it that jumped like lightning. A blue creature, a cross between the Loch Ness and the Cookie Monster—it was furry and scaly both, and had a huge spike fin down its back—rose, flailing, from an old-fashioned bathtub without water.

Oneida's mother laughed. "She said she'd do the water in post. Guess she never did."

Arthur didn't react at all. He pressed two fingers against his nose, and squinted like it hurt, and said, "Hey—hey, Max. Stay on eighty-one. I know a better way to get there."

Then Oneida's mother and Arthur turned to face each other, staring straight through the space where Eugene's head should be, which frightened him for a moment because he didn't know if he would be crushed or absorbed or what if they got any closer, so he closed his eyes and when he opened them, they were gone. The little man in the suit was sitting closer.

"Hi," Wendy said. "I'm Wendy. You can call me Eugene. Or Wendell. I think I'm going to go by Wendell from now on. I like the way it sounds."

"My name is Joseph Cornell," the little man said.

"Oh, hey." Wendy's voice squeaked. "Hey, I know you! I know all about you!"

"That's nice," the little man said.

"Is it true you died a virgin?"

The little man sat up straighter, pulled down on his vest.

"I'm sorry, that was rude. But seriously, is it true? It's so awful."

"I screwed Dolley Madison." The little man tilted his head as though trying to remember the particulars of that occasion.

"It was hollow and meaningless. I would have rather died a virgin, honestly."

"She was kind of hot," Eugene said.

"She was no Mary Todd Lincoln. Or Eleanor Roosevelt."

"Eleanor Roosevelt?"

Joseph Cornell sat up straight again. "One word," he said. "Mrowwr."

"Wow." Eugene began to feel slightly dizzy. "I have a confession to make."

"I know that you made a forgery for your father to pass off as mine. That's OK."

"Really?" Dizzy and ill. He was slipping down into the couch, lower, between the cushions, butt first. He couldn't say for sure whether he had a butt anymore or not. "I feel terrible about it. I think about it all the time. It seems so dishonest to me suddenly."

"It isn't," Joseph Cornell said. He handed Eugene a green glass bottle with a rolled piece of midnight-blue velvet inside. "Every artist steals from other artists. Do you honestly think you can say things that nobody has ever said before?"

"My father's going to go to jail, isn't he?" For some reason he couldn't hold on to the bottle, his hands didn't work, wouldn't grasp. His fingers melted, flopping like fettuccini. The bottle rolled away across the floor.

Eugene's knees were up around his ears as the couch sucked him in deeper. "It's my fault, isn't it?"

"We repeat ourselves," Joseph Cornell said. "We repeat ourselves because it reminds us of who we are. It reminds us where we came from."

Only Eugene's head was left above the couch cushions. He couldn't feel the rest of his body at all. He was very tired. He was very confused. He was very frightened.

Joseph Cornell stood up and knelt down in front of Eugene's head. He patted him affectionately, running his gnarled old artist's fingers through Eugene's full dark hair.

"Would you like me to tell your fortune?" Joseph Cornell asked.

Eugene nodded. The cushions on either side of his face battened his ears.

"You will grow up and die."

"That's a shitty fortune," Eugene tried to say, but the ravenous couch muffled him.

"On the contrary," Joseph Cornell said, leaning in closer. "It's the single greatest thing that will ever happen to you." And he kissed Eugene with soft full lips that didn't seem at all like the lips a dead introverted artist ought to have, that reminded him of other lips, familiar lips, lips that kept secrets from him. And for him.

He opened his eyes.

Oneida Jones was leaning over him in the dark of his hospital room, her glasses catching a sliver of light from the moon outside. She looked different: newer and older than he remembered. He didn't know her all that well.

But he wanted to. There was still time.

"I want to tell you something," she said.

"OK." He blinked. His eyelids felt funny, like he hadn't used them in a while. He didn't remember when he'd last been awake. "Tell me anything," he said.

She smiled wide. Her teeth were white in the dark. "There's so much to tell," she said. "Where to start?" And she actually climbed into his tiny little hospital bed with him: rolled him on his side and curled her body around his back, until they were a pair of nesting question marks. She draped her arm over his side and pressed her nose against the back of his neck, and Eugene Wendell had never felt so safe in all his life.

"You were right from the start," she whispered. "I'm named after a spoon."

᠅

"You want to tell me why you're doing that?" Max asked.

No.

Arthur rubbed a white daisy petal, fondant dried but still sweet on his tongue, between his thumb and the crook of his index finger. Then he tossed it out the window, into the black beside the highway, as he'd been doing every fifteen minutes since they left Ruby Falls.

"Where did you even get those?"

"Mona."

"Like a snack?"

Arthur handed him a petal. "They're edible. But don't bite down. You'll lose a tooth."

"Road trip! Woo!" Max said, voice garbled around the petal in his mouth. He smiled to show Arthur that he was still *so* fucking happy to see him; but he was kidding himself if he thought Arthur couldn't see straight through to the worry, to the anxiety he really felt.

Arthur had barely spoken since they pulled out of Mona's driveway. He'd spent the first hour on the one-lane highway to Syracuse staring at the two objects in his hands, his awakening brain stretching, yawning, percolating like a coffeepot. In one hand, he held the small parcel with Amy's ashes; in the other was the GPS device Max had rented with the car. Together with the bag of leftover fondant petals he found in the pouch of his sweatshirt, that he'd felt Mona slip inside when they said good-bye, they told him what to do next.

He smiled at Max, to show him everything was happening as it should. "Don't worry," he said. "I know exactly where we're going. And now the GPS agrees."

"Are you sure that thing even gets service out here? Wherever . . . we are?" Max craned his neck over the steering wheel, but there was nothing to see but highway and taillights and mile markers.

"We're taking the next exit, merging onto the Pennsylvania Turnpike."

"The—the what?" Max blinked. "Are we going into Pennsylvania? How does that get us to Massachusetts?"

"In all the time we drove around the city and county of Los Angeles, did I ever get lost?" Arthur's heart beat faster. "Trust me, Max."

To his credit—and Arthur's discredit, he thought; it was shameless to manipulate Max, who had come for him so quickly, without question, like this—Max didn't ask Arthur what the hell he thought he was doing until they drove into Philadelphia.

"I don't care if you don't want to go home, Arthur." Max had turned into the first gas station on the other side of the city. "I get that. But tell me. Don't trick me. Tell me where we're going."

Arthur looked down at the parcel that was Amy, cradled between his hands.

"We're going to release the Kraken," he said.

Harryhausen's Kraken, he told Max, was Amy's favorite monster. Its master and keeper Poseidon released it on Zeus's command—to destroy cities, to receive virgin sacrifices, and scare the shit out of Athenians—and when its work was done, it dove back to its home in the depths. Even when it was killed, when the head of Medusa turned its mighty bulk to stone, it crumbled to pieces and sank to the bottom of the sea, to rest in pieces, undisturbed.

He didn't mention that Amy, when she needed to hide, ran to the precise strip of sea they were approaching, or that Amy had spent the time between the first and second ages of her too-short life by that sea with the same woman who had so recently helped Arthur live through a similar half-life. None of that seemed important to tell Max, who was only too happy to head toward the ocean of Arthur's choosing once Arthur told him half of why. They drove across northeastern Pennsylvania into New Jersey, the land flat and grassy, low and watery, as they approached the shore.

They entered the town limits of Ocean City at one in the morning.

The streets, off-season, were dark and deserted. Max drove in the general direction of the water, following signs for overflow parking lots, weaving down the narrower roads behind the boardwalk, looking for an empty curb. He parked illegally thirty feet from a boardwalk ramp. Ray Harryhausen, out of his carrier in the backseat, lifted his head at the sound of the cut engine, sighed deeply, curled himself into the world's largest cinnamon roll, and fell back asleep.

Arthur had been to plenty of New England beaches, but Jersey beaches were different, which he knew as soon as he opened his door. They *smelled* different: saltier, warmer, even for October. Wind ruffled his hair and he started walking, clutching the parcel of Amy to his tender chest, and then he began to run up the wide wooden ramp, old boards creaking beneath his pounding feet, and it was there, it was all there at the top: to the right and to the left, as far as he could see in the darkness, were the pizza stands and the junk shops, boarded for the night or the season, he couldn't tell, that Mona had brought to life for him. This was the place where Amy and Mona had been children, where they had discovered choice and possibility, had tasted freedom and the rest of their lives. There were streetlamps the length of the boardwalk but they were weak fireflies compared to the moon, enormous, full but for one flattened edge, closer than Arthur had ever seen it, so large and bright it momentarily cowed him. He was pinned by its light, stunned and immobilized by the enormity of time, of everything that had come before his tiny speck of a life and everything that would come after. And then he heard it—the ocean—turning over, moving, breathing, and he freed himself from the moon's thrall and remembered why he had come.

He waved Max closer. Max was staring up at the moon too, bewildered in the light.

Arthur crossed the boardwalk and his sneakers were off by the time he descended the stairs on the opposite side, down into the sand, cool and damp. He mashed it between his toes and couldn't stop smiling—at the sound of the ocean, at the light of the moon. At the memory of his wife flopping around, a naked Deborah Kerr on the edge of the surf, white foam surrounding her in a liquid cloud, laughing, drunk, and lovely.

He unwrapped the parcel. The tin was cold in his hands, and the sand was cool and flat where the water had covered it. His feet made small dry dents that disappeared moments after he left them. Arthur lifted the lid on the box that held his wife and didn't feel horror or sadness to see her like this, the last shape she would ever take; he felt triumphant, as though she'd been made complete, had finally taken a form that suited her true nature. His wife was as inscrutable and flawed as the gods of Olympus, and now she was other than human, other than God. She was a Titan, an immortal, an elemental force who could no longer be killed.

He walked parallel to the sea, his feet splashing in the shallow water, and tipped the box and poured Amy out in a fine ribbon of dust that trailed behind him as he gained speed, as his legs pumped higher and his feet splashed harder into deeper surf. He released Amy and he flew, faster, lighter, as she released him. When he felt so light he thought he might fly off into the night and, like a helpless moth, be drawn up to his death against the gaping moon, Arthur Rook, gasping for breath, stopped and turned to see the distance he had come. Half a mile of beach lay behind him, sand pale and water blue as ink in the moonlight. A wave crept up the beach, farther than any waves had come before, and Amy, unbound, drew herself back to the depths.

Max waved to him and Arthur, breath calmer, waved back. Max Morris was an excellent friend. He needed to let Max know that, and apologize for hoodwinking him into helping him bury Amy here, in this place that must have always been her home. They would drive up to Boston and Arthur would spend perhaps a week with his mother and father and brother, and then Arthur thought he would fly to Los Angeles, but not to stay. To pack his belongings. To finish that life.

And when he returned, as he now knew he could, there would be a trail of white sugar petals to follow, a dotted line lighting the way home in the dark.

Eight Years Later

Oneida was the last to see Amy.

She was twenty-three and a first-year graduate student in art history. She thought she might specialize in preservation and archival technique—she was good at remembering and organizing, always had been—and the past eight years of Arthur teaching her how to look at the world had made her a visual adept. She saw things that had only just decided to be seen, Mona said once. "You're a little spooky, kid, but I love you anyway." And then Mona turned to Arthur, reading the paper with his bare feet on the kitchen windowsill and said, "This is all your fault," and Arthur said, "It's half my fault."

Oneida hadn't wanted to go to the new admit luncheon. It was a beautiful spring day, the kind made for lazing in the sun with a book, trying to forget about the multiple brilliant papers she needed to write by next Thursday. Her roommate Barry, a third-year Ph.D. in archaeology with whom Oneida suspected she was plainly and perfectly falling in love, convinced her free food was always worth it.

"It's not even your department," she said. "What do you care?"

"Aren't SOs invited?" Barry had a widow's peak and a nervous habit of tugging on his right earlobe. "Aren't I a Significant-enough Other to attend?"

"Play your cards right," Oneida said.

Professor Howard Rice, who specialized in impressionist painting but, as a devout child of the sixties, had a weakness for pop art, was hosting the luncheon at his museum of a house. Oneida shook the hands of a dozen admitted students, doing her best to woo bodies to the university, which amounted to telling them all the same thing: *I've had a wonderful experience thus far—challenging, yes, but thrilling,* words just truthful enough to keep her gag reflex in check. Most of the admits were much older, and she could tell they thought she was strange: odd, and very young. And yet some of them saw themselves in her. They would come to school here next year, Oneida knew, and she told them as much before moving on to the next. "See you in the fall," she said, and they all looked puzzled but smiled, having just realized for themselves that, yes, they *would* see her in the fall.

After an hour of telling fortunes, Oneida, warm with white wine, wandered off to explore Rice's house. It was old and labyrinthine, every blank wall covered with a tapestry or a painting or an antique mirror. And there, in the hall that led off the main vestibule to the library, Oneida saw her mother.

She squinted and leaned closer. Yes. It *was* Amy, just as she had been the first time Oneida ever saw her: a faceless mystery, lying naked on a beach with her hair carried out to sea and to space.

Howard Rice, coming out of the library, paused and leaned in beside her.

"You've a good eye," he said. "That's an exceptional work."

Oneida hadn't yet had Rice for any of her course work, but still she knew he was a clueless windbag, harmless, really, but totally out of it—sort of like Sherman Russell, which predisposed her to treat him with particular kindness. Sherman, despondent and distracted after Anna finally moved out of the Darby-Jones, had slipped on a patch of ice in the high school parking lot and broken his leg in five places. Now he got around using Bert's old cane, which belonged to the house—like all of Bert's possessions—after she finally passed away, peacefully, in her sleep one Christmas Eve.

She smiled at Rice and asked what he meant.

"It's a lost Joseph Cornell." Rice grinned like a kid and pointed at the white painted mesh. "One of his later pieces. You can tell from the more abstract expressionistic touches. The mesh. The fields of white paint."

"Where did it come from?" she asked. "How did you acquire it?"

Rice smiled again. "Private sale. Cornell was always making little things and sending them off to people he admired, people he loved from afar. It was the only way he could tell them how much he cared about them. Lost Cornells pop up once in a great while, though in the past five years they've been springing up like daisies. And the pieces themselves have been more elaborate and exceptional, like this. Supply has created more of a demand, I'd think. A bit of a vogue."

Wendy, Oneida thought. Wendy, following in his father's footsteps. The more she considered it, the more sure she became. The last time she and Wendy spoke, a year after they graduated from high school, he had told her he was going to do something totally nuts, just for the hell of it.

There's a shocker, she'd said, and hugged him, hard, because even then she knew it might be the last time. He'd been dating Dani for a year at that point—Dani and Wendy had just finished their freshman year at Syracuse—and even though Oneida could see that they belonged together far more than she and Wendy ever had, being the third wheel on their bike was too difficult. She kept Dani; she let Wendy go. And then so did Dani.

"It's quite enigmatic and quite moving, though, isn't it?" Rice said. "Who do you think she is?"

Oneida looked through the glass at Amy. She saw her own jaw, her own long legs. And she saw Arthur and Mona building wedding cakes together in the kitchen and driving off in the old station wagon, *Jones & Rook, Baking and Photography*, detailed on the side. She saw her mother on her own wedding day, laughing hysterically for no reason when Arthur showed up in his tuxedo shirt, adjusting cuffs that drooped under the weight of a pair of enormous ruby-red cuff links. She saw Dani crying on a giant blue beanbag in the prop loft and, in a photograph taken in Zimbabwe, her arms high above her head to catch a red rubber ball of a sun. She saw Wendy, eye blacked by Andrew Lu; she saw Eugene, loping away from her on that last day, longer and leaner and assless as ever. She imagined him in a closet of an apartment in New York City, the tools of his trade spread before him: wood, glue, and a thousand memories made of paper and glass and plastic. Telling the world he loved it, one work of art at a time.

She saw herself, reflected in the glass—her eyes large and dark and open to see all the world. Older, but not quite as old as her own worthy soul.

Getting there.

"She's the beginning," she said. "Of everything."

Acknowledgments

Thanks are due

To my editor Marjorie Braman, for her insight and energy, and everyone at Henry Holt, for being so enthusiastic from day one.

To my agent Bonnie Nadell, for her guidance.

To Lee Konstantinou, for being the linchpin.

To my friends, for their tireless cheerleading, and especially my early readers, for their feedback: Megan Frazer Blakemore, Jason Clarke, Karen Daugherty Clarke, Grace Hsu, Rob Kloss, John Mullervy and the Boston Writing Workshop, Katy Pan, and Laura Quinlan. And to my kindred BAWs, for their love, support, and inspiration: Manda Betts, Sandra Lau, and Jenna Lay, who holds the other half of my brain and keeps it sane. None of this without you, either.

And to my parents and my family, for their sense of humor, their excitement at my successes, their unconditional love and understanding, and their goonieness. Every day, you all remind me where I came from, why it matters, and why I'll always love coming home.

About the Author

KATE RACCULIA grew up in Syracuse, New York. She has been a bassoonist, a planetarium operator, a proposal writer, a designer, and a karaoke god. She received her MFA from Emerson College and lives in Boston, Massachusetts. This is her first novel.

THIS MUST BE THE PLACE

By Kate Racculia

About the Author

- A Conversation with Kate Racculia

Behind the Novel

- "Writing *This Must Be the Place*"
  An Original Essay by the Author

Keep on Reading

- Recommended Reading (and more)
- Reading Group Questions

For more reading group suggestions,
visit www.readinggroupgold.com.

ST. MARTIN'S GRIFFIN

 # *A Conversation with Kate Racculia*

Who are your favorite writers?

I love Kate Atkinson, Michael Chabon, Margaret Atwood, Jane Smiley, Richard Russo—I could go on. And there's nothing in the world like a vintage Stephen King and a glass of iced tea on a lazy summer day.

Which book/books have had the biggest influence on your writing?

Ellen Raskin's *The Westing Game* blew my ten-year-old mind with its multiple characters, multiple plots, multiple red herring, try-to-solve-it-yourself mystery. And years later, John Irving's *The World According to Garp* was an object lesson in absolutely stuffing a book to bursting—with characters, with ideas, with absurdity—and yet making it all ring true. *See author's Recommended Reading list to learn more.*

What are your hobbies and outside interests?

I watch movies all the time: the good, the bad, the unspeakably awful (the better to mock; thank you, *Mystery Science Theater 3000*).

I'm also a collector of everything from old records to antique postcards. I've never met an antique mall I didn't like.

What is your favorite quote?

"Still and all, why bother? Here's my answer. Many people need desperately to receive this message: I feel and think much as you do, care about many of the things you care about, although most people do not care about them. You are not alone."
—Kurt Vonnegut

What is the single best piece of advice anyone ever gave you?

My father once told me to never forget that TUMS spelled backward is SMUT. I'm not sure how to quantify the ways in which this advice has changed my life, but I've never forgotten it.

What inspired you to write your first book?

This Must Be the Place was inspired by many, many things: the art of Joseph Cornell; the Pixies's *Doolittle* album; the true story of John Myatt, an art forger who happened to be a single father (which got me thinking: What would it be like to have a forger in the family?); and a burning desire to justify the student loan payments I owed on my MFA.

Where do you write?

I like to write in noisy cafés. Anywhere there's plenty of ambient energy and easy access to a great cup of coffee.

What is the question most commonly asked by your readers? What is the answer?

Where did you get your ideas? And the answer is: I...kind of don't know. Does anyone? I imagine my brain as a melting pot of everything I've absorbed about the world—from my family, my friends, my coworkers, and my teachers; from movies and music and books—that simmers quietly, just waiting for me to decide to see what's cooking.

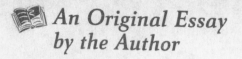

An Original Essay by the Author

"Writing *This Must Be the Place*"

BEGINNING

I started writing *This Must Be the Place* in the summer of 2006, at the very end of the repayment grace period for my student loans. This was not a coincidence. I had just moved into a new apartment in Cambridge, Massachusetts, with one of my oldest and dearest friends. I was flush with the heady joy—read: financial solvency—of my first grown-up job. After approximately twenty years of school, it felt pretty magnificent to be earning a wage; but it also felt pretty *this-is-not-all-I-want-to-do-with-my-life*. I had played bassoon for years in youth orchestras; had a degree in illustration; had minors in art history and English; had stacks of notebooks full of stories and the beginnings of novels; and had a brand new graduate degree in creative writing. After all that time spent reading and analyzing and performing and imagining—and loving every second of it—I was now a full-time cubicle drone, writing fifty-odd page marketing proposals about (wait for it) equity investment strategies and compliance policies.

Nonetheless, I decided there were two things I would emphatically not do. One: I refused to send Sallie Mae a monthly loan payment without doing something to justify it. And two: I refused to let what I did for money—which was, all things considered, an extremely decent gig—define me.

I have always been stubborn. I have always loved to make things up and to write. The former trait has occasionally made my life difficult, but in deciding to write a novel, the two worked a kind of alchemy in concert. My MFA thesis, a novella about a young pianist returning home for her childhood friend's funeral, felt like a completed work. I wanted to take on something new. I knew it would be a novel, knew

I wanted the writing to last and grow over time, but I couldn't make the project insurmountable. It needed to be something I could do for the love of it, small scale and personal, that would remove me from the stresses of my nine-to-five and validate those loan payments one sentence at a time.

I'd already written a story about a school-picture photographer living in a boardinghouse who was poisoned by his landlady's daughter (it didn't make much sense, but trust me when I say the daughter had the best intentions). The photographer's name was Tim, I think; he became Arthur. He had a wife named Audrey who was dead when the story started. They lived in north Hollywood, not far from where I spent a summer working on an internship credit for my graduate degree. They had a cat named Ray Harryhausen and an overbearing landlord named Mac.

Then someone broke into my apartment and stole my laptop with the first chapter on it.

NEMESIS

Wait. Let me back up. The new job, the loans, the stolen laptop—that's not the beginning. The real beginning of *This Must Be the Place* was an art project I did in the first grade. We were making collages. I don't recall the point of the assignment or the actual conversation I had with my first-grade teacher—a lovely woman I actually saw last summer when she came to a reading in my beloved hometown of Syracuse—but I imagine it went something like this:

Mrs. S: You make a collage by cutting out pictures from magazines and pasting them together on a piece of paper.

Me: You mean...all together? Touching? Overlapping?

Mrs. S: All together!

Me, had I possessed the vocabulary: *WHAT INFERNAL ANARCHY IS THIS, WOMAN?!*

Collage was my nemesis. I was the kind of child who thought hospital-food trays, with their neat compartments separating the mashed potatoes from the meat, were the standard to which all plates should aspire. How could I possibly be expected to participate in an endeavor that was, as indicated by the work of my contemporaries, about haphazardly gluing as many pictures as possible of Barbie, Optimus Prime, and/or adorable lion cubs on a single sheet of oak tag? What was the point? Why couldn't I draw a tiny city populated with anthropomorphic cats (as was my wont) instead of creating this hellish "collage"?

The tide turned, as it must to make the story worth telling, in high school. My art teacher assigned another collage project, only this time the finer points of the medium were explained to me. If you'll allow another imagined conversation:

Mr. T: The point of collage is to create patterns and suggest meaning by placement.

Me: You mean, everything touching and overlapping, but with a point? An underlying meaning?

Mr. T: Yes, that's correct.

Me, now possessing the vocabulary, but unable to speak because my mind has been *blown*.

I went to the University of Buffalo and majored in illustration, primarily working in mixed-media collage. I understand collage now—not only as my preferred medium for visual artistic expression, but as a way of understanding my world. Everything we know about ourselves is itself a form of collage, a composite of experiences, memories, details, smells and sounds and sights; and how we interpret the patterns and connect the underlying dots is how we come to

understand our lives. It's how we find method in our madness.

Writing *This Must Be the Place*, then, was an act of self-collage, assigning method to the madness of my life up to that point, which had essentially been my childhood. Not to imply that my childhood and adolescence were overly dramatic. Sure, middle school was a little hairy, but—my love of order and partitioned food vessels aside—I had an extraordinarily happy, safe childhood. My gratitude for my luck, my parents, my family, my friends, and my teachers I was (and am) blessed enough to have by my side, guiding me, knows no bounds; especially since *they* are the real reason I was able to write *This Must Be the Place* at all. When the people around you say, over and over again, *you can write that story; you can paint those pictures; you can try out for that orchestra; you can go to school for art*; and, most important, *you are loved*; you're bound to grow up believing that anything is possible if you try, if you want it and you work for it.

Sometimes I look back and think my childhood was stupidly happy, like, living in a quirky eighties sitcom—happy, with wacky neighbors and catchphrases and the occasional moment of slapstick, like that time my mother and I broke two different chairs in one afternoon because I was too big to be sitting on her lap anymore but that didn't stop me from trying. Or that *other* time when I tripped over my bike because I was playing dryland Marco Polo in the middle of the street, and ended up needing two stitches in my chin. I have a shockingly clear memory of Glenn Frey's "You Belong to the City" playing on the radio while we drove home from the emergency room—floating through Syracuse at night, my chin bandaged and swollen and realizing, *grasping*, that I *did* belong to this city. Hadn't I shed blood, however moronically, on her streets that very night? I was exhausted, probably still in shock, but safe and awake enough to have a profound revelation (for an eight-year-old) about my place in the world in a dark moving car.

That memory is *absolutely* what informed Arthur, Mona, and Oneida's midnight run from the emergency room.

WHERE IT ALL CAME FROM

In 2006, I was twenty-six, officially done with school, vaguely unsatisfied with my job, and ripe for a quarter-life crisis, or at the very least an extended mental vacation frolicking with the loves of my youth. Like: Ray Harryhausen monster movies (Medusa was and is the biggest movie badass, ever, hands down, no contest). The music of the Beatles, which completely defined my life between 1993 and 1996. The songs of Foreigner and Journey, which I didn't realize were tattooed on my soul until I rekindled my love for them during the Napster revolution. The delicately inscrutable shadow boxes of Joseph Cornell and the dreaming mysteries of Salvador Dalí introduced to me in my art history classes and by my father, respectively. And the places—Ocean City on the Jersey Shore, where I traveled every summer with a high school concert band. Ruby Falls, which isn't based on any one place in particular but is itself a collage of all the little towns in upstate New York where I spent the first eighteen years of my life—full of huge old houses and strange characters, breathtaking in the autumn. To my characters I gave the world I grew up in; my characters themselves were built from bits and pieces of myself. Arthur got my eye for art, which is also where he got his name. Oneida got my antisocial only-child tendencies and my curiosity, and took her name from the lake I've vacationed on since I was three. Eugene got my love of music and

my (would-be) rebellious streak. Mona got my sense of humor and my love of food, especially cake. Amy, even, is me—the stubborn part, the workaholic part, and the dreaming-it-into-reality part.

LOVE STORY

When I set out to write a novel, knowing that two of the main characters would be a single man and a single woman, I promised myself I would RESIST romantic comedy conventions. I was *not* writing a love story. It was *not* a foregone conclusion that Mona and Arthur would end up together (in other drafts, they didn't). I was writing about people in a small town unraveling their pasts into the present, caroming off each other like soap bubbles, who might fall in love or might not; I was writing about art and expression and growing up and not knowing who you are, at least not yet, and being lucky enough to meet and recognize a kindred.

Which doesn't mean it's not a love story. In fact, I think it means it *is*; it just isn't the kind of we-know-where-this-is-going-nothing-new-to-see-here kind of love story I never wanted to write. But more than that, it's a love *letter* to the places and experiences I knew growing up, recombined and collaged into something new.

I am a repressed romantic. I violently eschew schmoop. I cry foul on flowers and hearts. But at the end of the day, like the Beatles said, I truly believe that all you need is love.

TO SUMMARIZE

Between 2006 and today, I've changed jobs twice and moved three times. Friends have gotten married. Babies have been born. People I love have moved away and moved closer; people I love have gone. I've drunk over two thousand cups of coffee; eaten several hundred turkey, pesto, and cheddar sandwiches at Diesel Café in Somerville, where I wrote most of *This Must Be the Place*; and had my laptop stolen twice (the second time from the aforementioned café, and yes, there are two unfinished versions of this book floating around Cambridge). The stock market tanked and my day job in investment marketing became about a thousand times more stressful. We elected a new president. Zombies lost their cool; vampires were hot; zombies are making a comeback. I became utterly obsessed with *Gilmore Girls, Twin Peaks, Mad Men,* and *Doctor Who,* in that order. Start to finish, from a Word document on my laptop to a paperback on my shelf, writing this book has been the most excellent of adventures, one even my wildest daydreams couldn't have foreseen—with a cast of amazing (real live) characters who made it all possible, whom I can never thank enough.

But I don't think *This Must Be the Place* is a book I could write again, the same way that you can only grow up once (even though it might end up taking longer than you expect). If, in the end, parts of it feel a bit uneven, I'd like to think that's because it's the story of how I got here and where I came from; that I'm simply not done cooking. That this is only the end of my beginning, and there's a long way left to go.

Kate Atkinson, *Behind the Scenes at the Museum*

The gold standard in novel-as-collage.
Traces (and unravels) multiple generations of
an English family in the insanely captivating first-
person voice of one Ruby Lennox, youngest of the
clan, who begins narrating at her own conception.
Kate Atkinson is a phenomenal writer, and this
(her first!) is one of the best books I've ever read.

Margaret Atwood, *Cat's Eye* and *The Robber Bride*

I want to be Margaret Atwood when I grow up.
These two novels—along with *The Handmaid's
Tale*—are probably my favorites of hers, if any book
that crystallizes the many ways girls and women
can be cruel to each other can be called a "favorite."

Beaches

Because sometimes you need a really sincere, totally
unironic sobfest. I'm glad I saw *Beaches* for the first
time when I was too young to be cynical and make
fun of it; consequently, now I never can.

Guster, *Ganging Up on the Sun*

The album that had the most direct influence on the
writing of *This Must Be the Place*—from the name of
the town (Ruby Falls), to being haunted by the past
("One Man Wrecking Machine") and the unbearable
unknowableness of others ("Satellite"). I hear this
album and Darby-Jones comes alive in my head.

*Keep on
Reading*

John Irving, *The World According to Garp*

Garp didn't directly inspire *This Must Be the Place* so much as show me how immersive a novel can be, and all the tricks a writer can pull to make it that way. There's so much going on in *Garp*—so many characters, so many ideas, so much perverse tragedy and heartbreaking comedy—and yet it hangs together, all of a piece, like a symphony of kazoos that moves you to tears.

Lorrie Moore, *Who Will Run the Frog Hospital?*

Another story about an intense friendship between two teenage girls that is anything *but* "another story." Moore can write a novel about a paper bag and I would show up to read it.

My So-Called Life

I didn't watch *My So-Called Life* when it was actually on television, even though, age-wise, I was the target audience—I was nerdier than I was angsty at the time, so I was watching *Star Trek: The Next Generation* and *The X-Files* instead. I was twenty-seven when I finally saw it on DVD, and it took my breath away. This show is an EXACT representation of how it felt to be a teenage girl in the nineties, painfully, joyfully, and completely.

Richard Russo, *Empire Falls*

Nobody writes upstate New York like Richard Russo. Nobody writes like Richard Russo, period—every sentence is a phrase of music, every paragraph a song. You lose yourself in his words.

Reading Group Gold

Ben Sisario, *The Pixies' Doolittle (33 1/3 Series)*

Essays and stories about each song on one of the weirdest, greatest albums of all time.

Charles Simic, *Dime-Store Alchemy: The Art of Joseph Cornell*

Simic distills the inspiring enigma that is the art (and life) of Joseph Cornell in short works of criticism, fiction, and poetry. A dream you can tuck in your pocket.

Rebecca Stead, *When You Reach Me*

An incredible book about growing up, friendship, family, New York City in the seventies... and time travel. My number-one recommended read of the past year.

Un Chien Andalou

Because some brands of crazy you simply must experience for yourself.

Keep on Reading

Reading Group Questions

1. Very early on, Max Morris says to Arthur that "sometimes you let the people you love believe what they want to believe." Do you think that's true? How does that statement play in to the rest of the novel?

2. What role does food play in the novel? Mona bakes cakes for a living, and also feeds her tenants each night—it's pointed out several times that both Mona's meals and cakes are especially delicious. Do you think her skill with food is meant to imply something about her personality as well? Is she a nurturing person in general?

3. The novel opens with a young Amy on a bus headed toward Hollywood. What were your initial perceptions of teenage Amy? How did your opinion of her change over the course of the novel?

4. We never get to see Amy as an adult, except through Arthur's eyes. Do you think she was a different person as an adult with Arthur than she was as a teenager with Mona? Or are Mona and Arthur's perceptions of Amy just different? Are they reconcilable? Do you think it's possible for people to ever change in any fundamental ways?

5. Mona notes fairly early on that "the past was never past. It always came back to kick your ass." Is that true for the characters of the novel? In what ways?

6. The novel follows the development of several romances, some between adults and some between teenagers. Think of Oneida and Eugene's relationship and compare it to Mona and Arthur's. How do age and maturity alter the development of each relationship? How do the teens act differently? Do you think there's anything to be said for the naïveté that the teenagers bring to their relationship? Or the experience that the adults bring to their relationship?

7. Secrets play a large role in the novel. Do you think that any of the secrets that are revealed should have been kept? Do you think that one person can ever truly know another? Or are we all bound in some way by the secrets that we keep?

8. When Oneida's real parentage was finally revealed, were you surprised? How does Oneida deal with the revelation? Do you think that it changed her feelings about Mona in anyway?

9. Eugene tells Oneida that "life is art." What do you think he means by that? How does the novel illustrate the point?

10. Art is a major theme of the novel. Many of the major characters are artists: Amy, a puppeteer and animator; Arthur, a photographer; Astor, a forger; Mona, a baker. How does each person's chosen medium suit his or her personality?

11. The novel also deals closely with misconceptions— how do art and misconceptions relate to one another? What do you think the novel is trying to say about art? What do you think of the fact that Oneida goes on to become an art historian? That Eugene becomes a forger?

12. In Eugene's dream, Joseph Cornell tells him that he will grow up and die, and that "it's the single greatest thing that will ever happen to you." What do you think this is supposed to mean? How is this a novel about growing up? Do all of the characters mature in one way or another— even the ones who are already "grown up"?

Keep on Reading